Books by Elisa Braden

RESCUED FROM RUIN SERIES

The Madness of Viscount Atherbourne (Book One)
The Truth About Cads and Dukes (Book Two)
Desperately Seeking a Scoundrel (Book Three)
The Devil Is a Marquess (Book Four)
When a Girl Loves an Earl (Book Five)
Twelve Nights as His Mistress (e-Novella – Book Six)

There's much more to come in the Rescued from Ruin series! Connect with Elisa through Facebook and Twitter, and sign up for her free email newsletter at www.elisabraden.com, so you don't miss a single release!

The Truth About Cads and Dukes

ELISA BRADEN

This is a work of fiction. Names, characters, places, and incidents are products of the author's imagination or are used fictitiously and are not to be construed as real. Any resemblance to actual events, locales, organizations, or persons, living or dead, is entirely coincidental.

Copyright © 2015 Elisa Braden

Cover design by Kim Killion at The Killion Group, Inc.

Excerpt from *Desperately Seeking a Scoundrel* copyright © 2015 Elisa Braden

All rights reserved. No part of this book may be used or reproduced in any form by any means—except in the case of brief quotations embodied in critical articles or reviews—without express written permission of the author.

For more information about the author, visit www.elisabraden.com.

ISBN-13: 978-1-54-085389-9
ISBN-10: 1-5408-5389-6

Dedication

*This one is for my brothers:
Because, in spite of girl cooties,
a serious deficit of athletic skill,
and frequent tattling to Mom,
I am your favorite sister.
You didn't always say it, but I always knew.*

Chapter One

"Humiliation is a sign either of poor judgment or poor timing. Or, in your case, both."

—The Dowager Marchioness of Wallingham to her nephew, upon his premature departure from Oxford for activities of a highly inappropriate nature.

May 5, 1817
London

Jane Huxley fervently hoped she had the correct address. To be caught with one's backside hanging out of the wrong house's window—clad in men's breeches, no less—would be most unfortunate.

She wanted to laugh at her own predicament, but at the moment, air was in short supply. In truth, she was stuck:

folded double, her right half inside a stranger's London town house, her left half outside that stranger's ground-floor window, and her generous middle squeezed until she could scarcely afford a shallow breath. She fancied she was beginning to see spots, but the darkness made it hard to say for certain.

Perhaps this is a bad idea, she thought, not for the first time.

Bracing her hands on the sill in front of her, she thrust her shoulders upward with all her strength. The window dug painfully into her upper back, but it did not budge. She took a breath, panting weakly. Brilliant. Suffocated by one's own corpulence. If she had forty years and forty thousand sheaves of paper, she could not invent a more humiliating demise. Earlier, assessing the window from outside, she'd been sure she could fit through the opening—simply climb a short ladder retrieved from the stable, step through one leg at a time, and there you have it. She'd been mistaken.

It doesn't matter. You must get through, Jane. If you are caught here, ruination shall be the least of your worries. She could almost hear her mother's sobs upon witnessing one of her daughters being carted off to Newgate for burglary. Or, worse yet, Bedlam. The thought was shudder-inducing. Even injury would be better, and Jane was emphatically opposed to pain.

She leaned forward until her face brushed the opposite casing. The new position completely closed off her air and threatened to scrape off her spectacles, but it flattened her enough that she could feel her shoulders slide an inch or two farther into the room. Bending her neck sideways at an unnatural angle, she grasped the wall on either side and gave a mighty shove.

After her backside hit the wooden floor with a bruising thud, and her spectacles flew off to ping into a shadowy piece of furniture, Jane allowed herself to lie with one ankle still propped on the sill, pausing to wheeze air back into her burning lungs and let the pain throbbing in her cheek and ear subside. Heart pounding, she listened for sounds of an uproar in the house, signs that a servant had heard her grunting, graceless entrance into Lord Milton's house.

All was quiet—for now. But the night was far from over.

Shaking her head and laughing silently at her own stupidity, she reached up to adjust her mask. It was a simple piece of cloth, cut from one of her brother's old coats. An old *woolen* coat. The thing had been itchy when she'd first put it on, but after an hour of nervous sweat, it had grown unbearable. It was one of many reasons she could now reasonably declare herself the Worst Burglar in the History of Man. Or Woman. Could women be burglars?

She glanced down at her present ensemble—her brother's boyhood breeches, a stable lad's castoff coat, and a worn pair of riding boots she'd discovered in an attic trunk. Aside from the mask, it was all rather comfortable, the breeches in particular. The freedom of movement was something of a revelation. She arched a brow and sighed. Yes, she supposed women could be burglars, but in Jane's considered opinion, it was not so much a daring profession as a daft one.

She rolled over and felt around the floor for her spectacles. Oak floors, plush carpet, the leg of a chair. Dash it all, they could not have gone far. Now on her hands and knees, she scuttled to her right, running her hands in wide sweeping motions. "Ow!" she hissed as her knuckles whapped into something hard, probably a table leg. Shaking her fingers vigorously against the sharp pain, she soon resumed her sweep.

There! Feeling the familiar curve of the wire rims against her fingertips did much to settle her thumping heart. She tested the lenses. Intact, thank heavens. Returning the spectacles to their rightful place, she pushed to her feet and struggled to get her bearings. It had been a full moon only a few nights past, but London's thick layer of coal smoke and clouds made the darkness inside the room nearly impenetrable. Again, she wondered how she had allowed herself to be persuaded into this foolishness.

She shook her head. Now was not the time.

Slowly, as her eyes adjusted, she made out the bulky forms of a large desk, several chairs, three bookcases, and a small table near the window where she had entered. This must be Lord Milton's library. "Hmmph," she grunted, recalling her recent observations of the simpering fribble. Not precisely a scholar, that one. She'd be surprised if this room was used for more than enjoying the occasional brandy. As a book lover, she found it an appalling waste, but in this case, a reliably empty library worked in her favor.

She crept toward the opposite end of the room where she imagined the door must be, skirting around the edge of the desk and only slightly bruising her hip on the arm of a stout chair. Rubbing the spot absently, she felt along the wall until she reached a series of raised panels. Ah, yes. The door. She paused, listening for any noise. Nothing. Aside from her thunderously loud heart, that was. Hand slick with sweat, she struggled to turn the knob, managing to crack the door an inch and peek out at a dimly lit corridor. Empty. No footsteps. Of course, it was past midnight, and Jane had been assured Lord Milton was away for several days, so finding servants wandering about would have been surprising.

Taking a deep breath, she opened the door wider and stepped out into the hall. Fine tremors shook her arms and threatened to buckle her knees. A bit of moonlight from a window at the end of the long corridor allowed her to count the doors. The one she sought was the third on the right. Or was it the left? Her stomach dropped as nerves made her doubt herself. No, it was the right. She scratched at her mask and adjusted her spectacles.

You are a dashed fool, she scolded, carefully sidling along the wall. *This is it. No more reaching beyond yourself. Those days are over. O-V-E-R. You are Plain Jane Huxley, and that is that.* It was sound advice. However, it did nothing to get her out of her current illicit act. That had been a promise made to a friend.

And Jane Huxley always kept her promises, even when it was hard.

Deep breath. Door two.

A few more feet. There, now, door three.

Air whooshed out of tight lungs as she realized she had arrived. Her task was nearly finished. All she had to do now was open the door, find the necklace, and return home. Simple. She reached for the knob.

The sound of whispering stopped her hand, her breath, her heart. It froze her feet to the oak parquet. She flattened herself against the wall, glancing frantically side to side. No one had entered the corridor. But she could still hear the sound, faint and undeniable. It stopped, but only for a moment. She put her ear to the door. There. Whispering and ... and movement, like rustling clothing and shifting feet. Many feet.

Oh, dear heavens. Someone was in that room. More than one someone, if her ears did not deceive her. Ice bloomed beneath her skin. It should have been empty. She'd been told it would be empty. Swallowing hard, she backed slowly toward the library.

Hands grabbed her arms from behind, squeezing hard into the fleshy parts just above her elbows. "Hold there," an effete, refined voice sounded above her head. She squawked, tried to twist against the man's grip, but he simply shoved her forward like a bit of seaweed on the crest of a wave. The third door on the right opened, he shoved her again, and she stumbled into the room. "Light it up, gentlemen!" the voice ordered. "Let's have a look at our intrepid intruder, shall we?"

Suddenly, two lamps were simultaneously lit, and she could see what had been awaiting her. Men. More than a dozen. She squinted at them, unable to believe the sight. Everything moved slowly, as though in a dream. *Or nightmare,* she thought with distant horror. For, as her mind began working again, she realized some of the men were familiar. The short, prematurely balding one was Sir Christopher Flatmouth.

Another she recognized as the second son of Lord Gattingford. She glanced right. Leaning negligently against a settee wearing an elegant gray coat and an unreadable expression was the thin, inexplicably attractive Viscount Chatham. She did not have to look behind her to confirm the man who had shoved her into the room was Lord Milton; she would know that lisp anywhere. To a man, they were all sons of the aristocracy. And to a man, they were all wastrels, the dissolute, perennially bored scoundrels of the ton.

Presently, their surprise at seeing her was wearing off, because many began to laugh uproariously. She even thought she heard a few "huzzahs" amidst the glee. She did not understand it. Why were they laughing? Cheering? Her answer came moments later when one of their members was shoved to the front of the crowd.

Her eyes widened, shock moving through her with tidal force. Curling blond hair tumbled artfully above sheepish blue eyes. His boyishly handsome features did not appear pleased, despite the backslapping congratulations coming from his friends. His face was ruddy, his posture unusually slumped—he looked like a child caught in the middle of mischief.

She had done this for him. She was standing amidst this briar patch of rakes and cads, dressed as a fat, incompetent highwayman. Because of him.

Heat shimmered along her neck and cheeks, but in all other aspects, numbness settled over her, as thick and paralyzing as ten feet of snow. *Please let this not be happening.* Dear God, this humiliation was intolerable. Nothing made sense. She only knew she could not get enough air, could not move from where she stood.

Her breath caught as she stared into his blue eyes. All around, the others seemed to be crowding closer, their laughing chatter louder, their wild gestures intruding into her small bubble of space. *I must leave. Now. Before this gets any worse.* By force of will, she took a scraping, stumbling step back toward the door. Once again, hands stopped her. A lisping voice mocked, "Where are you off to, little thief? Stay a while. The entertainment has only just begun."

The blue-eyed man she had once considered a friend shoved violently at the man next to him and charged forward. "Release her," he barked. "The wager is won. You have what you came to see. It is done."

"Wager?" she murmured hoarsely, but it was lost among the loud guffaws and protests of the gentlemen.

"Ballocks! Can't let her go 'til she's unmasked," Sir Christopher declared sloppily. Clearly, his evening's "entertainment" had begun early.

"Just so! How else are we to know for certain the conditions of the wager have been met?" shouted another man.

A third—Lord Gattingford's son—replied, "Who else would wear spectacles on the outside of her mask?" That generated a new round of guffaws from the crowd. Jane reached up to touch the edge of the rims.

"Lost ten quid on this one," another man remarked, resentment flinting his voice. "Should have known he could charm the chit. The fat ones are always so eager to please."

The room began to rock and tilt. Heat and shame squeezed like a coiling snake around a fresh kill. She shook her head automatically, unable to stop the motion. She spun to face Lord Milton, a whey-faced, wiry man who over-plucked his eyebrows into thin, straight lines. He still had hold of her arm, but was preoccupied with amusement. Almost without thought, she lowered her shoulder and rammed it into his solar plexus. "Ooof!" She was rewarded by the shock bulging his eyes and loosening his grip.

Tearing herself free, she ran for the door, still partially open. Two steps away from freedom, it slammed shut, a lean, elegant hand braced on the panel in front of her. Slowly, she allowed her gaze to travel up the gray-clad arm to meet a hooded set of turquoise eyes. Chatham.

Without a word, he stepped in close, seemingly wrapping her in his arms. "Wh-what are you ...?" she began. Clean linen and citrus and the faint odor of whisky surrounded her. He was surprisingly warm for such a cold man, she thought absently. She felt a sharp tug at the back of her head. "No!" she shouted hoarsely, suddenly realizing what he was doing. She tore at the fine wool of his sleeves, shoved at the hard bones of his chest. But it was useless.

The mask fell away, along with her spectacles and several hair pins. Her hair came down, a fall as straight and dark as her ruined pride. The chatter ceased. She pushed away from Chatham, turned to the man who had engineered her humiliation. He was a blur. A blond, deceitful blur who had made her into a laughingstock. In the silence, she could not stop what happened—the dollop of cream on the strawberry of her day. There, in the middle of Lord Milton's London town house, surrounded by cads of every sort, wearing her brother's breeches and a stable boy's coat, Plain Jane Huxley did what she had sworn she would never do in public: She let the tears come.

Chapter Two

"Any book portraying 'true love' as a reason for marriage should be given the same credence as the rantings of a bedlamite. It is termed 'fiction' for a reason."

—THE DOWAGER MARCHIONESS OF WALLINGHAM to Lady Jane Huxley upon spying said lady's fourth copy of *Pride and Prejudice* hidden inside an urn.

Six weeks earlier
Piccadilly, London

FOR LADY JANE HUXLEY, THE LITTLE BELL ON THE DOOR OF Norton's Bookshop on Piccadilly sang a song of welcome unlike any other. She breathed deeply the beloved scent of paper, ink, and leather bindings, pulling it into her lungs as if she could make it part of herself. Ah, yes. Blissful.

"You are not planning to spend a *lot* of time here, are you?" The sullen question came from Eugenia Huxley, Jane's second youngest sister.

Jane glanced over at the dark-haired girl. Genie had grown over the past year. Come autumn, she would be fourteen, and while she was more than six years younger than Jane, they were currently the same height: barely five feet. It was strange to think of her bratty little sister becoming a proper young lady who, in only a few short years, would be making her debut.

Sherry-brown eyes met her own. "Leave it to you to find the most boring place in London and trap me here for hours on end." Genie's face scrunched with disgust as she swept her gaze over the shelves crowding the small, dusty store's main floor. "You promised me shopping. Books are not shopping."

Jane sniffed and adjusted her spectacles. "Nonsense. One must buy books, just as one must buy ribbons. The fact that it is not something you *wish* to purchase does not change the definition, Genie."

She felt Genie's glare land on her cheek, but she ignored it to search for the proprietor of Norton's Bookshop. He rushed in from the back room, a blur of thinning hair, woolen twill, and wire spectacles. "Mr. Higginbotham! G-good afternoon. I am looking for—" Jane began, only to be interrupted by an upraised finger.

"Not now, gel." Bustling by, long wisps of his ever-sparser hair flying high, Mr. Higginbotham did what he usually did: ignored her in favor of a male customer.

"I don't like him," Genie commented, her narrowed eyes following the thin man to the front of the shop.

Jane sighed. "That is his way. He is looking after his interests."

"He is rude. Does he realize who you are? At the very least, he should pay heed to how much you spend in his shop. To treat an earl's daughter in such a way is simply boorish."

At times like this, Jane was grateful to have sisters. Genie might seem a frivolous brat, but against outsiders, she was fierce in defense of Jane—or any of their siblings, really. Jane squeezed her arm and nudged her toward the back corner. "Come. If you behave, I will take you next door when I'm finished." Next door was Genie's favorite hat shop. But her fondness for bonnets must have dwindled, because she tugged Jane to a halt and gave her a look of queenly hauteur.

"Do not speak to me as if I am a child."

Now Jane remembered why having sisters was a two-edged sword. "You don't wish to go next door, then?"

"Don't be ridiculous. Of course I wish to go."

"Then what is the problem?"

Genie looked stymied for a moment. Inside, Jane smiled. Being twenty, as opposed to Genie's almost-fourteen, gave her certain advantages—namely, the ability to win an argument with circular logic.

The queenly posture returned in due course, and Her Majesty peered down her royal nose at Jane. "I shall not wait longer than an hour. After that, you may find me next door."

Giving her a placid look, Jane replied, "Don't forget to take Teddy with you."

Red bloomed on Genie's cheeks, rising along her forehead and painting her throat in blotchy color. Teddy was the handsome new footman who had accompanied them on this excursion ... and Genie's latest impossible fancy. "Hmmph," Genie grunted, turning on her heel and stomping toward a low shelf full of navigational references.

While her sister pretended a fascination with all things nautical, Jane hid a grin and made her way to the far back corner of the shop. It was a dark and quiet spot, as the shelves rose to very near the ceiling, forming a small room. Jane paused, simply breathing in silent anticipation. Her gloved fingers drifted slowly toward the neat row of spines, slid over their smooth surfaces. She knew what she had come for: A copy of *Emma* to send to her best friend, Victoria Lacey. Well, now Victoria Wyatt, Lady Atherbourne. Had it been only last year that their friendship began in earnest? Jane smiled and shook her head. It seemed longer.

Jane's parents, the Earl and Countess of Berne, had been friends with Victoria's parents, the Duke and Duchess of Blackmore, before the latter couple died tragically in a North Sea shipwreck. Two years ago, Jane's mother became Victoria's sponsor and chaperone in London, and last year, after a disastrous scandal forced Victoria to marry Lucien Wyatt, Viscount Atherbourne, Jane had been recruited into the effort to restore Victoria's reputation. Only then did Jane and Victoria converse regularly enough to become friends. In fact, they'd found a rapport Jane hadn't felt with anyone apart from her sisters—perhaps not even them.

Recalling Victoria's most recent letter, Jane's mouth curved upward again. Thankfully, while her friend's marriage had begun in scandal, it had quickly grown into a true love match, and they were now settled at Lucien's Derbyshire estate awaiting the arrival of their first child. That was what had brought Jane to Norton's Bookshop today: Unquestionably, a woman in confinement needed a good book to pass the time.

Jane moved to her right, examining the titles: *Mansfield Park*, several copies of *Waverley* and *Robinson Crusoe*, some volumes of poetry by a man she had never heard of. But no *Emma*. Dash it all, it was the most delightful novel, a rival for Jane's all-time favorite, *Pride and Prejudice*. She had written Victoria glowing descriptions of its many charms, had promised she would send a copy along with her very next letter. It would be such a shame to disappoint her.

Jane adjusted her spectacles and glanced at the upper shelves, hoping to spot the book. On her third sweep, she thought she might have found it, but there was only one volume—*Emma* came in three.

"Blast," she muttered under her breath. Not only was two-thirds of the book missing, but the third that remained was located on the highest shelf. This called for much stronger language. "Bloody hell," she whispered, just to try it out. There. That was more satisfying.

"My, my. I had no idea cursing restrictions had loosened this dramatically. How marvelous." The teasing, masculine voice came from mere feet behind her, slightly to the left.

Frozen in place, Jane prayed he was speaking to someone else. Although, in this little alcove, there was no one else. Perhaps he was addressing one of the shelves. Or talking to himself. Perhaps if she did not move or respond, he would not notice her. Perhaps ...

"Lady Jane, isn't it? Lady Jane Huxley?"

Bloody hell. Inside her head, the curse did not have the same impact. But, then, she suspected nothing short of being divinely transported to another location would make her feel better about this moment. In truth, Jane was shy. Not the ordinary sort of shy—more the sort that tied her tongue, causing her to stumble and bumble over her words, to be stricken with paralysis every time someone unfamiliar spoke to her. Replying to even the most banal expressions of polite inquiry was an exercise in fortitude, but knowing that a stranger had overheard her uttering profanity and apparently knew her name ... well. That was mortifying.

It took her a full minute to face him. He waited patiently. Blast. She'd hoped he might leave. But, no. When she finally turned around, he was there, tall, lean, and amused. Golden-blond curls tumbled above sky-blue eyes. A small, straight nose and refined features gave him a youthful, almost feminine beauty—a beauty that was familiar.

Her embarrassment receded in favor of surprise. She knew him. He was Lord Colin Lacey, the younger of Victoria's two brothers. (The older one was the Duke of Blackmore, but Jane preferred not to think about him.) Lord Colin, to Jane's knowledge, was a hopeless drunkard, a wastrel with few redeeming qualities apart from boyish good looks. At least, that was her impression from the one occasion when she'd been close enough to form a judgment—she had been seated next to him at Victoria's wedding breakfast. Deep in his cups a full hour before the meal was served, he had behaved with all the decorum one might expect from such a condition—none at all. The event had come to an abrupt end, in fact, when Lord Colin had made a dreadfully inappropriate comment to an entire table full of guests.

What was he doing here in a dusty corner of Norton's? She would not have thought him much of a reader. And yet, here he was, upright, sober, and rather smartly attired in a light-gray tailcoat and striped lavender waistcoat. Quite puzzling, given that Victoria had recently despaired, "Colin is so far from the shores of dignity, I fear he shall never find his way back again." Today at least, he appeared quite ... well, *dashing*, she supposed.

"Are you not going to reply, Lady Jane?" He flashed a grin that was both boyish and endearing, like a cherub offering a wink. A handsome cherub. "I was hoping to hear more epithets to add to my collection."

Jane felt herself flush, knowing the ruddy color did her no favors. "L-Lord Colin," she rasped, quickly clearing her throat to cover her nervousness. "A pleasure to see you again."

His grin widened, a sparkle entering his eyes. "And you, Lady Jane Huxley." He sketched a deeper-than-necessary bow. It made her wonder if she was being mocked. Gentlemen rarely spoke to Jane, and when they did, they never smiled charmingly or engaged her in witty banter. Usually, if they did not ignore her entirely, they avoided her gaze, as she avoided theirs, saying as little as possible and departing for prettier pastures as swiftly as politeness would allow. But not Lord Colin. Not today.

"It has been too long," he said warmly. "Victoria's wedding, if I am not mistaken." He glanced around the small space enclosed by books. "Searching for your next favorite novel, I presume? Or perhaps a reference on the vulgar tongue?"

Normally, she would have assumed such a remark was intended to be derisive, but his tone suggested a jest shared between friends. Warily, she nodded, then changed her mind and shook her head.

Eyes crinkling at the corners, he chuckled, the sound as warming as a cup of chocolate. "Feeling contradictory, are we? I cannot blame you. Choosing between fiction and profanity is most challenging. As amusements go, each has its merits."

"I—I am ... neither, actually." Her fingers automatically fussed with her spectacles. "I was searching for a gift. For Victoria."

"For Tori? Really? Her birthday is not until July, you know. You have ample time. No need for cursing—unless it is simply for fun. In which case, I heartily endorse it."

Feeling more at ease, Jane released a small laugh. "It is not for her birthday. I promised I would send her a copy of *Emma*, so she might read it during her confinement."

For a moment, Lacey's smile froze, something like surprise, then regret, moving through his eyes. Then it was gone. "Ah, yes, of course. And the babe will be coming ... soon."

It sounded almost like a question, so she found herself nodding, although he must surely know. Victoria was his sister, and this her first child, after all.

"Quite right," he continued briskly, clapping his hands together. "Shall we find this *Emma*, then?"

"You—you intend to help me locate the book?"

His brows arched in surprise. "Naturally. You are a damsel in need of assistance. What sort of man do you take me for?"

Her mouth quirked. "I'm not certain you wish me to answer that." The response escaped before caution could filter it. Immediately, she felt herself blush, and her hand flew up to cover her mouth. *Too late for that, you ninny.*

He laughed. "Well done, Lady Jane. Indeed, given my past

misdeeds, you may be correct on that score." For a moment, he appeared almost bashful. "I can only hope to improve your opinion of my character. Perhaps offering my assistance is a way to begin anew."

Dropping her fingers, she hesitated before giving him a nod, then pointed to the top shelf. "I have managed to spy one of the volumes up there, but I have not seen the other two."

He moved the few feet necessary to reach the book, close enough that his sleeve brushed her shoulder. Stretching a long arm up, he plucked a third of *Emma* from its hiding place with the enviable ease of a tall man. She took it from him, running her fingers over the cover, and marveled at the pleasantness of not being ignored. "Thank you, my lord."

He waved his hand dismissively. "Let us dispense with formalities, shall we? We are, for all practical purposes, family. Please call me Colin."

She paused, considering his request. On one hand, he was right—their families were closely connected, and given her friendship with Victoria, formality did seem a bit, well, formal. On the other hand, she was an unmarried woman in her third season, and calling a gentleman by his given name implied a certain intimacy. That could lead to assumptions, which could lead to scandal. *Hmm.*

On the other hand (drat, she was running out of hands) who would possibly care? Jane was hardly a diamond of the first water—more like a stone at the bottom of a river: round, plain, and utterly unremarkable. In some ways, it allowed her greater freedom than many other young ladies, as she escaped the scrutiny assigned to those with better prospects.

Lord Colin tucked in his chin and gave her a questioning smile. "Still thinking about it?"

She pressed her lips together. He really was rather charming. "I shall call you Colin when we are alone," she decided aloud. "But amongst company, you shall be *Lord* Colin, as is proper. Fair?"

"Perfectly so. And I will continue to address you as Lady Jane." He tilted his head toward her. "Perhaps one day, I may earn the right to call you simply Jane."

His eyes sparkled the way Victoria's did when she gave someone a sincere compliment. It warmed the recipient right through, and Jane was not immune. Apparently, this sort of charm was a family trait. An image of their older brother, the Duke of Blackmore, sprang to mind, and immediately she revised her assessment. Clearly, charm neglected to land on *some* branches of the family tree.

She focused on Colin, who had returned to perusing the shelves for the other two parts of *Emma*. "Lord ... er, Colin," she began haltingly. "I must say, while I am grateful for your assistance, I cannot help wondering ..."

He stopped and looked over his shoulder. "Yes?"

"Well, why?"

"Why what?"

"Why would you bother?"

He sighed then was silent for a long while, his gaze falling to his feet. "Have you ever made a mistake, Lady Jane? I mean a mistake so grievous that you doubt redemption is possible?"

My, my, she thought. *When did this conversation become so grave?* She shook her head, but he wasn't looking at her. Then he turned, and he was.

"I have. More than once. For far too long, I followed a path of darkness, realizing only recently that redemption shall never be possible if I do not pursue it. And to do that, I must change my course."

"Are you intending to join the clergy, then?"

He reeled back and clutched his chest as if she had struck him. "Good God, no! What an appalling notion."

She gave him a mischievous grin. "Well, all this talk of darkness and redemption. What else am I to surmise?"

Slowly, he laughed and wagged a finger at her. "You are a cheeky one, aren't you? No, I only meant that, henceforth, I have resolved to behave as a gentleman, as I have not done in some time."

"So, you are being kind to me as a gesture of good manners."

"I am helping you because you deserve to be treated with kindness, and any gentleman worthy of the title should do the same."

Her heart gave a little flutter. Apart from her brother and her father, no man even looked at her, much less thought she merited such generous courtesy. It felt like summer had come a month early—warm and unexpected.

"Thank you," she whispered. "Colin."

He smiled gently and nodded. "It is my pleasure."

By the time they located the two remaining volumes—inexplicably scattered on the bottom row of the rear shelf—they were chatting and laughing together as though they had been friends for ages. In some ways, he reminded her of Victoria, except he was a man, and a rather attractive one, at that.

"My lady, it appears our partnership in this endeavor has been a success," he said, handing her the final volume. He glanced over her shoulder toward the front of the shop. "I fear I must take my leave. But perhaps we shall have occasion to talk again soon."

"I would like that."

He smiled, his eyes crinkling and twinkling. Giving her a tip of his nonexistent hat, he bowed gallantly and strode away.

She was sighing, watching the door close behind him, when Genie poked her head around one of the shelves. "Your time is up, Jane," she hissed. "I can feel the dust of this dreadful place settling into my very soul."

"A tad overdramatic, don't you think?"

"No. I do not think."

Jane sniffed and raised her chin. "Note that I am letting that pass without mockery. It is entirely too easy, and beneath my dignity."

Genie refused to be distracted from her central complaint.

"I am surrounded by boredom. Tedious, dusty, *wordy* boredom. We must go now, Jane. *Now.*" She stamped her foot on the last word, the whine in her voice reminding Jane that her sister was still quite young, indeed.

And thank goodness for that, she thought as they made their way to the counter where Mr. Higginbotham was sorting his stacks. Apparently, Genie had not noticed Jane's long and chummy conversation with Lord Colin. Jane would prefer not to answer questions about it, especially since she had few answers, herself. Better to keep this from her sisters. And her mother. *Oh, dear, yes.* Her mother would surely get the wrong idea.

"Sooo, Jane …" Genie's voice was a casual inquiry.

"Mmm?"

Jane's sister blinked at her innocently. "That gentleman you were speaking to. Is he your suitor, then?"

Jane froze.

"No. That's silly. If you, of all people, had a suitor, surely Mama would know. She would have an apoplexy if she were not informed, considering she has despaired of you becoming a spinster."

Jane's eyes narrowed behind her spectacles. "What do you want?"

"A new hat; an *expensive* one. And your promise never to bring me to this wretched place again."

"Done." Thank goodness Genie was still young enough to be so easily bribed. Jane could not bear to hear her four sisters and her mother volleying this about like a lively game of cricket. It was too uncertain, too new. Too precious and fragile.

"Oh, that is just the beginning. Did you think to purchase my discretion so cheaply?"

For the third time that day, a vile curse entered Jane's mind. *Bloody hell.*

Chapter Three

*"Never wager that which you can ill afford to lose.
Unless, of course, your opponent is too deep in his cups
to recall the stakes. Then, by all means, wager the moon."*

—THE DOWAGER MARCHIONESS OF WALLINGHAM to Lady Reedham
while partnered for a rousing game of whist.

IT WAS VERY LATE AND COLIN LACEY WAS VERY DRUNK. Normally, being in such a state was jolly good fun. But not tonight.

"I presume the wager is going well?" a dry voice inquired from across the table.

Colin lifted his head from where it had dropped onto his forearm. When had Chatham sauntered in? And when had he begun that strange, weaving dance he was performing? Colin shook his head. The world moved sickeningly. Ah, yes. It was the brandy that made his friend sway and ripple in his chair. A dreadful lot of brandy.

Snorting sloppily, Colin replied, "No. Not well at all. But you knew that."

Lazy, elegant fingers gripped a glass of whisky and tossed a shot down Chatham's throat. Colin wondered if Chatham was drunk, too. He could never quite tell for certain. Benedict Chatham, Viscount Chatham, was a deuced controlled man, even deep in his cups. One never knew if he was furious or thrilled beyond measure. His demeanor remained the same, whatever the circumstances: World-weary cynicism and biting wit accompanied by frightful intelligence and a curious magnetism that women found irresistible, despite being bone-thin and linen-white. Colin had been his friend for over three years, and still, he often seemed a virtual stranger, albeit an amusing one.

Wiping a hand over his face, Colin attempted to sit upright. "None of thish would be necess—necessh—there would be no wager at all if my brother were not such a moralizing prig."

"Careful there," Chatham replied, his posture negligent, one slim leg slung over the other, a hand propped on his knee. A single finger of that hand lifted to indicate the bottle of brandy some club employee had conveniently left on the table. Colin's elbow had nearly knocked it to the floor. "It would be a shame to damage the valuables."

"You are brilliant, do you know that, Chatham?"

"You're only saying that because you're drunk."

Colin shook his head emphatically. "No! No, no, no. Brandy is dreadfully expensv—exshpen costly. That's why I swore it off. Stopped it like that." He snapped his fingers, but they seemed to miss each other, because the sound wasn't right. "Can't afford the stuff. Can't even afford decent boots. Bloody Harrison cut off my funds."

"Yes, your brother is not one to suffer fools forever, it is true."

"Tha's right! It is *his* fault I am in this predic—predicam—mess. Now the wager grows more bloody impossible with every new chap who adds his name to the book." Colin waved to the sideboard, where the betting book lay open, waiting for the next gentleman to up the ante. Thankfully, this particular book was being kept here, at the exclusive gambling hell known as Reaver's, in a private room accessible only to those Chatham allowed inside. As the future Marquess of Rutherford, Chatham could afford to arrange such conveniences—fortunately for Colin. And Lady Jane Huxley, he supposed.

Graceful as a cat stretching after a nap, Chatham stood and retrieved the book, glancing down at the growing list of notations. "I fail to see your complaint. The more who join the wager, the greater your reward."

"Never meant to ruin anyone."

Chatham turned his vivid turquoise gaze on Colin. That particular look—a cold, measuring sort from eyes that were hooded beneath low, dark brows—always gave him the shivers. It was like being examined by a wolf who was not especially hungry at the moment, but wanted to reserve the right to assess his options. "Then perhaps you should not have wagered in the first place." Chatham's voice was soft, expressionless.

Colin snorted and glanced down at the marble tabletop. "You sound like the duke."

"Does he know about the wager?"

He laughed mirthlessly and shook his head. "If he did, he'd cut off far more than my funds."

In truth, he wouldn't blame Harrison for delivering violence upon his person. The more time Colin spent with Jane, the worse he felt about what he had to do. Take that very evening, for example. Before arriving at Reaver's and getting thoroughly sotted, he had attended a ton event at Lady Reedham's town house—a musicale, or some such. Given the nature of ton events, it was sometimes difficult to discern the difference. In any case, there had been a great deal of dreadful music, and although his brain was pleasantly foggy at the moment, he thought he recalled a gangly young woman at the pianoforte, banging away as though sorely vexed with the composer.

But that was not the important part. The critical bit came a few minutes later, when he spotted Lady Jane Huxley seated in the third row of chairs, her head bowed as if in prayer. It took some time to spot her—she was quite short in stature, and two additional rows of gawkily tall women sat between him and her. He'd been determined, however, and at the next opportunity, when the girl at the pianoforte took a blessed break, and the ladies next to Jane bolted for the refreshment table, Colin slipped in and took a seat beside his quarry.

Glancing down at her lap, he quickly realized that she hadn't been praying at all. "Good book, Lady Jane?"

She jerked and fumbled with the thing, snapping it closed and adjusting her spectacles. Then she cleared her throat and turned to stare at him with wide, mahogany-brown eyes. "Lord Colin," she said with admirable steadiness. "How unexpected to see you again. I did not realize you were a lover of Mozart."

"Oh, I'm not."

She blinked slowly, her lips quirking. "Perhaps that is best, given the performance."

Groaning in agreement, he chuckled then glanced around. "Are you here with your mother?"

She nodded and stroked her hands over the book cover. "She insisted we should attend in support of Miss Blythfield, who is a friend of my sister. This evening is her musical debut."

"The one playing the pianoforte?"

"Yes."

"You are supporting *that*?"

A helpless grin tugged at her mouth, breaking wide as she shook her head at him. "Perhaps 'supporting' is a bit strong, upon further reflection." When she smiled, little dimples appeared in her cheeks, a sweet surprise in what could only be described as a round, plain face.

He rewarded her with a wink. "Hence, the book, I gather."

"You are most discerning, my lord."

"I have been called worse."

She laughed, a pleasant, slightly husky sound. "One shudders to imagine."

Deliberately, he leaned toward her, lowering his head near hers. "I came to see you, Lady Jane."

Eyes flaring wide, a flush rising from her generous bosom to her face, Jane sputtered, "M-me? Whatever for?"

Two chairs away, an elderly woman of considerable bulk cleared her throat pointedly, drawing his eye past Jane and causing him to straighten under the matron's stern gaze. "Perhaps we should discuss this elsewhere," he murmured, glancing around the room. The guests must have been anticipating a second round of musical torture, because many were heading back to their seats. Quickly, before Jane's mother could return and mistake him for a suitor, he surreptitiously covered Jane's hand with his own. "Wait until the music begins again, then meet me in the front hall."

Judging by her frown, it seemed Jane would protest, so he squeezed her hand. She looked down at where they entwined and stopped, her teeth worrying at her lower lip.

Marshaling his most persuasive expression—the one his sister, Victoria, had dubbed his "sweet-as-a-spring-lamb face"— he whispered, "Please, Lady Jane. Won't you grant me this favor?"

Her eyes met his, full of doubt, discomfort ... and something else. There, in the dark-brown depths magnified by her spectacles, was the hidden spark of longing he'd noticed during their conversation in the bookshop. Lady Jane Huxley, like any other female of her age, *wanted* to be courted, to be admired and whispered to in a dark corridor. To be pursued.

Most men overlooked her, this short, plump, brown-haired,

plain Jane. And those who did not were eventually dissuaded by her studious absorption in whatever book she had in hand. Even when a gentleman bothered to engage her, she rarely offered more than a few polite words. Given how infrequently men paid her any mind at all, Colin would not blame her for being skeptical of a suddenly ardent suitor. But if he was to be successful, he must gain her trust. And soon.

He could almost hear his brother's cold sneer. Bloody hell, he'd said it to himself often enough: *A man is never so loathsome as when he deceives an innocent for his own benefit.*

But he had no choice.

Colin's breath stopped as he waited for Jane's assent. They could not have the conversation he needed to have with her here, where members of the ton crowded within earshot. He must get her alone.

She glanced behind him then gave his hand a return squeeze before sliding hers away. Slowly, she nodded, pretending to return to her book. "Very well," she whispered. "My mother is approaching. You should probably go."

A rush of elation drove him to his feet and toward the back of the room where a long table acted as a repository for the refreshments.

He was close. He could feel it.

Suddenly, his skin itched. Especially his neck beneath his cravat. He ran a finger between the cloth and his throat, feeling the telltale dampness there. Rolling his shoulders, he sidled past a pair of velvet-clad matrons and avoided the flirtatious gaze of one of their charges.

Since the atrocious months following Harrison's decision to cut off his funds, his body had almost entirely adapted to its forced sobriety. In truth, as the fog of drink had cleared, he'd even begun to appreciate its benefits. For one thing, he was less likely to be hunched over a chamber pot upon waking. And the odds that his sister would wish to claim him as an uncle to her firstborn improved with every day he did not do something to embarrass her. Of course, she did not know of his plans for her dearest friend. Or why such a thing was necessary.

A twinge of pain tightened his throat. He swallowed hard to quell it.

Behaving in a *loathsome* manner, necessary though it might be, made him long for the comforts of oblivion. Right now, he would gladly forsake certain body parts—the smallest finger on his left hand, for example—for one blessed bottle of brandy. Lady Reedham did not offer his chosen beverage, so he downed a cup of orgeat punch and propped his shoulder on the wall near the room's entrance. Then, he waited for his shy wren to gather her courage.

As expected, she did not rise until well into the second set. He watched as she tiptoed past the row of her sisters and moved to the double doors near where he stood. A footman bowed as she passed into the corridor, bowed again as Colin followed a minute later.

Frowning, he searched the dark hall, lit only by two tapers. Where had she gone? He had told her to meet him here, had he not? He scratched his head. Yes, he distinctly recalled saying—

"Psssst. Lord Colin." The loud whisper came from his left. A white glove appeared from an alcove behind the stairway. It waved him closer.

He grinned. This was going to be easier than he'd thought.

Approaching her slowly, he grasped her hand in his and gave it a tender kiss, as a knight might do for his lady. Or, at least, that was how a typical female might imagine it, he supposed.

But Lady Jane was not the typical sort. She immediately jerked her hand away, leaving him kissing air, and hissed, "Are you *foxed* again? I have no use for drunkards."

Perhaps the wooing was not going quite as well as he'd imagined.

He let his arm fall back to his side and adopted a sheepish expression. "I humbly apologize, my lady. I do not fault you in the slightest for believing the worst of me. My only intention was to demonstrate my sincere regard."

She was quiet for a long minute before sighing. The darkness of the alcove made it difficult to gauge her expression. He couldn't see much more than the occasional reflection of light off of her spectacles. When at last she spoke, her voice was hushed and restrained, as if she only half believed him. "What did you wish to speak to me about?"

Suddenly, his tongue stuck to the roof of his mouth. Sweat sprang forth on his palms. He pressed them against the inside of his gloves and cleared his throat. "Right, well. Yes. That is … you—you know I have a great many regrets."

She did not reply.

"And that I have recently made it my ambition to reform—er, rectify matters. To set things back in order, so to say."

Still, nothing from Jane. Well, perhaps a bit of honesty would tug on her heartstrings. Or at least her vocal cords.

"The truth is, Lady Jane, my sister has not spoken to me in some time. She was most dismayed by my prior behavior. I cannot blame her."

A soft snort of what sounded like agreement came from Jane's general vicinity.

"I had lost hope of regaining her affection until last week, when you and I encountered one another in the bookshop." Somewhat blindly, he reached out toward the white of her gloves. "You are her dearest friend, are you not?"

A sniff, then one of the gloves rose to fuss with the rim of her spectacles. "One may say so, as she is mine."

"I hesitate to ask, for it is no small request, but for the sake of restoring the familial bond between Victoria and me, would you consider speaking to her on my behalf?"

"Me? What would you have me tell her?"

"Simply that I am attempting to deserve her regard once

again. Perhaps that you have seen my efforts with your own eyes."

White-gloved arms folded across a darker bodice. He couldn't remember what color dress she wore—a dull brown, perhaps—but he knew it was dark because her gloves looked like they floated in the deep shadows. "You and I have spoken twice, Lord Colin. And while those conversations have been ... pleasant, I would hesitate to give an endorsement on such paltry evidence."

And just like that, his shy little bird took the bait. "That is why I have sought you out, my lady. For, I believe, were you to spend more time in my company, you would be convinced of the sincerity of my efforts."

She stood for a while, thinking. He could practically *hear* her thinking.

"Entirely proper, you understand. I have the greatest respect—"

"Why me?" Jane interrupted.

"Victoria trusts you."

"No, I mean, why do you not simply speak to her yourself? Or, for that matter, why do you not attempt to make amends with the duke? I have heard he is in town."

Blast. This wager was going to kill him before it was over. His family was not a subject he relished discussing, the duke in particular. "My brother is not the forgiving sort," he said quietly. And that was the bloody damned truth of it.

"Yes, I can well imagine." Her instantaneous, heartfelt agreement was surprising—and encouraging. Most women lusted after Harrison, or at least the chance to leg-shackle a powerful duke. Apparently, Jane was the exception. In fact, he was finding her to be the exception in many regards. She was different than the usual run of wallflowers. Once a man got past her thorny walls of shyness, she was actually quite ... nice. And not at all dull. The opposite, really. He liked her.

He lowered his head and spoke, mimicking a confiding

posture. "I have made overtures, but he will have no part of it. Even threats of revealing his grace's rather *graceless* dunk in the Blackmore fish pond have failed to bring him 'round."

This time, her snort was obviously muffled laughter. Her voice rippled with it when she said, "What I wouldn't give to have witnessed such an occurrence. Akin to an eclipse of the sun, both rare and awe-inspiring."

"Oh, his grace was the picture of dignity, I assure you. One might even say he was *soaked* in it."

That got Jane laughing so hard, she bent double and braced her hand on his arm to steady herself. "The duke ... drenched ... with a l-l-lily pad ... on his beautiful, golden head."

He raised his brows. She had a dashed good imagination. "I hadn't thought of that. He could wear it like a crown. Suits him perfectly. Harrison Lacey, the eighth Duke of Blackmore. King of the Fish Pond."

She waved her hand at him, gasping for breath as another round of laughter consumed her. Clearly, Jane found the idea of Harrison meeting with misfortune exceedingly humorous. Come to think of it, so did he.

Taking several deep breaths to regain control, she patted his arm. "I do enjoy your company, Lord Colin. I—I would not be opposed to spending more time together. So long as our visits are proper."

His heart thudded sickeningly against the wall of his chest. She had agreed. It was what he'd come here to achieve. Now, winning the wager was possible.

Abruptly, he wanted to retch.

Instead, he nodded and smiled down into her flashing spectacles. "You shan't regret your decision, Lady Jane," he lied.

After watching her disappear back into Lady Reedham's music room, he'd gone straight to Reaver's and gotten roaring drunk.

Which was where he presently sat. Drunk. At Reaver's. Watching Benedict Chatham sip his second glass of whisky and thumb through the bleeding betting book that was five pages longer than it had been a fortnight ago.

Chatham arched a brow and glanced up at Colin. "Breeches?"

Colin's stomach heaved with nausea. He let his head drop back onto his arm where it rocked back and forth in despair. Chatham chuckled before remarking reassuringly, "Well, at least they did not specify a color. Now, *that* would be a challenge."

Chapter Four

"Courtship has no room for honesty, boy. By its very nature, it is a sly trick rooted in wishful thinking and self-delusion."

—THE DOWAGER MARCHIONESS OF WALLINGHAM to her son, Charles, after said gentleman's dismal attempt at conversation with Lord Willoughby's widow.

THREE WEEKS AFTER AGREEING TO SPEND MORE TIME WITH Lord Colin, Jane was heartily confused. He had sent a note the morning after Lady Reedham's musicale, requesting that she join him for a ride in Hyde Park. She had agreed, taking her maid, Estelle, along as chaperone. Remembering how excited she had been, the pains she had taken in choosing her riding gown—most uncharacteristic, she acknowledged—it had been rather disappointing that he'd behaved so ... well, oddly. Instead of attempting to charm her, as he had seemed to do on their previous encounters, he had been quiet, distracted. Then he had asked her if she'd ever considered traveling abroad or doing something daring, something no one would expect. She, of course, had asked him if he was feeling quite right.

Two days after their ride, she met him at the British Museum, where they viewed the Elgin marbles and laughed together over further tales from the Duke of Blackmore's boyhood. She should not relish *quite* so heartily Colin's description of his brother's breeches splitting after being thrown by his mount into a hedge. But she simply could not help herself.

Later in the afternoon, Colin had begun to tell a peculiar story about a missing necklace belonging to his mother, but they were interrupted by Genie, who, upon viewing the Greek statuary, declared that Athenians could not have been terribly civilized, as they had little to offer in the way of hats. With that, Jane had decided to take her leave, and Colin had bowed, looking rather pinched around the forehead.

The last time she had seen him, standing motionless just outside the British Museum, he had been staring after her and Genie and Estelle as they climbed into their carriage. She did not know what to make of his silence. Or of him, for that matter.

"Do you suppose I shall meet *him* this evening, Jane?"

Blinking, Jane turned from the window of the Berne carriage to her sister, Maureen, seated beside her. With soft brown eyes, rounded-yet-symmetrical features, and light-brown hair that always appeared lit by the sun, Maureen was indisputably the prettiest of the five Huxley daughters, so Jane answered easily, "If not this evening, dearest, it shall be another. Do not fret."

Maureen nodded and gave her a wistful smile. Jane patted her arm. Since the previous summer, when their oldest sister, Annabelle, had married Lord Robert Conrad, Maureen had taken to spinning fantasies around finding her own true love. At two years younger than Jane and in her first season, she sometimes needed reassurance.

From the opposite side of the carriage came a tart admonishment from their mother. "You did not bring a book along, did you, Jane?"

Jane felt her mouth tighten. "No, Mama."

"How do you expect to acquire a proper suitor in the pages of a novel? I daresay it is impossible."

"Yes, Mama."

"I should not need to remind you this is your *third* season."

"No, Mama."

"You must seize upon every opportunity. Goodness knows how much longer these occasions shall present themselves."

"Yes, Mama."

Their father, kindly man that he was, took Mama's hand in his own and squeezed. "Let her be, Meredith. She agreed to come along, did she not?" He gave Jane a wink.

In truth, Jane had not precisely *agreed* to attend Lady Gilforth's ball. Instead, she had been informed it was occurring, that she was expected to accompany her parents and Maureen, and that she was forbidden to bring the novel she'd been reading when Mama had entered the library. Before a protest had reached her lips, her mother had held up a hand and said, "I trust you understand fully," with brows arched expectantly over wide brown eyes.

What else could Jane say, other than, "Yes, Mama"? For the last two seasons, she had disappointed her sweet, good-humored mother to the brink of desperation. The specter of spinsterhood for her second-oldest daughter had added more than a few strands of white to Meredith Huxley's brunette coiffure.

Briefly, Jane had contemplated telling Mama about Colin Lacey, if only to ease concerns that she was incapable of cordial interaction with a gentleman. She had rejected that catastrophically bad idea an instant after it had occurred. Lord Colin's behavior, while charming, was not that of a suitor. He was kind and amusing but often distracted, as if his mind was preoccupied with other matters.

Having witnessed a number of love matches play out before her eyes, including those of her best friend and her sister, she understood the difference. She refused to raise her mother's hopes when he obviously intended friendship, rather than romantic attachment. Fortunately, Genie had proven a rather clever ally in disguising the purpose of their outings. It had cost Jane nearly her entire allowance, of course, but she was learning much about her sister's hidden talent for subterfuge.

She sighed and resumed staring out the carriage window at the bustling lane. Lady Gilforth lived across Mayfair from their London residence on Grosvenor Street. It was a tolerably brief carriage ride, she supposed, providing one was not required to listen to one's mother worry aloud about otherwise sensible girls who chose "storybooks and poetry over securing a sound match."

Jane did not fault her for her consternation. In looks, she and Mama were much the same: more plump than was permissible; a short, round nose most would describe as a pug; and coloring that blended nicely into wood paneling. But in every other way, Jane and her mother were a study in contrasts: Lady Berne was effusive, gracious, warm. Since her youth, Mama's humor and kindness had shone from her, attracting numerous friendships and the eye of Jane's father, the future Earl of Berne, in her first season. Annabelle, the oldest of the five girls, shared this disposition, as did Maureen and Genie and even young Kate, albeit to lesser degrees.

Jane, to put it simply, did not.

Little wonder Mama was confounded by Jane's inability to attract even one suitor. *She* had never been consigned to dwell on the fringes of ballrooms with the old flowers and the wallflowers—or, as Jane had privately dubbed them, the Oddflowers.

She sniffed and shifted subtly in her seat, feeling the carriage slow as they approached Lady Gilforth's town house.

How was she to endure an entire ball without a book to keep her company? Was she expected to gaze out at the crowd, marveling at Sir Barnabus Malby's ability to recall the steps of a dance while mesmerized by a passing bodice? Or perhaps she should admire Penelope Darling's braying chortle at every tedious quip from Lord Mochrie.

Truthfully, it was enough to make any "otherwise sensible" girl dash out to the nearest terrace. Of course, Victoria had tried that, and she had been quite thoroughly ruined. So, perhaps not the best idea.

"Jane, are you coming?"

Her head swiveled back toward the open door of the carriage, through which she could see her mother, father, and sister staring at her expectantly.

"Of course," she murmured, scrambling down from the carriage. Adjusting her Kashmiri shawl across her shoulders, she could not suppress a shiver of dread.

Maureen looped an arm through hers. "Imagine. This may be a night we remember for the rest of our lives."

Casting her sister a sideways glance, Jane lifted a skeptical brow.

"I saw that," came Mama's customary reprimand, followed by a hushed warning. "Kindly demonstrate you are capable of being pleasant and agreeable, Jane. I will not have it said my daughter is a churl. Lady Gilforth's influence is swiftly growing, and Lord Gilforth is much admired within the House of Lords. All of the finest gentlemen shall be in attendance." The martial gleam in her eye was alarming, for Mama was typically a jolly sort. Soon, however, the reason behind her fervor was revealed: "I have it on good authority *his grace* is expected."

Maureen's gasp was echoed in Jane's heart, though likely for different reasons.

"Wellington? I thought he was still in Paris," their father interjected.

Mama's fan tapped Papa's arm as she tsked. "Not Wellington. Blackmore."

The dawning realization on Papa's face was followed swiftly by an amused twinkle. "In that case, you girls should be on your best behavior."

"Precisely." Mama directed her emphatic affirmation at Jane, who clutched her shawl a bit tighter as they waited for the other guests crowding Lady Gilforth's door to move forward. This was shaping up to be a crush.

Sighing prettily, Maureen remarked, "He is very handsome. And distinguished."

And insufferable, Jane added silently. *A judgmental, pompous ice king who needs nothing so much as a sharp blow across his ... pride.*

"The fortune and title add a certain appeal as well, I daresay."

Jane frowned at Papa, who grinned at her as if they shared a private joke, then held his arm out for Mama so they could enter Lady Gilforth's foyer. Sometimes, she did not understand her father's jests. To her mind, the Duke of Blackmore was the least amusing topic imaginable, unless one pictured him receiving a well-deserved comeuppance.

Last season, Blackmore had even dared reprimand Jane directly—in her own home, no less. It was only the second time they'd had occasion to speak. Granted, she and Genie had been squabbling, as sisters tended to do, but how was she to know the blasted eighth Duke of Blackmore would be lurking in the shadows of her family's drawing room, awaiting a visit with Lord and Lady Berne? Only after she'd threatened to throw Genie bodily into the fireplace had he revealed himself, hands clasped behind a rigid back, jaw locked tight against possible cracking—wouldn't want a shred of emotion to escape, after all. Had he been anyone else, she would have described him as bristling with disapproval. But Blackmore did not bristle. He was like a blade—merciless and precise. It had taken mere seconds for him to reduce Jane to feeling all of ten years old, caught nipping Papa's cognac or stashing a toad in Mama's silver teapot.

Taking a deep breath, Jane reminded herself that, even if he deigned to attend Lady Gilforth's ball, he would be too busy fending off marriage-minded young ladies and their voracious mothers to take any notice of her. Certainly, for politeness' sake, he would greet Mama and Papa, probably even bow to her and Maureen, but that was likely to be the extent of their interaction.

She sniffed and adjusted her spectacles, then lightly smoothed the yellow primrose silk of her gown along one hip. *You need only curtsy, Jane. Give him a "your grace," and nothing more.* Feeling the tightness in her belly ease, she waited for Lady Gilforth's butler to announce them, her eyes quickly examining the edges of the long, spacious drawing room. Along one pale-blue wall sat a row of cream-colored settees and dark-blue velvet chairs, already half-populated by familiar figures: Sallow, thin Miss Sutherland, now in her fifth (and probably last) season. The aged Lady Darnham, whose face appeared to be formed entirely of smile-shaped creases. The alarmingly tall, redheaded Miss Lancaster, with her unfortunate tendency to crush gentlemen's feet while dancing ... and walking ... and, oddly enough, while dining.

Ah, yes. A wry grin tugged. *The Oddflowers are well represented this evening.* Her eyes drifted to a pair of open doors on the far wall, through which lay the dining room where Lady Gilforth had set up the refreshments. *Hmm.* If she were to sit at the near end of the Oddflower wall, she could occupy herself with an occasional trip to the refreshment tables. Hardly a thrilling journey, but an acceptable way to distract oneself and help time pass more quickly. *Yes, indeed. A sound plan.*

A sharp nudge in her ribs brought Jane's eyes around to Maureen.

"Mama was right," her sister whispered theatrically behind her fan. "He is here. Do you suppose he is seeking a wife?"

Jane followed Maureen's gaze. He was not difficult to

spot—taller than John, their brother, who was an even six feet, Blackmore stood half a head above most other gentlemen. She also had to admit—grudgingly—that Maureen had not exaggerated when she'd called him handsome.

He was. Quite so.

The jaw that favored a locked position was strong and square and lean. A straight, refined nose acted as a symmetrical anchor between lofty cheekbones, which sat beneath a piercing pair of blue-gray eyes. On the whole, if she was bound by honesty, his blond male beauty was undeniable, in much the same way as the Elgin marbles were objectively masterful. Jane imagined if the English nobility possessed a pantheon of gods like that of the ancient Greeks, he might be considered their Apollo, except Apollo had never been as powerful as the Duke of Blackmore, nor as intimidating.

"Well, whether he is here to find a duchess or not," Jane finally answered, "I recommend keeping your distance. I understand frostbite is rather painful."

An hour later, Jane was thankful for her strategy of making occasional trips to the refreshment tables. Lady Gilforth had outdone herself. To quench revelers' appetites until supper, two long sideboards were strewn with a wide variety of tidbits, from tiny cheesecakes to flaky biscuits. Anyone who had attended a ton ball knew how it felt to be famished by the time supper was announced. Such interim offerings were most welcome. Additionally, at the center of each sideboard sat a silver bowl of delicious punch—sweet, tangy, and a bit spicy.

Jane poured her fourth cup, wondering if this time, she might place that elusive spice. Cinnamon? She shook her head. No. Not cinnamon. But perhaps it was a blend of orange and mulled wine. That made more sense. Clove, cinnamon, and nutmeg might together produce the heady flavor. Perhaps even with a dash of peppercorn.

Peering through the doors into the drawing room, she watched dancers swirl around the center of the floor in a quadrille. How many quadrilles had she witnessed over the past three seasons? Too many. Waltzes? Too many. The motions of every season were the same, and Jane had grown deeply weary of each and every one.

Sighing, she took another sip and longed for a nice, distracting novel.

Being an Oddflower gave one a unique perspective on the spectacle of the standard ton event, as she was able to observe the motions and repetitions without direct participation. Her brother, who was on his grand tour of the continent, had recently sent a crate full of treasures to Berne House, including a fascinating clock that, when striking the hour, extended a tiny bird on a branch from a crevice above the clock face. The bird, having no will of its own, was controlled solely by the regular movement of the clockwork mechanism.

That was how she regarded the motions of the London season: rote gestures orchestrated by an apparatus immune to its objects. Curtsy, whirl, bow, titter, fan, smile, tilt, and again. And again. The same motions. The same routine. She supposed there was a point to it all. Ladies must find husbands and gentlemen must find wives. But, being all but locked outside the process, she could not help noting its monotony.

Inside her mind, she began a letter to Annabelle, who was now blessedly free of such obligations, having married last August. Of course, Annabelle had adored the season with all its trappings, insisting on enjoying two of her own before marrying Lord Conrad, whom she had loved devotedly since childhood.

Dearest Annabelle, Jane would write. *Lady Gilforth's refreshments are magnificent. For nearly two minutes in every twenty, I cease pining for a novel that will allow me to forget my misery, and simply relish her ingeniously spiced punch. I suspect it contains more than a minor quantity of wine.*

She glanced down, seeing the remnants of her fourth cup. Feeling pleasantly warm, she placed it on a tray and braced herself for the long journey back to her seat along the

Oddflower wall. As she entered the drawing room, a masculine shout of pain arose from the center of the quadrille dancers, drawing her attention.

"Oh, dear, Sir Barnabus, was that your nose?" Charlotte Lancaster's flame-red hair was visible above most of the other ladies' heads, and even those of many gentlemen. "I do beg your forgiveness. I fear my elbow has a mind of its own. Are you quite all right?" Jane had heard her apologize for habitual clumsiness before, but Miss Lancaster ordinarily sounded more sincere. Sir Barnabus Malby's misplaced nose was probably less to blame than his wandering eyes. Miss Lancaster had rather modern notions about such things. Come to that, so did Jane. But even the portly, malodorous Sir Barnabus did not ask Plain Jane Huxley to dance. *Well*, she decided, *there are benefits to being ignored, after all.*

Tucking her lip between her teeth, she rose up on her toes to see if she could get a glimpse of the man's face. Perhaps Miss Lancaster had bloodied his nose. *Now, that would be interesting.* A black lapel appeared in front of her. She moved to her left, but so did the masculine wall wearing the black coat and white cravat. And now it was closer, so it obscured even more of her line of sight. She scooted to her right. Again, the gentleman glided in the same direction. Huffing in exasperation, she looked up to see who was so blasted determined to place himself between her and the commotion.

"One might have hoped for improved comportment in a lady entering her third season," the precise, clipped, unmistakable voice of her nemesis intoned from his lofty height. "Perhaps I expect too much."

Eyes widening, heart thudding hard against bone, Jane felt the hated heat of embarrassment burn through her in a wave. Blackmore. The great, golden god of ton propriety was reprimanding her for having simple, natural curiosity. The last time he had done something similar, they had been standing in her family's drawing room. She and Genie had been arguing over a book Genie had stolen. Jane had made an empty threat about throwing her sister into the fireplace.

"What book is so precious, I wonder, that it draws threats of burning one's sibling?" She remembered his voice, slicing flinty and cold across the room. *"Nothing to say for yourself, then?"* And she had been struck dumb, frozen by the shame of the accusation, never mind how unfair it might be.

It was the same now, as if an entire year had not passed, as if, instead, her only task had been to continuously stand before him, awaiting his harsh assessment. How dared he? Not even her father or brother, either of whom would be within his rights, would castigate her so. Who was the bloody Duke of Blackmore to her? No one. He was Victoria's brother, not hers. *Therefore, he is Victoria's problem. Not mine.*

Backing away one step, she cleared her throat, gathering herself to deliver an equally icy greeting before escaping back to her Oddflower seat. But the "your grace" that she intended refused to emerge. Her mouth worked, but her voice did not. She swallowed, feeling the crimson fire beneath her skin intrude like another presence.

She felt his blue-gray eyes travel over her gown, then back up, pausing at the modest neckline and returning to her face. Cool and remote, they seemed to be cataloging her features as a stable master might note the condition of a mare. "Have you danced yet this evening?"

Blinking slowly, she wondered at the question, which had sounded grudging, like he did not wish to be there at all. What in heaven's name was he doing? Why was he continuing to speak with her? This was the sort of thing a gentleman might say if he was trying to persuade a lady to ... no. It was impossible. She needed to provide him an acceptable opportunity to withdraw. That was all.

She shook her head and swallowed, eyes darting between him and the doorway to the dining room. "I—I'm afraid the heat has caused a frightful thirst. I was just going to retrieve another cup of punch when you arrived."

A single aristocratic brow elevated. "Again? Is this not the fifth such venture?"

For the second time that evening, Jane was struck straight down to her slippers by a statement from the Duke of Blackmore. Had he been *watching* her? A strange shiver burned over her skin, different than the flush that had engulfed her earlier, but just as heated.

"No one should require so much refreshing," he stated assuredly. "Perhaps if you were to dance, you would not be inclined to consume in such quantity."

And the Ice King returns, she thought. *Well, at least he is predictable.*

Blackmore's shoulders straightened further, his jaw tilting to an arrogant angle. "A waltz shall begin soon. Will you consent to dance it with me?"

Upon further consideration, perhaps not so predictable.

She would have gasped, but she couldn't seem to find her breath. Or the ability to move. He had just asked her to dance. *He,* the unanimously agreed-upon Catch of the Season—every season—had asked *her,* the quintessential Oddflower, to dance a waltz.

Growing visibly disgruntled by her silence, the tall, blond Apollo of the aristocracy, bit out, "When a lady is asked to dance, it is customary to answer."

He was right. She must answer him. And she would. Clenching her teeth, Jane marshaled every scintilla of courage to be found inside her plain, round, Oddflower body, and gave him the answer he richly deserved.

"No." It emerged as a whisper. Swallowing past all trepidation, she repeated the word in her normal voice, pinched though it might be. "No. I don't believe I shall dance with you, your grace."

Chapter Five

"She is her own worst enemy, Meredith. Mark my words, one day you will have no choice but to agree with me."

—THE DOWAGER MARCHIONESS OF WALLINGHAM to Lady Berne while discussing Jane Huxley's prospects for future spinsterhood.

IT WAS PAINFULLY OBVIOUS THE DUKE OF BLACKMORE WAS unaccustomed to rejection. A scowl dawned on his brow; perplexity narrowed his eyes. As though expecting her to correct her own statement, he glared down at her, waiting.

They stood as an island of silence amidst the din of chatter and music.

Jane felt an overpowering urge to squirm, but she forced herself to continue meeting his gaze and say nothing. Perhaps her red glow would eventually disgust him, and he would leave her to her spiced punch and velvet settee.

"Your grace!" Her mother's exclamation made Jane's heart lurch and pound. *Oh, dear.* Waving at them, Mama marched out of a cluster of matrons near the edge of where Miss Lancaster had brought the dancing to a temporary halt. "A most unexpected pleasure. Why, it has been an age." Mama sidled up to Jane and curtsied to Blackmore, who bowed stiffly, his scowl easing into a frown.

"Lady Berne," he said simply.

One might have thought his tone rather chilly, but Jane suspected for Blackmore, it was nothing out of the ordinary. Certainly, it did not faze her mother, who gave the man a broad, beaming smile. "Lady Gilforth assures me a waltz shall begin momentarily."

His body stilled, lips flattening into a grim line.

"Perhaps, if you are not otherwise engaged, my Jane would be a suitable partner?"

Oh. Oh, no.

In the past, Mama had pressed Jane into conversing with gentlemen, had encouraged her to more actively seek their attention, had insisted on buying her new, more flattering gowns each season. But never—*never*—had she directly solicited a dance on Jane's behalf. And to do so from the all-mighty Duke of Blackmore was ... words failed. *Excruciating* came close, but did not quite capture the resounding nature of her mortification.

Apparently, Blackmore was inclined to view the suggestion as a putrid smell wafted before him, because his hard-edged chin angled further upward, and his nostrils flared in displeasure. "I have made such an offer, madam, and it has been declined."

Wondering idly if she would survive this night, Jane watched Mama's eyes fly wide, her head tilt, her lips tighten. This was bad. Very bad, indeed.

Abruptly, Mama adopted a pleasant smile. Wrapping her hand surreptitiously through the crook of Jane's elbow, she dug in harder than necessary and sent another beam up at Blackmore. "Nonsense," she declared. "A misunderstanding, that is all. She would be *delighted* to dance with you." The claws grew sharper, almost painful. "Wouldn't you, Jane?"

Well, in the interest of preserving her arm, and quite possibly her life, Jane supposed one dance with the Ice King was not too much to ask. She nodded her assent.

Stiffly—it seemed he did everything stiffly—the duke bowed and held out a white-gloved hand. "Lady Jane."

She slid her own hand into his, and he smoothly transferred it to his arm. The motion pulled her much nearer to him than she had ever been. Dimly, she noted that he smelled good, like freshly laundered bed linens dried in the sun. *Must be the starch in his cravat,* she thought. *Plenty of that, no doubt. The thing could stand and salute Wellington all on its own.*

Glancing to the side, she was struck by their differences. He was more than a foot taller. Strong and lean, though much broader at the shoulders than one perceived from a distance. Handsome as Hades—on second thought, Apollo was probably more appropriate, so she would stay with that comparison. Regardless, he was everything she was not.

We must appear a ludicrous pairing. Her gaze darted around the drawing room. *Just as well I am too short to see past the crush.* She did not relish the jeering dismay she was bound to find on every face.

Pulling her into the dance, Blackmore managed to make the unevenness of their heights less awkward than anticipated, shortening his strides and smoothly leading her through the turns of the waltz. Again, a great, yawning silence stretched and sagged between them. Two minutes on, however, she had to admit the dance itself was rather ... lovely. Controlled. Graceful.

Before she could think better of it, her observation slipped out of her mouth. "You—you dance quite well, your grace. Surprisingly so."

His brows arched, then his firm, straight lips tightened. "If you perceived me as a poor partner for the waltz, perhaps that explains your earlier rudeness."

Her body stiffened, slowing their turn, but he applied pressure at her back, and they continued with nary a pause. "It is not my manners which should be in question, but yours," she muttered furiously.

"Only a child would believe so."

She shot a glare up past his infuriatingly perfect jaw, colliding with blue-gray eyes that flashed like sunlight glinting off new ice. "I am not a child. And I will thank you to cease treating me like one."

"Age is merely a number denoting the passage of time, Lady Jane. One's maturity is best measured by one's actions and comportment—areas in need of improvement, where you are concerned."

Her jaw worked as she struggled for breath. "You are a rare creature, your grace. I fear I have never encountered anyone as pompous and appallingly rude."

His scowl deepened. "It is hardly rude to state the truth."

"Then, allow me to return the favor. You are insufferable."

The barest hint of a flush crept up along his cheekbones. "What I am, Lady Jane, is at the end of my patience. This is the last time I agree to grant a favor for my sister when it involves cheeky misses who lack the sense to discern between a duke and a dray horse."

The statement stopped her cold. Even Blackmore's nudging could not make her move. Breathless, arms heavy and limp, Jane asked, "What has Victoria to do with anything?"

For the first time that evening—or ever, that she could recall—he looked distinctly uneasy. After blinking several times, he cleared his throat. "She requested, if I should see you during the season, that I partner you for a dance."

Before he finished his statement, her eyes slid closed against the truth, her head dropping forward to hang between them. It hurt. Deeply. Even her best friend thought Jane so pitiful that she must recruit her brother to offer a dance. Breathing through the tight ache in her chest, Jane attempted to tug her hands free.

"What are you doing?"

The music continued to play, but little of the song remained. Surely she could retreat to her settee in the far corner of the drawing room and return to blessed obscurity. Surely he would let her go.

But he did not. His back faced the crowd, hers a wall. His arms remained in place, refusing to release her.

Likely worried I will embarrass him. Mustn't have that.

Suddenly, it was all too much. *He* was too much. She must say something to convince him to let her go. Eyes locked on his well-starched cravat, she gathered her breath and her anger and her courage. "Perhaps you are right, your grace," she said quietly. "Perhaps I do not have the sense to tell a duke from a dray horse. But such a thing might prove easier if the former did not so perfectly resemble the latter's backside."

The music ended. His arms fell away.

Turning, she stumbled and pushed along the edge of the room, sidling past a group of young bucks discussing an excursion to Tattersall's, and five young ladies fanning themselves furiously in a bid for attention. They were all a blur to Jane.

Dimly, she heard Penelope Darling laughing too loudly at one of Lord Mochrie's witticisms. Then, a gruff apology from an elderly man as he elbowed Jane in the shoulder. She did not feel it. Her sole mission was to return to the dining room, and from there out into the corridor, and from there ...

From there ...

She did not know.

As an earl's daughter, she was not permitted an escape route.

The dining room entrance loomed. She slipped out of the tightly packed drawing room and immediately thanked heaven for allowing her a breath of less-stagnant air. In front of her, footmen worked quickly and efficiently to set long tables for supper. To the left, a set of doors stood open, beckoning her into the corridor.

It was not a perfect solution, but at least it would give her a temporary reprieve, some privacy away from the tittering fools of the ton. She stepped out into the darker, hushed space. Two maids passed her without bothering to curtsy. Jane was accustomed to such disregard of her position. Many, many people seemed nearly incapable of noticing her. Most often, she found it alternately amusing and annoying. Tonight, she found it relieving.

Lady Gilforth's home was not terribly ornate or ostentatious. Rather, it was quietly elegant, the walls of the corridor paneled in dark wood—walnut, perhaps. Her drawing room and dining room were coordinated in shades of blue and green, accented by moldings in white and furnishings in rich, jewel-toned fabrics. None of the rooms Jane had seen were overlarge, and yet they felt spacious and bright. But here, in the quiet corridor, the warm, dark wood seemed almost a friend, a promise to keep her secrets. She made her way to the end of the hall, tested a knob on a discreet door. Turning it slowly, she opened the door a mere inch, noting the lack of illumination in the space beyond.

Ah, yes. Perfect.

Many town houses in Mayfair had been built along similar lines as Berne House, and in her home, there was a closet in this very spot at the end of a corridor. She glanced behind her to make certain the duke had not decided to do something outlandish—following her, for example.

What she saw when she turned caused her to jerk around and slam her back against the door. It closed with a loud bang. Wincing, she blinked and adjusted her spectacles. No, she was not imagining things. There, his blond head swiveling to and fro as he searched the hall, was Victoria's *other* brother, Colin Lacey.

The racket of the door closing must have alerted him, because he squinted in her direction, then charged forward as he recognized her. "Lady Jane!" A grin split his face, displaying white teeth in the dim light. "It seems I forever find you in corridors."

She held up a hand. "Lord Colin, I must warn you, I am not favorably disposed toward anyone of your bloodline at present."

He stopped. "I don't understand."

"Did Victoria send you as well? Is that what all of this has been about?"

Coming within feet of her, he dared to appear both baffled and concerned. "Send me? I have not spoken to Victoria in months."

"Why assign only *one* brother to the distasteful task of taking pity upon poor, Plain Jane Huxley, when you can send two?"

He took a deep breath to respond, then apparently at a loss, released it in a whoosh as he shook his head. "You have me at a disadvantage, Lady Jane. I haven't the slightest idea to what you're referring."

His puzzlement seemed genuine, forcing her to reconsider her assumptions. "Victoria did not ask you to feign a courtship?"

The sudden gurgle of laughter that burst from Lord Colin caused an uncomfortable flush to prickle its way across Jane's cheeks.

Seeing it, he immediately waved away her embarrassment. "Please do not mistake my laughter for mockery. It is not at your expense, but my own. Victoria would sooner deliver a basket of poisonous asps to your door than request that I pledge my suit to you." The mirth slowly disappeared from his voice, replaced with something like regret. "My sister has a rather low opinion of my character. Deservedly so."

"Oh."

He smiled gently. "Tell me what happened."

She sniffed and clutched her shawl a little tighter across her arms. "That is not important. It is sufficient to say I have noted stark contrasts between you and your brother."

His brows arched.

"And it gladdens my heart that you are not *him*."

Another smile curved his lips, this one slow and conspiratorial. "You cannot fathom what I have been forced to endure."

"He is insufferable."

"Stuffy."

"Heartless."

"Sanctimonious."

"Tall."

He chuckled. "Tall?"

Nodding emphatically, she explained, "He looms over me like a great, towering oak. A frigid, disapproving oak that does not even wish to be in my presence, but is merely tolerating such a trial because his *sister* ..." Catching herself winding up for a potentially disastrous tirade, Jane stopped and clamped her lips together.

Colin's eyes crinkled in sympathy. "I understand. Harrison is at his worst when he believes he is doing what is best—never mind what we lesser creatures might wish for ourselves. The Duke of Blackmore knows better."

"That is it precisely! Who is *he* to stand in judgment?"

"Only a man."

Jane swallowed, realizing that here was someone who understood—*truly* understood how galling it was to be the object of undeserved derision. She wanted to weep at finding a kindred spirit in the precise moment she needed one. Had she been the weepy sort, she just might. But she was not. It could be too easily perceived as weakness, and she had more than enough of that to contend with. "It can't have been easy for you."

"Having Harrison for a brother?"

She nodded.

His eyes grew serious, then sorrowful. He swallowed visibly and looked away, coming back with an empty grin a moment later. "Have I told you of my most recent interaction with the duke?"

Shaking her head, she felt her curiosity pique. Would this be another amusing tale ending in Blackmore's abject humiliation? Surely, that was just the balm she needed after this dreadful night. A good laugh before she must return to the dining room and breathe the same air as His Royal Iciness during supper.

Colin cleared his throat. "It involves a necklace. My mother's necklace. Or, rather, *our* mother. His and mine. And Victoria's, of course."

"Yes, yes. Your mother. Do go on."

His nose wrinkled on a sniff. He plucked idly at his coat sleeve and glanced down at his boots. "I lost it."

She frowned. "You lost your mother's necklace?"

The look he sent her was sheepish, but also something else. Nervous, perhaps. "It is a family heirloom, meant for the future Duchess of Blackmore."

"How did you lose—"

"I'd been drinking. A great deal."

"Ah. Yes, well. That explains it."

A quiet smile warmed his eyes. "Not entirely. A former friend, Lord Milton, was curious about it and dared me to show it to him. So, I took it from Clyde-Lacey House and brought it to his town house." Seeing her dismay, he quickly interjected, "A dreadful mistake, one of many I am now attempting to set right."

She sighed. "Go on."

"Somehow—I do not recall how—I left and returned home without the necklace. When I later asked Lord Milton about it, he claimed that I took it with me, but I know that is untrue. My belief is that he deliberately stole the necklace as retribution for his own ill fortune with cards."

"He stole a family heirloom as recompense for your defeating him at the gaming table? What sort of gentleman—?"

"The low sort. As I have stated—"

She waved a hand. "Yes, yes. You are attempting to reform."

He nodded. "To that end, I recently confessed the loss of the necklace to Harrison. He was ... displeased."

Releasing an inelegant snort, she asked, "What did he say?"

"That I should not speak to him again unless I was prepared to return what I had lost."

She crossed her arms beneath her bosom, a single finger tapping along the edge of her long glove, just above her elbow. "Do you know, I have a brother and four sisters, each of whom has vexed me greatly at one time or another. But I never once considered cutting them from my life."

Colin shrugged, implying he had long ago given up battling against his brother's inflexibility. "It is his way. One can scarcely blame him. At least he has granted me the opportunity to repair the damage I have caused." Smiling weakly, Colin shifted from one foot to the other.

"Have you a plan to retrieve the necklace?"

He had lowered his head to once again examine his boots, but at her question, he glanced up, his gaze oddly bright. "Yes." He straightened his shoulders as though bracing himself. "I have determined the location where Milton is hiding the necklace. It is still in his house, here in London. But I cannot retrieve it while he is there, as he will surely be watching, knowing that I suspect him of the theft."

She frowned. "Then, how will you gain access to his home?"

"I will not have to. All I need do is lure him away, leaving the house empty and unguarded for several hours, during which anyone could easily slip in and take back what is rightfully mine, with no one the wiser."

By the time he finished, his gaze was intensely focused. On *her*. The implication was unmistakable.

"Oh, no. No, no, no. I agreed to convey my favorable impression of you to Victoria. I did not agree to become your partner in burglary."

"I would not dare ask it of you—"

"Is that not what you just did?"

"—but you are my only hope, Lady Jane. It must be someone I can trust not to simply flee with the necklace, someone who would not raise suspicion, nor be particularly associated with me. I promise you will not be in a moment's danger; I will make all the arrangements. You need only enter Milton's house, retrieve the necklace, and return it to me the next day."

"I'm sorry, Colin. I cannot h—"

"Harrison has given me an ultimatum—retrieve the necklace within a week, or he shall never speak to me again. And he will advise Victoria to do likewise. No doubt he expects me to fail, and this is merely his excuse to cut all ties." Colin reached for her hands, forcing them out away from her body and squeezing them in his own. "Please, Lady Jane. You are my only true friend."

His urgency was, indeed, severe. She felt it radiating from him in waves. He was desperate for her help. But how could she agree? If she were caught in such an illicit act, the consequences for her reputation would be nigh immeasurable.

On the other hand, she could not help picturing the Duke of Blackmore's face upon being presented with the necklace he had demanded as the price for his loyalty, imagined him being forced to retreat from his rigid position, to bend toward forgiveness. It would be humbling to a man of his nature to be proven wrong.

For some reason, that mattered to Jane—more than it should. The Duke of Blackmore. Humbled. And, unbeknownst to him, she would play a role. She, Plain Jane Huxley, could bring the Ice King to his knees. All she must do is be a little daring.

Unfortunately, "daring" was one of many things she was not. She had read about daring, dreamed about it occasionally, witnessed it a few times. But it simply wasn't her.

Colin squeezed her fingers, reminding her of the need to respond. She looked into his eyes. A half-shade less green than Victoria's, and a half-shade less gray than Blackmore's, they were quite a lovely blue. And quite troubled.

In the end, that was what convinced her.

"Very well," she said, squeezing in return. "What would you need me to do?"

Chapter Six

"Allow me to demonstrate the distinction between an error and a scandal: Mistaking one's husband for the footman is an error. Mistaking the footman for one's husband is a scandal."

—THE DOWAGER MARCHIONESS OF WALLINGHAM to her son, Charles, upon news of a certain widow's unfortunate predilections.

"BREECHES?" INCREDULITY ELEVATED ANNABELLE'S VOICE A FULL octave.

"Breeches," Maureen confirmed, patting Jane's hand where it rested in her lap. "And a mask."

For her part, Jane could not bear to look at either of her sisters, opting instead to stare blankly out the window of her bedroom.

It was the morning after the greatest mistake of her life. And Annabelle could not seem to grasp the simplest of concepts. Yes, breeches and a mask. And, yes, she'd been caught attempting to burglarize the London house of Lord Milton. What was so difficult to comprehend? It was untenable, granted, but hardly complex.

"Well, I don't believe it. There must be some error. Jane would never ..." Trailing off as Maureen shook her head solemnly, Annabelle slowly moved to sit on Jane's opposite side on the divan. They were like parentheses, her sisters, surrounding the bumbler between them. Annabelle slid her hand over Maureen's, which remained over Jane's.

What a bloody tangle.

"If you were in need of funds, you had only to say so. Robert would gladly grant me an increase, and then I could give you whatever you required. Truly, there was no need to go to these lengths—"

Before Jane could utter a word, Maureen answered, "This was not about funds, Annabelle. She was deceived by a dastardly pretender."

Annabelle's eyes, so similar to Jane's own, flew wide. "Who?"

"Lord Colin Lacey." The answer came not from Maureen, or even Jane, but from Genie, who had poked her head into the room.

While Annabelle gasped, Maureen inquired, "What are you doing in here, brat? I thought you were occupied with your music lesson."

"Papa asked me to fetch Jane. He wishes to speak with her in the parlor."

Jane's stomach plummeted down what must surely be an entire flight of stairs. Papa was a kindhearted, good-humored sort, but *this*—Jane's hideous error in judgment—would try the most saintly of fathers.

Fortunately, Jane had sisters to help her to her feet, sisters to brace each of her elbows as she somehow navigated out into the corridor, down the stairs, and to the closed parlor doors.

There, she stood flanked by Maureen and Annabelle, with Genie hovering behind. Together, they gazed blankly at the golden-brown wood, perhaps expecting it to convey a different sort of message. One in which Jane's folly, rather than being the cause of her certain ruination, was seen as a lark, blithely dismissed by those in the ton who made such judgments.

"Perhaps you could come and stay with me and Robert for a spell," Annabelle whispered as they all waited for a miracle to occur. "It shan't be long before having an auntie around the house would be welcome."

Marvelous. I shall be the spinster auntie living on the largesse of my brother-in-law. Although she was grateful for the offer, she did not relish becoming a charitable project. Besides, it would do nothing to solve the central problem: If she was ruined, Maureen and Genie and even little Kate would find their marriage prospects severely diminished.

Taking a deep breath, she knocked on the door. At her father's quiet, "Come," she stepped through. Papa turned from the window, his usual grin absent, supplanted by exhausted resignation. Suddenly, he was no longer her doting Papa, but a man of many years, with thinning, graying hair and creases along his forehead. Hazel eyes that normally crinkled and danced with laughter now were shadowed and drawn.

Swallowing a lump, she rasped, "I'm sorry, Papa."

Hazel eyes softened and warmed. A small, gentle smile lifted his mouth. "I know, Poppet." He glanced away for a moment then gestured to the striped sofa across from his favorite green chair. "Let's sit and see about negotiating our way through this labyrinth, shall we?"

As they sat across from one another, Jane wondered if it was even possible to extricate oneself from the trap she had blithely—and blindly—sprung. Victoria had been thoroughly ruined last season, and with the aid of Jane's family and Mama's good friend, Lady Wallingham, her reputation had been restored. But *she* had been offered marriage by Lord

Atherbourne, which had helped immensely in neutralizing her indiscretions. Jane had no such prospects. Colin Lacey was as likely to come up to scratch as he was to sprout wings and lay eggs for breakfast.

Papa rested his hands on the arms of the chair and sighed his weariness. "I wished to speak with you before your mother and Lady Wallingham arrive."

"Lady Wallingham is coming here?" She shook her head, denial and despair warring within her. "Must we involve her, Papa?"

Victoria referred to the Dowager Marchioness of Wallingham as "the dragon." It was an apt description. As Mama's bosom friend and a powerful figure within ton gossip circles, she had readily assisted Victoria, a duke's sister, when asked. But she had never seemed to have a high regard for Jane, criticizing her shyness and bookishness as "a lengthy, self-serving sulk waged against one's own interests." Aside from the dragon's likely disinclination to help, Jane failed to see how even a matron as influential as Lady Wallingham could possibly reverse the damage. The mistake was simply too grave.

"Your mother insisted," Papa answered. "Now then, we have greater concerns before us. What were you thinking, Jane?" His present exasperation was closer to what she'd expected. She remained silent to give him the chance to release it.

Last night, still reeling with shock, she had managed to explain the bare facts of the situation, but had been too distraught to elaborate more fully. Having assured themselves of her safety, both he and her mother had agreed to delay further explanations until this morning. Now, Papa desired a thorough accounting. She could scarcely blame him. Her stupidity astounded even her.

"You have always been a sensible girl. This scheme was, to put it kindly, as addlepated as any I have ever heard. What could Lord Colin possibly have promised in exchange for placing not only your reputation, but your sisters' future prospects in jeopardy?"

Cringing, Jane muttered, "Nothing. He offered me nothing."

His hands spread wide, beseeching heaven for answers. "Help me understand. Because right now, I simply do not."

"I believed him a friend. He required my help, or so I thought. He gave me his word I would be in no danger."

"Did it not occur to you that a *friend*—let alone a *gentleman*—would not ask such a thing of you? Would not conceive of placing you in such jeopardy?"

She blinked. "I supposed the circumstances to be extraordinary. He had prevailed upon my generosity before, and so I believed—"

Papa straightened in his chair, leaning his elbows on the arms. "Did he dare to take liberties—?"

"No! It was nothing like that, I assure you. He behaved as a proper gentleman." It took her merely a second, and her father's disbelieving expression, to revise, "Well, until last night. Deceiving me in order to win a wager cannot precisely be termed 'gentlemanly,' I suppose."

Thankfully, Papa seemed mollified by the reassurance and relaxed back into his chair. "Your mother is apoplectic. I shall do what I can, but you must know she is quite beside herself. And quite determined."

Swallowing and squeezing her hands into fists where they rested beside her hips, she nodded and sighed, "I expected as much."

"... aware he requested privacy, Godwin. I doubt very much he intended to exclude his wife." The doors to the parlor swung wide as Mama entered. But it was the woman beside her that caused Jane to tense. Small and birdlike, Lady Wallingham was an aged, thin wisp of a woman—a dragon contained within a white-haired, fragile form.

Sharp green eyes instantly found Jane and sank into her flesh like talons. "Did I not tell you to cease reading those fanciful storybooks, Jane Huxley?" Lady Wallingham's voice was approximately twice as loud as one would expect from her tiny frame. Jane occasionally wondered if she was a bit deaf, but she showed no other signs of it. "True love and stirring adventure. Pure balderdash! Little wonder you were fooled by the first passably handsome scoundrel who cast a glance in your direction."

Before Jane could respond, Mama ignored Lady Wallingham and charged toward her. Jane shrank back into her seat, but her mother was not deterred. She immediately clutched Jane in a tight hug, pressing her face into her bosom and knocking her spectacles askew. "Oh, Jane," she wailed, rocking them back and forth. "How has it come to this? My own daughter, disgraced. I shall never forgive that man."

"You do realize she disgraced *herself*, Meredith," came Lady Wallingham's tart rejoinder.

Mama finally loosened her grip and sank down onto the sofa, which thankfully rescued Jane from death by smothering. Her arm remained firmly around Jane's shoulders, however. "Nonsense. Would she have been in Lord Milton's house at all, were it not for the lies of that despicable creature? I think not."

Lady Wallingham seated herself regally in the chair beside Papa. "Any friend of Benedict Chatham is suspect. She should have known better from the outset."

This caused Mama to pause as she absently rubbed Jane's shoulder. "Come to think of it, why was it Lord Chatham who brought you home, Jane?"

She had wondered when one of them would ask. He had not accompanied her to the door, but his carriage was clearly marked, and by the time she had arrived at Berne House, Maureen had already discovered her absence and alerted their parents. They had been on the verge of launching a full-scale search of Grosvenor Street, and so had rushed outside when Lord Chatham's coach pulled up. Once she had been bundled into the house, she had only managed to confess the essentials of her misadventure before dissolving into tears once again. It had not been her best night.

"Af-after I was unmasked, Chatham said the terms of the wager had been met, then insisted on escorting me home. I told him I could walk, as Lord Milton's house is not far, but he was most adamant."

Lady Wallingham harrumphed. Loudly.

Papa grumbled, "One might consider him chivalrous but for the fact that he took part in the scheme."

Jane shrugged and fussed with her spectacles, which still had not regained their proper shape after her journey through Lord Milton's library window and Mama's effusive hug. "I do not know why he did it," she said. "Perhaps he regretted his participation in Lord Colin's plan."

A second Wallingham harrumph was followed by, "If that is true, I shall eat my hat."

"It matters little how you were returned to us," Mama declared. "Only that you are safe."

"And then my slippers!"

Rolling her eyes at Lady Wallingham, Mama squeezed Jane's shoulders comfortingly and continued, "Don't fret, Jane. For every problem, there is a solution. Lady Wallingham and I will not rest until we discover it."

This time, Lady Wallingham raised her brows at Jane's mother. "*I?*" she queried dubiously. "It is not *I* nor *you* who should be responsible for rectifying this appalling circumstance, Meredith."

Papa snorted in disgust. "If you imagine Colin Lacey will set things right, my dear lady, I fear you shall be disappointed."

"I expect nothing of the sort," Lady Wallingham scoffed. "The one who should be held to account for that whelp's scurrilous behavior is Blackmore. So much the better that he owes us a debt for our efforts on his sister's behalf."

Jane's stomach lurched sickeningly at the mention of the duke. It took her a moment to catch her breath, but at last, when she did, she managed to squawk, "No!" All eyes turned to her. "Lady Wallingham, I beg of you, please, *please* do not involve the Duke of Blackmore in this ... this debacle."

The dragon sniffed dismissively. "It is already done."

Jane groaned and dropped her face into her hands.

"Spare me the dramatics, girl. And cease your tiresome worry. As always, I have a plan." This statement caused a fresh round of despair. "It is better this way. Leave the thinking to those of us with a facility for it."

If Jane were reading about this in a book, she would not have believed it. Surely, her life could not possibly get worse than being duped into burglarizing a man's house, being caught there in a mask and breeches, and being escorted home by one of London's most disreputable rakes. But yes, apparently it was possible. Because now the Duke of Blackmore would not only be informed of her stupidity, but obligated to help remedy it. All of his worst suspicions about her character would be confirmed. She could envision his haughty, superior sneer even now.

Her mother stroked her back and murmured soothingly, "Trust Lady Wallingham, dearest. She knows what she's about."

Yes, Jane thought. *She's about to turn a debacle into an unmitigated disaster.*

When one had the Blackmore legacy in one's charge, scandal was very much like poison. And yet, for Harrison Lacey, the eighth Duke of Blackmore, the last three London seasons had been cursed with that vile malady.

First had come his own: a duel with the previous Viscount Atherbourne—which had ended disastrously in the man's death. The following year, in a bid for revenge, the brother of the aforementioned viscount had lured Harrison's sister, Victoria, into a ruinous liaison. And now ... this.

The expensive parchment crumpled in Harrison's hand, the words written in Lady Wallingham's bold scrawl fading into a reddish haze. Squeezing his eyes shut, he willed his unruly anger to recede. Quickly, he released the letter, allowing it to settle back onto his desk.

He should have known it would come to this. Colin had been veering dangerously out of control for years now, growing increasingly petulant, rebellious, and reckless. And yet, to deliberately destroy an innocent—albeit vexing—young lady, particularly one from a respectable family with close ties to his own, was simply unfathomable.

"Your grace, Mr. Drayton has arrived," Digby announced quietly from the study doorway. "It appears he has located Lord Colin."

Harrison glanced up and nodded at the sandy-haired butler. "Show them in."

His throat was uncomfortably tight. Rising, he clasped his hands behind his back and paced to the window, then to the bookshelves on the opposite side of the room, then back to the window. They were his responsibility, Victoria and Colin. His failure, at least in Colin's case.

Boots clomped and squeaked on the polished floor of the corridor. "... love of God, Drayton. Leave go before I darken your daylights."

The Bow Street runner answered by giving Colin Lacey another shove, sending him stumbling into the room. Once he'd regained his balance, Colin tugged at his coat and glared at Harrison. "Call off your hunting hound, *brother*. An invitation would have done just as well."

"I doubt that," he replied softly.

Swiping a hand through his hair, Colin looked over his shoulder at the rumpled Drayton. He waved his other hand in dismissal. "Shove off, then. There's a good hound."

Drayton, a rangy, haggard man who had proven indispensible to Harrison over the past year, ignored the order, standing silently in the corner of the room. The runner knew his employer well.

"Sit down, Colin."

Turning back to Harrison, Colin snorted. "Right. Time for another lecture, no doubt. What is it now? You've already cut off my funds. Is transportation next?"

Harrison moved forward, sidestepping the desk and standing directly in front of the pale, red-eyed boy—for he could not properly be termed a man—who had created so much destruction. "I. Said. Sit. Down."

He sat, though grudgingly. Harrison rounded the desk and did likewise. "Explain the wager."

Colin stilled then plucked at the fabric of his waistcoat. "Wager?"

Silent as a stone, Harrison simply glared and waited. His brother shifted, avoided his gaze, and attempted to keep his own silence. But Harrison was patient. Colin had never possessed the discipline to outlast him.

"It was nothing, really."

Harrison waited as ruddy color moved up his brother's neck.

"A small lark. With some friends. No concern of yours, certainly."

"A lark," Harrison said softly.

Colin threw up his hands. "Very well! It was a colossal lapse in judgment. Is that what you wish to hear?"

"I wish to hear the truth. Tell me what happened."

"You cut off my funds," he replied, crossing his arms. "What else was I to do?"

Again, Harrison let Colin's words hang in the silence. A full minute passed. Finally, Colin glanced away. "I did not intend to harm her."

"That refrain is both familiar and tedious. It does not matter what you intended, only what you have wrought."

Swallowing hard, Colin dropped his gaze to his hands. "Is it very bad, then?" he asked in a thin voice. "Will she be …?"

"Ruined? Oh, yes," Harrison confirmed, managing not to shout the words by the merest thread. "Quite so."

Colin pinched his forehead between finger and thumb. "It wasn't supposed to be … Damn it all, Harrison, it really did begin as a lark. Milton jested that I had become a dreary humdrum without the brandy, and that he did not believe I could entice even Plain Jane Huxley to a turn about Hyde Park. He offered up a few quid, and the wager was set. Other gents added their bits. Before a fortnight passed, the thing had gone a trifle mad."

"Yet, at no point did you call a halt."

"I needed the funds. You haven't any notion how dire—"

Harrison's hand slammed onto his desk. "I am not interested in your excuses. Tell me what occurred last night."

Colin stared at him, eyes flaring.

"Now!" His command was a gunshot. Harrison did not often raise his voice, but the circumstances were rather extraordinary.

Attempting to appear casual, his brother shrugged. "I spun a tale about our mother's necklace. Claimed Milton stole it, asked Lady Jane to help me retrieve it."

"What necklace?"

"The one intended for the next Duchess of Blackmore."

Harrison frowned. "There is no such necklace."

"As I said, I spun a tale."

"Why did she agree to help you?"

Colin shifted in his chair, rubbing his palms on his thighs. "I played upon her feminine sensibilities. I am not proud of it."

A strange shaft of darkness, cold and stunning, crept through Harrison's body. The light in the room dimmed until the only bright thing was his brother's face. "You seduced her?"

The question, quiet though it was, must have revealed something of Harrison's current state, because Colin froze as though cornered by a predator. "No," he protested, then more emphatically, "No! Nothing of the sort. I befriended her. We are *friends*." His gaze slid away from Harrison's. "*Were* friends, rather."

In Harrison's experience, plain young women with no suitors and few prospects were unlikely to interpret the sudden attentions of a man like Colin as mere friendship. But his patience was thin, and so he moved on. "I ask you again, what happened last night?"

Sighing, Colin let his head drop back against the chair and loll to one side. "She did everything I asked. Wore a coat and breeches. A mask." He chuckled, the sound affectionate and sad. "Had to wear her spectacles over top. A bit awkward, that. But Jane is ..." He glanced at Harrison and immediately straightened. "She entered through the library window. We were waiting inside the drawing room. She must have heard something through the door, because Milton had to fetch her and bring her back. I wanted to end it there. But the gents had other ideas. They demanded she be unmasked, so Chatham—"

"Benedict Chatham was involved?" Harrison snapped.

"He pulled off her mask." Colin's throat worked visibly on a swallow. "She—she wept, Harrison."

The shaft of black, writhing shadow slithered through him again. This time, it pushed him from his chair with such force that the thing slid back into the wall eight feet behind him. His hands landed with a brutal crack on the desk, and he hung his head between his shoulders. That coil of rage gripped like the serpent it was, setting fire to the walls that contained it, tempting him to squeeze his brother's throat in his hand. Instead, his hands formed fists on the polished surface of his desk.

Colin's voice was thin when he confessed, "Once I saw it—saw her—standing there, her hair fallen down, her spectacles gone, I knew how wrong it was. I should never have allowed the men to gather like a pack of—"

"You bloody well should never have done *any of it!*" The magnitude of Harrison's roar caused Colin to leap up and drop back several steps. Drayton, who had been standing silently in the corner, flinched in surprise then moved to stand in front of the doors, preventing Colin's possible escape. After a thick, lengthy silence, Harrison pushed away from his desk and paced to the window. He could not look at Colin. He was afraid of what he might do. When he finally spoke, the words were like stone—heavy, hard, and cold. "I can only be grateful our mother and father are not alive to witness what has become of their son. For my part, I have never been so ashamed to call you my brother."

For a long time, they stood in the same room, both simply breathing and absorbing the enormous, jagged chasm that had formed between them. In age, they were separated by only six years, but the distance between Harrison and his brother had grown steadily as he had waited for Colin to show signs of true manhood, only to be bitterly disappointed. His brother was now five-and-twenty, but behaved like a reckless youth of five-and-ten. Last year, Harrison had learned that Colin's callous treatment of an innocent young woman had led to the girl's suicide. That was when he had cut him off, hoping the measure might force him into sobriety. Based on Drayton's reports, it had worked. But not well enough to prevent another scandal, another victim of Colin's selfishness.

"You *should* be ashamed." The quiet statement stunned Harrison enough to turn and look at his brother. Colin was white as milk, his hand braced on the back of the chair as though too weak to stand on his own. "I disgraced myself. I betrayed a friend. I was desperate, but you are right. That is a paltry excuse for my actions. I shall offer for her this very day."

Harrison blinked. "No, you shall not."

Colin's head came up. "You said she is ruined."

"She is."

"And I am to blame."

"Despite her participation in this preposterous enterprise—against all good sense and at grave risk to her reputation, I might add—spending her life shackled to a penniless scapegrace is too severe a punishment."

His hand clenching and unclenching on the back of the chair, Colin seemed prepared to argue the point. He opened his mouth, only to close it a second later. Then, ceding greater wisdom to Harrison, he half-smiled and nodded in wry, humorless agreement. "I know you don't believe me, but I have been attempting to reform. I have refrained from excess at the tables and the brandy bottle." At Harrison's dubious look, Colin revised, "For the most part." He rubbed at his chin and sighed. "Your sanctimony always brings out my worst tendencies, but in this, you are correct. The wager was an unforgivable mistake. I needed the funds to leave England"—at this news, Harrison shot a questioning look to Drayton, who frowned and shook his head; apparently, it was the first he'd heard of it as well—"but I never should have agreed to involve Jane. She deserves far better than that. Than me."

Rarely had Harrison seen his brother this way—serious and reasoned enough to analyze his own actions. It was disorienting. "Where will you go?"

Colin shrugged wearily. "Caused too much strife for England to contain. Perhaps America will have an improving effect." His smile was weak and quickly faded. "You'll take care of her then? Jane?"

Harrison gave a single nod.

"Good. Treat her well, Harrison. She's rather more remarkable than one would suppose."

Again, the affection in Colin's voice made Harrison wonder at the nature of their supposed friendship. "Don't concern yourself with her welfare. I've grown accustomed to cleaning up your wreckage. You can best help her by keeping your distance."

His mouth tightening, Colin acted as if he wanted to say more, but then glanced back at Drayton. "If you wish me to leave, you will need to leash your dog."

Harrison gave Drayton a nod, and the man moved back to his corner. Colin went to the doors and paused. Without turning, he said quietly, "I am sorry for what I have done. You may not believe that, but it is true. I was sorry even before I did it." He waited, possibly expecting Harrison to cheer and clap his shoulder in felicitations at finally achieving some measure of adulthood. Instead, Harrison said nothing, leaving Colin to utter, "I wish you well, brother," and slip away.

Moments later, Drayton sent him an inquiring glance, and Harrison nodded. "Watch him." The runner immediately disappeared to follow Colin's trail.

Frowning, Harrison returned to his desk, realizing his chair was feet away, against the wall. He dragged it back and sat, taking up a pen and fresh paper. After several minutes, he was satisfied with his two messages and called to Digby, who appeared instantly.

"Yes, your grace?"

Harrison addressed and sealed both letters and held them out to the butler. "See that these are delivered without delay."

Digby glanced at the envelopes. "Lord Chatham and ... Lord Berne, your grace?"

"Indeed," he answered absently, his pen already at work again on a note to his solicitor. After that, it would be a letter to Victoria, and perhaps one to Aunt Muriel. "I've always believed in paying one's debts promptly."

Chapter Seven

"Might I suggest you abandon this penchant for reckless imbecility before your options are reduced from limited to nonexistent?"

—THE DOWAGER MARCHIONESS OF WALLINGHAM to her nephew regarding his reinstatement at Oxford following said lady's heroic intervention on his behalf.

JANE HAD TRIED EVERYTHING. CURLED UP IN HER FAVORITE chair, near the window of her favorite room—Berne House's cozy, oak-paneled library—she sipped at her favorite morning beverage (coffee stirred with a jot of cream and sugar, though everyone thought her mad to take it in such a way), and read her favorite novel.

None of it helped. Two days had passed, and still, she could not get comfortable. Like a subtle itch beneath her skin, the knowledge of her recent escapade and its dreadful consequences refused to leave her in peace, even for a few hours. Tales of that night already had traveled from the men present in Lord Milton's drawing room to the ladies of the ton. The latter wasted no time in tearing her to pieces.

Her family's only hope, according to Lady Wallingham, was Blackmore. Jane had not asked *how* the duke might intervene on her behalf; he was one of the most powerful peers in England, but even he could not stop determined gossips with a bone between their jaws. She could only surmise that perhaps by forcing his brother to publicly apologize and defend Jane's honor, her reputation might be repaired sufficiently to remove the taint from her sisters. Still, although he had agreed to speak with her father, she was less than optimistic.

Reaching beneath her spectacles, she rubbed her tired eyes. When she slept at all, her slumber was fitful and filled with disturbing visions of Colin Lacey laughing and mocking while his brother's cold gaze silently condemned her. A shiver ran up her spine. She toed off her slippers and leaned against the chair's wing, then tucked her feet beneath her lap blanket. Sighing, she returned to her book. Surely Mr. Darcy could make her forget about the insufferable Duke of Blackmore.

Blast. Why must I constantly dwell on that man?

Her high-backed chair was turned away from the door, so she did not see it open, only heard the click of the knob turning and felt a draft of air. This was followed by the voice of their butler, Godwin. "Lord Berne will join you momentarily. Would you care for tea?"

"No."

Jane froze as that one deep, frost-coated syllable pinned her in place.

"Very good, your grace."

The door closed and silence fell. She could not hear him move. Was he even still in the room? *Ninny. Of course he is.* Should she say something? Spring from her chair and directly into a curtsy? What would he say? No doubt it would be infuriating. Or humiliating. Or some combination thereof. Absently, she placed her cup back into its saucer with a soft clink.

Suddenly, the sharp rap of boots moved toward her, approaching at a commanding clip. *Bloody hell.* She squeezed her eyes closed then opened them when the boots stopped.

"Lady Jane," he said tightly, his jaw incapable of mobility, it seemed. He wore green today—a dark-green superfine tailcoat along with a buff waistcoat and trousers. If she did not know what a high-handed, supercilious horse's backside he was, she might be inclined to melt and sigh over his handsomeness.

Were she prone to such silliness. Which she was not.

Knowing the duke's less admirable qualities only too well, she ignored the dictates of good manners and chose to remain seated. "Your grace," she said casually, reaching for her coffee and taking a small sip. "You've come to meet with my father, I presume?"

A part of her—the part that was heartily tired of being the pitiable Oddflower—reveled in the calm, cheeky way she delivered her message. *Shy little Jane won't be so easily cowed as all that, will she?* But another, more cautious part fairly screamed that she should get up, curtsy, apologize, and leave the room as expeditiously as simple physics would allow. The Duke of Blackmore was not a man to trifle with.

Particularly when her family was relying upon his assistance.

Saying nothing, he simply stood with his hands clasped behind his back, staring down at her from his great, lofty height. His eyes sharp and cold enough to pierce her midsection, that blue-gray blade ran her up and down, slicing through her in a wave of bright, shivery tingles.

It was dashed disquieting.

Setting her cup on the side table once again, she cleared her throat and slid her feet to the floor. Then she clutched her book to her chest, turning slightly to discard her blanket and rise. She curtsied, hoping he did not notice her lack of slippers.

But he wasn't looking at her feet, or even her face. His eyes instead were fixed on her hand. She looked down. A perfectly ordinary hand—her left one, as she'd needed her right to set aside the blanket. Perhaps he was noting her book.

"Have—have you read it?"

On anyone else, she would have judged his expression a blank stare. But surely the vaunted Duke of Blackmore was not so absentminded.

"*Pride and Prejudice*," she clarified. "It is one of my favorites."

"A novel?" he said finally.

She nodded.

"I do not waste time with such fribbles."

Her mouth quirked. "Of course not."

Frowning, he elaborated, "On the rare occasions when my schedule permits reading for purposes of leisure, I prefer subject matter which is both practical and edifying. Fiction is neither."

"Naturally."

"You sound as if you do not believe me."

Jane raised her eyebrows. "I assure you, your grace, I believe every word."

His frown deepened, eyes narrowing in suspicion. He stepped closer, now less than two feet away. "Are you mocking me, Lady Jane?" The words were spoken softly, but with a dangerous edge that sent gooseflesh rising. Suddenly, it did not seem particularly wise to poke this particular lion.

"N-not at all."

He stepped forward again, forcing her to retreat until the backs of her legs brushed against her vacated chair. *My, my,* she thought. *He is so much larger than one anticipates from a distance.* Examining her face, her throat, then dropping to where her hand clutched her book and back up to her spectacles, he eyed her with an intensity she felt as a stroke of flame. Automatically, she reached up to touch the metal rims at her temple. His gaze tracked her movement like a predator. "Someone should teach you better manners."

He was alarmingly close, mere inches from her. She could smell his sunlight-and-starch, feel the warmth of his body. An odd ache settled between her heart and her stomach, probably because she needed to breathe. Yes, that was it. Her lungs were burning.

His head tilted. "Your husband, perhaps."

That absurd statement caused her to suck air into starving lungs on a choking gasp. "H-husband," she coughed, shaking her head. "I do not know what you've been told, your grace, but I fear marriage is quite imposs—"

"I know everything."

She paused. "Then you must know I have destroyed any chance—slight as it was—of making a proper match."

His eyes flashed as though she'd said something both pleasing and disagreeable. "You blame yourself?"

She stared up at him, wondering at the question. "It was my fault. Whom else would I blame?"

"My brother."

"Colin lied, it is true. But he did not force me to dress in a lad's coat and breeches, put on a ridiculous mask, and creep through a man's window. Those regrettable choices were mine and mine alone."

He seemed genuinely perplexed by her statement, perhaps expecting her to dissolve into tears and hysterical recriminations of his deceitful kin. Then his expression cleared, becoming tighter. "You should not defend him."

"I did nothing of the—"

"He is unworthy of such devotion."

"Yes, well, plainly—"

"And he is leaving England."

She blinked, momentarily stunned. "L-leaving? Where—"

"It does not matter." His shoulders—appearing broader than normal, perhaps due to his proximity—straightened as his head came up in a now-familiar arrogant pose. "You will forget about him, beginning now."

Why, oh why, dear God, was her temper so easily and terribly ignited by the one man her family needed most? She had to grind her teeth and take a bracing breath to prevent herself from striking back with a childish retort. The words were there, clamoring at the back of her throat, held captive by caution. Ordinarily, her shyness might trap them inside, but lately, she did not feel shy with Blackmore. He infuriated her too much—burned right through her self-doubt and left no room for hesitation.

Perhaps that was why, as he opened his mouth to speak, the words she'd been fighting not to say burst forth from her lips, the ropes binding them weakened by heat. "How would you propose to ensure my forgetfulness, your grace? I daresay the only way to determine whether I have complied with your demand is to be present inside of me. And who would volunteer for that proposition? You?"

He seemed flummoxed by her outburst, nose flaring, eyes flashing, lips parting. There was even a hint of color rising along his cheekbones. Ah, yes. She had him there, didn't she? Simple logic, really. He should not go about tossing out directives that he could not enforce. He would have to be inside her mind to know whether she had forgotten about Colin, and that was impossible.

Swallowing hard, he appeared at a loss for words.

Her triumph soared. "Further, if you are not inside me, you cannot possibly exert your will over mine in order to achieve what you desire. Perhaps next time you wish to have your way, you shall think of this and wield your tongue more wisely."

Well, this was most strange. Now his breathing appeared just a bit labored.

"Enough," he rasped. "I must meet with your father. Where

the bl—" He cleared his throat forcefully, then pulled a gold watch out of his waistcoat pocket and flicked open the cover. "What is keeping Lord Berne? Does punctuality mean nothing in this house?"

"There is no need to be insulting. I am certain Papa will be here shortly."

"How is it an insult to point out what has become patently obvious—"

The door opened, and her father entered with a jovial smile. "Your grace! I see you and my Jane are becoming better acquainted. Excellent, excellent."

Jane gave Blackmore a triumphant grin of her own. "You see? All one requires is a bit of patience." She reached behind her to retrieve her blanket, draped it over her arm, and dipped a curtsy. "I shall leave you gentlemen to your discussion." With that, she crossed the room to Papa, stood on tiptoe to kiss his cheek, then continued to the door. She would have exited in near-perfect victory—except *he* would not allow it.

"Lady Jane," Blackmore said, his voice a command to stop and turn back.

When she did, her heart gave a little flop, and a flush bloomed beneath her skin.

For, there stood the duke, dangling her plain, well-worn slippers from two fingers. "Forget something?"

Damn and blast. Bloody damned duke and his bloody *unnatural perspicacity*.

As Jane entered the passage to the kitchen minutes after leaving the library, she lamented the fact that no amount of cursing alleviated her vexation with that man. Granted, she now wore her slippers, and that was helpful on the stone floors of the kitchen. But he had deliberately embarrassed her.

"... the price of pheasant, and I said for that kind of coin, I could hire a hack to Hertfordshire and pluck two or three myself!"

Jane followed the sound of her mother laughing with the housekeeper, Mrs. Jones, and the cook, Mrs. Dunn, as they all huddled around the central work table, apparently debating the supper menu. Mama preferred a very personal approach to meal management, as she often expressed her pleasure or displeasure with Papa by incorporating either his favorite or most despised dishes into their daily menus. Jane thought it one of Mama's more amusing idiosyncrasies, but then, she neither swooned over roasted pheasant nor paled at the sight of parsnips, as Papa did.

A maid entered behind Jane and nearly collided with her. "Oh! Begging your pardon, my lady. Didn't see you there." The girl scarcely paused to curtsy before hurrying off to the dining room with her armful of linens.

Mama looked up from the list she was holding. "Jane? Where have you been hiding this morning?"

Giving her mother a weak smile, she approached the trio of women. Typically, ladies of quality did not spend time in the kitchen with the servants. But her mother was far from typical, and Jane appreciated the result—a household that was more welcoming and comfortable than that of most ton families. "I was in the library, reading a bit."

Sympathy stole over Mama's face. She tsked and hugged Jane, then patted her shoulder. "All will be well. You mustn't allow yourself to sink into despair, dearest."

"I know. Do not fret over me, Mama. Actually, it was quite pleasant to pass the time in solitude." A little frown pulled at her brow. "Until the duke arrived."

Mama gripped Jane's forearm. "He arrived? When?"

Jane glanced down at her mother's hand. "A short while ago," she said cautiously. "He is presently in with Papa."

Mama's grip tightened while her other hand sprawled flat across her bodice. "Mrs. Dunn, Mrs. Jones," she said crisply. "We must take inventory."

With that, the three women sprang into action, with Mrs. Jones scribbling in her small notebook, Mrs. Dunn calling out ingredients from the adjacent larder, and Mama breathing a bit fast, apparently overcome with excitement.

"Mama, are you quite all right?"

Mama did not glance away from her task of monitoring Mrs. Jones's list-taking abilities. "Hmm? Oh, yes. Top of the trees, you might say. Why do you ask?"

"You are behaving as though we are expecting the Prince Regent to dine with us."

She laughed lightly and waved her fingers. "One never knows when one shall be called upon to host a ball or other significant fete. Best to be prepared."

Jane had little doubt her confusion showed on her face. "Is there some news I have missed?"

At last, her mother looked in her direction, and, apparently unable to restrain her enthusiasm any longer, she broke into a brilliant smile and rushed forward to grasp Jane's hands. "I should wait to tell you, but I cannot." She shook their clasped hands up and down like an overeager pup with a discarded stocking. "I expect we shall be planning an engagement ball *very* soon."

Stunned, Jane felt her jaw go slack; behind the wave of shock came a small twinge of hurt. "Why did Maureen not tell me she had a suitor?"

"Maur—" her mother began, only to realize her own mistake. "Jane. It is not Maureen who is soon to be married. It is you, dearest."

Jane stared at her mother, wondering when she had begun imbibing copious quantities of wine with her breakfast. Before the attempted burglary, Jane had been a plain, shy, bookish Oddflower with an overgenerous amount of flesh and exceedingly poor eyesight. Afterward, well ... her odds of receiving an offer of marriage from anyone, let alone the kind of gentleman that would send her mother into raptures, would have a hill to climb before reaching zero—a fact Mama did not seem to realize.

"I—I am not betrothed, Mama. You do comprehend—"

"Not *yet*," she whispered theatrically, giving Jane's limp hands another shake. "But even now, your father is accepting the duke's offer for your hand."

Was the light dimmer, of a sudden? It certainly seemed so to Jane. And Mama's voice was fading in and out a bit. Perhaps Jane was coming down with some sort of illness, because she would have sworn her mother said—

"Only imagine it, dearest. My Jane, the Duchess of Blackmore. Won't it be splendid?"

Chapter Eight

"Luck is a sop for those of poor vision and scant intellect. In the end, superior players win despite, not because of it."

—THE DOWAGER MARCHIONESS OF WALLINGHAM upon losing four shillings to Lady Colchester during a game of piquet.

THE GODDESS OF FORTUNE HAD NOT SMILED ON COLIN IN months, but today was particularly bad. He glared up at the figure of her likeness, a sculpture of Fortuna pouring gold from a cornucopia. She stood inside the foyer of Reaver's, a feminine, mocking reminder of the lure of false hope, or so he had always thought.

"My lord, if you would care to wait in the dining room, Lord Chatham has said he will join you momentarily."

Colin glanced over at the lean, dark-skinned majordomo. "Thank you, Shaw."

When he entered the dining room, he found it empty of all but a few gentlemen quietly sipping their morning coffee. Unlike White's and Brooks's, Reaver saw no need for restraint in his club. Every surface shone with blatant luxury, from gold silk walls and draperies to sparkling crystal chandeliers to ornate gilded mirrors. It was decadent. And misleading—no one became wealthy here except Reaver. Colin chose to sit with his back facing the wall at a table in the far rear corner, where they would have the greatest privacy.

Inside, he felt the quaking begin, that crawling, writhing sensation that made him want to rise, to run. Pulling air deep into his lungs, he forced himself to calm. Not yet. He must see Chatham first.

With his usual ghostly grace, the dark-haired viscount arrived, wielding his walking stick with an insouciance that made the casual observer underestimate him. Colin had seen what the man could do with the carefully disguised weapon, so he made no such assumptions.

"My, my. You are looking a bit worn at the edges, old chap." Cool and unreadable, Chatham sat, propping his cane against his chair.

"Do you have it?"

"Of course."

Colin slumped as relief flooded his body. For the first time in weeks, he could breathe without wondering if it would be the last time. "Thank God," he whispered.

Chatham reached inside his coat and withdrew a pouch. He slid it across the table with a lean, long-fingered hand.

"The final sum?" If Colin were fortunate—which, again, had proven an elusive quality of late—it would be filled with over a thousand pounds, more than enough.

"Not as much as you would like, I'm afraid. Flatmouth denies everything. Claims Phillips put his name in without his consent." Chatham shrugged and sighed. "What can be done?"

Frowning, Colin nodded, running a hand through his hair.

He tore the pouch open and counted the notes. Blinking, he counted again. Frantically, he dug into the leather pouch to see if he had missed something. No.

No, no, no.

"Where is the rest of it?" he demanded.

Chatham raised a brow. "That *is* the rest of it. What you hold is all you have."

"This is only four hundred. It is not enough."

"Yes. Unfortunately, Flatmouth was not the only one to renege after the fact. Do you know, I believe your friends may be less than honorable fellows."

Colin leaned forward over the table, his voice low and deadly. "Where the bloody hell is my money, Chatham?"

The other man's eyes were flat and emotionless. "As I said, you have what I managed to gather. The rest, well. After your brother's efforts on the lady's behalf, I venture you shall never see it."

Colin's head snapped back at the mention of Harrison. "What has he done?"

"Made it abundantly clear he will destroy any man associated with the wager. Naturally, many whose names were in the book chose to invoke a lapse of memory, and now recall the circumstances of that evening a trifle differently than you or I. Lady Jane's brief foray into thievery was merely a Banbury tale told in jest. Or so it now appears."

"How does he know the contents of the book?"

One corner of Chatham's lips lifted subtly. "I gave it to him."

Sitting back in his chair with a hard thunk, Colin stared at the viscount, wondering if the man had gone stark staring mad.

"Or, to be more precise, I sold it to him."

For the briefest of moments, Colin had dared to imagine he might finally be safe. All the air he had breathed during that blessed idyll fled in a hiss. Harrison would break each and every man listed in the book. Slowly and with devastating purpose. Colin had seen it in his brother's eyes when he'd told him about Jane's humiliated tears. He wouldn't stop because a man denied participating in the wager—that would mean nothing. Those who had reneged did not understand. But they soon would. Refusing to pay their debt would not save them from the Duke of Blackmore.

It would, however, consign Colin to a worse fate. Palms covering his eyes, his fingers forked through his hair. "I am bloody well dead," he groaned. "Dead."

"Yes, I imagine that is true. Incidentally, do you still have that book of maps I lent you?"

He dropped his hands, shooting his former friend a hostile glare.

Chatham smiled. As usual, it did not reach his eyes. "Better to retrieve it prior to your demise, wouldn't you say?"

Minutes later, Colin left Reaver's with less than half of what the wager should have paid. Four hundred eighteen pounds. It was perhaps sufficient to leave. It was far from enough to stay.

Tucking the pouch inside his coat, he made his way out of the quiet square and onto the bustling St. James Street. In front of him, a coach-and-four lumbered past, followed by a coal cart. The racket of the wheels and the horses and all the various shouts of those going about their daily routine was both comforting and disconcerting. He needed to get to the docks. He needed to disappear. His neck was crawling.

Wasting no time, he turned north toward Piccadilly, walking faster, heart pounding. He could scarcely believe what had happened. Four hundred eighteen was no small sum, but to him, it was a death sentence. Syder would never accept half of what he was owed. And Colin had run out of time.

A lad and his aged companion strolled past, the old man's cane thudding on the ground. A horse snorted and clopped behind him. Every sound, every movement was sharper, more startling. His senses told him to run, but he knew that would only draw unwanted notice.

He reached Jermyn Street, pausing to wait for an opening to cross. If he could get to the coach stand at Piccadilly and Bond, he could take a hack to the docks. From there ... he didn't know. Perhaps one of the new steam packets. He would have to leave London; that much was certain. But how far must he run? Here, Syder seemed all-powerful, a black-hearted monster with tentacles stretching from the hells of Pall Mall to the slaughterhouses of Whitechapel.

Four hundred eighteen would not sustain Colin for long without connections. He knew no one in America or Canada. He had an aunt in Edinburgh, an old school chum in Dublin, a former mistress in Paris. How many miles would Syder consider too many for the pleasure of killing the man who had cheated him?

He didn't know. He didn't know a bleeding thing.

Glancing behind him, his breath stuttered, his heart slamming inside his chest like a hawk trapped inside a wooden crate. Drayton. He thought he'd shaken the houndish, haggard runner. Bloody hell.

Veering right onto Jermyn, he quickened his pace. Ahead was a small alley between two shops. Drayton lagged far enough behind that if Colin ducked into it at the right moment, he stood a chance of losing him. Letting a man behind him elbow past, Colin watched a post-chaise amble by before dashing into the alley. It was darker there, the brick walls looming close on either side. The long path stretched like a corridor, but he could see more light at the end. Colin loped deeper into the narrow space toward the brighter, open mews, hoping it would lead him out onto an adjacent street. He glanced over his shoulder to see if Drayton followed.

And felt his head explode into darkness.

Black brightened to red, faded darker, then lightened to gray. The quiet snick of a pistol cocking reached Colin's ears, but blood pounded so loudly and grotesquely inside his skull, it scarcely registered.

"Death is dreadfully final. Might I suggest retreat?"

Coming from above him, the voice was icy and nonchalant. Chatham? No. Couldn't be.

"Syder'll hear 'bout this." That voice, deeper and rougher, also sounded familiar.

"Perhaps he will. Or perhaps you lost Lord Colin's scent after pursuing him to the docks. I recommend the latter."

"Men what lie to Syder end up skinned like cattle."

"Hmm. And what happens to men who fail in their task because they were stripped of their prize before it could be delivered?"

Only Colin's sickening, pounding head filled the silence that followed. It rushed and throbbed against the cold, hard damp pressing his cheek. Heavy, booted footfalls slowly retreated. Colin's stomach roiled, the pain sending his gorge rising. Distantly, he heard the first voice murmuring to someone, another click, and the quiet tap of a cane on hardened mud. But soon, he felt his stomach heave, and the contractions of his body forcefully emptying itself caused his head to explode again. After that, the red returned, then the black, then nothing.

Chapter Nine

*"Some stains cannot be removed. In that event,
most would consider the cloth ruined, but that is because
they are not clever enough to realize the whole garment
can simply be dyed a matching color. No more stain,
and a new gown. An ideal solution."*

—The Dowager Marchioness of Wallingham to her newest
lady's maid while instructing the girl on the proper administration
of her duties.

Jane was going to be sick, quite possibly all over the wine-red silk laid out before her. Surrounded by her sisters, her mother, and Lady Wallingham, she sat at a small table in the Bond Street shop of Italian-born modiste Renata Bowman. She could not imagine a greater misery.

"The color is much better, yes? No more yellow for this one." The dark-haired, elegant dressmaker did not bother to glance over at Jane as she made her statement. Instead, she waggled her fingers in Jane's direction as though referencing a sofa in need of new upholstery.

"Oooh, I never considered red for her. It is quite dramatic. Do you think it's a bit *too* bold?" Annabelle asked Mrs. Bowman, who harrumphed dismissively.

Maureen proffered her own opinion. "She is to become a duchess. Stronger colors will be more suitable, particularly once she begins acting as Blackmore's hostess."

Jane's stomach twisted, her breakfast of baked eggs and biscuits threatening to reappear with unseemly haste.

"Jane!" snapped Lady Wallingham. "You shall not vomit on such lovely damask. If you must cast up your accounts, do so elsewhere."

All eyes turned to her as she covered her mouth with her hand. "Are you unwell, dearest?" Mama inquired.

Swallowing hard against the gorge in her throat, Jane took two deep breaths and muttered, "I am fine."

"You don't appear fine," said Genie, briefly turning away from a display featuring a pink gown surrounded by five hats. Jane dropped her hand and glared at Genie, who shot her a cross-eyed look meant to tease her out of her doldrums. Jane sighed. Nothing was likely to accomplish that feat.

Meanwhile, the others continued their discussion of Jane's extravagant trousseau, which was a joint effort of Mama's fondest wishes and Blackmore's funds. Annabelle ceded ground on the darker, richer colors, sighing over a midnight-blue velvet pelisse, while Maureen cooed her approval of a russet silk day dress. Mama expressed dismay at the scarcity of ruffles in the designs Mrs. Bowman was recommending. Mrs. Bowman released a string of Italian phrases then pointed at the waistline in one of the illustrations.

"You see this, Lady Berne? Your daughter, she is ... how to

say ... *round*." The dressmaker's long, elegant forefinger ran the length of the gown then tapped the hem. "And *breve*."

Jane blinked. Mrs. Bowman thought her brave?

"She is short," the woman clarified, adding, "We must lengthen." She demonstrated by pinching her fingers together and separating her hands vertically. "We must create waist. And we must *simplify*."

"Oh, but I quite like ruffles," said little Kate from behind Mama's shoulder. "Rosettes, as well. Can she not have a few rosettes, Mama?"

Would it not have drawn too much attention, Jane might have groaned. She loathed dress shopping—inevitably it led to mortification and discomfort for someone of her figure—but doing so in the current circumstance was nigh unbearable. This was going to cost the duke an absolute fortune.

While Papa was far from a pauper, his income was perhaps one tenth of Blackmore's. And with five daughters to outfit for multiple London seasons, a trousseau of this scale would have beggared the family. Fortunately for Jane's mother and sisters, who relished the thought of shopping for an inordinate number of gowns, silken underclothes, hats, gloves, shoes, and other sundries fit for a duchess, Blackmore had insisted on paying for it all. He had not, however, consulted Jane.

Not on the trousseau. Not on the wedding. Not on the marriage.

She had neither seen nor spoken to the man in the week since she had snatched her slippers from his hand and stomped out of the Berne House library. Indeed, by the time her mother had informed her of Blackmore's purpose, he'd already concluded his business and departed.

She had rushed from the kitchen to the library, surprising her father by bursting through the doors, wheezing and shouting, "Papa, you mustn't agree!"

But Papa had simply shaken his head and crossed the room to enfold her securely in his arms, just as he had when she was a child. "It is done, Poppet," he had whispered against the top of her head. Pulling back, he had braced his hands on her shoulders and given her a loving but stern look. "You must accept this match. And be grateful."

"Grateful!" she'd squawked.

His hands firm, his voice firmer, he'd given her a tiny shake and replied, "Blackmore is attempting to right a wrong in which he took no part. His miscreant brother has sullied his family's honor, and he wishes to rectify matters by giving you the protection of his name and title." She'd started to protest, but he had continued adamantly, "It is a noble sacrifice, Poppet, and yes, you should be grateful. Blackmore has just saved not only you but your sisters from a good deal of misery."

Stricken, Jane's head had felt detached from her body, her need to deny the truth strong. But she could not deny it. Her father was right. Blackmore was sacrificing himself, throwing the considerable power he wielded within society—a great, towering lot of it—over her and her family like a protective shield.

It was the only event significant enough to overshadow her bungling-burglar escapade among gossip circles—the Duke of Blackmore, at long last, had chosen a bride. Making *Jane* his bride established in no uncertain terms that he did not believe the rumors and would not tolerate scandal being attached to her by anyone.

She simply could not fathom why he would do such a thing. Victoria had spoken of Blackmore's overdeveloped sense of honor and pride, but the Apollo of the aristocracy shouldn't even be *dancing* with Plain Jane Huxley, much less marrying her. *Noble sacrifice, indeed.* They were an appalling mismatch. Besides which, she did not wish to be a duchess. More specifically, she did not wish to be *his* duchess.

"Am I to have no say in this?"

Her father's expression had grown grave, though his voice had remained gentle. "I fear you've had your say, Jane. When you climbed through Lord Milton's window, endangering yourself and your sisters, your decision was made. Now, you must set things right. You must do this for them."

Tears had flooded her eyes, spilling in twin streams down her cheeks. She could see the glare of daylight flashing over the wet trails. Her chest had felt hollow, scraped out clean and left gaping.

Her father had clasped her close again, his hand cradling the back of her head, his arms tight. "He is a good man, Poppet. I would never have agreed to the match if he were not."

Perhaps he was—the Duke of Blackmore could have married anyone. She could name at least seven beauties of high station, all diamonds of the first water, who would have proven a better fit for him. To settle for the likes of Jane was an inexplicable act of selflessness.

Blackmore was so far above her, he might as well be the moon.

In the end, however, she had agreed to wed him. Because her father was right—she could not toss her sisters' futures on the rubbish pile simply to escape a marriage she dreaded. Maureen and Genie deserved their chance to dance the waltz and shop for bonnets and wield their fans flirtatiously during their own London seasons. They deserved to do so without the specter of Jane's horrid mistake clinging to them like a spider's sticky web.

Now, for the same reasons, she had agreed to this shopping excursion to purchase a trousseau she did not want for a marriage she did not want to a man she … well, a man for whom she was tragically ill-suited. Presently, she heard Mama exclaiming over an illustration of an emerald-green riding ensemble and felt her stomach roll threateningly. Mrs. Bowman explained she would be dropping the waistline on all the gowns a bit more than was fashionable, as it would help Jane appear "less dumpling, more duchess."

That was when Lady Wallingham chose to insert herself into the discussion, declaring, "Yes, yes. This is all very well. But what of her wedding gown, Mrs. Bowman? Princess Charlotte wore a magnificent confection of silver net. I insist Jane wear nothing short of gold."

Mrs. Bowman shook her head emphatically and raised a finger. "Gold is too much yellow. No, no, no. For Lady Jane, it must be richer." She pulled a pencil from her pocket and snapped her fingers at her assistant, who hovered in the background. A small sketchbook appeared instantly. Mrs. Bowman flipped it open and began with quick, decisive strokes. "Bronze. Silk. A bit of ribbon along the bodice."

Lady Wallingham's green eyes sharpened on the modiste, who appeared lost in her own thoughts, mumbling occasionally in Italian. "She shall have gold netting. Put it over whatever you like. But Lady Jane Huxley shall wear gold on her wedding day."

Mrs. Bowman stilled, glancing up at the Dowager Marchioness of Wallingham. A glint of grudging respect entered her dark eyes before she raised her brows and shrugged. Returning to her sketch, she murmured, "A wide sash to extend waist. And gold netting over bronze silk."

Jane looked at Lady Wallingham, who nodded imperiously. This was much too grand. It was too costly. It was … not her.

She knew that, in some sense, they were all correct. She should be grateful to the duke. She should look forward to becoming a duchess. Even Mrs. Bowman was probably right—she should wear richer colors and lower waistlines and simpler forms. But Jane did not want to wear bronze or emerald green. She did not want to be a duchess.

Most of all, she did not want Blackmore to look at her with the resigned regret she knew she would see on his face for the rest of their lives.

She wanted to run.

To hide somewhere far away.

To lose herself in a story—any story—as long as it belonged to someone else.

Mrs. Bowman held up the sketch for everyone to view. They all sighed and cheered while Jane squinted at it in misery. Surely such an exquisite gown would look ridiculous on her—like stuffing a barn owl into one of Genie's more elaborate bonnets. Her only solace lay in the thought that perhaps the wedding gown was Mrs. Bowman's crescendo, the highlight that signaled the end of this Bond Street nightmare. But, as she soon discovered, such wishful thinking was a path to disappointment.

"And now," the dressmaker announced, flipping to a fresh page, "a few things for the wedding night, no?"

Chapter Ten

"Men are driven by two forces: lust and power. Marriage is the only polite institution which serves both purposes at once. Otherwise, I daresay, we would have a devil of a time dragging them to the altar."

—THE DOWAGER MARCHIONESS OF WALLINGHAM to Lady Berne while discussing her son Charles's intractable lack of interest in remarriage.

"GOOD GOD, MAN, PUT THAT THING AWAY."

Harrison glanced up from his watch and turned a raised brow to Henry Thorpe, the Earl of Dunston. Dust motes floated on the morning light streaming through the window of St. George's, pluming around Dunston's brown head. Having known the man since well before Oxford, Harrison was accustomed to his friend's exasperation.

"It is three minutes later than the last time you looked. She will appear when she is ready. Have patience."

"She is late," Harrison replied flatly, closing the watch with a snap and sliding it back into his pocket.

Dunston sighed, his affable nature likely strained by the full twenty-minute delay of Harrison's wedding. "Her mother and sisters are attending her. Ladies require ample time to prepare."

"She was given ample time. Five weeks, to be precise. Any longer is simply petulance."

Standing in the rear of the church, out of sight of those gathered in the oak pews, they spoke in hushed tones. Harrison had no desire to incite alarm.

"As usual, I'm afraid Lord Dunston has the superior argument, Harrison."

He turned to see his sister strolling toward him. Having borne his nephew only eight weeks earlier, she looked remarkably healthy—glowing, in fact—in a gown of soft green silk trimmed with cream-colored lace. The tightness that had settled around his lungs eased a bit. "Victoria."

When he had written to her of his decision to marry, she had insisted on traveling to London for the wedding, despite his specific instructions to remain in Derbyshire. Her husband had proven worthless in dissuading her, of course; Atherbourne was woefully besotted. If she but asked, he had little doubt the viscount would leap headfirst off the cliffs of Dover.

Giving Harrison a radiant smile, she tugged his black sleeve to straighten it, even though his valet made the gesture unnecessary. The servant was paid handsomely for his impeccable standards and skills. "Be patient, my darling brother. I am certain your bride simply wishes to look her best."

"My patience is not at issue. The wedding was scheduled for nine. It is now"—he pulled his watch from his pocket, noting Dunston's exaggerated, eye-rolling sigh—"twenty-five past."

Victoria's hand, which had settled gently on his arm, gave him a small pat. "Why don't I go and see if I may hasten her arrival, shall I?" She said it in the tone one would use on an unreasoning infant.

"Yes!" Dunston answered before Harrison could reply. "Thank you, Lady Atherbourne. That is the ideal solution."

She grinned at the earl and gave Harrison's arm another pat. "Don't worry so." Reaching up to stroke the space above the bridge of his nose, she teased, "You're developing a crease."

After she left, Dunston remarked, "Your sister appears well."

"She is."

"Interesting."

Harrison shot him a questioning look, which Dunston answered with a shrug. "Considering you killed Atherbourne's brother in a duel, and that he later blamed you for that death as well as the death of his sister, I would not have predicted their marriage would go on quite so happily."

His voice was flat when he replied, "The matter has been settled. As you well know." Dunston also knew Harrison did not like to discuss the atrocious dawn when he had shot Gregory Wyatt, killing a good man and setting into motion the vicious scandal that had torn Victoria's life asunder.

"Yes. You and Atherbourne are civil now; it is true. But that is precisely my point. Marriage is unpredictable. *Love* is unpredictable."

"Rubbish."

"Which part?"

"Marriage is entirely predictable. It is designed to be so. The husband protects and provides for the wife, who then sees to his comfort and bears his children. A simple agreement."

Dunston's forehead dropped into his fingers, which rubbed as if he had a megrim. "You honestly believe it is no more complicated than that, don't you?"

Raising a brow at his friend's clear vexation, Harrison replied, "Of course."

Dunston sighed, shook his head, and let his hands fall to his sides. "Grant me one promise."

"Yes?"

"Never say such a thing to your wife."

Harrison scowled and opened his mouth to argue, but Dunston clapped him on the shoulder and paced away toward the large column where the pews began. He returned with a report. "The guests are a trifle restless. Why did you invite so many? When my cousin married, I counted myself fortunate merely to have been informed."

"Lady Wallingham insisted. Claimed it was essential to our aims."

"When did you begin taking direction from Lady Wallingham?"

Harrison's glare communicated his displeasure without the need for words.

Minutes later—six minutes, to be precise—the sound of the church's organ alerted them to his bride's arrival. Finally, *finally*, this damnable wedding could begin.

Fifteen minutes earlier …

HUDDLED INSIDE A SMALL, WHITE CHAMBER OF ST. GEORGE'S, Jane was having a great deal of trouble breathing. A quiet knock at the door preceded her mother's muffled, "Dearest? Your father would like to speak to you. Won't you come out?"

She was not trying to be difficult. It was just that she worried about moving too far away from the chamber pot. "I am not feeling especially well, Mama."

The next voice she heard was her father's. "Poppet? You shan't be alone. I will be with you every step."

She squeezed her eyes closed, nearly crumpling at the quiet reassurance. "I know, Papa." He would be there, his steadying arm holding her upright as she walked down the aisle to Blackmore. But who would be there for her when it was over? Who would hold her upright when the duke looked at his new duchess with pity and resentment?

Hearing whispers outside the door, she waited, perched on a small wooden chair, dressed in the magnificent bronze gown Mrs. Bowman had made, wondering when someone—*anyone*—would come to their senses. She glanced over at the chamber pot in the corner. There was nothing left in her stomach, but nausea still rolled through her like a storm.

Another gentle knock. "Jane?" This time, it was Victoria. "I am coming in."

She would have protested, but Victoria gave her no chance. Her best friend's golden-blond head peeked around the door before she finished speaking, followed by large, sweet, blue-green eyes. "Oh, Jane," she sighed. "You look so very lovely." Stepping fully into the small chamber, she closed the door and leaned back against it, her lips pursing in a sympathetic smile. "And so very miserable."

"How did you do it?" Jane knew she was both pale and sickly, so she dismissed all but the last part of Victoria's statement. What she needed now was advice on how to survive an unwanted wedding.

"My circumstances were a bit different. Lucien and I ... well, let us say we were already acquainted well enough to know we would suit."

"Still, it cannot have been easy for you."

Victoria's smile was gentle. "No. It was not. I'm afraid I have no secret knowledge to offer. This is simply one of those moments you must endure with as much dignity as you can manage."

Jane grunted. "I feared you would say that." Sighing deeply, she braced her palms on her knees and let her head fall forward. Soft rustling was followed by warm, gloved hands coming to rest over hers.

When she looked up, Victoria was kneeling before her. "He is a fine man, Jane. Loyal, honorable. Far kinder than he lets on." At Jane's dubious expression, she chuckled. "It's true. I know he seems a bit stuffy—"

"He is the coldest man I have ever met. No, wait." Jane paused, pretending to calculate all the men she had ever known in her head. "Yes, the very coldest. He disapproves of me to such an extent, I will be astonished if he does not employ a governess to instruct me on proper behavior."

Shaking her head, Victoria asked, "Don't you suppose there might be more to him than what he appears upon casual acquaintance?"

"No. And if there is, I have seen little evidence of it."

Victoria's mouth quirked. "Hmm. After the wedding, I daresay you will have ample opportunity to discover his more endearing qualities."

Suddenly, Jane's chest felt abnormally tight. She flipped her hands over so that they now grasped Victoria's. "He and I are dreadfully mismatched, Victoria. Can you not see this?" The words felt pulled from her by force—the truth spoken plainly and urgently after being stifled for five weeks. "Everyone in this church, everyone in London, in England itself, understands. Why are you all behaving as if it is not the most laughable pairing ever to be suggested?"

"Jane," she began soothingly.

"Please do not deny it. I cannot bear to hear you to lie to me."

"I would not lie to you."

"Then tell me, before this year, who did you imagine he would select as his duchess?"

"He had not yet begun the search for a w—"

"It was Lady Mary Thorpe, was it not? Dunston's sister."

The look on Victoria's face spoke the truth.

"Precisely," Jane confirmed for her. "With good reason!

Even you thought it necessary to request that he grant me a waltz—something I still have not forgiven you for, incidentally."

"Jane, I only meant—"

"Your pity was insulting, but it was not entirely unwarranted. I will make an appalling Duchess of Blackmore."

"Oh, that is simply not—"

Jane released Victoria's hands to enumerate her points on her fingers. "First, I am short."

"You are only three inches shorter than I, and two shorter than Mary Thorpe."

"Second, I am plump."

"You are pleasantly rounded. Many men appreciate a shapely figure."

"Third, I am shy."

Victoria smiled. "You are not shy with me. Once you feel comfortable—"

"Fourth, I wear spectacles."

"Well, you could remove them, I suppose, if they bother you so much."

Jane stopped. "They do not bother me. I cannot see a whit without them. I am speaking of how others perceive me."

Carefully, Victoria backed away, rose to her feet, and straightened her shoulders, her hands folded serenely at her midriff. "Stand," she said firmly.

Jane blinked. It was not like Victoria to give orders. But Jane complied, rising obediently from her chair, partly because Victoria looked every inch the daughter of a duke, and partly because it seemed she would not speak until Jane did so.

"Now, will any of this nonsense alter what is to happen today?"

Jane hesitated before shaking her head.

"No," Victoria confirmed softly. "After today, you shall *be* the Duchess of Blackmore. You. Not Mary Thorpe. Not anyone else. Whatever expectations others might have had are meaningless. The new Duchess of Blackmore is an intelligent, charming, shapely woman who wears spectacles and reads entirely too much."

"Don't forget short."

"Your height does not signify."

"It will when my husband resembles a tree standing beside a mushroom."

"Jane."

Jane sighed. "Very well. Perhaps you are right."

"No 'perhaps' about it." Victoria slowly grinned, then reached out and pinched Jane's cheeks gently. "There, now. A little color. I am sorry I asked Harrison to dance with you. I did mean well, you know."

"I know."

"Are you ready to become my sister?"

Jane threw her arms around her best friend. They held each other tightly for long seconds before Jane whispered, "You know that is the only thing good to come out of this absurdity, don't you?"

Victoria sniffed and then pulled back to cup Jane's face between her palms. Her eyes were swimming with tears. "We have long been sisters of the heart, now we shall be in truth."

With her thumb, Jane mopped the single drop that spilled down Victoria's cheek and gave her a wry smile. "Is it producing an heir that turns you into a complete watering pot?"

Chuckling, Victoria shooed away her hands and took a deep breath. "Ready?"

"No."

"Steady on, dear Jane. You are about to become a duchess. Best begin acting accordingly." The falsely stern tone was lightened by Victoria's playful smile, but Jane knew she was right. She must become a duchess—his duchess. And she could delay no longer.

Her stomach cramped, flopping painfully around inside

her abdomen like a fish thrown onto a riverbank: out of its depth, struggling to breathe, instinctively knowing its place was elsewhere, but unable to do a thing about it.

"Very well," Jane said hoarsely. She cleared her throat, straightened her spectacles with shaking hands, and put on the bravest face she could muster. "Fetch Papa. It is time to show the world what the new Duchess of Blackmore looks like."

HIS BRIDE WORE A BRONZE GOWN OVERLAID WITH SHEER GOLD that shimmered in the light from the church windows. She was far from a beauty—"plain" suited her perfectly. But the gown was flawlessly formed, drawing the eye to her ample bosom, then down to her newly discovered waist, where a dark-bronze sash cinched becomingly.

Harrison scowled. Perhaps this explained the extravagant bill he had received from Bowman's on Bond Street.

His eyes traveled upward to her face. She was pale. Jane's eyes were not on him, but darting fretfully from her bouquet of ivory roses to the guests in the pews. Lord Berne had his hand over hers on his arm, but she still lagged slightly behind her father, as if he was dragging her forward against a current.

Finally, her dark eyes met Harrison's. She walked into a shaft of sunlight and halted for the briefest moment. The reflection of light on her spectacles flashed before she moved forward again; after that, she did not look away from him.

"Dearly beloved ..." He heard every word of the ceremony, spoke his vows, knelt when asked. But all the while, his focus remained on her. Jane.

Her voice had the faintest rasp. It was something he had noticed at Lady Gilforth's ball, though at the time, he'd been more vexed with her than intrigued. As he listened to that voice promise to love, cherish, and—most especially—obey him, a sensation ran from his scalp, over his skin, and down his spine. In the part of him no one knew, satisfaction thrummed and preened, unexpected and unwelcome.

It returned again as he slid his mother's ring onto her finger. At last, after the third prayer for their fruitfulness, the priest ceased his droning and completed the ceremony. Harrison offered his arm to his wife. Despite severe efforts to squelch it, that fugitive satisfaction stole through him a third time. Now, it filled his entire body.

His wife. She was his wife.

Her hand slid inside his elbow, the touch light and cautious. The music of organ and choir resounded inside the cavernous church as they retreated down the aisle.

He should not be so pleased. She was far from beautiful, far from the elegant and dutiful bride he had long presumed he would choose when the time came—which had always been "later." He frowned. Perhaps that was the reason for this puzzling gratification. He would no longer be forced to endure the marriage mart. Any gentleman with a title and fortune would be thankful to escape that madness.

Glancing down at her dark hair, parted in the center and gathered at the back of her head, graced with gold ribbon and creamy pearls, his frown deepened. Slowing as they reached the last column at the end of the pews, they stood together and waited for the parish clerk in the shadowed corner of the church.

She heaved a great sigh and glanced idly up at his face. Her brows lowered, and she blinked owlishly before dropping her gaze to his chin and muttering, "Do not scowl at me. This is your doing, not mine."

And that's when he knew. It was more than the relief of removing himself from the husband hunt. It was *her*. Jane. She was quite possibly the only woman who had ever challenged him so directly. She did not treat him like a duke. She treated him like a man, and one who vexed her as much as she did him. The thought of gaining control of her quenched a hidden need he rarely acknowledged, much less indulged.

He wanted to subdue her, bring her to heel. The impulse was base. Primitive. But as soon as it entered his mind, it burst outward from its source, rushing down his veins to effervesce beneath his skin. Feeling his groin tighten in anticipation, he clenched his jaw and pushed back against the unseemly instinct. He must not let the feeling linger. She'd married him for one reason: to secure her reputation. He had married her for one reason: to restore his family honor. Allowing their union to become anything more would be a dangerous mistake.

It was inappropriate to feel such things for his wife.

To imagine her kneeling before him.

To picture her surrendering to his pleasure and hers.

No, he must snuff out these primal urges like the brushfires they were.

Else watch as they both burned to a cinder.

IN JANE'S EXPERIENCE, FEW PROBLEMS COULD NOT BE BETTERED with a good meal. Today was proving the exception. Her wedding breakfast had been an unmatched feast—Mama's doing, of course. Salty, succulent ham, tender brioche, sweet plum tart, omelets delicately flavored with shallots and thyme, and a dizzying selection of other dishes, each more tempting than the last. By the time the wedding cake was presented, Jane feared she might burst.

But none of it lessened her misery. Nor, it seemed, had it comforted the Duke of Blackmore. Her husband. *Blast, I will never grow accustomed to that.* Even now, two hours on, he retained the same expression of strain and consternation she had witnessed just before the parish clerk had escorted them into a small office where they had signed the register, finalizing their ill-begotten union.

She sighed, sipping her coffee and eyeing the guests who milled about her family's drawing room. They all appeared to be enjoying themselves more than she. Laughter and conversation created a general din that floated around and above her like mist over the moors.

In truth, she should be thankful to be seated on this small divan tucked away in an innocuous corner of the room. Sometimes it was pleasant to be ignored. The past two hours had been horrendous. All that smiling and nodding and "my lord"-ing. At one point, she'd feared her knees would buckle from the strain of curtsying, especially after the dratted priest had kept her and the duke in their kneeling position for nigh on a half-hour while he droned on and on and *on*, pleading to the Almighty for her fertility. Really. A simple prayer for a fruitful union was more than adequate. Three lengthy entreaties struck her as undignified.

Now that she thought about it, the chance to sit here and rest, drink her coffee relatively undisturbed, and have no one approach was quite nice.

A few feet away, Lady Wallingham loudly declared gold the ideal color for fashionable brides. The dowager wore a brilliant blue gown with a matching, plumed turban. Flamboyant, yet somehow always elegant, Lady Wallingham managed to be both outspoken and powerful. She was eccentric, yet widely accepted—even respected—by other matrons.

Jane straightened when a notion tickled the skirts of her mind. In the role of duchess, she was bound to fail spectacularly. Everyone knew this. But what if she became an eccentric? An Original, as it were—the duchess who loved books more than balls, the one who rarely spoke, rarely appeared in London, never hosted a single ...

Her gaze snagged on her new husband's golden-blond head, where he stood near the fireplace speaking with Lord

Dunston. He looked forbidding. He looked like the Blackmore who would never countenance the indignity of an eccentric wife. She slumped as her small ray of hope died a premature death.

Jane's mother pulled Lady Wallingham away, and a group of Annabelle's friends sauntered by, ignoring Jane as usual. Behind them, another band of five young ladies gathered, their blond circle enclosing a familiar figure with lovely auburn hair. Jane stiffened as she recognized Lady Mary Thorpe, sister of Lord Dunston.

As Annabelle's giggling crowd moved away, Jane could not help overhearing Mary's friends discussing—of all things—Jane herself. "I was astonished, simply astonished!" whispered the spiteful Lady Phillipa Martin-Mace. "What could Blackmore have been thinking to wed an ugly, fat nothing like Plain Jane Huxley? A horrid choice, to be sure, but even worse when he could have offered for *you*, Mary."

Jane winced, then quietly set her coffee on the low table in front of her, feeling a sudden return of her earlier nausea. Really, this was only to be expected. She should have been prepared. But to hear the truth so baldly stated felt like the sudden slash of a cold knife.

"*Should* have, you mean. She preyed upon his gentlemanly honor," Adorra Spencer interjected, her abnormally large teeth making her diction less than crisp. "We all know Blackmore is obsessive about it. Otherwise, he doubtless would have offered for you this very season."

The lightest blond of them all, Miss Cecilia Barkley, refused to be outdone. "He is rightfully yours, Mary dearest. *You* should have been the Duchess of Blackmore."

A warm presence depressed the cushion next to Jane, drawing her attention away from the yellow-haired palace guard surrounding a demure, unprotesting Mary Thorpe.

"I wondered where you had disappeared to," said Victoria casually. "Hiding in plain sight, I see."

Jane's gaze dropped to her hands, where it snagged on her wedding ring, a sizable emerald flanked by a dozen diamonds and wreathed in gold. It had belonged to his mother, the last Duchess of Blackmore. She twisted the thing a full revolution before consciously stopping and folding her hands. "From time to time, invisibility is beneficial."

Victoria leaned closer, nudging Jane's shoulder with her own. "Pay them no mind. Envy is the ugliest color in the palette. I am a painter. I should know."

"Are they not correct?" Jane whispered. Before Victoria could answer, she continued, "Even I had heard he was on the verge of offering for Mary Thorpe before ..." With a small motion, she gestured to her left hand. "... this happened. Perhaps she is right to feel betrayed."

Victoria wasn't having any of it. "By now, you know Harrison well enough to know this: If he had made promises to her, he would have kept them. He did not. And so if Mary now feels betrayed, that is the result of her own fancy."

"Yes, but—"

"Jane, do you remember how Mary behaved toward me when my reputation was in tatters?"

She nodded. The cinnamon-haired girl and her gaggle of blonds had given Victoria the cut direct. Recalling the grief in Victoria's eyes as Mary had led her group to cross Bond Street in an obvious attempt to avoid passing near Victoria, Jane felt a resurgence of the angry indignation she had experienced at the time.

"And do you suppose I would prefer to spend the next forty years exchanging pleasantries with someone I know to be, at best, inconstant? Or rather, would I prefer someone who has proven loyal and true?"

"Er—the second one?"

"Precisely." Victoria gave a little shudder. "My nieces and nephews shall learn better character than that at their mother's knee, thank God."

It took Jane a moment to realize she was referring to Jane's future children—with Blackmore. For which, it would be necessary to ...

She felt a flush rise in her cheeks.

Oblivious to Jane's inappropriate thoughts, Victoria concluded her supportive rant with, "However it came about, I am most grateful it is *you* who wears my mother's ring."

Jane met her friend's eyes, knowing she meant every word. "Thank you," she rasped.

Victoria squeezed her hand briefly. "This has been a difficult time, but you are not alone. If you should ever have need, come to Thornbridge." A soft smile curved her mouth. "Oh, it is wonderful, Jane. You could stay for as long as you like. Lucien has so many books—"

"Perhaps she should get settled at Blackmore Hall before she takes up residence with you, dear sister." The quiet, clipped voice drew their eyes swiftly up to Blackmore's face. He did not look pleased.

Victoria gave him a brilliant smile, which he did not return. "I was simply inviting Jane for a visit. We are friends, you know."

Ignoring her, Blackmore turned his iron gaze to Jane. "We should depart before the hour if we are to reach the inn by nightfall."

Head swiveling in surprise, Victoria protested, "Harrison, you cannot possibly expect your bride to spend her wedding night traveling in a carriage."

"No," he said flatly. "We shall stay at the inn. I believe I said as much."

Shooting Jane a look of sisterly exasperation, Victoria said, "I would attempt to reason with him, but once he is set on a course, nothing persuades him to abandon it."

As they made their way upstairs to Jane's bedchamber to prepare for her departure, Jane felt the chill of dread settle beneath her skin.

Once he is set on a course ...

Most of what Jane knew about her new husband came from Victoria's descriptions, a handful of less-than-cordial interactions, and his reputation as an exacting and powerful duke. Much of her resistance to their marriage was based on her unsuitability to fulfill the role of duchess. It had consumed her thoughts to the exclusion of all else.

Until now.

Now, she must consider that, in addition to being the eighth Duke of Blackmore, he was also a man. The deeply uncomfortable conversation she'd had earlier with Annabelle about the "joys of marital relations" played again through her mind as Victoria, along with Jane's sisters and mother and maid, Estelle, all flitted about her like a flock of butterflies.

She swallowed hard, her ears heating and buzzing.

He was a man.

Handsome. Commanding. Virile.

Oh, dear God. Why had she not realized sooner? All along, she had worried she would be found lacking as his duchess. What should have concerned her most were her imminent failures as his wife.

She struggled to recall what Annabelle had told her. Something about "transporting" and "utter bliss." Her sister had mentioned that a man had an appendage, and not to be alarmed, as it needed to harden. When Jane had asked how such a thing could occur, Annabelle had assured her that if a man found a woman pleasing, it would happen naturally.

Her lungs seized.

What if he did not? Find her pleasing, that was.

"... grace?"

She shook her head and blinked into Estelle's face, which hovered inches from her own. "Oh, b-beg your pardon, Estelle. Were you speaking to me?"

The maid, a thin woman of forty whose friendly, matter-of-fact manner had made her one of Jane's favorite companions, just smiled. "New title might take a while to get accustomed to, eh?"

Jane blinked again and nodded absently.

"Are you quite all right?"

Jane did not respond.

She couldn't.

She was too busy dashing for the chamber pot, where her mother's magnificent wedding breakfast made an early—and unpleasant—reappearance.

Chapter Eleven

"Spare me your tiresome droning. Travel's discomforts are surpassed only by its inconveniences. And you are swiftly becoming one of the latter."

—The Dowager Marchioness of Wallingham to her nephew on their journey from Oxford to London.

Harrison's wife had not spoken a single word in over three hours. And she was on her seventh sigh. They sat beside one another in his coach, traveling the Great North Road for Blackmore Hall in Yorkshire. Although Harrison often preferred silence, hers was broken only by the turning of pages, the rumble of carriage wheels, and that incessant sighing.

He glared down at her short, round nose where it failed to properly hold her small, round spectacles in place. She pushed them up in a now-familiar gesture. Inexplicably, it sparked a flare of heat inside him. Perhaps irritation. Perhaps something more.

Strictly speaking, Jane was everything plain and drab and ignorable—her hair was brown and straight, her eyes brown and wide, her nose too short, her skin more milk than cream, and her figure too plump to be considered beauteous. His eyes dropped to her generously rounded breasts, lovingly outlined by the bodice of her emerald-green traveling gown. *Upon further consideration, that trait does have its advantages,* he thought.

She sighed again, a subtle grin playing about her lips, which were neither too thin nor too full, too narrow nor too wide. They were simply a set of lips—quite fine, with a slight bow along the upper, but hardly worth noting. Why their slightest quirk or lift or moue should be so bloody riveting, he had no idea.

The carriage jostled through a deep hole, causing them both to sway. Her right hand braced on the wall beside the window frame, then almost immediately returned to grasp her book. Her left hand delicately turned the page, her fingers sliding lovingly over its surface then rising to nudge the edge of her spectacles—again. His mother's ring winked and flashed in the late-afternoon light.

But that was not what caught his attention. It was her hand—or rather both of her hands. They were exquisite: small, silky, delicate, white. She had removed her gloves because, as she had explained shortly after their departure from Berne House, she preferred to feel the slide of paper beneath her fingertips.

He had nearly groaned. The mere thought of her hands made him restless. Imagining what else she might savor and stroke with those naked hands turned him hard as stone.

Again, the sheer inappropriateness of his thoughts alarmed him. Lust was for mistresses, not wives. He had dismissed Marguerite, his mistress of three years, before he had offered for Jane. Perhaps that had been unwise. He was a man of strong appetites, which Marguerite had previously tended discreetly, regularly, and enthusiastically. After six weeks of abstinence, it only made sense that his hunger might drive him to fixate upon his new wife.

Still, he mustn't allow the aberrant thoughts to continue. Wives should be shown the utmost care and consideration for their delicate sensibilities. Jane was an innocent. His task would be to introduce her to the marital bed gently and with great restraint.

Certainly, he could not demand that she stroke his cock with those white hands, then take him between her unremarkable lips and deep into her saucy mouth. Nor that she later cup her full, luscious breasts so that he could suckle them until she was soaked between those fleshy thighs.

He gritted his teeth and gripped the leather strap above the window, turning his gaze out to the green, rolling fields of the countryside. The whisper of a turning page followed by her eighth sigh drew him back to her like a lodestone.

"If you desire a more pleasurable amusement than admiring the farmland of Hertfordshire, your grace, I will gladly lend you one of my books," Jane said without glancing up from her novel. She must have sensed his focus upon her. Perhaps it had caused her discomfort. God knew it had done so for him.

"Fiction, I presume," he said, his voice embarrassingly hoarse.

Finally, she raised her head to meet his eyes. "Yes."

"No," he answered gruffly. "I do not care for novels."

"Perhaps poetry would be more to your liking."

"Frivolous nonsense. An utter waste of time."

Her mouth quirked. "Well, your grace, seeing as you have an overabundance of time to waste at present, perhaps you will gain a new appreciation for fiction. It is a fine distraction, if nothing else."

He had no answer to her very salient point, and simply glared down at her. Taking his lack of response as agreement, she set her book on the seat next to her, braced a hand on the window frame, and pushed herself up into a stooped position.

What the blazes was she doing?

Turning until her backside faced him, she bent forward and tugged at a basket that apparently had been tucked beneath her feet. "I have just the thing," she muttered, her round, lush backside bobbing mere inches from his face. "Wordsworth is far too lyrical. What you need is something with vigorous action. Something to get the blood pumping."

That was it. She was torturing him intentionally.

Her rump bounced and swayed enchantingly as she dug through the basket. He swallowed, unable to turn away, though he knew it was wrong ... so very wrong to imagine grasping her hips, raising her emerald-green skirts and showing her just what vigorous action—

"Ah-ha! I knew it was here!" Her left hand stretched out triumphantly, clutching a trio of volumes tied together with a bit of twine. He could make out the word "Waverley" along the faded spine.

Suddenly, the carriage lurched hard, the wheels groaning as they hit one of the deeper craters in the road, throwing Jane off-balance and sending her sprawling backward.

Right into his lap.

She squeaked in alarm. He groaned in surprise.

The instant she fell, his arms automatically wrapped around her waist and across the upper swell of her breasts. Now she was pressed tight, cradled inside the curve of his body. His head lowered against his will until his lips hovered an inch from her milky-white neck. She was all softness. Every. Damn. Inch.

Gritting his teeth and taking a deeper-than-necessary breath, he fought against the agonizing pleasure of her wriggling bottom caressing his cock. This close, her scent filled his lungs, fresh and sweet and warm like the buttered apple tart he remembered from Blackmore Hall's previous cook.

His mouth watered.

"Oh, dear me. I—I do beg your ... oh ..." Her breathless rasp sent yet more blood rushing from his head to the highly appreciative part of him celebrating her proximity with unseemly glee.

The carriage rocked again as it trudged through another hole. Fortunately, the abrupt motion jarred him out of his lustful fog long enough for reason to take hold. Clenching his jaw tight, he slid his hands to grip her waist just above her hips, lifted her and set her down next to him, back in her proper place.

"Oh!" she squeaked, her hands brushing over his as he withdrew.

Past all patience, he growled, "Reading does not interest me. Kindly keep your books and your seat."

"I am sorry, your grace," she began, straightening her spectacles above flushed cheeks. "It was not my intention to—"

"Regardless, such mishaps are the natural result of improper behavior, a lesson you should be well versed in by now."

Her face went from blushing to bright red. "I shall bear that in mind."

"Please do. Now, I would like to sleep. Pray, allow me the courtesy of an hour's peace and quiet." With that, he could no longer look at her. Even breathing near her was painful, as her scent still filled his head with its inebriating vapor. He was reeling with it, his senses caught and flailing like a bit of linen on a line, battered by a fierce wind. He crossed his arms over his chest and closed his eyes, his head lowering in a pretense of sleep, his hand discreetly draping the tails of his coat over his lap. Likely she was too innocent to understand what had been prodding her backside insistently. Even so, he did not wish to answer questions about it.

Although she did not respond to his rebuke immediately, he soon heard the swish and snap of a page turning, along with an under-the-breath retort that sounded suspiciously like, "Try a tomb. Plenty of peace and quiet there, you insufferable ..." Her voice trailed off on a fuming sigh, followed by the silence he had requested.

If only this untimely, unsuitable, utterly disastrous desire to leap upon his new wife's lush body like a ravening wolf could be ended so easily.

JANE ATTEMPTED MIGHTILY TO DISAPPEAR INTO HER BOOK, but it was little use. She had read the same sentence five times and scarcely a word of it resembled English.

Blast. It was that man. Her *husband*.

She slanted him a narrow-eyed glance. He was hunched away from her, pretending to sleep. His hair glinted in the fading light, light brown at the roots, burnished gold at the tips. It was slightly darker and more ashen than Victoria's, but perhaps that was because it was cropped short. Had he grown it long, likely the gold would take precedence. She let her eyes slide down over his jaw. It was like a blade, so crisp and hard. He was, in fact, hard everywhere. His shoulders. His chest. His thighs. Those, especially. When one viewed him from a distance, he appeared lean and elegant. But when one drew close, he was a good bit larger and more imposing, broader of shoulder, thicker of arm.

How could such a beautiful man hide such a frigid and rigid soul?

It had been utterly unnecessary to react so harshly to her overture and subsequent tumble. She'd been trying to do the man a favor, as he had been alternately gazing out the window and then down at her for nearly three hours. Clearly, he had been languishing in boredom if he'd been attempting to read her book over her shoulder. That must have been what he'd been about, because she could not fathom any other motivation for his palpable staring. Finally, the heated chills of his gaze grew unbearable, so she had offered him a book of his own.

A simple courtesy. Any polite person would do the same. But did he see it as such? Certainly not! The Ice King could not sully his pristine mind with the low romanticism of novels. Perish the thought! Aside from his literary snobbery, he had blown her little tumble entirely out of proportion. How was she to know that patch of road would be full of holes and ruts?

She turned another page, just so he would not suspect she was fuming. In need of an outlet for her outrage, she began planning a letter to his sister, who was woefully misguided when it came to the duke's character: *Dearest Victoria*, she would write. *I fear you are woefully misguided as to your brother's character. Permit me to enlighten you: Far from kind, he is both curmudgeonly and rude. Lady Wallingham is kinder. The proprietor of Norton's Bookshop is kinder. I suspect even Monsieur Bonaparte is kinder. When I offered him a book to pass the time on this interminable journey, his response was to shout me into silence.*

She paused, reconsidering her description.

Well, in fairness, perhaps "shout" is overstating it slightly. Blackmore never shouts, does he? That, too, is an annoyance. He is ever cold and quiet and cutting.

Shaking her head, she attempted to resume her original point.

That is a complaint for another day. This day, I shall demonstrate his penchant for rigidity. When I tumbled into his arms—

Oh, dear. That did not sound right.

—quite by accident, mind you—

There, that was better.

—do you know what he did? After holding me rather firmly for a good while, he set me back onto my seat as effortlessly as he would transfer a basket of turnips! Can you imagine? Lift and plop, as though I were an infant, not a full-grown woman a trifle over-fond of cream and sugar.

She paused, recalling the feel of his muscled arms around her, his hard chest behind her, and his hard, hard thighs beneath her. He had wrapped her up, tucked her into himself, his warm breath on her neck. She had scarcely dared breathe—in fact had not for several seconds—as the most peculiar sensations had washed over her.

The feeling of his arms about me was extraordinary, I must say, she continued. *Rather like standing beneath the ripe sun of late summer, watching a hundred swans suddenly take flight from a golden field. It rushes over your skin, both spark and tingle. A springle, if you will.*

She snickered a bit at her newly invented word then eyed Blackmore cautiously. He remained oblivious. So much the better.

Quite unlike anything I have ever known. And then, to transfer my not-insubstantial person without so much as a breath of exertion! He is freakishly strong, your brother. I find it both disturbing and intriguing. What is wrong with me, Victoria?

Shifting in her seat, she swallowed, suddenly feeling a bit parched. A tad overheated. A trifle nostalgic for an open carriage where a cool breeze could usher away her sudden flush. Perhaps she would revise the letter before posting it. Yes, a fair and thorough analysis of Blackmore's character required much closer examination. For accuracy's sake, of course.

Chapter Twelve

"A traveler is much like a man in his cups. Ordinarily, he would see a coaching inn more as a source of disease and infestation than rest and sustenance, but after days on England's dreadful roads, the entire world outside one's carriage resembles a palace."

—THE DOWAGER MARCHIONESS OF WALLINGHAM to the proprietor of a Wiltshire coaching inn upon being presented with her bill.

THEY ARRIVED AT THE COACHING INN OUTSIDE BIGGLESWADE shortly after dusk. It was an hour later than Harrison had anticipated, but the coachman had been forced to drive more slowly due to the unusually bumpy road. Several days of rain followed by more days of sun had done their work well, resulting in long stretches of road made perilous with craters and ruts. He should have accounted for it. Ordinarily, such details did not escape him, and it was disappointing to realize the upheaval of the wedding had diminished his usual thoroughness. However, he was pleased to see the other two traveling coaches carrying their servants and belongings had arrived safely ahead of them. At least one part of this day was going according to plan.

The carriage rocked as the coachman climbed down from his perch. From the road, the Pig and Plough appeared small, its original structure a Tudor-era, wattle-and-daub farmhouse. But from inside the central courtyard, one could see the more recently added, two-story brick structure extending from each side in a large, open square. Inside, he knew the food, while rustic, would be quite good, as would the ale. The lodgings would be clean and orderly. And the price would be reasonable, since it sat outside the village proper, back from the main road, surrounded by farmland.

Although it was a fine inn—one of his favorites along the route between London and Yorkshire—and he had stayed there many times, he doubted he had ever been so glad to arrive at the Pig and Plough. This had been a most trying journey.

A quiet rumbling sound from his wife's side of the carriage preceded her muttered, "I would give every book I own for a meal of substance."

"That won't be necessary," he said dryly. "I do believe they accept pounds and pence."

"Did you just make a *jest*, your grace?"

He did not appreciate the incredulity in her voice. Contrary to Colin's frequent accusation, he did possess a sense of humor; he simply chose to exercise restraint. Not everything in life should be subject to one's amusement. "The Pig and Plough serves an excellent hare stew."

She stilled, uttering the faintest, feminine moan.

Oddly seductive, he longed to hear it again. For a moment, he wrestled with the prurient impulse. It was wrong to allow himself such indulgences. He really should not ... "The broth is rich, redolent with salty flavor," he continued, his voice acquiring a slight rasp. "And it soaks most pleasingly into bread heated and freshly risen from the oven."

This time, her moan was unequivocal. It was followed by a catch in her breathing.

"At the finish," he described in a low voice, enjoying the sound of her delicate panting, "sweet, ripe berries drenched with cream accompany a pudding of the utmost tenderness."

"Stop," she protested hoarsely. "Please. I am famished, your grace. I cannot bear another word."

Neither could he. Fortunately, the coachman chose that moment to open the door, and they exited gratefully from the carriage onto the cobblestone courtyard.

Shaking her skirts, then rubbing absently at her lower back, Jane eyed the elaborate wooden sign over the door. It featured a fat, pink sow standing upright to drive a plow, playing the part of farmer rather than livestock. "Mmm," she murmured. "Do you suppose they serve bacon?"

Ignoring the question, he ushered her inside and spoke briefly to the innkeeper, Mr. Moffat, who bowed and y'grace'd numerous times before showing them to the dining room. Eight tables crowded the interior, where a low fire in the oversized brick hearth sent flickering light dancing over its plastered walls, timbered ceilings, and worn plank floors. An elderly couple chatted over half-full bowls in one corner, but otherwise, the room was empty. Harrison and Jane sat at the second table flanking the fireplace.

Short and stout, the bald Mr. Moffat crossed thick arms over a barrel chest and assured them, "Plucked the hares from the meadah m'self this morn. Stew's nevah been finer, I'd say." The man's rapid-fire country accent must have sounded garbled to Jane, because she blinked up at him blankly then dropped her gaze to the table.

"We'll each have a bowl," Harrison answered. "Some of

your ale, as well. And puddings, if you have them."

"Do I have them? They'll be comin' straight away, y'grace!"

Ten minutes later, Jane had spoken not a word, only nodding her thanks to the innkeeper then devouring half her bowl of stew along with a significant quantity of bread. To Harrison, her eye-closing, soft-sighing appreciation for her meal was disturbingly erotic.

He wondered if something was wrong with him. Frowning, he considered the possibility. Was it a fever? Certainly, he felt hot. Flushed. But no fever had ever caused him to grow and remain painfully aroused at the sight of a woman's hands or the sound of her satisfying an empty stomach. Perhaps it was some sort of ague.

Two plates, each holding a currant pudding topped by a small dollop of cream, appeared on their table, delivered by the shockingly tall, thick-boned Mrs. Moffat. She planted large hands on larger hips and half-smiled. "Here you are, Duke. This yer new duchess?"

He raised a brow and sent her a wry glance. "Gracious as ever, I see."

Mrs. Moffat snorted. She was not one to stand on ceremony. Or basic good manners. "Notice you didn't answer."

Jane, who had been sitting still and quiet since Mrs. Moffat approached, touched the rim of her spectacles, swallowed visibly, and nodded toward the woman without meeting her eye.

He frowned. Was she intimidated? By the innkeeper's rough-hewn wife? The woman was rather towering, and quite forward for one of her class, but surely an earl's daughter—

"Well, Duchess, it's glad to meet you, I am." She pointed a thumb at Harrison. "Duke here's been comin' round Pig and Plough for—what now?—nigh fifteen years, I'd say. Nevah thought he'd be bringing by the likes of you."

The more the woman talked, the more Jane shrank into herself, her face growing blank, her eyes remaining downcast, her body motionless like a rabbit fearing Mr. Moffat's stew pot.

"Mrs. Moffat," he snapped. "The Duchess would prefer to dine in solitude, if you don't mind. As would I."

Again, another snort. She gave Jane a knowing look. "He's a mite sharp about the rules, this one. Must be all that starch in his neckcloth. Not to worry, though, Duchess. Once you get him alone, that part comes off quick enough." At the woman's broad wink, blotchy color ascended Jane's throat and face.

Watching his wife's reaction, Harrison's stomach began to burn as though he had swallowed a jug of vinegar. His voice grew softer. Deadlier. "I shall not ask again."

Finally, it seemed the thick woman's senses returned. She straightened, her arms dropping to her sides, her smile disappearing. She sniffed, nodded, and turned to depart.

"Th-thank you, Mrs. Moffat." The quiet words came unexpectedly from Jane, bringing the woman's head around. "The stew was sublime. And the p-puddings look heavenly after our long journey."

Mrs. Moffat smiled warmly, revealing a missing tooth. "Ye're most welcome, Duchess."

As she ambled to the elderly couple's table to clear their bowls, Jane plucked her pudding up and began savoring its delightfully buttery texture. "Mmmph," she said, rolling her eyes in ecstasy. Her free hand flattened over the center of her chest, drawing his focus to the generous swell of her breasts. She swallowed and licked the crumbs from her lips. "This is divine. You must try it."

Brows lowering, Harrison wondered at Jane's reaction. Not to the pudding, which he knew to be delicious, but to Mrs. Moffat. He had known she was shy, but he'd assumed it was primarily with those of her own station, usually most pronounced at balls and other crowded gatherings. However, it appeared her nervousness around those she did not know extended to everyone, even servants and innkeepers' wives. He must remember this in the future, for as her husband, it was his duty to see to her comfort.

To that end, after their meal, when Jane's satisfied sigh was followed by a covered yawn, he suggested it was time to retire. "Our room shall not offer luxury, but it will be clean and reasonably comfortable."

"*Our* room?" Jane's eyes rounded, her voice rising to a squeak. "Singular?"

"We are married. Would it not seem peculiar if we required separate chambers while traveling?"

Lips tightening, she nodded. "I suppose you are right." While her words agreed with his point, her shoulders tensed visibly.

Her tension did not improve as they made their way upstairs to the inn's largest chamber. In fact, as he turned from closing the door, he saw her standing in the center of the room, wringing her hands. He stalked toward her until they were only a foot apart. "You are distressed. What is it?"

Glancing around the room, he could not determine the cause. Compared to most inns, Pig and Plough's best room was moderately spacious. There was a small double bed with a yellow-and-blue checked coverlet against the wall, a screened-off area in one corner with a chamber pot and washbasin, and a large window framed by faded yellow curtains. Certainly nothing to generate this sort of alarm.

She refused to look at him. Instead, her eyes were fixated on the bed. "N-nothing. I am simply a bit nervous."

"Why?" he demanded.

Shooting him an exasperated look from beneath her lashes, she resorted to sarcasm. "Oh, I cannot imagine, your grace. Perhaps it has something to do with this being my wedding night."

"Wedding night ...?" Suddenly, her reaction made a good deal more sense. "You thought I would demand my husbandly rights tonight? When you are clearly exhausted? At a humble Bedfordshire coaching inn?"

She sniffed and touched the corner of her spectacles. "Well, when you put it in those terms, perhaps I presumed incorrectly."

"Yes, it is safe to say so."

She nodded, her eyes glued to his cravat. "But we shall both be ... sleeping. Together." She glanced behind her, then back to his cravat. "In that bed."

Why must she say it that way? Until this moment, perhaps unwisely, he had not much dwelt on their sleeping arrangements. Now, he could focus on nothing else.

"You are very tall," she accused.

"And you are not," he retorted.

"Additionally, I had previously misjudged the broadness of your shoulders. But they are quite so. Broad, I mean."

He noted her breathing had grown faster, her eyes soft as she examined the aforementioned shoulders. "What of it?"

She blinked. "Hmm? Oh! Just that the bed is a trifle small. And you are—apologies, your grace—not."

Glancing toward the bed, then back into her deep brown eyes, he attempted to stifle the many inappropriate responses that leapt into his head. All considered, the one he uttered was rather tame by comparison. "We shall fit perfectly."

Her tongue darted out to moisten her lips. She swallowed hard.

Before he did something foolish like taking hold of his virginal wife and showing her just how well they would fit, he clasped his fists behind his back, and informed her of his plans. Plans he would adhere to, damn it all, in spite of this vicious lust that assailed his self-control mercilessly. He would *not* be ruled by crude instincts. "You needn't concern yourself that I shall seek to consummate our union while on our journey. I had anticipated waiting until we arrive at Blackmore Hall, where we may both find comfort and recover from the rigors of travel before such demands are made."

"Oh," she said in a small voice, appearing unburdened yet deflated. A shadow moved through her eyes. "How considerate."

He stepped back, putting some distance between them. "The servants are in the rooms down the hall. I shall ask your maid to attend you. Estelle, is it not?"

She nodded, the corners of her mouth turning down, her throat working on a swallow.

He suspected he had somehow upset her. But he did not ask. Instead, he turned on his heel, opened the door, and fled the room before he did something both of them would regret.

JANE WAS AWAKENED BY TWO THINGS: A DISGUSTINGLY cheerful, persistent song from a bird perched too close to the window. And something squeezing one of her bosoms with a fair amount of enthusiasm. Otherwise, she was quite comfortable, especially given her hard, lumpy pillow and heavy, overly warm blanket. Normally, she preferred a softer bed and a lighter covering, as she disliked having her sleep disturbed by too much heat. But, in this case, it was lovely being so tightly wrapped inside her cocoon, her legs weighed down, her waist secured, her backside snugged and prodded by the hard, lumpy folds of the heavy, hot blanket. And her bosom, squeezed and cradled and teased by …

Her eyes popped open. Oh, dear. It was not a blanket. Nor a pillow. Nor even her corset, which she had removed before climbing alone into bed. *Alone*, mind.

Quite when her husband had joined her, she could not say, having fallen asleep before he'd returned from wherever he had gone. Now, she was grateful for that small blessing, as their relative positions were faintly embarrassing.

They were tangled up like vine and tree. Near as she could deduce—for, she could not see anything but a gauzy outline without her spectacles—one of his arms was stretched beneath her head. The other curled around her waist and wound upward so that his large, lean hand could have its way with her breast. That part felt … quite pleasant, actually. His palm was warm and firm, sliding over her hardened, sensitized nipple as his long fingers gently squeezed, generating little *springles* of sensation that made her want to catch her breath and slide her legs along his. She wriggled her hips experimentally. The lump that had been pressing into her backside thrust forward and pressed harder.

What *was* that?

Could it be his appendage? Eyes wide, she considered the possibility. Yes, it was conceivable. She remembered Annabelle mentioning something about mornings and the appendage. But she had been trying very hard not to listen, and so did not recall details.

Immediately, she knew she must formulate an urgent letter to Annabelle. She was sorely lacking in key information. *Dearest Annabelle,* she would write. *I awakened this morning to a most disturbing—*

No, that wasn't it.

—discomforting—

Hmm. Not quite right, either.

—extraordinary circumstance. I found myself positively engulfed by my new husband. We were both sleeping soundly, until a bird desirous of an early demise disturbed my slumber. While his grace slept on, I could not help noticing a certain pressure, a prodding of sorts, coming from the region below his waist.

Dear heaven, this was disastrous. Perhaps she should simply come to her point.

Perhaps I should simply state my point: You attempted to explain the male appendage before my wedding. Would you be so kind as to explain it again? This time, pray do not spare any detail. I suspect I shall require all the knowledge at my disposal.

Ever your grateful sister,

Jane

P.S., The sensation of being held and stroked by the Duke of Blackmore has necessitated the invention of a new word, as I fear the English language fails to provide a term sufficient to describe it. I have dubbed the feeling "springle"—half spark, half tingle. I am rather pleased with it, though I suspect he would not approve. He is sadly a stickler for tradition.

The tradition-stickler's nose nuzzled her neck, and his thumb raked sinfully over her nipple through the linen of her gown. Her thighs squeezed together, trying to quench the warm, glowing ache that bloomed between them. He inhaled deeply against her skin, absorbing her scent. A low groan rumbled in his chest, echoing down her spine. She couldn't stop the insistent stroking of his thumb, couldn't stop her hips from grinding back to push harder against him, couldn't stop the small, brief moan at the top of her next breath.

And that was what woke him.

His thumb stopped. Her hips froze. Neither of them breathed.

Then, she realized sleeping people should not stop breathing. So, deliberately, she closed her eyes, breathed slowly, and pretended to sleep.

Carefully, he removed his arm from beneath her head, his hand gently easing her onto a pillow. Next, he withdrew his legs, sliding them from between and over the top of hers. Then, his hips receded, taking his heat and his appendage with him. The very last part to disentangle itself was his hand, which lingered on her breast like it needed a long farewell. Perhaps it did.

Finally, it, too, slid away, the bed jostling as he left. She heard his footsteps recede along the squeaking wood floor toward the screened corner of the room. Next came intermittent splashing. Rustling of cloth. Clinking of a razor against the basin. The window opening. The bird flapping away. Water being tossed, then splashing as it was replenished from the pitcher. More footsteps, this time with boots, but careful falls reluctant to disturb her.

They paused.

Curious, she opened her eyes the smallest fraction and

peered toward the door. She could not see much—a dark blur with golden hair in front of a brown door. He was standing there, motionless. Staring.

At her? No. It couldn't be.

He must be examining his timepiece, of which he was inordinately fond.

Yes, that was much more likely. To think he had been watching her sleep was pure foolishness. *Her.* Plain Jane Huxley. Well, Jane Lacey now, she supposed. Then again, perhaps that was it precisely. He had married a plain woman, and if this very morning had been the moment he realized how permanent that was ...

Suddenly, she was very glad for her poor eyesight.

Very glad, indeed.

Chapter Thirteen

"Indeed, the wealth of one's husband is only important if one prefers frequent meals over starvation."

—THE DOWAGER MARCHIONESS OF WALLINGHAM to Lady Maureen Huxley in response to said lady's assertion that a suitor's funds are of less concern than his sincerity.

THREE DAYS LATER, LYING IN A COPPER TUB WITH STEAMING water lapping just beneath her chin, Jane considered that perhaps this marriage was not such a bad bargain after all. The tub, for example, was positively splendid. Deep and long, it had been placed before the carved marble hearth in the dressing room adjacent to the Duchess of Blackmore's chamber. *Her* chamber. Inhaling the apple-blossom perfumed steam, she allowed the water's heat to soothe away her lingering stiffness and sighed with bliss.

Before arriving at Blackmore Hall the previous evening, Jane would have insisted there were few, if any, advantages to the title. Clearly, she had miscalculated. While the luxury of her new home should not have come as a surprise—Blackmore was one of the wealthiest peers in England, after all—seeing it for the first time had overwhelmed her senses.

As their carriage had approached along the drive, the sunset had limned the winged, Palladian sprawl of pale limestone a bright gold. Centered by a pediment and columns, the house rested on a rise above a large, picturesque fish pond. It was surrounded both by a heady wealth of gardens and further by a green landscape of gentle hills and expansive fields.

Once inside the entrance hall, despite her exhaustion, she had spun in place, wondering at the grandeur of peacock-blue silk walls, white columns flanking a shell-shaped niche, and a frescoed ceiling opposite polished marble floors. It made Clumberwood Manor, her family's country house in Nottinghamshire, seem a shabby peasant's dwelling. And the entrance hall was merely the first of more than a hundred and twenty rooms, some of which she had spent the morning and afternoon exploring with the kindly housekeeper, Mrs. Draper.

Jane enjoyed comfort. She relished a hot bath, a feather-soft bed, a blazing fire on a chilly night. But she had never dared to anticipate such lavishness being hers one day. Becoming the Duchess of Blackmore might prove an awkward fit in every other aspect, but in this, she would wallow until her fingertips wrinkled like an apple in the sun.

"Are you ready for a rinse, your grace?" Estelle's voice came from behind her head.

Jane sighed wistfully. "Can I not lie here for the remainder of the day?"

The snap of a towel being briskly shaken was followed by Estelle's chuckle. "Bound to get a mite peckish, I suspect. Don't want to be late for dinner, do you? They say the cook here is a mad Frenchman, but his meals are delivered straight from heaven's door."

She groaned at the mention of food. "That does sound lovely. Give me just a few minutes more, Estelle. I believe my backside has yet to recuperate from our journey."

Indeed, despite the sumptuousness of Blackmore's coach, traveling the rutted road from London to Leeds had not been pleasant. After the first day's contrariness, the duke had elected to ride his horse, rather than sit inside the carriage with her. At each stop, although he was polite and always saw to her comfort, he had grown remote and taciturn, scarcely uttering a word to her, other than ordering her inside for meals and such. After the first night, he had arranged for them to sleep in separate rooms, remaining true to his promise of delaying their marriage's consummation.

However, even after arriving at Blackmore Hall last night, they had slept separately, with him citing her obvious exhaustion. She had wondered if he was vexed with her, but he had not appeared so. Which left only one conclusion: He regretted their union and dreaded the intimacy of the marriage bed.

She glanced down at her body, buoyed by the water. It was all whiteness, softness, roundness. How could she blame him, honestly? Most men preferred a more refined form. Everyone knew that.

He would have to meet his manly obligations eventually, just as she would do her wifely duty. But perhaps he had decided a longer—maybe even indefinite—delay would give them time to reconcile themselves to the onerous task. Yes, that was likely. And probably wise.

A weight settled inside her chest, causing it to ache and squeeze all the way up to her throat. Swallowing hard, she reprimanded herself for her foolish emotion. *No sense in going all weepy.* She sniffed and half-smiled. *You should be relieved. Yes, relieved. He shan't bother you; you shan't bother him. It is the perfect arrangement. Quite sensible, really.*

With that comforting thought, she finished her bath and dressed for dinner. As usual, her arrow-straight hair refused to take a curl, so Estelle simply parted it in the center and anchored it at the back of her head. "There, now," the maid said, stabbing one last pin firmly along Jane's scalp. "All finished."

Jane stood and stared into the mirror of her dressing table. Her gown was exquisite—the gentle green of a meadow at sunrise. The sleeves extended to her elbows, the square neckline adorned with filigreed ribbon in a darker green matching the sash at her waist. Truly, with only the dress, not her face, visible in the small mirror, she scarcely recognized her own form. Mrs. Bowman, for all her bluster, was a masterful talent.

"Here you are, your grace," Estelle said, draping a soft, ivory shawl over Jane's arms. "You look a picture. Best not delay. I hear his grace is awaiting you in the dining room."

Jane nodded, tiny flutters in her belly prefacing an increase in her pulse. As she had seen little of him yesterday, and nothing of him today, perhaps a bout of nerves was to be expected. Why, it was a wonder she could recall his features, so carefully had he avoided her.

Upon entering the dining room, she received a devastating reminder. He wore blue—deep, midnight blue. And he was heartbreakingly handsome, standing so tall and straight beside his chair, his shoulders broad and squared, his hair shining in magnificent, candlelit glory, his brows lowered in a steely glare ... at her.

"You are late," he growled.

Blinking to clear the sudden fog that had descended, she retorted with all the wit she possessed in that moment, "Am I?"

"Five minutes. At Blackmore Hall, we dine at seven. Did Mrs. Draper not inform you?"

She stared at him from her position inside the doorway, for right then, she could do nothing else. Really, it was not as if she had never seen him before. Why did he appear so much more handsome than usual? Strange, indeed. Perhaps he was simply much refreshed after recovering from their travels. "Seven?" she repeated. "Oh, yes, of course. Mrs. Draper did say so."

"If you knew, then why are you late?"

She looked around the dining room, noting they were the only souls present, aside from the footmen attending them. A single brow arched. "My apologies, your grace. I do hope our guests will not be offended by my poor manners."

Either he did not understand her sarcasm or he chose to ignore it, because his only response was to pull out the chair to his right and say coldly, "I trust it shall not happen again."

Mouth quirking, she shook her head and moved to take her seat. It had been two days since she was this close—close enough to smell him. She took a deep breath, gathering sunshine and starch into the cellar of her lungs. Her eyelids fluttered. When had starch become so delicious?

"Did you sleep well?"

The question started over her head then moved to the chair beside her. She nodded. "Quite. And you?"

"Mmm. Better tonight, I expect." His face was expressionless, his blue-gray eyes restlessly exploring her hair and dress. "You look ... well."

There went that fluttering again. In her belly. In her eyelids. It was silly, like when she drank too many cups of coffee. "As do you, your grace."

With a wave, he invited her to eat the asparagus soup that had been placed in front of her. She blinked, realizing that perhaps for the first time in her life, she had completely ignored food. And delectable food it was: Veal filet as tender as a new blade of grass, with a rich, creamy béchamel sauce; succulent salmon with a lushly balanced, earthy sorrel sauce; a gooseberry tart that was sweet and tangy and made her eyes roll and lips pucker. Before the meal was over, nine dishes had been offered, all as heavenly as Estelle had reported.

As she slid one last bite of juicy-tart gooseberries into her mouth, the duke, who had been largely silent throughout the meal, asked, "Do you play the pianoforte?"

Biting down and letting the sweet tang explode on her tongue, Jane held up her finger, closed her eyes and savored for just a moment. Finally she swallowed, and turned to Blackmore. His eyes were a bit glazed, his cheekbones a bit ruddy, and his breathing a bit fast. She could only conclude he, too, was reacting to the meal. It really was exceptional. Tomorrow, she would have to meet this mad Frenchman who managed the kitchens. He was an artist. "Yes. Actually, I quite enjoy it, so long as I am not playing before too many people."

His eyes dropped to her hands, his chest suddenly heaving on a deep breath. "Are you finished?"

Puzzled, she tilted her head. "I suppose I am."

"I will show you the music room."

Frowning, she searched his face. He looked pained. Was he still overtired from their journey? Certainly, he seemed a robust sort, not one to require long periods of rehabilitation. Most perplexing.

"And the library."

"Oh!" She smiled, remembering the two-story, mahogany-paneled room with curved bookcase alcoves and a ceiling painted to resemble a cathedral's, complete with heavens teeming with angels. She had thought the motif rather appropriate. "It was the first room I viewed with Mrs. Draper this morning. Magnificent, your grace."

"Did she show you the old library or the new one?"

Wide-eyed, she leaned toward him. "There are two? What's the difference?"

His grin was slow and unexpected. It made her mouth go dry. "If you have to ask, then you must see it for yourself." He stood and pulled out her chair. "Come, I will show you."

And he did, taking her on a head-spinning tour of the old and new libraries. Apparently, the one she had seen earlier in the day was the new library. The old library was tucked away in the back corner of the ground floor, just down a narrow corridor from his study. As he held the door open for her to enter, she could not say what she had been expecting. What could possibly be more magnificent than the new library?

She held her breath, feeling him move in close behind her. So close, the heat of him felt like summer on her skin. "Do you like it?" The low, rumbling question spoken next to her ear sent a shiver down the slope of her neck, over the hills of her breasts, and back up the curve of her spine.

"It is wondrous," she whispered, so breathless she could barely form words. She wasn't speaking of the room, although she could have been. It was half the size of the new library, dark and intimate where the other was palatial and grandiose. Walnut paneling stained nearly black was offset by three large windows looking out onto the rear gardens. A fireplace anchored one wall, along with two winged leather chairs and a green velvet sofa. A writing desk sat beneath the center window. The room was perfect. Almost sacred.

"Come," he said hoarsely. "You must see the music room."

Turning, she bumped into his chest, her nose landing in his cravat. His hands automatically came up to brace her. "Oh, I beg your ... par ..."

She looked up—very far up—into his eyes. Before a storm gathered, blue water would transform, grow troubled and take on a steely light. That was the color of his eyes: blue water before a gathering storm. He held her upper arms snugly, his hands wrapping entirely around them and pulling her closer so that the tips of her breasts brushed against his coat.

Footsteps sounded in the corridor. A footman, tending to the candles. Blackmore set her away several inches and swallowed before dropping his hands to his sides. Then, he bowed and waved her ahead of him.

As they walked the length of the house to find the music room, he cleared his throat and began describing the history of

Blackmore Hall. "There has been a structure of one sort or another on this land since the time of William the Conqueror. Blackmore Castle still stands, though it is something of a ruin."

"Really? A castle? I would love to see it."

He glanced down at her, the corner of his mouth lifting faintly. "Tomorrow, perhaps. I shall take you."

She smiled. "I should like that very much."

Nodding, he continued his history. "This house was built and rebuilt four times."

"Gracious! Four?"

"Mmm. The most recent renovation expanded Blackmore Hall to its current size. My grandfather employed the finest craftsmen of the time. Robert Adam." He waved a hand toward the grand staircase as they approached the front of the house. "Thomas Chippendale." For this, he pointed to a mahogany table holding a vase of roses. "Capability Brown."

"He was a designer of gardens, was he not?" Maureen had spoken of him often, as she adored gardens.

"Quite a skilled one, yes."

They arrived at the music room. Much like all the other rooms, it was impressive: Cream silk walls with a leafy motif. Elegant, round-backed chairs upholstered in deep-gold brocade and edged with dark wood. The same fabric was used for the draperies. The enormous, square carpet featured a radius design in dark blue, red, and gold.

And then, there was the pianoforte. It occupied a corner of the room, its golden-brown wood polished and gleaming. She shot a questioning look up at the duke. He nodded toward the instrument. "Please."

She grinned, shrugging off her shawl and handing it to him absently. Seating herself on the matching bench, she brushed the keys lightly with her fingertips. Then, pausing to take a breath, she played a simple country tune she had committed to memory. About halfway through, she sensed him moving close to her, his shadow playing over her hands. But it was rare that she was able to play such a finely tuned, beautifully crafted instrument, and so she did not lift her fingers from the keys until the very last note had departed the room.

She sighed. "This is quite the loveliest surprise I have received in ages. Thank you, your grace."

Smiling up at his face, she was shocked at how closely it resembled stone. His fist strangled her shawl. His eyes burned over her hands.

Nervously, she reached up to adjust her spectacles. He followed the movement then locked on her mouth. "It is time to retire." His voice was little more than a low growl, almost menacing in its intensity.

One of her hands settled nervously over her waist. "Oh, but I am not particularly sleepy. Perhaps I could play one m—"

"Now." The growl was deeper.

Oh, dear. She did not know what had upset him, but clearly something had. The wild gleam in his eyes spoke of barely-contained emotion. She had seen it twice this evening—at dinner, and now here. Whatever the cause, she was not keen on testing his mood. Nodding, she accepted the shawl he handed her and allowed him to escort her upstairs to the Duchess's chamber. Feeling awkward, she opened the door before turning back to face him—only to find him glaring over her shoulder.

"Oh, your grace! And your grace," said Estelle from behind her. "I was just preparing the duchess's dressing gown."

Turning back to the maid, Jane answered, "Very good, Estelle. Thank you."

"I'll just leave you alone now to ... retire ... shall I?"

Before she could respond, Blackmore said stiffly, "No. Stay and assist the duchess in preparing for bed." With that, he inclined his head to Jane and backed away. "For now, I shall bid you good evening."

Watching her husband's broad back disappear down the corridor, then into the Duke's chamber, which adjoined her own, Jane shook her head in confusion. "He is the most confounding man, Estelle. I do not know if I shall ever understand him."

The maid wore a secret smile.

"What?" Jane demanded.

"Nothing. I'd say only this, your grace. Men are simpler creatures than you might think. Chances are, given a fortnight, all will come clear."

"Well, I do hope you're right."

Estelle's smile grew. "I am, don't you worry. Now, let's prepare you for *sleeping*, why don't we?"

Chapter Fourteen

"You may delay, if you like. But eventually, dear boy, you shall give me what I want, or resign yourself to a life of misery."

—The Dowager Marchioness of Wallingham to her son, Charles, upon his continued resistance to producing a grandchild.

An hour later, curled up in a cozy chair next to a crackling fire in her bedchamber, Jane's heart rolled like a ship at sea. Would he declare his love for her? Would he at last break his long silence and tell her the truth of his devotion?

Hurriedly, she turned the page. Yes! He would. He did.

"'I cannot make speeches, Emma,' he soon resumed; and in a tone of such sincere, decided, intelligible tenderness as was tolerably convincing. 'If I loved you less, I might be able to talk about it more.'"

She closed her eyes and pressed the book to her chest. Even upon the fifth reading, that line still thrilled her to her toes. "*If*

I loved you less, I might be able to talk about it more." She sighed, savoring the words like a fine port, then continued the story.

A firm knock followed by the sound of a door opening and closing interrupted the emotional scene. Without looking up, she waved a hand in the direction of the intruder. "Not now, Estelle. I am just getting to the good part."

The throat being cleared had a distinctly masculine ring to it.

Freezing mid-sentence, Jane slowly raised her gaze, finding first a pair of large, stocking-clad feet, then a pair of black trousers, and finally the whole of Blackmore standing less than six feet from her, wearing an unreadable expression. Awkwardly, she scrambled to her feet, dropping *Emma* on the floor. "Oh, dear." She bent forward to retrieve it, managing to bump the side table with her hip and slosh chocolate from china cup into china saucer with a clink. "Oh, *dear*," she repeated, straightening abruptly and twisting to glance behind her at the mess.

"Jane."

She twisted back. "Yes?"

"Calm yourself."

Adjusting her spectacles, she dropped the book onto her chair and folded her arms across her waist. He had removed his cravat and tailcoat and waistcoat. His white linen shirt gaped open at the neck, revealing a triangle of skin and a hint of hair rising from the muscles of his chest.

Her hands dropped to her sides where they pressed against the claret silk of the lace-trimmed peignoir Estelle had laid out for her. Earlier, Jane had wondered at the choice, but most of the garments provided by Mrs. Bowman were equally decadent, so she had shrugged and slipped it on before sitting down to her nightly cup of chocolate and a good book.

Blackmore's eyes narrowed and dropped to her uncorseted bosom, his nostrils flaring on an indrawn breath. The heat of his focus caused her nipples to harden, the embarrassing reaction, in turn, generating a warm flush.

"I—I wasn't expecting you," she stuttered. "What are you doing? Here. Tonight. I thought ..." Her voice faded as he took two steps toward her, bringing with him the scent of sunlight and crisp air and ... oh, simply *him*. Weakness flooded her legs, fluttered in her belly.

"You thought ... what? That I would wait forever?" His low rasp rippled over her skin. "I am your husband. It is my right to enter this room whenever I choose. Particularly for the first time since our wedding."

Bloody hell. She had suspected his motives the moment she saw him standing in her bedchamber, half undressed. But not before that. Not the slightest bit. She had, in fact, decided he might very well intend to wait forever. Obviously, she had presumed incorrectly. Her stomach twisted, the feeling akin to plunging from a sheer cliff. Her skin went cold, then hot. Her teeth pressed into her lower lip. She could not seem to catch her breath.

He took another step closer, leaving mere inches between them. One of his hands came up to stroke her hair, which Estelle had brushed and left loose and straight. The sensation of his fingers sifting through the strands caused shiver after shiver to run over her skin like rain droplets on a leaf.

"What book were you reading?"

His scent surrounded her, making her dizzy. Making her melt. "Book?" she breathed. "I ... it is called Emma. It is the story of a girl whose father ..." She ran out of words the moment his fingers stroked softly behind her ears, caught on her spectacles, and lifted them ever-so-gently from her face. "Never mind," she sighed, letting her eyes drift closed.

His hands came back to cup the sides of her head. Something warm brushed over her forehead, her eyelid, her cheek. Drifted down to the corner of her mouth. Then moved against her lips with a tender pressure. He was kissing her, she realized. The Duke of Blackmore was kissing her.

"Jane," he whispered, his heated breath washing against her chin.

"Hmm?"

"This will go easier if you relax."

Her eyes popped open. She was close enough that she could see some detail of his face. It appeared he was grinning slightly. "Are you laughing at me?" she demanded.

"Not at all."

"I don't believe you."

His hands busied themselves untying the sash beneath her bosom, his knuckles brushing against the cushion of her breasts. "Why would you think so?"

"I can hear it in your voice. It is grossly unfair. You know I have never done this."

He slipped her robe off her shoulders and tossed it over the chair. "Yes," he answered. "I am aware."

"Then you should also know I have little notion of what is expected."

"I am relieved to hear it," he said.

She frowned and squinted up at him. "Relieved? I thought you were amused."

"A wife should be innocent when she first comes to her husband. It is only right."

Sighing in exasperation, she glared up in the general direction of his eyes. "I don't know what I am supposed to do. That leaves me at a disadvantage. Besides which, I cannot see a thing without my spectacles. You are a blur. Quite handsome. But a blur, nonetheless."

He was quiet for a moment before saying thoughtfully, "Would you prefer to wear your spectacles?"

Her relieved, "Yes, I would," was answered immediately with the frames being smoothly slipped back into place on her nose.

"There," he said, his chiseled jaw blurry no longer. "Better?"

She nodded, suddenly feeling his proximity at double its customary force. She could see the shadow of his beard beneath his skin, the slight flush along his cheekbones, the reflection of firelight in his eyes, which were darker than usual.

Perhaps she should have left the spectacles off.

"Now," he said in the manner of a tutor instructing a student, "let's begin with kissing. Allow your lips to soften and accept the caress of mine." He proceeded to demonstrate by cupping her cheeks in his palms and bending to stroke his lips over hers. She tried to keep her eyes open—how much could she learn without sight, after all?—but they drifted closed of their own volition, just as her hands automatically rose to stroke the backs of his where they held her face with such gentleness.

Warmth like she had never experienced began to glow inside her as his lips nibbled and caressed hers. It started low in her belly, blooming outward like a flower seeking the sun. Just as the feeling emboldened her to begin matching his pressure, meeting his caresses with some of her own, he pulled back, dropping his hands.

She opened her eyes. They widened as soon as she saw what he was doing. He was removing his shirt, pulling the thing off over his head. "Oh. Oh, my, your grace," she breathed. He was even more thoroughly muscled than she had suspected. Being so tall and lean and distinguished when clothed, it was easy to dismiss the man's physique as typical of an aristocrat. But, as she had learned in the carriage and, really, whenever she came into close proximity, he was almost unnaturally strong. And now she understood why. He looked like one of the Greek figures depicted in Lord Elgin's marbles, but with a bit of light-brown hair along the upper half of his chest.

"What is wrong?" he demanded, glancing down at his own torso. She didn't blame him. It was most captivating.

"N-nothing. Nothing at all. Are you much accustomed to exercise, your grace?"

He frowned. "I enjoy fencing. And riding, of course. Why do you ask?"

"Oh, no particular reason."

"I shall never hurt you, Jane."

Her eyes flew up to his. Of course he wouldn't. The thought had never occurred to her. Why would he say—?

"No more than necessary, in any event."

"I beg your pardon?"

His color deepened, and he lifted one hand to rub the back of his neck. The movement caused the smaller muscles along his belly to tighten and ripple in a riveting fashion. She swallowed hard. He answered, "There will be some discomfort the first time. Thereafter, you should find it less trying."

"So, the discomfort is all on my part. Do I understand correctly?" She asked the question only to poke at him a bit. Annabelle had already explained the pain she would experience.

"Yes."

"Hmm."

"It is unavoidable. But I shall take every care to lessen your difficulty."

"How?"

"By helping you to relax." He glanced over his shoulder at the green-silk canopied bed, then back at her. "Perhaps we should lie down."

She paused, considering his suggestion, and then nodded. He walked to the bed and drew the covers back, waving her closer. She obeyed, moving to stand in front of him. Again, his hands stroked her hair, lifting it away from her shoulders and placing it behind her back. His slow, careful movements reminded her of a groom tending a nervous filly.

Bending to kiss her again, he held her chin between his finger and thumb, stroking her skin softly. She sighed against his mouth, moving closer until she felt his arms snake around her back, tightening so that her breasts flattened against the hard contours of his abdomen.

His heat was incredible, fairly burning her through the silk of her gown. Inside, restlessness took hold, forcing her hips forward to rub wantonly against his thighs. Something prodded her belly. A hard, swollen something of a rather insistent nature. His appendage, she concluded, growing a trifle alarmed upon recalling Annabelle's description of the consummation process.

Suddenly, the slick presence of his tongue glided along the seam of her lips, and on instinct, she opened so he could slip inside, where he stroked and pressed and pleasured her mouth. He tasted cool and warm all at once, like mint and vanilla. Her arms stretched up between them to wrap around his neck. She desperately wanted more. Tightening her grip, she attempted to pull him closer, to increase the pressure of his mouth against hers.

He groaned, his arms squeezing forcefully around her waist until her feet left the floor. Placing her on the bed as if it were nothing, he maneuvered them until she laid flat on her back and he rested half on top of her, half on the bed. His legs scissored between hers, his thigh rubbing in the most delicious way along the juncture that ached and clenched for him. She moaned and dared to thrust her tongue insistently against his, craving his flavor, needing him to do ... something.

Only, he did not do as she wished. Instead, he broke the kiss, his chest working fast with his panting. For a moment, his head hung between them as if he needed to gather himself. Rolling onto his side, he sat up to douse the lamp beside the bed, casting their portion of the room into deep shadow.

She felt him leave the bed, heard the sound of cloth sliding over skin, then felt the mattress depress as he returned to lie beside her. Her arms automatically circled his neck, but he gently clasped her wrists and placed her hands beside her shoulders.

"It is better this way," he rumbled, his voice nearly unrecognizable. "Just lie back and let me touch you."

Touch her he did, first with his lips against the side of her neck, nibbling and suckling. Then with his hands, sliding his palm over her breast, stroking her nipple through the silk of her gown until she moaned and writhed, her lungs laboring to take in more air. Several times, she lifted her hands to brush his face or clutch his hair, but each time, he returned her arms carefully back to her sides, causing her to grunt in frustration.

Finally, he began to bunch the skirt of her nightgown further up her thighs, which gave her a chance to rub her bare legs against his hairy ones. It was an intriguing sensation, one she did not have time to dwell upon. For, the next thing she felt were his fingers stroking her inner thigh. When they brushed against her most intimate place, her whole body jerked in surprise. They lingered, however, soothing the flesh there, drawing forth what felt like an unusual amount of moisture. Was this normal? She did not have breath enough to ask, feeling as winded as she did after racing her sisters up the long, snowy hill near their country house.

Only, she did not feel cold now. Indeed, she was heated through until her bones melted, leaving her liquid and malleable in his hands. His thumb swirled pleasurably around a sensitized spot within the folds of her intimate place, ratcheting up her restlessness to an unbearable degree. She wanted to arch into him, to moan and beseech him to take action. But clearly, her husband was not comfortable with her making demands. His movements were all slow, careful, deliberate. He controlled both himself and her, binding them in this limiting dance.

He moved between her thighs, gripping her knees and splaying them up and wide apart for his hips. Finally—*finally*—she thought, squirming to accommodate his weight and unaccustomed presence. A hot pressure parted her, slowly entering. Stretching. Stretching unbearably. She grunted and bit her lip at the burning pain.

He lowered his face into the crook of her neck and thrust his hips forward in a swift, controlled movement. She wanted to whimper at the sudden heat and pressure and pinching pain. But she fisted the sheet beneath her and forced herself to remain quiet. He pulled out almost completely. She breathed a sigh of relief—which quickly became a gasp as he thrust heavily back inside her, repeating the motion again and again, the muscles in his arms and chest and neck distended and shaking as he supported his weight above her.

After the first few thrusts, her body began to ease, the pain to lessen, just as he had predicted. It even seemed to welcome the sliding fullness, the heated friction. But just as she began to think this process might be tolerable—even enjoyable—her husband stiffened and thrust one final time, groaning her name into her neck, his hips jerking twice more before collapsing atop her, obviously finished for the night.

Moments later, his chest heaving, he carefully slid out of her, his appendage softer for his efforts. Rolling away to lie on his back beside her, his breathing slowly returned to normal. "Are you well, Jane?" he asked, his voice rasping and raw, yet eminently polite.

"Of course," she answered neutrally. "You were most considerate, your grace."

Her comment was met with a long silence. Within minutes, she felt him leave the bed, heard him pick up his shirt and trousers. The door between their chambers quietly opened and closed.

Reaching up, she removed her spectacles and blindly placed them on the bedside table. She hadn't needed them after all. It was too dark to see anything. She suspected he had not wished to look at her. Else, why douse the light? Why leave her gown in place until the last moment? She still wore the thing, gathered in folds above her hips.

A tight ache settled deep into her chest, twisting and burning, centered around her heart. It overshadowed even the soreness between her thighs. She fisted the blanket and drew it further over her body as she turned onto her side and curled inward, suddenly chilled after all that unsatisfying heat.

Annabelle had lied to her. She did not know why. Perhaps

her sister had worried that Jane would balk if she knew. But in her mind, she penned a scathing rebuke to her eldest sibling. *Dearest Annabelle*, she would write. *This night, I discovered a most disturbing fact—that you are only too capable of misleading me, and to my great dismay, I am fool enough to have listened. However, the truth must be stated: Marital relations are approximately as "transporting" and "blissful" as taking a hack to Piccadilly. After the initial excitement and anticipation have passed, the journey is fraught with jarring motion, odd smells, and general discomfort. And in the end, dear sister, one is left with only this—the distinct feeling of having been robbed.*

Chapter Fifteen

"When it comes to men, my dear, it is advisable to keep one's expectations low and one's compensatory indulgences high."

—The Dowager Marchioness of Wallingham to Lady Berne during a discussion of Lord Berne's less endearing qualities.

It was a disgrace—outright highway robbery, Harrison thought as he examined the household accounts. The bill for spices had increased tenfold in the two weeks since their arrival at Blackmore Hall. Tenfold!

"Your correspondence, your grace."

He glanced up to see Beardsley, the estate's butler for the past four years, entering his study. Nodding, he indicated the tray on his desk designated for new correspondence to be reviewed. The butler was even shorter than Jane, but he was the most efficient and competent man ever to hold the position. Victoria had hired him shortly after taking over their mother's duties. It was one of many reasons he still missed her. He did not possess her gift for understanding people. Take their cook, for example. Why would the Frenchman suddenly require ten times the usual amount of spices? Certainly, the size of the household had not increased proportionately.

Sighing in disgust, he set the bill aside and retrieved the first letter from the stack of correspondence. He sliced it open and quickly examined the message from Dunston, who reported he and his mother and sister would be passing through the area next month and would take Harrison up on his offer for a visit.

Frowning, Harrison considered this news with some concern. Jane was only now beginning to overcome her shyness with the servants. Last week, they had received a visit from the vicar and his wife. She had scarcely spoken more than a handful of sentences. While not precisely rude, her discomfort had been obvious, and the vicar had kindly cut his visit short, offering his felicitations on their marriage.

He tried to imagine Jane playing hostess to the sociable Lord Dunston, along with Dunston's mother and his sister, Lady Mary. It would be most trying for her, especially given that their visit would last days or weeks, not the mere hour the vicar and his wife had spent.

Harrison despised seeing his wife in such a state. With him, Jane was unreserved, even cheeky, though often subtly so. Her lively sense of humor, quick wit, and clever, observant nature were most endearing. In fact, having accompanied her on several explorations of the estate, including the gardens, the ruins of Blackmore Castle, and along the river that wound through the surrounding countryside, he had grown quite fond of her company, craving it at odd times over the course of each day.

Her personality was unusual, in his experience, but could not be faulted as unappealing. Quite the opposite, in fact. It was simply stifled and trapped in the presence of anyone unfamiliar.

Recalling her reaction to the vicar's visit, he felt anger rise again. She had been seized by silence and self-doubt, clearly ill at ease with anything more than the bare niceties. Inexplicably, he had found himself growing agitated, glowering at the vicar, who had done nothing other than wish them well in their marriage and encourage them to attend Sunday's service. Jane's discomfort made him want to tear something—or someone—apart. An unreasoning response, but undeniable.

Shaking his head, he reminded himself that she must learn to handle visits such as Dunston's sooner or later. Perhaps, as her husband, he could ease her path by handling all the arrangements in advance, ensuring she need only make occasional appearances for meals and such. Yes, he decided. That was the proper course. He would plan everything for her, remain by her side whenever necessary, and reduce her obligations to those of an honored guest. An excellent solution.

Satisfied, he quickly penned a response to Dunston then dealt with the remaining correspondence. By the time he had finished, his desk was cleared of all papers except the household accounts and the bill for spices. His earlier frown returned.

Upon closer examination, he realized the quantity of spices had not, in fact, increased tenfold. Instead, his cook was now spending truly exorbitant sums on chocolate.

"Beardsley!"

The butler answered his bark almost instantly. "Yes, your grace?"

"Fetch Mrs. Draper."

When the housekeeper arrived, Harrison held up the spice merchant's bill and demanded to know what had prompted the outrageous increase.

"I—I am given to understand Monsieur Renaud wished to ensure he did not run out, your grace. Her grace—the duchess, that is—she is mighty fond of chocolate. Takes it every evening."

"*Every* evening?"

"Yes, your grace. Some mornings, too. Though, she prefers coffee then."

Jaw tightening, Harrison dismissed the housekeeper and looked again at the bill. Such extravagance was preposterous. He must confront Jane about her indulgence. As he strode the corridor between his study and the old library—the room she occupied with an almost religious devotion—a small voice in the back of his mind questioned whether he was exaggerating the importance of the expense as an excuse to seek her out. But immediately, he rejected the notion. She was his wife. He could speak to her whenever he wished. He did not require excuses.

Naturally, he had placed limits on himself when it came to spending too much time with her. The woman was pure temptation. It had taken every ounce of restraint he possessed to visit her bed only once per week, the frequency he had deemed appropriate for marriage. And as painful as that was, even more excruciating was preventing their passions from inflaming beyond his ability to control. But if he did not restrict himself, he would give in to his baser instincts and never let her leave the bedchamber. What sort of man would treat a proper wife so? No, he must continue to show her the respect she deserved by controlling his primal nature and keeping an appropriate distance.

As expected, he found her curled up in one of the chairs between the fireplace and the window, her brown slippers lying on the floor, her russet silk skirt tucked around her knees, and a large book cradled in her lap.

When he closed the door, she looked up. And then she smiled. Dark eyes sparkling, dimples emerging, her face went from plain to riveting in a flash. "Oh, your grace, you have no idea of the treasures you possess."

On the contrary, he could think of at least one.

"This Bible is sublime." Indeed, her voice held a hushed

reverence, her fingers lightly stroking the pages. "It is sacred art from a hand that obviously adored its subject."

The feelings that seized him in that moment were anything but godly. Profane, perhaps. Sinful, certainly. He fought it, as he always did. And, as usual, the battle left him little patience or softness when he next spoke. "I received the bill from the spice merchant. Because of your chocolate habit, it has increased tenfold."

Her smile disappeared, replaced by a confused wrinkle between her dark brows. "My chocolate habit?"

"Yes. You have been partaking every evening, and it must stop."

Carefully, she closed the Bible, stood up and carried it back to the bookcase, sliding it reverently back into its home. Turning to face him, she braced her small, white hands on the back of the chair and asked, "Are you short of funds, your grace?"

His head recoiled, his temper flaring. "That is not the point."

She came around the chair, moving closer, her color rising, her hands now planted on her hips. "If you like, you may feel free to use my dowry to cover the cost of my *habit*, as you say."

"It may not be sufficient, if this profligacy continues."

"Profligacy?" She pressed her lips together then nudged her spectacles higher on her small, round nose. "Tell me truly: Do you not think it unusual for a *duke* to concern himself with such minutiae as a minor increase in chocolate consumption?"

"I would not call a tenfold increase 'minor.' And do not change the subject. We were not speaking about me."

"Well, perhaps we should be. Might I suggest you take up archery or hunting? I understand some dukes enjoy these very *appropriate* pastimes."

He moved closer. "You are implying I do not have sufficient activities to occupy my time, I take it."

"Either that or you cannot afford to employ a steward, which may be even more alarming than your outrage over chocolate."

His ire rising with each passing second, he attempted to regain control of the conversation. "Enough," he snapped. "You will cease drinking the stuff every night. From now on, you may have it once per week. That is all."

Her flush grew and her eyes flashed, signaling her fury. "Given the quantity of starch required to keep your cravats sharpened, you are in no position to issue such commands." Stomping the final two steps between them, she poked a stiffened finger into the offending garment, glancing off his chest beneath. "For the same cost, I could bathe in chocolate every night and still have enough left for a plate of biscuits."

He tried—oh, how he tried—not to envision her naked form covered in chocolate. But it was there, playing through his mind like a demon's trick, tempting him beyond his endurance. The part of himself he had too long denied howled and struggled for dominance. And the part of him that had begun to harden the moment he'd entered the old library and seen the smile that twisted him inside out—that part turned to pure stone, ready to take what was his.

Perhaps if she had stopped there, he could have resisted, pulled the primitive animal he feared back into its cage. But she was not finished.

"*You* may prefer to indulge yourself on a weekly schedule, your grace," she snapped, obviously referring to his once-weekly visits to her bed. "But I believe the pleasures of life were not meant to be meted out in so miserly a fashion."

Her statement broke him. He had tried so bloody hard to control himself—until he thought he might die from the strain of it. And did she appreciate all he had done to protect her? No. Instead, she accused him of denying *her* pleasure. She had poked his pride, his authority, his manhood—even his cravat—one time too many.

The light grew sharper, her face clearer. His skin tightened as red edged his vision. The tide of lust and obsession and dark need pushed against the wall of his will, stretched muscle and bone, causing a heavy, burning ache throughout his whole body.

It would take so little to snap the tether, to let the tide and the animal run free.

So. Very. Little.

And then, just like that, it happened. Watching the subtle lift of her saucy, sarcastic mouth curving into a satisfied smirk, everything he feared suddenly unleashed.

Without thought, his hand wrapped around the nape of her neck, gripping hard and pulling her mouth up to meet his, letting the pressure force her lips open, invading with his tongue. The other arm crushed her against him, his body roaring its approval at the cushion of her sweet, full breasts, the endless softness of her waist and hips.

If she had resisted, he would have stopped at a kiss. But she did not. Instead, after a brief moment of surprise, she met his fire with her own. Now, she was *there* with him, his body exulted. Her mouth suckling his tongue. Her hands threading through his hair, yanking him down tighter. Her dusky moan a wanton invitation, echoing through his lips.

He lifted her off the ground, stumbled toward the desk, set her on its surface. His mouth eating at hers, he pulled her thighs apart, wedged his hips between them, ground his aching cock against the warm notch at their juncture. But it wasn't satisfying. He needed to be inside. She was his. *His.*

Grabbing fistfuls of russet silk, he yanked her skirt higher, his hands fighting the fabric for access to what was his. He broke the kiss, heard her whimper in need, sucked air into his chest, pulled her sweet apple smell into himself. His vision spun. His mouth dropped to her throat. He needed more. More of her skin and her scent and her hands clutching his neck as they did now, as though she would never let go.

His lips slid down over her collarbone. His tongue found a trail to her breasts. His hands won the battle with her skirts, fingers finding her damp curls, gliding through slick folds, sinking deep and true into her tight, wet sheath. His sheath. *His.*

Using his other hand to yank at the edge of her bodice, tugging her sleeves off her shoulders, forcing one plump breast to overflow so his lips could capture the ripe, red nipple, he then suckled hard, raked her with his teeth. Moaning and gasping, she squeezed his hips with her thighs, squeezed his fingers with her wet sheath, writhed and pushed her breast deeper into his mouth.

He tore at the fall of his trousers. Freed his engorged cock. Bent his knees. Removed his fingers. Released her nipple with a wet pop and a lingering lick against the very tip.

Looked into his wife's molten eyes.

Then, deliberately, he notched the head of his cock against her. Paused to listen to her gasp for breath, whimper with longing. And he thrust with all his strength. Her mouth worked open as her eyes squeezed shut, a scream of boundless pleasure emerging like a siren's song. Now, he was drowning in fire, her sheath clenching and clinging to him. He retreated then thrust again, the desk banging against walnut paneling. Again, harder. Her fingers clawed into his nape, sharp and stinging and perfect. Again, deeper. He growled her name, the sound a guttural claim. Again, faster.

Jane. His Jane.

Again. And again. Deeper. Faster. Harder. More.

He wanted to burn himself into her, saturate her body with his.

Her breasts, bared to him, shook with every thrust. Her throaty moans echoed across his skin like a symphony, gathering into a crescendo. She seized upon him, clenched hard, rippling all around him. Her beauty in that moment of climax—milky skin pleasure-flushed, mouth swollen and open on a gasp, bottomless brown eyes closed in ecstasy as she uttered a final thready cry—it drove him mad, his arms wrapping her tight against him while he buried his face in her throat, buried his cock to the furthest depths of her body's hot, welcoming embrace.

He felt the peak coming, felt it like a geyser at the base of his spine. Knew it would change him forever. When it came, the intensity was a lightning storm, thundering and crackling along every muscle and nerve, forcing his hips to hammer at her, working his cock hard inside her. The frenzied movement could not be controlled. It would not be stopped. Together, they were a force of nature. Shouting his triumph and growling his satiation as he shot his seed deep within her core, he knew beyond all doubt. It was true. She was his.

His by right. His by God.

As she gently stroked his hair and his neck with her hands, laid her lips softly against his temple, his only thought was that she was his.

And he would never let her go.

JANE WAS NOT ENTIRELY SURE WHAT HAD JUST HAPPENED. Still trembling in the aftermath of furious ecstasy, she could only cling to him, feeling similar tremors ripple beneath his skin. He remained a full presence inside her, his hips wedged tightly between her thighs, his arms cinched around her back, squeezing her almost painfully to his chest, his hot breath dampening the skin between her neck and shoulder. It was as though she had tried to leave, and he held her prisoner.

Except that she did not want to escape. For the first time since their marriage, she wanted to stay. Just like this. Her body slick and pulsating in remembered pleasure. With him standing raw and bare and stripped of his title, his manners, and his bloody starch.

His every muscle shook, his chest heaving as he fought to regain his breath. She understood, for she felt the same. It had come on like a raging tempest, so sudden she had barely managed to hold onto him. One second, she'd been incensed at his ridiculous accusations over chocolate, and the next, his eyes had flared with fearsome heat, his mouth and body virtually consuming her.

After his third visit to her bed—was it only last night?—she had resigned herself to not-unpleasant, but ultimately rote and unfulfilling marital relations. Each time he'd touched and kissed and stroked her body, her hopes had risen, only to be dashed by the end of his husbandly duty. She hadn't wanted to complain. After all, he was the very picture of courtesy—cool, controlled, blasted *frustrating* courtesy.

But that was before today, before she'd known what she was missing. Before he'd revealed what he'd been hiding from her—ferocious passion buried beneath layers of ice. Even now, she could feel him withdrawing, his arms loosening around her, his body pulling free of hers. As he retreated, he gently shifted her bodice up, lowered her skirts to cover where they had been joined, then discreetly tucked himself away and buttoned the fall of his trousers. His head, while no longer buried in her neck, remained bowed. He would not meet her eyes.

"Jane," he rasped, his voice almost completely gone, his hands resting lightly on her silk-satin-covered knees. "I ... I am sorry. Did I ... are you ...?" His finger came up to stroke the skin at the side of her throat where the bristles of his jaw had chafed her a bit.

She had never seen him so uncertain, so vulnerable. "I feel positively splendid," she replied softly.

Troubled, searching eyes flew to hers. Remorse and surprise mingled there. His throat worked on a swallow. "I lost control. To treat you, my wife, in such a way is an unforgivable lapse. It shall not happen again."

She began to protest that it should—and would—happen again, if she had anything to say about it, but he did not give her the chance. He braced his hands on her waist, lifted her down from the desk like she weighed no more than a pillow.

She squeaked in surprise at the move, her skirts falling back into place. Before she could utter a word, he straightened his spine, steeled his shoulders, turned on his heel, and left her swaying on jellied legs in the old library, certain now of only one thing: The eighth Duke of Blackmore was a fraud.

Chapter Sixteen

"England is simply crawling with scoundrels and ruffians. Why, only last week, I was insulted twice—once by an exceptionally rude innkeeper and again by my own nephew!"

—The Dowager Marchioness of Wallingham to the Home Secretary, Lord Sidmouth, in a strategic discussion about securing domestic order and tranquility.

A crust of bread landed on the scarred table in front of Colin while loud bickering sounded behind him. A husband and wife sniped at one another over whether to continue on to Manchester or head south to Warrington, where her mother lived. This was why he did not want to marry. Eventually, every woman became a shrew haranguing a man over his dislike for her kin.

Rubbing his forehead between finger and thumb, Colin

took a swig of bitter, musty ale and stood. As he left the taproom of the dank old public house and pushed outside, the midday light hit him hard, sending needles of pain arcing through his head. He pulled his hat lower, hunched his shoulders, and headed for the stable.

Even after weeks, sudden movement and bright light bothered him. He recalled little of how he had escaped Syder's man. Three days after his injury, he had awakened in a boarding house in Richmond, west of London. A large, gruff, middle-aged woman with a love of knitting and the unlikely name of Fern had been hired to care for him. By whom, she would not say. He suspected either Chatham had experienced a rare attack of conscience or Drayton had found him and assumed Harrison wouldn't want his only brother—and current heir—dead. No matter. Once he'd regained his feet, he had paid Fern handsomely for her trouble and her silence, then had purchased a horse and headed north.

He hated traveling. Too damn much time to think. Thinking hurt abominably.

A scream and the sound of glass shattering came from inside the pub. The door slammed open and the husband was shoved outside, wheeling backward to land on his ass in the muck. The wife threw a wad of cloth in the man's lap, screeching about how her mother had been right about him all along.

Pulling his hat lower over his eyes, Colin cringed and felt grateful never to have been caught in a woman's leg shackles. He hurried on to the ramshackle stable where his horse was waiting. She was a fine little bay mare, gentle and calm.

Nickering softly at him as he entered, Matilda accepted the small bit of apple he had saved from his meal. "There you are, old girl." She nuzzled his hand in a bid for more. He chuckled. "Aren't you a demanding little thing? If I had more, I would give it to you. Of that you can be certain." A wave of dizziness came over him, and he leaned his head against her neck for a moment. He still wasn't right. Fern had warned him about leaving Richmond too soon, that he wouldn't heal unless he rested fully.

But he had felt the itch before. Felt the wormy sensation of being hunted. They were close. And so he'd run. First to Southampton. Then, after a near-miss with a dock worker who was apparently receiving funds from Syder, all the way to Liverpool. Bought passage to New York, only to learn his ship to America was delayed for unexpected repairs; it wouldn't depart for ten days. Then he had spotted six men combing the waterfront. Syder's men.

Southampton wasn't far enough. Liverpool wasn't far enough. Perhaps even America wouldn't be far enough.

"Running ain't the answer, Lacey."

The low, graveled voice came from behind him. He turned, his head swimming, to see the tall, rangy man who had trailed him relentlessly from one end of England to the other. "Drayton."

Come what may, Harrison's damned hound was on his scent. It was a bloody nuisance.

"Aye." Craggy and disheveled, the runner looked as he always did—worn threadbare. "Think you Syder'll give up? Best think again."

"What do you know about it?"

In a blink, the runner's eyes went from flat and weary to dark and fierce. "I know that butcher all too well."

"Then you know running is the only answer."

Drayton dropped his eyes and shook his head. "Head for Blackmore. Tell the duke the truth. Give your apologies to the duchess."

"Duchess?"

The look the runner shot him made Colin blink. *What an ass I am,* he thought. *Of course Harrison would marry her.* "Lady Jane," he whispered to himself.

"Aye."

He groaned and rubbed his forehead.

"Head to Blackmore," Drayton repeated. "You might believe you're dodging notice, Lacey, but a boy in leading strings could track you."

"That is precisely why I will not head there, you dolt."

The man shrugged. "Don't mean much to me, mind. My task is to watch you. Get paid for that whether you're asleep on your horse, hanging from a hook in Whitechapel, or lying in a dirt hole staring at your Maker."

Colin cringed at the blunt litany of his likely outcomes.

"Were it my debt and my skin, I'd be looking to the one man who gives a bloody damn whether I live or die."

"And what happens when they follow me?" He shook his head. "No. I have done more than enough without placing my brother and his new wife in danger."

Drayton shifted sideways so he could look out to the muddy road. "You prefer death, do you?"

His jaw tightened along with his gut. "Yes."

The man's shaggy head hung forward. "Ballocks," he muttered. He glanced back at Colin. "I can give you a week's lead. Perhaps a fortnight."

Colin squinted. "How, precisely?"

The runner grinned. It was not a pleasant sight. "They'll be chasing ghosts." He turned his back and walked to the entrance, pausing with a hand braced on the timbered frame. "Make haste, Lacey. If I know Syder, you'll need every minute. And for Christ's sake, stay off the stage roads."

Watching Drayton shamble through the muddy courtyard into the public house, Colin considered the idea. Blackmore. He hadn't been home in over a year. Not since before Harrison had cut him off. Harrison, who was ashamed to call him his brother, but who also continued to pay Drayton to watch him. Evidently he did not want Colin dead. It was a small comfort.

Matilda nibbled his hat, forcing him to pull away from the stall. Absently, he reached back to rub her nose. "Fancy a long ride, Matilda? I cannot promise an easy journey, but if we reach our destination in good time, you shall have the finest stall in the finest stable in Yorkshire."

Her nose pressed his hand insistently. The smell of rotting hay and horse dung was sharp and vile. Sighing with his decision, he gave her one last pat. Then he saddled Matilda, mounted up, and headed back out into the daylight.

Ignoring the pain of it, he turned east.

Toward Blackmore.

Toward home.

JANE STARED OUT THE LIBRARY WINDOW, WATCHING Blackmore mount his horse for yet another ride. The truth was now undeniable: Her husband was avoiding her. Four days after their explosive tryst, merely entering the old library gave her a heat flush that was slow to abate. It made reading (and sitting and sleeping and *breathing*) dashed difficult.

But Blackmore did not appear to suffer the same malady. He had, in fact, spoken to her only once in those four days, and that because they'd nearly collided at the top of the staircase. One word—"apologies"—muttered solemnly before he backed away and waved her onward; that was the only time she had heard his voice. In four bloody days.

Jane was heartily sick of it. He took his meals in his room, his rides nearly a half-day from the house, and his beautiful, confusing self away from her presence as though she were covered in honey and he standing on an anthill.

Glancing down at the letter from Annabelle, received this morning, she reread her sister's stark advice. *"You must press for what you desire, dearest. Marriage lasts a lifetime. That is far too long to accept less than the happiness you deserve."*

Of course, Jane had written her two weeks ago, so

Annabelle did not know about the old library. She did not know what Blackmore had done to Jane, how he had revealed himself and, in turn, changed her fundamentally.

He was not cold. Far from it. He wanted her. *Her.* The Oddflower. The round, bespectacled, short, bookish, shy *her.* Unbelievable, she admitted, but also true. Why, in heaven's name, he did not simply allow his desire free rein, she could only guess. *Some misplaced sense of propriety, most likely. Well, that nonsense must stop.*

She pressed her thighs together to stifle the ache of emptiness there as she watched him ride away.

And it must stop today.

What she needed was a plan of seduction, a way to break his everlasting control. The problem was she had no idea how to accomplish such an aim. Last time had happened purely by chance.

As she scoured Annabelle's letter for clues, her eyes caught on the third paragraph. *"Consider his preferences. Offer him more of what he seems to enjoy."* Of course, Annabelle was speaking of meal planning, not marital relations, but perhaps this sound advice could be applied to more intimate matters.

Jane sniffed and folded the letter neatly. First, she would have to determine what would tempt his appetite. She tapped the folded edge of the paper against her chin, trying to recall what precisely had set him off four days ago. She'd been reading a passage from The Song of Solomon. He had stalked into the room looking stern and commanding and tall and broad ... oh, dear. She squeezed her thighs together again. There went that flush.

Attempting to concentrate, she closed her eyes. He'd been vexed with her because of chocolate. No. Before that, he had been riveted. On the Bible she held. No, that wasn't quite it, either. He had focused on her hands.

Her eyes popped open. He did that a lot. More than a lot. Almost constantly. She held out her hands, flaring her fingers and examining them in the light from the window. They were perfectly ordinary. Pale, small. The skin was quite smooth, and her fingers were well shaped, but she could see nothing that would cause him fits of passion.

Hmm. Most perplexing. But, certainly, if the duke favored the sight of her hands, she would be happy to employ the knowledge for their mutual benefit.

What else might appeal to him? Instantly, she thought of her bosoms. Undoubtedly, he appreciated those. She glanced down. They had always seemed rather cumbersome to her, like great, fleshy globes that made dress fittings a misery. However, the duke seemed to like them quite well, if his lingering glances at her bodice were any sign.

Come to think of it, he stared at her a great deal: in the carriage on the way to Blackmore Hall, on their excursions around the estate, even at dinner. *Especially* at dinner. Or any meal, really. Many times, she had looked up after savoring a delicious bite to find his eyes on her. She had always concluded that his staring was a form of judgment, that he was examining her for flaws, which he could then demand she correct.

But what if that had not been the cause at all? What if he had been watching her because …

She swallowed.

Oh, dear. The flush was getting worse. Now weakness invaded her limbs. She staggered toward one of the chairs and plopped down into the seat, fanning herself with her sister's letter.

Suddenly, she knew how to seduce her husband. It would take planning and a fair amount of daring. Her teeth worried her lower lip. Could she do it? If she was right, and he could be tempted, then she must try, for she could not bear to continue on as the polite strangers they had been for the past few days. So, that meant leaving the library and implementing a bold, inspired plan of action. And the first step involved a mad Frenchman.

Chapter Seventeen

"A Frenchman's talents must be twice that of an Englishman's to compensate for the significant increase in arrogance and unpleasantness."

—THE DOWAGER MARCHIONESS OF WALLINGHAM to Lady Reedham upon said lady's complaints about her French cook.

THE MAIN KITCHEN AT BLACKMORE HALL WAS SO ENORMOUS, three long work tables—not one—stretched down the middle. The room swarmed with scullery maids, all rushing about, chopping this and that, and being shouted at in French-accented English by the man at the center of it all: Monsieur Renaud. He was surprisingly young, even handsome, with swarthy skin, black hair, and a long nose, which often wrinkled in disgust at the results of his maids' efforts. His arms bulged as he transferred a large haunch of meat from one table to another. He spat onto the first table's surface, cursing the poor girl who had previously used it to scale fish.

Jane, having gone unnoticed upon entering, cleared her throat. No one looked her way. She tried again, louder this time. Still nothing. "Monsieur Renaud?" she called out, her voice a bit more wavering than she would like. Half the maids stopped to stare, then whispered and elbowed one another. Before long, they were all curtsying. But Renaud did not stop what he was doing. Instead, he wielded a knife on what appeared to be mutton, muttering to himself in French, most of which was terribly vulgar.

"Monsieur Renaud, I would like to speak with you, if you don't mind."

He waved at her without glancing away from his work, the knife flashing in the afternoon light from the high windows. "Speak away."

She moved farther into the room, coming to stand on the opposite side of his work table. "I would like to request a picnic be prepared."

Finally, he stopped, his knife hand dropping, his other arm coming up to swipe his forehead, which glistened with sweat. "A picnic." The way he said it, with such disdain along the two syllables—"peek-neek"—implied he did not approve. But perhaps it was simply a language barrier.

"Yes. That is, I would like to have a meal prepared which can be enjoyed out-of-doors. In a basket, if you please."

He snorted then resumed carving his meat.

For a moment, she wasn't certain whether he understood that she intended the picnic to be packed straight away, for he did not exhibit much urgency. Or any urgency, really. "M-monsieur, I shall need the basket soon."

Another snort.

"Within the hour."

He stopped. Slammed his knife on the table. Threw his hands up in a wild gesticulation as a string of French expletives exploded from his mouth.

Her eyes widened. Never had she heard such colorful language spoken in her presence. It was most enlightening. She'd had no idea such things were possible—much less desirable—between Englishmen and sheep.

"Monsieur Renaud," she interrupted calmly, holding up a finger. "Certainly, I do not wish to cause disruption. But this is quite important, or I would not have requested it."

Another spate of vitriolic epithets. *Really,* she thought. *This is bordering on absurdity.* Perhaps he was unaware that she spoke fluent French.

Again, she inserted herself in the midst of the tirade, her words serene and deliberate. *"Peut-être vous préférez quitter l'Angleterre et retourner à votre pays d'origine. Je peux certainement arranger ça."*

He froze mid-insult, his mouth pinching and sputtering, his face reddening. She had simply offered him the opportunity to leave England, as he appeared to be rather vexed with its inhabitants, and to assist him in returning to his home. His reaction seemed overly dramatic to her. But then, she recognized the tempestuous flair of someone longing to be the center of attention. Genie was her sister, after all.

His heavy brows collided in a fierce glower. "You speak French?" he muttered.

"Oui," she replied, giving him a placid smile and touching the corner of her spectacles. "Now then, if a simple picnic is too much for you, perhaps one of the kitchen maids can assist me. It need not be elaborate. Some bread, perhaps. A few berries."

His eyes narrowed, and he folded his muscular arms across his chest. "*Non.*"

"No?"

"This is not acceptable. Bread. Berries. Food for peasants!"

"Then, what would you suggest?" she inquired innocently.

His hand smacked the work table, and he tossed orders at the maids, who scrambled to do his bidding. When he was finished, he looked back at Jane. "You are a clever one," he said resentfully.

She smiled, careful not to reveal her triumph. "I must say, Monsieur Renaud, I am positively obsessed with your mince pies. Might you have some to place in the basket?"

He scoffed, shouting, "Add two mince pies!" at his harangued assistants.

Two hours later, she found herself climbing the hill toward the ruins of Blackmore Castle, lugging the weighty basket, and cursing herself for choosing this particular location. On one hand, it presented the privacy required for her quest. On the other hand, it was located on a forested hillside thick with blackthorn and hazel underbrush, making the trek slow going. Previously, when her husband had brought her to the castle, he had cleared the path ahead of her, using his large frame and long arms to ensure she encountered no difficulty.

Today, she was forced to wade through the brambles on her own, the occasional thorn catching at her skirt and the sleeves of her dark-blue spencer. Fortunately, she wore gloves, which protected her hands. Unfortunately, the day was warm with only the lightest breeze rustling the trees. Perspiration trickled down her spine, causing her skin to itch. Her spectacles continuously fell lower on her nose, necessitating constant adjustments from her free hand. The frustration added to her exertion. She hoped he did not reach the castle first, for she would like a few moments to refresh herself after her strenuous climb.

At last, she spied the gray, mossy remains of Blackmore Castle between the branches of a looming beech. A trio of ravens launched themselves from one of its ramparts. In truth, it was quite a small castle, not nearly so grand as she had once imagined. Gray stone with a handful of miserly slits for light, only half the thing still stood at its original height. The rest lay on the ground, squared boulders covered in moss and brambles.

Her legs and lungs burning, she panted and huffed, heaving

the basket ahead of her to clear the path. Then, she heard the whinny of a horse.

Drat. He was there already.

Having inquired with the stable master where her husband had gone riding, she'd been gratified to realize he'd gone to meet with the vicar regarding a new roof for a poor cottager in the village. Knowing he was only a quarter-hour ride away, she had immediately sent a message with one of the grooms to ask Blackmore to meet her at the castle for a very important purpose. At the time, she'd been deliberately vague, as she had reasoned urgency without detail would be her best strategy. Apparently, she'd been correct. He must have ridden quite fast in order to arrive ahead of her.

"The man is too bloody efficient," she muttered, brushing a leafy branch away from her face. Stomping up the rest of the overgrown trail, she entered the space that would have once been the great hall.

"What the blazes were you thinking?"

She spun to her left, where her tall, blond, angry husband bore down on her like a bird of prey. He stepped over rotted timbers and stones with no more effort than she would navigate a gravel path, coming within inches of her before she had a moment to catch her breath. Relieving her of the heavy basket, he set it on the ground with one hand then stooped to reach for her skirt, deftly removing a thorny branch snagged in the sky-blue muslin.

His sunlight scent wafted up to her nose, filling her starving senses. Oh, mercy, he was so close—

"Perhaps I was unclear, but as I recall, I specifically told you *not* to go wandering about the estate without me." He did not shout, but his voice cut like a razor.

She sighed as he rose to his full, broad-shouldered height. A melting sensation in her lower body—particularly between her thighs and belly—signaled that her troublesome heat flush was becoming rather indiscriminate. In truth, she now found even his disapproval arousing. Something must be wrong with her.

"Jane," he snapped. "What is the matter?"

She tore her gaze away from his shoulders, currently encased in a handsome brown riding coat, to answer his question. "Not a thing, your grace. I thought we might enjoy a nice picnic together."

He stared at her, his jaw tight. "A picnic."

"Yes, a picnic. Why do all the men around here keep saying it like that?"

Eyes sharpening to diamond hardness, he bit out softly, "What men?"

A shiver slid over her skin as his big body inched closer, looming over her and bombarding her with intensity she had not felt in four days. Her stomach swooped. "I–I only meant Monsieur Renaud. The cook. He prepared the basket." She gestured to where it lay on the ground.

His eyes followed her hand then came immediately back to her face. "I do not have time for a picnic. I thought you were in distress. Your note said so."

"I am in *great* distress," she said, nudging her spectacles back into place and removing her bonnet. She moved a few feet away to set the simple straw hat on one of the larger stones—and to catch her breath. "My husband has been neglecting me."

He went still and silent, his face inscrutable.

"Additionally, I am too warm. I believe I shall dispense with some unnecessary layers."

Staring directly into his eyes, she unfastened the braided frog closures along the front of her spencer. Though her hands trembled, there were only five, so it did not take long. Shrugging out of the blue kerseymere, she peeled the long sleeves away from her bare arms. Beneath, she wore a thin, short-sleeved muslin gown originally designed to wear with a chemisette, as the neckline was quite low. If one wished for modesty, it was an important addition, particularly with a figure such as hers. However, she had not chosen to wear a chemisette. She had even debated leaving off her stays, but decided they helped enhance the visible part of her bosoms, which was, of course, slightly more than the upper third.

"Jane," her husband ground out.

"Hmm?"

"What are you doing?"

She blinked at him innocently. "I don't know what you mean. I am simply cooling myself." She stroked her collarbone with her still-gloved fingers. "It is dreadfully warm today."

A muscle in his jaw flexed.

"I think perhaps it is the gloves," she continued. "Do you suppose that could be it?" Ever so slowly, she stripped the soft, supple leather from her hands, folding it gently away from each wrist, loosening individual fingertips, then slipping the whole of it off, letting the leather gently drag against her skin. "There now," she said. "Much better."

"Put them back on."

She had to steel herself against the urge to obey his harsh command. He was quite intimidating in this thunderous mood. Instead, she ignored him and moved toward the basket, leaving her gloves, spencer, and bonnet lying on the stone. She bent forward to dig through the items for their outdoor luncheon, deliberately presenting him with her backside. It was not a certainty he had any interest in that part of her, but she reckoned it was worth the attempt.

A hiss of air sounded from his vicinity. *Excellent.* She smiled to herself. *Another valuable piece of information.* "We have a veritable feast on offer. But first ..." She turned toward him, holding a thick, woolen blanket. Her heart stuttered and the air left her body. He was right there, less than six inches from her, his body as rigid as the stones surrounding them.

"We must leave," he said, his voice rough, his eyes dilated. She noticed he clasped his hands behind his back, as though afraid of what he might do were they loose.

The look on his face sent *springles* running to every part of her body—her nipples, her thighs, between her thighs. Even her lower back experienced the little peculiar sensations of shivery heat. "Why must we?" she asked, her voice husky.

His mouth tightened. "You know why."

"Tell me." She tossed the blanket.

The barest flash of agony shifted through his eyes, tugged at his brow, before it was controlled. "What happened before ..."

"In the library."

His chest heaved and his jaw hardened. "Yes. It was unforgivable."

She crossed her arms beneath her bosom, unintentionally lifting the rounded flesh to swell further above her neckline. "According to whom?"

He blinked, his eyes darting between her bosoms and her face, seemingly unable to decide where to land. "To me. It is my duty to protect you."

"You are my husband."

Sighing, he dragged his gaze fully to hers. "Precisely."

"And I am your wife."

Now, wariness crept into his expression. "Yes."

She smiled. "Would you not say it is also your duty to provide for my every need?"

Sensing a trap, he tried reasoning first. "As long as you are not harmed in doing so, yes."

"Then we are in agreement." She held her arms out to her sides, inviting him to look his fill. "Do I appear harmed to you?"

A crease formed between his brows. "You appear underdressed."

She sniffed. "Entirely suitable for the weather. And my purpose. Which is to ensure my husband provides for my needs as I provide for his."

"Jane—"

"First, we shall eat Monsieur Renaud's marvelous feast."

He ground his teeth together.

"And then we shall discuss all the other needs we might satisfy together."

"Jane," he gritted. "I will not be moved in this. You cannot tempt me into ravishing you."

A slow grin curved her mouth. She inched closer, letting her bosoms barely brush his abdomen, enjoying his sharply indrawn breath. With a mischievous glance from beneath her lashes, she asked, "Would you care to wager on that, your grace?"

Chapter Eighteen

"Every man since Adam has feared the power of a woman's temptation. Every woman since Eve comes to understand they are right to fear us. Be thankful we are merciful creatures."

—THE DOWAGER MARCHIONESS OF WALLINGHAM to her local vicar after a fiery sermon on the dangers of lust.

RESPONDING TO HER CHALLENGE BY CAREFULLY STEPPING back, the duke tightened his lips in apparent disapproval. "I should think you would seek to avoid wagers," he retorted softly.

She narrowed her eyes at him. Evidently, he thought angering her would cause her to retreat from her course. He was mistaken. "Let's eat, shall we?" She stooped to retrieve the blanket then spread it out with a snap and sweep of her arms, laying it on a smooth patch of ground cushioned with grass, moss, and vines.

"I am not hungry."

"Pouting is unworthy of you, your grace."

"You have drawn me away from important—"

She turned from where she was unpacking the basket, her hands landing on her hips. "Rubbish. Is your will so weak that you cannot even bear a simple meal with me? I thought you stronger than that."

This provocation appeared to anger him, as his eyes snapped and flashed. "Be careful how you challenge me, wife. You may not like the consequences as well as you believe."

Ignoring the peculiar twist in her belly, Jane promptly replied, "Don't be silly," and then lowered herself onto the blanket. "We are dining together. It is not a challenge. It is a meal." She waved him over and patted the blanket next to her. "Come sit, your grace. The sooner we finish, the sooner you may resume your day's tasks."

Reluctantly—very reluctantly—he joined her, sitting on the far edge of the blanket, directly across from her. She smiled and leaned forward to hand him a mince pie wrapped in a napkin then took one for herself. "See? Isn't this pleasant?" she sighed.

He did not answer, instead taking a resentful bite, his arm propped negligently on one upraised knee.

She was not, in fact, terribly hungry. At least, not for food. But she made a show of savoring each tidbit, each flaky, buttery bite. First, her mince pie. Then, a sweet apricot tartlet. Finally, the plump, juicy strawberries. By the time she pulled the small flask of wine from the basket, his eyes were glazed with what she now recognized as pure lust. He had taken only three bites, preoccupied with watching her lick crumbs delicately from her fingertips.

As her fingers slid over the flask, she tsked. "Oh, look. Now I am all sticky."

Suddenly, in one swift motion, he pushed himself onto his feet and paced away from her to the stone wall, all the way across the wide space, his hands braced on his hips, his shoulders stiff. "Jane," he said roughly. His voice was muffled, since he stood more than twenty feet from her with his back turned. "You must stop."

"Why must I?"

He shook his head, waiting a long time before offering an answer. "What I want from you, it is not ... not appropriate to demand of a wife."

Rising onto her knees, she carefully stood, shook out her skirts, and picked her way over the remnants of their meal to move nearer to him. Mindful that pushing him too far could work against her, she halted a few feet away. "Is it not conceivable you are exaggerating the delicacy of my sensibilities just a bit?"

His head fell forward and shook back and forth as one arm straightened to prop against the stone wall. "You don't understand."

He sounded so despairing, she could not bear it another second. Within moments, she had slipped silently between him and the wall, the moss cool against her back, his chest radiating heat against her front. "Then I propose a solution," she said as his eyes came up to meet hers. They were as volatile as an ocean squall. They drove the air from her body, made her ache deep inside. She wanted to soothe him, to ease his obvious torment. "Tell me your desires. Describe them, one by one. And I shall inform you if anything you say causes me offense. Surely words alone are permissible, if only to establish where the boundaries lie."

She could see his mind working, mulling her suggestion. He was not a man easily dissuaded from a course he had already set, as Victoria had rightly observed. However, she was counting on a combination of logic and lust to push him into bending. Just a bit. For her.

"Words are powerful, Jane. With your love of reading, you should know this better than most."

"We shall leave them here, at the castle, then. They will live among the moss and the ravens." She reached for the hand still propped on his hip, and he let her take it in hers—a promising sign. Stroking the back of his strong, lean hand, then lacing their fingers together, she met his eyes fully and said, "I give you this promise. Whatever you say to me here shall remain ours alone. And, should you desire, we need never speak of it again."

He appeared mesmerized by her hand cradling and caressing his. For a long while, he said nothing, the rustle of leaves and the rush of their breath the only sounds between them. When he broke the silence, his voice was dusky and low. "Your hands are exquisite. Do you know?"

Her breathing quickened, her pulse following suit. "Are they?"

He nodded. "I dream of them often."

"What do you dream?"

"Your touch upon me."

"I dream of that, too."

Closing his eyes briefly, he took a deep breath. "Not like this."

With her free hand, she laid her palm directly over his heart. "For me, it always begins here," she whispered. "I very much admire your chest."

His mouth curved into a small half-grin. She sensed she had surprised him. "I'm afraid my fantasies are not quite so chaste."

"Tell me."

The smile disappeared, replaced with hunger. "You do not wish to hear this."

Frustrated with his reticence, she swatted him lightly. "I do. Tell me."

And then he did, his voice stark and challenging, daring her to object. "I dream of you naked. Completely. Of your hands caressing me."

If he expected her to scream and run away after that, he was sadly—

"Between my legs."

Oh, she realized. *His appendage.* She had not thought much about touching it with her hands. She'd not even had a close look at it, what with his penchant for shrouding them both in cloth and darkness.

But he wasn't finished. "I long for your hands to stroke me there, to take my cock between your lips—"

"Cock? Do you mean your appendage?"

He blinked as if awakening from a dream, only to find a spider crawling upon him. His dismay was comical. "My what?"

"Your appendage. The part of you between your legs, which you insert inside m—"

He coughed, swallowed hard, and firmed his lips. "You refer to it as my appendage?"

"Yes. You, apparently, do not. I don't know what you find so amusing. Is cock a better word? I think not. Appendage is more descriptive and gentler to the ear."

His lips quirked and trembled. "By all means, call it whatever you like."

She sniffed. "Do go on."

Chest shaking with controlled laughter, he said, "I have forgotten where I left off."

"You wish me to stroke your app—your cock—with my hands, and then take it into my mouth."

All laughter, suppressed and otherwise, ceased instantly at her plain words. His hand squeezed hers reflexively, his eyes blazing down at her like blue flames. "Yes," he said, his voice raw.

"Frankly, your grace, I don't see the problem."

"I am not finished."

Her heart thudded against the bones of her chest, the arousal of his desires firing hers. "Continue. Please."

He crowded closer to her, bringing her hand up to his mouth. Tenderly dragging his lips across the skin on the back of her hand, he murmured, "First you would kneel before me."

He slid her index finger into his mouth, suckling it gently, his tongue swirling and playing before releasing it to lie helplessly against his lower lip. He allowed it to retract and rest against his chin. Meanwhile, his thumb circled her palm with tiny, thrilling strokes. "Then your beautiful white hands would squeeze my cock, sliding and milking. You would need to be firm about it. I am agonizingly hard for you. Always. The instant you enter my mind." He placed her palm against his jaw, holding her hand there. Her fingers cupped his cheek automatically. "When you take me inside your mouth, you will use your lips and your tongue to stroke and pleasure me. Then, with your hands, you will pleasure yourself."

She moaned, her heat flush raging out of control, weakness destroying her ability to stand. She had never imagined these things. These intimate, erotic, diabolically clever things. But she wanted them. She wanted him. This very second.

He frowned. "I have distressed you." He began to pull back. "I shall stop."

She clung to him, one hand reaching for his neck, the other grabbing a handful of riding jacket. "If you stop, I will kill you," she growled.

His face froze in a look of perplexity and dawning realization. "You are—you are not disgusted."

"Tell me more. Tell me everything," she panted, her fingers digging and pulling at him. She could not help it. He had lit a fire unquenched by anything other than him.

"You are aroused." He sounded astonished.

She groaned a protest at his bloody slowness. "Remove your coat," she ordered, tugging at the fabric. She had the thing halfway down his back before he began to assist her. Beneath it, he wore only his shirt and a simple, unstarched cravat. She buried her nose against the linen, breathing deeply of his scent, rubbing her aching breasts against his ribs, running her hands up and down the hard muscles of his chest. He was a feast for her hunger.

His hands came up to cup the back of her head, his fingers delving into the tight coil to dislodge her pins. Her hair fell loose down her back, a cool, heavy whisper sliding along her spine. Hands threading into the strands, he used his grip to tilt her mouth up to his.

She opened for his tongue, her hands gripping his nape and pulling herself higher along his body. He tore at the back of her dress, the delicate muslin shredding easily. Bodice now gaping, she shrugged off the gown and pushed it down over her hips as he stripped her of her stays and petticoat. At last, she stood before him, bare but for her spectacles.

His eyes—oh, his eyes—were fierce with lust, devouring her breasts, her rounded belly, her thighs and the swollen, aching juncture between them. His chest worked like a bellows, like a horse run too hard. His fingers ripped away his cravat. Muscled arms crossed over his chest to grip the hem of his shirt and draw it swiftly over his head.

Oh, he was lovely. His chest, padded with muscle, lightly dusted with hair, lured her eyes and hands to linger and touch and stroke with abandon. But there wasn't time. He dropped his shirt on the ground and immediately began working at the opening of his breeches. She grabbed his wrists, halting his frantic efforts, then fell slowly to her knees upon the discarded clothing at their feet. The warm summer air was like a silken caress on her naked skin as she unbuttoned his fall, her hands deliberately stroking the raging hardness bulging beneath the buckskin. Until it was revealed. His cock. Large and flushed, heavily veined and impossibly hard, it stood straight out from his body.

A loud groan emerged from her husband's throat as she grasped the hot, silken stalk in her fist, sliding her fingers up and down its substantial length. Unhesitatingly, almost on instinct, she leaned forward and enfolded the rounded head between her lips, suckling lightly and enjoying the musky, salty taste of him.

His hand fisted in her hair, for a bare moment pushing his length past her teeth and deeper into her mouth. He pulled back when she gasped, then slowly pushed forward again. Soon, she realized his need and relaxed her tongue, letting more of him slide in. Her hand squeezed him at the root, trying to better control the rhythm. His strangled cry of pleasure sent echoing sensations surging through her body.

"Jane," he panted. "I cannot take much more."

She did not want to release him, but he insisted, pulling her hand away and withdrawing from her mouth. Protesting that she wanted more of him, she fell silent when he dropped to his knees before her, cupping her face in his hands.

"I have to be inside you," he said starkly, taking her mouth with his before she could answer. Cradling her head, he lowered them both to the ground, laying her upon his coat and shirt, then kissing his way down her throat, his mouth suckling, his tongue sliding. She wrapped him in her arms, pressing her hard, aching nipples against him. One of his hands hooked behind her knee, spreading her legs to make room for himself. She scarcely noticed, for at the same time, his lips found her nipple and consumed it in the furnace of his mouth. Sucking with a fierce pressure, he compelled her body to arch into him, seeking more of the wild sparks flaring outward from the sensitized tip. His tongue swirled and provoked, laving and heating until she moaned her pleasure. As he gave the same treatment to the other breast, his hand cupping the weight of the flesh and holding it prisoner to his mouth, she sobbed and clawed at his back, begging him to be merciful. "Please," she cried. "Please, your grace. I want you inside. Come inside me. Now, please."

He released her breast, the damp tip cooling and beading even harder in the open air. "Jane," he grunted. "For the love of God, call me Harrison."

"Yes, your grace. Whatever you want. Just hurry."

His hands pulling her legs up to bracket his hips, he

positioned the tip of his cock at her opening, which flexed in ecstatic anticipation. Slowly, relentlessly, he sank his length deep inside her, his flesh stretching and invading in a deliberate slide. Just when she thought he could go no further, he pressed deeper, the base of him burning her opening, the thickness of him an almost painful ache. His arms gathered her tighter against his chest, one hand clasping her nape. "Do you feel that, Jane?" he whispered in her ear.

Her breath caught in her throat, and she nodded.

"That is your husband claiming what is his. What is *mine*. Do you understand?"

She moaned and arched her back, but he controlled her with his hips, staying rooted deep inside her, unmoving.

"If you understand, then say my name."

"Please," she whimpered, her fingers digging into his now-damp hair, her breasts rubbing frantically against his hard, muscled chest.

He licked her collarbone. His teeth tugged gently at her earlobe. His hips thrust even deeper, grinding against her. She moaned desperately. "Say it, wife. Who is inside you now?"

"You are. Harrison."

"Yes," he hissed, his hips jerking back and then pounding forward in a vicious, satisfying thrust.

She screamed her pleasure.

He thrust again.

She screamed his name.

And again.

She clawed and begged and screamed again.

Soon, the spiraling pleasure from the heat and power and speed of his thrusts gathered into a wave, rising and rising, curling and building, until her core exploded into spasms of incandescent ecstasy, seizing and spinning along her entire being, slamming her onto a golden shore over and over with its force. As the ripples echoed outward, she reveled in the feel of his continued thrusts, his hips hammering hers, his face beautifully stark above her, staring down into her eyes. The blue was engulfed by dark smoke, roiling with the ferocity of his culminating need. She cupped his cheek, brushing her thumb over his lips. At last, with three final strokes, his eyes squeezed shut. His teeth clenched, his head dropped to her shoulder, and he ended by shouting her name, his seed gushing inside her, his pleasure matching hers.

For a long while, they simply held one another, drifting in and out of sleep beneath the canopy of leaves and sky, their bodies sated and lazy in the sultry heat. Finally, his mouth found hers in a soft, lingering kiss. He stroked her hair away from her face, his hands bumping the rims of her spectacles. A grin tugged at his lips as he pulled back to hover above her.

"And what is that look all about, your grace?" she asked with a smile of her own.

"One day, I shall make love to you without your spectacles," he answered. "And my name is Harrison."

Wriggling until she was positioned more fully beneath him, she stripped away the spectacles, stretched out her arm to set them safely on a nearby stone, and then hooked her arms around her husband's neck, drawing his mouth back to hers. "Well, Harrison," she said. "I fancy 'one day' has arrived sooner than you anticipated."

Chapter Nineteen

"Fair play? Hmmph. Only children believe in such things."

—THE DOWAGER MARCHIONESS OF WALLINGHAM to the
Prime Minister, Lord Liverpool, during a discussion of
parliamentary decorum.

HER SCENT WAS DRIVING HIM MAD. AS WAS HER SIGHING.

"Perhaps you would be more comfortable in the library," he gritted.

Lounging on the sofa no more than six feet from him, she glanced up from her book and gave him a radiant smile. "Oh, but your study has the loveliest light." She waved behind her at the large windows looking out on a small rose garden. "Are you finished with your correspondence?"

Her question was phrased innocently enough. But he knew better. She was a siren. A bloody temptress in a blue dress and spectacles.

He grunted. "I have much to do." It was true, and it was a problem. In the past five days, he had rarely left her bedchamber. When he had, it was to make love to her in the old library. Or the new library. Or the music room, bent over the pianoforte. He had even taken her on the sofa where she currently lolled, waiting for him to finish his work.

This was one of many reasons he had resisted her in the first place. Aside from the indecency of ravishing one's wife in ways and to degrees one would scarcely consider with a mistress, Jane was the ultimate distraction from his responsibilities as the Duke of Blackmore. He had told her as much, to which she had replied, "Is my pleasure not your greatest duty, husband?"

He hadn't argued, as it was a fair point. And, of course, she had been straddling his lap at the time, so his thoughts had not been precisely clear. Even now, with her doing nothing more than breathing in the same room, he felt the tide of heat and urgency rising inside his body. How was he to concentrate on polite missives from the Prime Minister or agricultural reports from the steward at his western estate? In truth, he could not.

"Mmmm," Jane groaned throatily, her arms stretching above her head, her lush breasts pushing against her bodice. "I cannot seem to concentrate this afternoon. Perhaps another book would hold my attention."

As she moved toward the bookcase behind him, her fingers brushed playfully across his shoulder, whispering against his neck. She did that often, touching him in small ways, seeming to crave the contact. At first, he had not known how to react. Most people avoided touching him casually out of respect for his position. But Jane had no such reservations. Ever since their picnic at Blackmore Castle, she readily did so, frequently taking his hand in hers, stroking his face, brushing gentle kisses along his jaw, which was all she could reach when they both were standing. Her little habit both soothed and aroused him, even as he struggled with the foreignness of it.

She made a show of selecting a new book, which he tried mightily to ignore. The scent of her—ripe, sweet apples on a golden September day—hardened him to steel beneath his trousers. The letter between his fingers shook. He set it carefully on the desk.

"Oh, I have not read this one in ages! Harrison, have you read it? You must have done. Look, it is ragged and stained."

When he saw what she held, his breath halted for just a moment. Ice crystallized over his skin, the cold flush rising from deep inside the core of his body. His arousal disappeared between one breath and the next.

"It was well loved." She ran her fingers over the cover. "The signs are unmistakable."

He dropped his gaze to his desk. "Yes. I have read it." His voice sounded hollow to his own ears.

"*Travels into Several Remote Nations of the World by Lemuel Gulliver.* I attempted to read this to Eugenia once. She complained bitterly that Gulliver's reactions were unrealistic, and that he should have simply squashed the Lilliputians like the pompous vermin they were." Jane chuckled. "Genie does not mince words when she is displeased."

Carefully, he took up a letter from his stack and pretended to read.

"Where is the second volume? I don't see it here."

For a moment, he could not answer her. But this was an old pain, one he had battled and beaten long ago. Why it should reemerge today, he did not know. "It was lost. When Victoria was still a babe."

"Lost? What happened?"

"It was burned."

Her gasp was both audible and appalled. "No. What a dreadful accident. Whoever loved this book must have been devastated."

Stiffening, he did not respond. He did not look at her. He couldn't.

In the silence that followed, he heard the whisper of her

gown as she moved toward him, smelled her sweet skin when she stood behind him. Closed his eyes when she wrapped her arms across his collarbone, drawing him back into the cradle of her breasts. "Harrison," she murmured softly against his ear. "How did it get burned?"

He straightened before replying, "It has been decades, Jane. Why should it matter? It is only a book."

"I am curious. Tell me." Her hands slid back to rest on his shoulders, her breath tickling the skin of his nape.

"Leave it be."

Though he could not see her, he felt her flinch at his frigid snap. Her hands slid away from his shoulders, her warmth receding from his neck. Keeping his eyes locked on the paper before him, he waited for her impudent retort. It did not come. Instead, he heard the quiet click of his study door opening and closing.

Damn and blast.

She was vexed with him. He had spoken too harshly.

He attempted to read the report from the Home Secretary, Lord Sidmouth, about the successful thwarting of an uprising in Derbyshire, but his eyes repeatedly drifted to the study doors.

Where had she gone? The old library, perhaps. It had become her refuge.

Absently, he rubbed his chest, trying to ease the sudden ache there, along with constriction in his lungs. It felt like panic. He glanced again at the doors.

Perhaps he should find her.

Yes, he decided. He should speak with her, explain that he preferred not to dredge up the past, as nothing good could come of it. And then, once she better understood the proper limitations upon their conversation, she would resume her customary good humor.

He headed immediately for the old library. Which he found empty.

Blast.

The new library was the obvious next choice, but there, he found only Beardsley, instructing a footman on the repositioning of furnishings.

"No, your grace, I'm afraid I have not seen the duchess. Perhaps she is taking a turn about the gardens," the butler said in answer to Harrison's query.

The tightness in his chest increased as he exited the room. Where had she gone? If she was more distraught than he'd supposed, would she have retreated to her bedchamber? Or, worse, could she have taken it into her head to wander the grounds alone, perhaps even saddle a mount for a lengthy ride far from the house? Far from him?

He did not like the thought. She was his wife. She belonged here. Nearby. Where he could bloody well find her when he wished to speak with her. Or hear her dusky, seductive laugh. Or smell her intoxicating scent.

Striding the corridor toward the staircase, he contemplated imposing rules upon her to prevent future incidents of this sort. He should have access to her at all times. Barring that—as it seemed a trifle unreasonable to demand she remain within arm's reach for the duration—she should at least inform him of her whereabouts.

His thoughts were interrupted by faint music. The pianoforte. Steps accelerating, heart keeping pace, he headed for the music room. *Of course. Why did I not think to search there? She adores the music room.*

The door was ajar. Pushing it open, he approached slowly, not wishing to disturb her. She played a simple tune, dark and evocative, slow and melancholy. Her fingers stroked the keys with a lingering touch, and as she finished the final somber note, she sighed.

"It was not my intention that you should leave," he said quietly.

Shoulders stiffening, she refused to look at him, instead adjusting her spectacles and growing enthralled by the fine keys before her. "Contrary to what you may believe, your grace, I do not gauge my every movement according to your preferences."

Blast. She is your-gracing me again. Dire indeed. There is nothing else for it. I must apologize.

"Yes. A most vexing trait, that," he said. *Bloody hell. Why did I say that?*

The only benefit to his unusually unruly mouth was that she finally met his eyes. Hers were round and flashing. Then, her lips tightened. And trembled. And she burst out laughing. "For you, I am certain of it."

He breathed it in, the muscles in his neck relaxing for the first time since she had walked out the study door. "I am sorry, Jane," he said quietly as her laughter trailed off.

Her eyes softened, and she took his hand. As their fingers brushed and held, he felt his world right itself. When had her little touches become necessary to him? "I accept your apology," she said. "It was not *my* intention to resurrect difficult memories."

Dropping his eyes to where their hands clung to each other, he gave her the only explanation he could. "The book was dear to me as a boy. But that was a very long time ago."

She stood and kissed his jaw, slipping past him to head toward the door.

"Where are you going?"

Halting for a moment to give him a mischievous look over her shoulder, Jane grinned. "To retrieve a book. And to arrange a picnic. I am simply *famished* of a sudden."

As he watched her full, lush hips sway on her departure, he could not prevent a silent groan. *Bloody hell. Now I will never finish this day's work.*

THE STRAWBERRIES WERE HIS DOWNFALL. SHE COULD SEE THE break in his control coming. Delicately licking one of the sweet, ripe fruits, she held it poised on her lower lip for a breath. Then she engulfed it in her mouth, biting down with slow tenderness.

A fat bee buzzed near her nose. She swatted it away.

"Perhaps he wishes to share with you, Jane," came her husband's husky, amused voice. "I understand his sentiment."

She swallowed. "All you must do is read to me. Is that asking too much?"

He sighed, leaning back on his hands, his legs stretched out before him. They sat on a blanket beneath a tree on a grassy bank of the river that cut through Blackmore's vast parkland. "I don't know which is more alarming—your infernal persistence or your fondness for extortion."

She sniffed. "Extortion implies you will not enjoy the price to be paid. You liked reading once."

"I will enjoy the reward more."

"Harrison."

Moving to brace his back against the trunk of the tree, he picked up the book she had laid near his hand. *"My father had a small estate in Nottinghamshire,"* he began reading. *"I was the third of five sons."*

At first, his voice was stiff, resentful. But the more he read, the more she rewarded him, scooting closer on the blanket, trailing her fingers along his shoulder and neck. Eventually, she laid her head on his thigh, looking up at his beautiful jaw. Surprisingly, while he absently took her hand in his and kissed it, he kept reading about Gulliver and the presumptuous little Lilliputians. The muscles in his face relaxed, his deep voice growing more nimble over the words. Soon, even she closed her eyes, picturing Gulliver's exasperation at being tied and poked by people no larger than his finger.

"When the workmen found it was impossible for me to break loose, they cut all the strings that bound me, whereupon I rose up with as melancholy a disposition as ever I had in my life. But the noise and astonishment of the people, at seeing me rise and walk, are not to be expressed."

She giggled. "Can you imagine, Harrison? I fear I would not be nearly so patient as he."

When he looked down, a strange and powerful surge broke through her. His eyes glowed with blue light, sparkled with the pure joy of adventure and discovery and something else—connection, perhaps. For the first time, she felt she was seeing *him*. Not the duke. Not the man everyone else knew.

He was glorious. He stole her breath.

She reached up to stroke his face. He moved their linked hands so his knuckle could feather over her lips. In the voluptuous golden light, with the river sighing through the silence and leaves rippling above, her heart was seized by him. Spellbound. In thrall.

He was hers. Her Harrison.

A harder breeze blew past, and he dropped his gaze to the book in his hand. He set it carefully on the blanket. "My father burned it. The second half of the book."

His words chilled her, sent a shiver over her skin.

"I came to the river many times," he said, staring out at the lazy water. "For the fish. But also to lose myself in other worlds for a while. It was a comfort to me." A terribly sad smile pulled at his mouth. "He did not approve."

Swallowing hard against a growing ache, she slowly sat up, remaining close, stroking his hand with her thumb. "He was angry?"

He shook his head. "His grace would never be so crass. Anger is for those who lack discipline. No, he was *disappointed*. I was his heir. My time should not be squandered in unserious pursuits. He could not allow such fantasies to continue."

She felt a crass amount of undisciplined anger rising like a nest of furious bees. "So, he burned your book?"

He huffed a mirthless laugh, eyes still following the water. "Books. Plural. I had numerous favorites at the time. And, no."

Oh, thank goodness. For a moment, she had thought—

"He made me burn them. Every single one."

The hair on her neck lifted. Inside, she writhed with the need to scream, to stomp in outrage, to claw at his dead father. But she forced herself to remain still and silent.

Finally, he looked at her, giving her a tiny smile that sent her heart twisting inside her chest. "Except this one." He held up the book she had coaxed him to read to her. "This one I managed to save. I buried it inside a sealed box. Near the castle."

For a moment, she could not speak. Then, she did, because she wanted to understand. "How old were you?"

"Ten."

"You were ten."

"Old enough to know better, he said."

"Better than what? To read stories that any normal boy would cherish?"

His smile grew and warmed as it traveled her face. "So says the woman who stashes books in every nook of the house when she has two perfectly good libraries."

Unable to bear it a moment longer, she pulled herself onto his lap, fought her skirts until she straddled his thighs, cupped his face in her hands, and kissed him with all the tenderness inside her. Her lips moved ever-so-softly against his, sliding and pressing in small, nibbling motions. His caressed hers in return, but he seemed content to stroke her back and let her touch him as she pleased.

She pulled back, lightly resting her forehead against his. "It was wrong, Harrison. It was wrong." Her voice broke on the last word.

Beneath her, he tensed. "Your pity is unnecessary," he said, the duke returning to form. "It was a long time ago."

Rising up on her knees, she fisted his shirt and gave him a small shake. "Pity is the last thing I feel for you, your great, insufferable grace."

He relaxed slightly, even running his hand up to tickle her nape. "Duly noted," he said dryly.

She glanced to where he had set the book. "When did you retrieve it? The book, I mean."

"Four years ago."

His answer brought her head up. "After he …"

"Died. Yes."

"You waited all that time?"

In his eyes was weary acceptance and wry pain. "Had you known my father better, you would have no need to ask that question."

She hated his father. *Hated* him. The coldhearted bastard was fortunate he was already dead. But she thought it best not to say so. Harrison might take offense.

Distantly, she heard a horse whinny. A frown appeared between Harrison's brows. They both turned in the direction of the sound, but the rise of the land did not allow them to see who was approaching. Harrison gently, effortlessly lifted her from his lap—the man really was shockingly strong—and slid from beneath her to stand. He then absently offered his hand to help her to her feet.

After shaking her skirts to resettle them, she stood on her toes, trying to see over the rise, where a few more ash trees rustled and swayed in the increasing wind. Feeling a stark change come over her husband before the other man came into view, she shielded her eyes from the glare of the sun, and asked, "Who is it?"

He had gone cold. Rigid, hard, and ice-cold. "The prodigal," he answered.

Her eyes flew to the ridge, where she could just see the man's hat bobbing higher and higher above the grass. She squinted, trying to see his face. But she didn't have to, for her husband identified him first.

"It seems my brother has returned to Blackmore."

Chapter Twenty

"Unfortunately, we are not permitted to choose who shares our bloodline. If we were, this would be infinitely easier."

—THE DOWAGER MARCHIONESS OF WALLINGHAM to her son, Charles, during a discussion of her nephew's unsuitability to inherit the title of Marquess of Wallingham.

JANE HUGGED HERSELF AND PACED INSIDE THE LOVELY GREEN confines of the duchess's chamber. Glancing at the ormolu clock on the marble mantel, she noted that it had been over an hour since Harrison had stalked away, his demeanor darker and more thunderous than she had yet witnessed.

After Colin had appeared by the river, her husband had ordered her to remain on the blanket while he strode up the incline to meet his brother. They'd exchanged a few sentences—none of which she could hear—and before she could gather her wits to approach, Colin had turned his horse and headed for Blackmore Hall.

When Harrison had returned to her side, he'd immediately begun repacking the basket, his expression hard and remote. To her numerous questions, he'd said only, "We shall discuss it later, Jane."

On their return trek to the house, his jaw had been locked, his strides swift and long. She'd been forced to trot to keep up. Every so often, he had glanced back at her and slowed, but his thoughts were obviously tangled by Colin's sudden appearance. By the time they had climbed the steps of the rear terrace and entered the south hall, both Jane's breath and Harrison's patience had fled, and he'd taken only a moment to bark in her direction, "Wait for me in your bedchamber. I will join you there within an hour."

Now, left with little choice but to comply, she had paced here in her room, waiting as he had asked. Or, rather, demanded. She had composed at least three letters to Victoria in her mind, but nothing had eased her fretfulness.

"I must find him," she murmured to herself. After all, who knew what might have happened? Harrison could have killed Colin by now. A trill of alarm tripped down her spine. He was a very controlled man, but she had never seen him quite like this.

Spurred by a growing urgency, she hurried to the chamber door and threw it open. She gasped and stumbled back.

He was there. On the other side of the door. Looming, frowning, his hand raised to grasp the knob. "Where are you off to, wife? I believe I told you to wait for me here."

Huffing indignantly, she planted her hands on her hips. "You are late."

He crowded close, forcing her to back into the room, and shut the door behind him. "Colin and I had much to discuss."

His face was solemn and weary, his mouth flat. But he smelled the same, like fresh air and sunlight. His nearness weakened her bones. As he brushed past her to sink tiredly into an ivory cushioned chair, she breathed to clear her senses. "And?"

"He will stay here tonight. After that, I have asked him to leave."

"Why would you do that?"

His brows lowered further. "You wish me to turn him out immediately?" He shook his head. "I'm afraid I cannot, Jane, even for you."

"For me? No. I am asking why he should not stay longer."

Sharpening and solidifying like ice forming on a lake, his eyes locked on her as thick silence bloomed between them. Her statement had transformed him. She did not understand it. But she felt it, as cold and raging as a howler from the North Sea. "He tried to ruin you," he said, his voice silken and hushed.

Her skin prickled with a primitive urge to back away. She remained still, instead saying truthfully, "He deceived me, but equally, I deceived myself. The final choice was mine, not his."

Pushing himself from the chair, causing the wood to creak, Harrison rose to his full height. He came toward her, a volatile presence with the eyes of a stranger. "Why do you defend him?"

"It is not a defense. It is what happened."

"He lured you to Milton's house where he and his blackguard friends lay in wait."

"Yes, I remem—"

"He subjected you to their jeers and their insults. He allowed them to surround you like a pack of feral dogs. It wasn't only your reputation at risk that night, Jane."

She swallowed, feeling the blood flee from her face. "I know. I was there."

"Do you know what he stood to gain from that little farce?"

She shook her head.

"A thousand pounds."

It was an obscene amount. Most did not see such a sum in an entire year.

"To him, that constituted a fair trade for placing you and your reputation in very real danger. *This* is the man you consider worthy of your loyalty."

"You do not need to remind me of what occurred that night. I recall very well. And you are right—I do not owe him loyalty, nor am I excusing his deplorable actions."

With each statement, her husband had advanced toward her, step by slow step. But at this, he paused. The ice encasing him seemed to thaw just a bit at her reassurance. Perhaps it had been her admission that he was right. That tactic had always disarmed Genie during her tantrums.

Taking care not to allow her irritation to show, she continued evenly, "Harrison, like it or not, he is your brother. The fact that he came here, knowing how he would be received, indicates his situation is quite desperate."

His eyes dropped to her mouth, his nose flaring. Suddenly, he turned away from her, his hands clasping behind his back, and paced to the opposite end of the room and back again. "He needs funds," he said flatly.

She frowned. "More than a thousand pounds?"

Without looking at her, he replied, "The wager did not produce the full amount."

"I don't understand."

"The reason is not important—"

"Then it should not be difficult to explain."

She could see he did not want to tell her. He continued to pace, making her dizzy. Finally, he halted in front of her and squared his shoulders. "Those who participated in the wager have been persuaded to repent of their actions. Many have denied the events of that night took place at all."

Slowly, she approached him. His eyes tracked her cautiously until she halted within inches, tilting her head back to get a better look. As she examined her husband's hardened features, she realized what he had just told her was, in fact, a confession—one he had not wanted to give. The truth of what he had done for her caused her heart to squeeze painfully. "That is why the gossip waned so quickly, is it not? You threatened them, and they recanted."

"I could scarcely allow those vermin to revel in your destruction, much less to profit from it."

He stood stiffly, his chin raised as if he fully expected her to castigate him.

But she had no such intention. Without warning, she slid her arms beneath his coat and locked them around his waist. She laid her cheek over the linen of his cravat, closed her eyes against the sudden threat of tears, and held him as tightly as she could.

At first, he did not react, standing still as stone. Then, she felt his arms come around her, gently cradling her against him.

Victoria had been right. He was easily the most honorable man she had ever known, his kindness not the easy sort, but rather the most profound. Harrison—her Harrison—had protected a woman he barely knew, shielded her not only with his name, but with every weapon at his disposal. Before he'd had any cause to feel the slightest affection for her, he had placed himself between her and the consequences of her stupidity.

Gripping him tighter, fisting the silken cloth of his waistcoat at the small of his back, she fought the ache rising from her chest into her throat. When she spoke, her voice was a muffled rasp. "Thank you." In her mind, she finished the thought, though she could not yet speak it. *Thank you, my love.*

His arms tightened, his strong hand stroking her back, then sliding down to curve over her bottom, his long fingers pressing the cloth of her skirts high against the juncture of her thighs, where she was already beginning to weep for him. His other hand rose to draw tiny circles on her nape with his nimble, hypnotic fingers. "Gratitude is not what I need from you, wife."

Gracious, he was potent. Her breath quickened, her thighs squeezing. She lifted her eyes. "What do you need?"

In answer to her throaty question, he pulled her mouth up

to meet his. His tongue immediately slid inside, deliberately pulsing against hers in a rhythm familiar yet more aggressive than before, as though he needed to stake a claim. The hand at her nape moved between them to cup and squeeze her breast, lightly pinching her nipple through layers of fabric, sending shockwaves of pleasure arcing through her. The rich ache around her heart transformed and melted, softening for him, heating her from the inside out.

"I need you," he panted, pulling away only long enough to answer before plunging back in to continue ravishing her mouth. Using his grip on her buttocks, he lifted her until one of her knees came up along his hip. He bent his knees so he could grind his rock-hard staff against her.

Meanwhile, she desperately gripped his head, tore at his cravat, moaned her desire into his mouth. If he needed her, it could not possibly be more than she needed him—his naked skin against hers, his cock filling her emptiness. She wanted to melt completely and become part of him. She wanted to absorb him into her so they could never be separated.

By the time both of them were naked, the dark-blue silk of her dress was hopelessly mangled on the floor. They barely made it to the bed. He carried her only as far as the foot of it, laying her flat with her hips positioned at its edge. The coverlet was cool against her back, but she didn't feel it.

She couldn't. There was only him.

Immediately, he dropped to his knees, his lean, delicious hands sliding along the outside of her thighs, gripping them and hooking her legs over his shoulders. Then, he began to feast. His tongue parted her slick, weeping folds with a single swipe, circling around the small, sensitive nubbin at the center of her pleasure. She writhed at the building strain of so many sensations coalescing in one small place—the warm, slick tongue dancing against her, pleasuring and stroking, then delving inside her needy sheath before returning to its center to tease and torment.

Hard hands gripped her hips to hold her still.

She clawed at his head, begging for more.

Instead, he pulled away.

Too soon. It was too soon. "Harrison, please," she whimpered.

His answer was to rise, letting her legs fall to flank his waist. He forced them to splay wide, looking like the golden god she had once dubbed him. His eyes dropped to the wet, dark-veiled core of her, flaring with lust, then slid upward over her swollen breasts with their achingly hard nipples.

"I want to see your hands, Jane." His command was raw, his eyes fierce in the firelight. "Touch your nipples with those beautiful hands while I take what is mine."

The words made her moan and arch her back, gripping the blanket beneath her and squeezing with her legs.

Gently, he clasped first one wrist then the other, lifting her arms and laying her hands on her breasts. "Go on," he said. "Show me your pleasure."

Uncertain at first, she nevertheless obeyed, cupping her breasts and slowly running her fingers over her feverishly tight nipples. The sensations were not as pleasing as when he suckled them, but as she witnessed the ferocious satisfaction in his eyes, she grew bolder, squeezing her nipples between her fingers, surprising herself when the sensations intensified exponentially.

"Yes," he hissed. "Just like that."

He leaned over her, hooking her legs on his hips, wrapping them tightly around him, and slid his hard, thick cock deep inside its home. They both groaned at the rightness of it, the feeling of fullness and completion. Then he began to move, driving inside her with fierce, almost violent thrusts that rocked and jostled her body. Automatically, her hands squeezed her breasts, trying to appease them as they ached and pouted for his mouth.

But he was not giving her his mouth. He was giving her his cock—deep and hard, pushing her knees higher so he could pound into her core unfettered. The heat of their joining grew unbearable, her sheath clenching and seizing with every thrust, almost unable to keep up with the relentless rhythm.

Without warning, the fiery coil let loose, causing her to arch and sob his name as the unraveling ecstasy took her in its grip with wild, unexpected force and flung her upon the crest of wave after wave after wave. She seized upon him, her body milking and demanding as it spasmed again and again. In the next breath, he plunged thrice more and followed her into the same deep waters, growling her name, his body shaking uncontrollably and collapsing upon her with its precious weight.

She clung to his neck, her heart pounding, her throat closing with the beauty of it.

She loved him.

That was all she knew.

She loved him. And its power left her quaking like the last leaf of autumn.

HOURS LATER, JANE LAY IN HER BED, HER HUSBAND FITTED around her body like a glove over her hand. One strong, muscled arm was hooked beneath her head and across the front of her shoulders; the other banded her waist, pulling her hips back into his. His thigh rode high between hers, his cock nestled along the crease of her backside, quiescent for now. His breath stirred across her cheek, the rhythmic rise and fall of his chest against her back as comforting as a lullaby.

She adored sleeping naked with Harrison.

But tonight, she could not sleep. Could scarcely breathe.

What had she done? The answer came quickly: *You fell in love with your husband, you ninny.*

How could she be so daft? That answer was not forthcoming.

Carefully, she untangled herself from his grasp, moving slowly so as not to awaken him. She left the bed, pausing long enough to don her spectacles, then her nightdress, dressing gown, and slippers. Padding to the door, she glanced back at her husband, his big, long body a silvery outline in the moonlight. Her eyes lingered over his face—the patrician brow that often pulled into a frown of consternation; the beauteous cheekbones and refined nose; the crisp jaw that was home to his proud chin and clever mouth. She sighed, overwhelmed by an emotion she had never before experienced: a head-spinning blend of pure adoration and intense longing.

Before she could give in to it and run back to his arms, she turned the knob she'd been gripping and slipped out into the corridor. Thankfully, the servants had left a taper or two burning, so she easily found her way to the stairs. Perhaps a good book would distract her long enough for her mind to settle.

Three faint, forlorn notes of music drifted up to meet her as she descended. She stopped midway down, listening. They came again. She headed for the music room.

That was where she found him—seated at the pianoforte, plucking at the keys. A lantern's light played over his golden curls and loose linen shirt.

"Colin."

He froze, the minor chord hanging in the air between them. Then he faced her.

She gasped, her hand covering her mouth. "You look dreadful."

A grin that was more akin to a grimace twisted his gaunt features. "Never did mince words, did you, Lady Jane?" He closed his eyes for a moment then blinked them open again. "Your grace. It is your grace, now. Forgive me."

"What happened to you?"

His face was sunken and weathered, his eyes dull and defeated. "I shall save that tale of woe for someone I have not wronged so grievously." He turned back to the keys and stared down as if he did not remember how to play.

"Colin," she said softly. "Am I not deserving of the truth?"

"Of course you are. You deserve much better than anything I could ever give you."

It was an echo of the old Colin. The friend she remembered. "Then tell me what happened."

His shoulders rose and fell on a deep breath, his hand rubbing at his forehead. "I brought it all down upon myself. A disaster. I am a bloody disaster."

She moved closer to him, hugging herself against a sudden chill. "Stop. Just explain what happened."

"A girl fell in love with me. But I did not love her in return. How could I? My entire life, I have loved only myself."

She waited as he wrestled with the confession, his hands clenching on the edge of the pianoforte.

"I ignored her pleas. Burned her letters. She was ... fragile." His voice deepened, twisting at the pain of the next few words. "She took her own life. And that of the child in her belly. My child."

Jane felt sick. Victoria had hinted that Colin had done something unforgivable, but she hadn't gone into detail.

"The girl's brother believed Harrison was her lover. He accused him of it, of abandoning her. Harrison had no idea what the man was talking about, and said as much. They fought a duel. Harrison killed him."

Jane breathed out slowly with the revelation. Everyone knew about the duel from two years ago, though few spoke of it, and none knew why it had occurred. "Atherbourne."

"Yes. I was the reason for her death. I was the reason Atherbourne challenged my brother. I was the one who kept silent while Harrison was forced to defend his honor."

She groaned and swiped a hand over her mouth. "Oh, good heavens. Victoria."

He barked a mirthless laugh. "She suffered, too, because of me. Lucien Wyatt used her to take revenge for his brother's death. It is only by sheer good fortune that she and the new Viscount Atherbourne came to have affection for one another. Of course, I have not precisely been invited for Christmas pudding, but Harrison tells me they are happy in their marriage. For that, I am thankful."

Shaking her head, she clarified, "All of this occurred over a year ago."

He nodded. "That was when Harrison cut off my funds."

Ahh. Yes. Now they were getting somewhere.

His voice grew tired, his words sliding together a bit. "Could no longer afford brandy, or much else, for that matter. The drinking ceased by necessity. But I had nothing to live on. I had always been a hand at the tables, and for a while, gaming sustained me."

"Until it didn't," she said.

"Precisely."

"So, you have gaming debts."

He laughed silently, his shoulders shaking. "Let it suffice to say I owe a great deal of money to a very dangerous man. And he does not accept less than full payment."

Eyeing her husband's brother, she noted his shirt was stained and torn, his body thin and weakened. He looked frayed to the point of breaking. "How long have you been running, Colin?"

"What month is it?"

"July."

"Two months. God, two bloody months."

She crossed her arms beneath her bosom. "This man to whom you owe the debt, why would he pursue you to such a degree? Certainly, he will collect nothing if you are dead. Why would he not accept a partial payment?"

He winced visibly, turning on the bench and leaning his elbow on the keys, sending forth a discordant noise. Again, he rubbed his head and ended by cradling it in his hand. "You misunderstand. He will not kill me, at least not straight away."

Her scalp prickled in forewarning. "Then, what?"

"He will keep me for a while, cutting off bits here and there to send to Harrison, who will be forced to pay my debt, along with a substantial fee for the trouble involved."

She felt her gorge rise. Truly, she feared she would vomit right then and there.

"Oh, bloody hell, Jane, I'm sorry. I should never have told you that."

Putting up a hand to halt his stumbling apology, she swallowed down the nausea, breathing deeply and evenly to force it to abate. "This—" She swallowed again. "This is why you needed the wager. Why you deceived me."

A long silence greeted her question. Then, he answered, "What I did to you … I shall regret it for the rest of my ill-begotten existence. I would beg your forgiveness, but I do not deserve it."

Dropping her gaze to the floor, she wrestled with the memories of Colin before the betrayal. His warm regard, his humor and ease with her. He had been her friend. Until he wasn't. "Did you …?" She took a deep breath and started over in a small voice. "Was any of it real, Colin?"

He sighed deeply. "I liked you very much. Too much. At the beginning, when I approached you in the bookshop, the wager was harmless enough: a stroll in the park with Jane Huxley. Simple. My plan was to complete the terms within the week and collect enough to keep me at the tables. Once I conversed with you, I began to regret involving you in such a devious enterprise, and so I delayed. By the time I realized how dire was the threat from the man holding my marker, the wager had grown in size and complexity."

"And it became your way out."

His smile was filled with self-loathing. "To my utter shame, yes. I excused it by convincing myself that no one ever need know, that you might feel a bit embarrassed by the adventure, and certainly betrayed, but the men involved would maintain secrecy so as not to be associated with such a reprehensible wager."

She raised a brow. "You presumed this about Lord Milton and Sir Christopher Flatmouth and—"

"Yes, it was daft. My thoughts were quite muddled by panic, I'm afraid. Additionally, that was before they insisted on being present to witness the deed at Milton's house. By then, I had nothing to pay them should I fail in my task. And if I reneged, they would complain loudly about it, which would expose you to ridicule."

"So, instead, you exposed me to ruination. Or worse."

He looked away from her, staring across at the shadows on the other side of the room. "Apart from my role in Marissa Wyatt's death, that night is my greatest regret, Jane. I swear this to you."

Sighing, she moved to stand next to him at the pianoforte, lightly picking at the keys on the upper end of the scale. "Have you ever met my brother John, by chance?"

He turned to look at her hands, but would not meet her eyes. "We were at school together. Eton."

"One summer, John thought it would be great fun to drive our neighbor's phaeton. He piled three of us girls in the vehicle with him, and off we went, squealing and laughing. The problem was John had never before driven a phaeton. As the carriage moved faster and faster, we began to fret. John panicked, losing control and veering into a hedgerow. We were thrown when the phaeton overturned. Fortunately, no one was injured." She paused. "Well, Maureen's wrist was sore, and John's nose bloodied a bit. In any event, when we confessed to Papa, do you know what he said?"

"Bloody hell?"

She chuckled. "No. He said experience has a way of teaching us lessons that no admonition can ever duplicate."

"Hmm. At what point did he unveil the rod?"

Shaking her head, she grinned at him, her fingers absently plucking at the keys as he began harmonizing on the opposite end of the board. "Papa does not believe in such punishments. And, as it happens, he was right. John waited years before driving a phaeton again, determined to be in full command of himself before doing so."

"A delightful story. I am fond of happy endings."

She snorted and swatted his shoulder. "I have not yet come to my point."

Nodding, he waved a hand. "Proceed."

"John was twelve when this occurred. He was a boy playing at being a man. He endangered those he loved because he misjudged the risks of his own actions."

Colin's fingers froze.

Likewise, she let the tinkling notes she'd been playing dissipate into silence. "But he learned from it, Colin. He grew up. He made better choices."

"This is hardly a spill from a phaeton, Jane. And I am a good deal older than twelve."

"You and John have something important in common—you regret what you have done, hurting those you care for. That is the beginning. You must recognize your mistakes and work to do better."

"It is too late," he said, his voice a whisper in the now-quiet room.

"You can but try. You *must* try." For her husband's sake, Colin must change. Jane could not bear for Harrison to suffer the consequences of his brother's selfishness any longer.

From behind her, she heard the creak of the wooden floor.

"You are wasting your breath, wife," Harrison said, his voice an icy lash.

Chapter Twenty-One

"Like gunpowder, jealousy is a volatile element best handled with care and applied judiciously."

—THE DOWAGER MARCHIONESS OF WALLINGHAM to Lady Atherbourne upon hearing of Lord Atherbourne's sustained enmity toward Sir Barnabus Malby.

SHE SPUN TO WATCH HIM EMERGE FROM THE SHADOWS, HIS tall form clothed in the white linen shirt and buff breeches from earlier. He looked rumpled, as if he had thrown them on in a panic. "My brother is incapable of changing. He is like a plague. All one can do is attempt to limit the damage."

"He—he has made mistakes ..."

His long strides carried him into the lantern's light, where she glimpsed his face for the first time. Dear heaven, he was furious. With her.

"This is not where you belong."

"I know. I was just—"

"Come morning, Colin will leave here and never return."

"Harrison, I am not certain—"

His head tilted slightly, his jaw like stone. "It is not your decision. It is mine." His voice was hard and grinding, almost accusatory.

She did not understand his outsized anger toward her, and it sent her indignation rising. "He is your brother. Do you know what he has been through?"

His eyes flashed, nostrils flaring. "What *he* has been through?" While the words were quietly spoken, they might as well have been a roar.

"Er—Jane?" Colin muttered. "Probably best to let it be, for now."

Harrison shifted his glare to Colin. "Leave us."

"He is in *danger*, Harrison. Terrible danger. You cannot simply toss him to the wolves."

Eyes flashing, Harrison moved closer. Colin stood and placed himself between his brother and Jane. He held up a hand. "I will leave, as you wish. No need for argument. It was a mistake to come here in the first place."

"It is odd how frequently you realize your error only after the damage has been done."

Colin dropped his hand, slumping in exhaustion. "I bid you good night, brother."

After he left the room, Jane stared at her husband, wondering just what had come over him. His bitterness was understandable, perhaps, but his reactions went well beyond that. The undercurrent was a kind of volatile wrath, and seemed to be directed, at least in part, toward her.

"I cannot understand why you are so angry."

His silence was long as he stared at her, his eyes flashing in the low light. A muscle ticked next to his eye. "Can you not? I awaken to find my wife gone. I search for her, only to find her alone with a man for whom she once risked her reputation.

How much of a fool were you, Jane? Did you let him kiss you?"

"Don't be absurd."

"You are oddly adept at seduction for an innocent, wife," he murmured. "Did you practice your wiles on him? Did you touch *him* with your hands?"

"Wiles? Harrison, stop being ridiculous. I haven't any wiles to practice."

"That is a lie," he said softly.

Releasing a sigh of frustration, she tried again. "In answer to your preposterous questions, no, he never kissed me. You were the first. And I never touched him, nor did he touch me, in any inappropriate fashion. All the inappropriate touching I have ever experienced has been with you."

His face remained grim. "He claims you were friends. You frequently dress as a burglar and attempt to rob strange houses for mere *friends*, do you?"

"Harrison—"

"Answer me."

She did not want to. It was embarrassing. But she could see he was suspicious of her relationship with Colin, and she could not allow his doubts about her fidelity to fester. "I–I do not ..."

He waited then snapped, "Yes?"

"I do not have many friends." Cringing at her own confession, she continued reluctantly, "Only one, really, outside of my family. Victoria. So, yes, to me, friends are precious. And yes, if Victoria had asked, I would gladly have dressed as a burglar and attempted to rob Prinny himself if I thought she needed me to do so."

The hush of the room fell between them. The lantern light glowed across his features. Was it her imagination, or had he eased a bit? "Colin was never your friend. He deserves your scorn, not your loyalty."

Her imagination, clearly. "I do not deny that."

"Good. He will depart tomorrow, so you should have no further need to see him."

"Harrison, you must let him stay at least a few days," she said quietly. "He is being hunted."

"It is not your concern."

She stepped toward him, her chin rising with her temper. "Anything to do with you is my concern, you great lummox. How will you feel if he is attacked mere days from now?"

He blinked, seeming disoriented by her challenge. A muscle in his jaw flickered.

"Guilty, perhaps? Responsible?"

"He has brought this upon himself."

Moving close, she laid her hand carefully over his heart, and felt him flinch. "Of course he has. But you are a far better man than he is. Please do not make a decision in haste. It may be one you will mourn forever."

He swallowed visibly then covered her hand with his own. "Jane," he said in a low rumble. "Let us return to our bed."

"Harrison, I think—"

"I shall consider your argument and decide what is best in the morning."

He seemed calmer when she touched him. Perhaps that was the key. She nodded her assent, and together, they returned to her chamber and to each other's arms.

THE NEXT MORNING, BLACKMORE HALL WAS BUSTLING IN preparation for the visit from Lord Dunston, who was set to arrive in only two days. Maids polished the stair railing, footmen relocated furniture, and Beardsley and Mrs. Draper orchestrated the efforts like conductors of a master symphony.

Jane was a bit bewildered, as they had not bothered to consult her on a stitch of it, but for the moment, she had more important matters to consider.

He had changed his mind. Because of her.

Upon waking alone, she had hurried Estelle through her toilette, eager to find Harrison, who was in his study, meeting with his steward. He rose as she entered, stiffened as she asked for his decision, and finally informed her that Colin would be permitted to stay for the remainder of the week in a cottage on Blackmore lands.

Ignoring the steward, she had rushed to where her husband stood, taken his face in her hands and kissed his wondrous mouth. The kiss had gone a little long, considering a virtual stranger was watching. By the time she'd pulled away, Harrison's face was flushed, his eyes gleaming with lust. Feeling a trifle embarrassed, she had quickly left the room, hearing him clear his throat loudly and say, "Now then, where were we?" as she closed the study door.

At last, she could resume planning for Dunston's visit. Harrison had told her of his friend's intentions weeks ago, and she still dreaded it like a dress fitting with Mrs. Bowman. However, she consoled herself that it would be no worse than the London season with its balls and routs and musicales and endless entertainments.

Entering the kitchen, she immediately spied the mad Frenchman with the penchant for vulgarity. "Monsieur Renaud," she called above the hectic noise of maids chopping and hauling and gossiping. A cube of turnip landed at her feet. The cook glanced over his shoulder from his position at the oversized range.

"*Duchesse*," he grumbled brusquely.

She bustled forward, sidestepping a basket of onions to draw up beside him. "I am here to discuss the meals for Lord Dunston's forthcoming visit."

He eyed her balefully. "Hmmph. Did you speak with Madame Draper?"

"No, I am afraid she is occupied."

Moving to the work table, he barked at a harried blond

maid, "Thin! Slice them thin, you stupid girl. This is soup, not slop for pigs."

He sighed, leaning a hand on the table, retrieving a cloth from his apron pocket, and wiping his forehead. A dark lock of hair fell over one eye rakishly. He tossed his head and squinted at her. "What would you like to know?"

"Oh, you misunderstand. I would like to *plan* the meals. With your very wise counsel, of course."

His dark eyes dropped, and he rubbed the cloth over the back of his neck. "It is done, Madame."

"I beg your pardon?"

"*Le duc* has already made a list of his preferences." He waved negligently toward a long shelf beneath the high windows, where several sheets of paper were scattered.

"He ... he has?" She turned back to the cook, but he had resumed stirring at the range.

Her lips tightened. This was most peculiar. In every household she knew of—Victoria's, Annabelle's, her mother's—the lady of the house was responsible for meal planning. Every one.

When she had first arrived at Blackmore, the meals had already been arranged and were well managed by Monsieur Renaud and Mrs. Draper, both highly competent servants. She had felt no need to intervene; likewise with the general running of the household. However, a visit was a special occasion that required the guiding hand of the hostess.

Unless the host had determined she was incapable of attending to such a basic duty.

Hurrying back to the study, she gave a quick knock, pausing to adjust her spectacles and take a deep breath.

"Come," she heard through the door.

Pushing it open, she noted the steward was still there. The mild man with thinning hair and spectacles stood upon seeing her, as did Harrison. But her husband's perusal was a good deal more thorough. And more heated. Though his expression remained closed, his eyes traced a path of fire from her violet silk hem to her hair, coming back to linger over her bosom then settle on her face.

"Your grace," said the steward.

She nodded a greeting, but found it hard to tear her gaze away from Harrison's. "May I speak with you?" she asked breathlessly.

"Of course. That should be all for today, Mr. Talbot."

Taking the hint, Mr. Talbot bowed and left, closing the door behind him. The moment it clicked shut, Harrison moved from behind his desk, stalked toward her, wrapped her in his arms, and kissed her senseless.

She hummed a weak protest against his invading tongue, but quickly forgot why she was protesting. Then, she forgot why she had come into this room. And, for that matter, her own name.

"Jane," he whispered.

Oh, yes. That was it.

His mouth found the juncture of her neck and shoulder, nibbling deliciously. "Perhaps we should lock the door," he panted against her skin.

Her eyes popped open. Wait, wasn't there something …?

He was gathering up fistfuls of her skirt when she remembered. "Harrison."

His lips dropped to her collarbone.

"Harrison, stop." She pushed gently at his shoulders. He straightened and frowned at her fiercely, but he complied. "I need to discuss something with you."

He ran a hand through his hair and released a breath. "It cannot wait until after?"

For the briefest moment, she considered it. He was so very tempting, with his smoky-blue eyes and his strong, muscled shoulders and his—but no; it must be now. "I just came from the kitchen."

"Why would you visit the kitchen? That is not a proper place for a lady."

She waved that away. "Don't be silly. My mother visits the

kitchen regularly to assist with meal planning. It is a less formal practice, I'll grant you, but quite effective."

"Your mother," he said dryly.

She sniffed. "Yes. In any event, I consulted with Monsieur Renaud about—"

"I do not want you speaking to that Frenchman."

"Whyever not?"

"He is coarse."

"We get on quite well, actually."

His eyes sharpened, his mouth flattening. "Do you, now?"

"He informed me that you have already planned the menu for Lord Dunston's visit."

"Is there a problem?"

She frowned. "Well, I had assumed—"

A knock interrupted. It was Beardsley. "I beg your pardon, your grace. The footmen have moved the blue chairs into the yellow bedchamber. Mrs. Draper is inquiring if you would also like the green divan replaced."

Jane opened her mouth to answer, but Harrison replied over her head, "No. However, please tell her I shall speak with her shortly. The linens in the rose room are in need of changing."

The butler bowed and departed. She turned to see Harrison once again sitting behind his desk, opening a drawer, and withdrawing a sheet of paper.

"What—what are you doing?" she asked.

He did not stop writing. "I find it helpful to make a list of tasks for the servants."

She pressed her lips together and adjusted her spectacles. "Is there not something you would like for me to do?"

The pen halted. He glanced up with a devilish look. "Many, many things, yes." He resumed writing. "But I'm afraid that must wait. This evening, perhaps."

Clearly, he preferred to manage the household himself. Or he did not trust her to do so. But then, maybe she was overreacting. She tried again. "Harrison, I could help …"

"No need." He dipped his pen in the inkpot. "It is all well in hand. Perhaps you could find a book to read."

For such a small, inconsequential thing, his absent statement hit her with unexpected force, right around her stomach. The sensation felt similar to the time Genie had accidentally elbowed her in the solar plexus while they'd been struggling to cinch her first corset. In the same way, his casual comment knocked the breath from her lungs.

Was that the only skill he thought her capable of? Reading? Naturally, she loved to read, so she spent a good deal of time doing so, but she had been trained to run a household. She had expected to take on those duties when she married, as all wives did. Her husband, however, did not appear convinced of her competence.

Certainly, she had little doubt he desired her. But in the midst of her elation over that fact, she had neglected to consider that lust did not equal regard. *I am a fool,* she thought. *A plain, awkward woman who has forgotten how this marriage began.*

She examined his beautiful blond head where it bent over his list, daylight glinting off the short golden strands, his shoulders straight and broad beneath gray superfine. She swallowed hard against a sudden ache.

How could she forget? They had been a mismatch from the beginning. She was not meant to be a duchess. Not meant to manage an estate as magnificent as Blackmore Hall.

Quietly, she turned and made her way to the old library, with its dark wood and heated memories. There, she sank into her favorite chair, let her head ease onto its wing, and composed a letter to ... oh, she did not know. Herself, she supposed.

Dearest Jane, she would write. *You knew better once, did you not? I wonder how you managed to convince yourself that you were worthy of him. The truth was there the day he offered for you. Inside, as you busied yourself making the best of things, you have known all along. But his kisses turned you forgetful. His eyes caused you to see things that weren't there. Now, you've given him your heart. And all the while, the truth stands watch like a storm on the horizon, constant and patient. You may ignore it for a time, but not forever. Dearest Jane, wake up. The storm is waiting.*

She laughed at herself as a tear tickled its way down her cheek. Swiping it away impatiently, she could almost hear Lady Wallingham's trumpeting voice castigating her: *Foolish girl. Foolish, foolish girl.*

Chapter Twenty-Two

"Choose your guests wisely, for the ones you can least tolerate invariably stay the longest."

—The Dowager Marchioness of Wallingham to Lady Reedham upon hearing said lady's plans for a grand hunting party.

Pulled by six gleaming black horses, the traveling coach of the Earl of Dunston was a sight to behold, but no less so than its occupants.

"Cornelius!" came a feminine cry as the door was shoved open abruptly. A small, wrinkled body attached to great, flopping ears leapt clumsily to the ground and immediately set to sniffing in a series of circles.

"Dear heavens, I fear he has murdered us."

"Ladies, might I suggest we disembark before that fateful moment arrives?"

From Jane's position on the front terrace of Blackmore Hall, it appeared the small, rusty-brown animal was having a good bit of trouble, as it repeatedly trampled and stumbled over its own ears. It sat down firmly on the drive and scratched one of the offending flaps with a vigorous paw. An icy-green skirt of sprigged muslin appeared next to what she assumed was a dog.

Lady Mary Thorpe, wearing said skirt along with a pink spencer and a dashing, furbelowed hat, folded her hands at her waist and took a deep, though discreet, breath of fresh air. The pretty, cinnamon-haired young woman ignored the dog at her feet to gaze up at Blackmore. Her expression of wistfulness—as though she imagined both the house and the man being hers—came as no surprise to Jane.

"I have told you countless times. You must cease feeding that dog bits of cheese." As he bounded from the coach, Lord Dunston's brown hair gleamed in the midday light, showing hints of his sister's red. Lean and athletic, Dunston was not particularly tall, but his dark-green coat and gray trousers were expertly fitted, his waistcoat the fine patina of polished copper. He, too, appeared more handsome than anyone who had traveled the rutted road from Leeds should.

"Henry, I say. Help me down, you thoughtless boy."

Lord Dunston glanced back at the matron currently stooped in the carriage door's opening, waving a gloved hand beneath her slightly hooked nose. "Of course," he murmured, hurrying to comply just as the coachman came around to her opposite side.

The weighty woman garbed in head-to-toe pink wore a forbearing expression, but was somewhat pale as she descended. "Never bring that creature on such a journey again, Mary. I fear my brief time on this earth has shortened substantially."

The dog, exhausted from its whirling, sniffing explorations, stopped next to the carriage wheel, lifted its leg, and calmly urinated. When it was finished, Lady Mary knelt to lift the pup into her arms. "Nonsense, Mama. Cornelius is a good pup. Aren't you? Yes, you are a good, good dog."

Uncertain how long to wait for them to notice her standing on the front terrace, Jane took a resounding breath, tightened her stomach muscles to stifle the nervous flutters, and started forward. Before she reached the stone steps, she felt hands bracket her shoulders, slowing her progress. Her head swung around. "Harrison," she murmured. "I thought ..."

Over her head, he smiled at the earl. "Dunston, you always did enjoy adding unexpected guests to the list."

Lord Dunston grinned as Harrison brushed past Jane to meet him on the drive with a warm handshake. "Apologies, your grace. This time, you cannot blame me. Mary insisted."

The young woman kissed the wriggling puppy's head and slowly walked toward the men. A gradual, twinkling smile and flirtatious eye-fluttering preceded a honeyed protest. "I was certain you wouldn't mind, Harrison. You have always been so generous with your hospitality."

Jane's hand settled over her stomach. Was it possible to vomit from sweetness too revolting to witness? Perhaps if she vomited directly *on* the charming Mary, that sweetness would dissipate. It was something to consider.

Harrison bowed and grasped Lady Mary's outstretched fingers. "Lady Mary. Lovely to see you again." Was it Jane's imagination, or was her husband's voice significantly more melodious? Truly, it was a marvel. His words seemed almost a caress. "And Lady Dunston, a pleasure, as always. I do hope your journey was not too arduous."

"No journey is too trying to be with you again, Harrison," Mary, Queen of Sweets, simpered nauseatingly.

"Come, you must join us inside." Harrison waved them all toward the entrance. Toward Jane.

As they approached, they all slowed. Dunston was the first to reach her. "Your grace," he said with a quiet, warm smile. "Thank you for having us here."

"L-lord Dunston. You are most welcome."

Mary and her mother offered greetings as well, but theirs were unsmiling and only two words: "Your grace."

An hour later, Jane wondered if anyone would notice if she slipped away to the library. She didn't care which one. Anywhere that wasn't *here* would do.

They all sat together in the gold drawing room. Lady Mary and Lady Dunston had positioned themselves on an ivory sofa, sipping tea, the sleeping dog lying at Mary's feet. Harrison and Lord Dunston sat in chairs facing the fireplace. And Jane sat alone on a light-blue settee facing the two women, who conversed pointedly with everyone except her. Lord Dunston had attempted to draw her into the conversation a few times, but each time, it seemed Harrison would intervene, answering for her and drawing the conversation away again.

She loathed tea, and so she had nothing to do except fold her hands in her lap and stare over their heads out the window. It put her in mind of one of Lady Wallingham's luncheons, albeit slightly less vicious. And less stimulating.

"I offered him Ulysses' next foal. That persuaded him, at long last, to sell me one of his champion stock," Harrison said to Lord Dunston, describing his negotiations with Lord Wallingham, Lady Wallingham's son, who owned the finest stable in England.

"Ah, that would do it. I don't suppose you would consent to let me ride the old boy while I am here."

"Of course. If you are not too fatigued from your travels, perhaps we could go for a ride now."

Dunston took a quick sip of his tea and nodded. "Capital idea. Ladies, care to join us?"

Jane sat straighter, ready to bolt upstairs to change into her riding habit. *Anything, please, dear God, to extract me from this room.*

"Oh, heavens no. You gentlemen need time together without us ladies tagging along," Lady Dunston answered for them all. She waved her fingers in a shooing motion. "Run along now, and leave us here to our own amusements."

Jane noted Harrison frowned rather severely in her direction, but Dunston stood and bowed, so Harrison followed suit, though reluctantly. He paused at the white paneled doors, glancing back at Jane with that same perplexing expression. Then Dunston pulled him away, and she was alone.

With them.

"So," said Lady Mary brightly. *"Duchess.* How are you settling into your new role here at Blackmore Hall?" Her laugh tinkled through the air and down Jane's spine like a cat's claws on dry rock. "I daresay it is a far sight grander than your quaint home in—where is it?—ah, yes, Nottinghamshire. Becoming the Duchess of Blackmore must be quite a challenge for someone like yourself."

Jane's fingers pressed tighter together where they folded in her lap. "It—I have ..." She stopped to clear her throat. "It has gone well. Thank you for asking."

Lady Dunston took a leisurely sip from her china cup and set it back in its saucer with a delicate clink. "Yes, we were simply astonished when we heard Blackmore had offered for you. Imagine it. You had danced together only once. Your families were acquainted, but there was no indication of an alliance of this sort. So sudden!" She took another sip, her eyes gleaming and shrewd. "Naturally, we wondered if the unfortunate rumors played a part in the engagement. Scandalous accusations, simply scandalous!"

Jane did not respond. At the moment, her mouth was locked, her stomach cold and sick.

But Lady Dunston felt no such misgiving. "All of that has been laid to rest, of course. No one would dare accuse the Duchess of Blackmore of being a thief!" She said the last word in a whisper, too tawdry to speak aloud.

Mary raised one cinnamon brow imperiously, bent forward to set her cup on the marble-topped table, then gathered her sleeping dog into her arms. She stroked his brown, wrinkled head and smirked at Jane. "How very *fortunate* your engagement was announced at the precise moment when you were attacked by scurrilous rumors." All hints of a smile faded, and her eyes grew hard. "But, then, Harrison is more honor-bound than most."

There were so many things Jane wished to say. They burned in her throat—hateful, venomous things that would turn Mary, Queen of Sweets, as sour as a cask of vinegar. But she could not. The words were trapped by the knowledge that Mary was too bloody close to the truth.

When Jane did not respond, Mary glanced at her mother. "I am growing weary, Mama. I believe I shall lie down a while."

Lady Dunston nodded and set her cup on the table. "Yes, dear. I believe I shall do the same."

With that, they both rose from the sofa, Mary carrying her sleeping hound. Then they exited the gold drawing room without offering Jane so much as a nod for the sake of courtesy. If she were not terribly relieved to see them depart, she might just take offense.

THIS WAS RUBBISH. HE SHOULD CEASE FRETTING OVER HER. But her face as he had left the drawing room had made him long to toss Dunston and his family out on their backsides. Which was entirely unreasonable.

"... decided to wear the horse's shoes myself."

She'd been withdrawn, unsmiling, her skin pale in contrast with her dark hair. The memory of it still caused acid to churn in his gut. He did not know what was wrong, could only surmise that having unfamiliar guests in her home was deeply disconcerting to her.

"Not altogether comfortable, I must tell you."

The change in her was worse than he had anticipated, her behavior growing steadily more quiet and reserved over the past few days, until she was shrinking into herself whenever he came near. He had tried to kiss her last night, but she had turned away, claiming her monthly courses as an excuse to sleep alone. He knew better, but he had not wanted to press her when she clearly felt overwhelmed by their guests' imminent arrival.

"And then the saddle—oh, how it chafes."

Harrison tore his gaze from the trees in the distance and glanced over at his daft friend, who sat atop an ambling Ulysses. "What the devil are you on about?"

Dunston grinned. "A bit distracted, are we?"

Harrison grunted. "I would be enjoying a fine summer day if not for your nonsense."

Chuckling, the earl tipped his hat. "A pleasure to be of service."

As they approached the rise above the river, near the place he and Jane had picnicked the day Colin had returned, Harrison's thoughts flew back to his wife. In truth, they never strayed far from her.

"Perhaps we should turn back," he said to Dunston, who raised a brow.

"We have been gone for only a half-hour."

"I would prefer not to leave the ladies alone for too long."

Dunston covered a sudden cough. "You are concerned they shall perish for want of our company?"

Harrison sent him a well-deserved glare.

"Rest easy, old friend. The ladies are perfectly capable of drinking their tea and exchanging their gossip without our assistance."

Training his eyes forward, Harrison did not reply. What could he say? That the gnawing need to see Jane was afflicting him like a bad case of consumption? After only a half-hour?

"Ah," said the annoying Dunston. "You miss her."

"Absurd."

"Hmm. Yes, a bit. But also true."

Harrison pulled his horse to a stop in the middle of a grassy meadow above the river's rise. The field was covered in daisies. "I am not some besotted swain. Jane is ... She is ..."

Having pulled ahead, Dunston turned Ulysses around to face Harrison. "Your wife," he said softly.

Sighing in relief that Dunston understood, Harrison nodded. Yes. She was his wife. What he felt was perfectly normal. Part of a husband's duty was to protect her and provide for her comfort. It was not that he missed her. He simply needed to see her. To ensure that she was safe. And comfortable.

Dunston's hands overlapped and rested on the low pommel. "How are you getting along?"

He blinked. "Quite well, actually." Recalling the day she had teased and seduced him past his reticence at Blackmore Castle, he could not stop his mouth from lifting in a smile. "She often surprises me."

"Does she?"

"Do you know, she found a book I read as a boy. We read it again together." He nodded toward the river. "Just over there. Every time I think I understand her, she does something confounding."

"And you enjoy spending time with her."

His eyes riveted to their spot, where she had laid her head on his thigh, stroked his cheek with her soft, white hand. "Yes. She is so beautiful, Henry," he said absently. "Her laugh has a charming little catch just at the top. It makes you glad you are close enough to hear it. And when she smiles, her cheeks form these tiny dimples. Playful little things."

"I have seen them."

"Her voice ..." He paused to take a breath, his longing intensified by every word. "It changes like the pattern of light on water. When she is happy, the rasp is slight. When she is vexed with me, it deepens like a pup grumbling about being awakened from a nap." When she was aroused, it stroked over him like roughened silk, soothing and enflaming at once, but he could not tell Dunston such a thing. Aside from being inappropriate, the man would believe him hopelessly infatuated.

"I'm afraid I've not had much occasion to appreciate her voice. She has always been a bit on the quiet side," said Dunston, his expression oddly neutral.

"That is only because she does not know you well. She may be shy at first, but once you are her friend, you will quickly become enchanted by her winsome nature. Her wit is unlike any other female's. Did I mention her laugh?"

His friend smiled, his eyes crinkling. "Yes, you did. Not to worry, Harrison. I am certain as we grow better acquainted, I shall discover all the facets of her beauty, just as you have."

Focusing on Dunston's face, Harrison inquired sharply, "What are you implying?"

His eyes widened. "Nothing whatever!"

"It sounded distinctly like an implication."

"I find her quite lovely, Harrison. Others have called her Plain Jane, but I never have. You know that. Besides which, her new gowns have done wonders."

A slow, burning fist twisted around his stomach. "You have been eyeing her gowns?"

"Er—wait. Are you angry because I find her plain or because I do not?"

"She is not plain."

Dunston cleared his throat several times, requiring him to duck his head so that his hat brim hid his face from view and his fist covered his mouth.

"Plain implies she is ordinary. Unexceptional. Those words are the opposite of Jane."

"Oh, dear God," Dunston muttered. "Harrison—"

"When you must look at her, you will keep your eyes on her face. Not her skirts. And certainly not her bodice. Nor her hands."

"Her *hands?*"

Harrison reached into his waistcoat pocket to pull out his watch. It had been forty minutes. "We should return to the house."

Dunston began to protest, but Harrison had already turned his horse and headed toward home. He needed to see her. It was an ache inside him that would not abate. He pushed his horse from a canter to a gallop. Soon, the grass beneath him was flying past, the trees lining the hills a blur, but still, it was not fast enough.

They entered the stable yard at such a clip, the horse slid and stomped to a halt, its head coming up in protest. The animal's heaving breaths matched Harrison's as he dismounted in a leap and tossed the reins to the freckle-faced groom.

He needed to see her. To ensure she was well, and that her time alone with Lady Dunston and Lady Mary had not proven too discomfiting. To hold her close if it had, and perhaps offer a kiss as a distraction. To feel her hands stroking his face.

He did not even pause to wipe his boots, loping across the south terrace and straight to the gold drawing room. But he was too late. She wasn't there.

She wasn't anywhere. Jane—his Jane—was gone.

Chapter Twenty-Three

"Recently, I was reminded that granting favors rarely benefits the grantor as fully as the grantee."

—THE DOWAGER MARCHIONESS OF WALLINGHAM to her son, Charles, in reference to her nephew's continued misbehavior at Oxford.

ONCE AGAIN, SHE HAD CHOSEN A FRIGHTFULLY WARM summer day to trek across fields and through forests with a heavy, cumbersome basket. "I am bloody daft," she muttered, pushing up her spectacles as a leaf thwacked her breast. She pushed it aside impatiently and continued toward the cottage.

The little stone house sat cheerfully in a clearing, surrounded by ash and oak trees, its multi-paned windows lending it a welcoming air. It had once been the gardener's cottage, before Harrison's father had ordered a new one built near the walled garden on the opposite side of the fish pond. Apparently, the gardener had spent too much time trudging through these thick woods and not enough time tending his duties.

She wiped her forehead with the back of her wrist before knocking on the oak door. Inside, she could hear a muffled crash, like pots hitting the floor, then a quiet curse. "A moment, Boswell," the masculine voice shouted, referring to the footman assigned to deliver food and supplies each day.

Tapping her foot, she waited.

The door swung open. "You weren't due to return until tom—Jane!"

She smiled up at a round-eyed Colin. "I am certain you will see Boswell at his appointed time. But today, you have me." She raised the basket an inch or two, her arms burning from the effort. "And this monstrously heavy basket."

Shaking his head, he immediately took it from her and waved her inside. Thankfully, the interior was much cooler, the shade of the trees and the thickness of the stone walls a blessing in midsummer. It was neither large nor luxurious, with bare plank floors and few embellishments. But the simple wooden chairs were made more comfortable with pillows at the back, and the round table in front of a small stone hearth was topped with a matching cloth and a pitcher of daisies.

"I'm afraid I wasn't expecting anyone," he said sheepishly, setting the basket on the table and running a hand through his hair.

She glanced over his sparse attire—a simple linen shirt tucked into dark trousers—and shrugged. "You are not unclothed."

He chuckled, the sound a bit rusty. "It is good to see you, Jane."

Grinning, she cracked open the basket to begin placing items on the table. "And you, Colin. How are you feeling?"

"Better. A few days of rest, and my head no longer feels it is about to tumble off my shoulders."

"And this"—she held up a loaf of freshly baked bread—"should speed that along. Monsieur Renaud is masterful with all things, but anything baked is shockingly delicious."

As they sat and ate together, Colin's easy companionship soothed Jane in a way she could not explain. The cold lump that had grown and stretched against her ribs over the past two days eased and thawed, letting her breathe again.

"It wasn't until the fourth time she found a dead spider on her pillow that Victoria suspected it was I who had committed the dastardly act. Before that, she believed wholeheartedly the terrifying tale of the Ghost Spider that haunts the darkest corners of Blackmore Hall, preying upon small children who accidentally trample one of its offspring."

Holding her sides, Jane laughed harder than she had in ages, struggling to catch her breath. "Did—did she ever forgive you?"

"Oh, eventually. Victoria has a temper, but there are few people more loving on this earth."

Her laughter fading to a smile, Jane nodded. "She is extraordinary, your sister."

His eyes dropped to the table, his fingers tracing a crack beneath the cloth. "I have written her a letter. I haven't posted it, for obvious reasons. But I do want her to know how much I regret the harm I brought upon her and her husband."

Jane's hand covered his, which felt alarmingly thin and bony. "What will you do, Colin? Where will you go from here?"

He squeezed her hand in return. "In a few more days, I will return to Liverpool, and from there, sail to America."

As she gazed into his eyes, she could see him doubting his own survival, the blue brighter than it had been, but still shadowed by the knowledge of what chased him. "What if you had the funds to pay the debt?"

"Harrison offered me this place for a short time. I cannot ask for more than that."

She shook her head. "I have an allowance. It is not a

thousand pounds, but with the money from the wager and my funds, you could—"

"No."

"Colin—"

"I have taken enough from you. Bloody hell, Jane, you are too good for your own good."

Smiling, she gave his hand one last pat then withdrew to dig into the basket. "Perhaps you are right. But I will not stand by and see you tortured or murdered when I can do something to stop it. If nothing else, you are the brother of my best friend and my husband. That makes you my brother, too."

He was silent as she pulled out a reticule Genie had given her. Covered in a bevy of bows and little tufted feathers, all in pink, the thing was hideous, an experiment Genie had regretted soon after it was finished. But inside, was two months' worth of allowance, perhaps enough to save a man's life.

She held it out to him. "Here," she prompted. "It is yours."

"I do not want it."

"Don't be silly. The reticule is merely the package."

He crossed his arms over his chest. "I know that, Jane. I will not take your money. That is final."

She dropped the pink monstrosity onto the table with a plop. "Yes, you will. And furthermore, you shall repay me at a future date."

"Oh, shall I?"

"Double the sum."

"*Double?*"

She winced. "Very well. The total sum, along with ... fifty percent."

"That is highway robbery."

She folded her arms, mimicking his posture. "Then, what is a fair return, Colin Lacey, if you know so much?"

"Nothing. I am not taking your money."

Pushing back her chair, she stood. He did likewise. "Ask

Boswell to return the basket when you are finished with it," she said, donning her bonnet and walking to the door.

He grabbed the reticule and chased after her, holding it aloft before her nose. "Take it back. I do not want it, Jane."

She paused inside the open doorway, braced her hand on his shoulder, rose up on her toes, and kissed his cheek. Then, she patted his arm. "Fifty percent. I believe that is quite reasonable." And she left him standing there with the pink reticule and a look of consternation wrinkling his brow.

Smiling as she wended her way through the thick woods, she felt a glow in her chest that wasn't due to the weather. She sighed and looked up at the canopy of leaves, smelled the rich earth, loamy and ripe in the summer heat.

She might not be much of a duchess, but she was a good sister. A good friend.

About twenty feet before the edge of the woods, she heard a sliding rustle, like a foot slipping in the moist layer of leaves on the gently sloping ground. She turned, expecting to see Colin following behind her. But there was no one. Only trees and thick brambles.

She frowned, setting her spectacles higher on her nose. Squinting, she looked for an animal. Perhaps a bird had made the sound. She shook her head at her own imaginings.

Jane, you ninny, she thought as she resumed her path to the edge of the wood. *Soon, you'll be crediting the terrifying tales of the Ghost Spider, as well.*

"WHERE IS SHE, COLIN? IF YOU DO NOT TELL ME THE TRUTH, so help me God, you will pray you had."

Colin slammed his hand down on the table with a crack. "I told you, I do not know where she is. She left here some time ago. I assumed she would return to Blackmore Hall."

Harrison's heart was choking him, his insides twisting and pressing outward. She was gone. She'd been gone for hours.

When he had discovered the drawing room empty, he had searched her usual haunts—the libraries, the music room, her bedchamber. With each successive room, his urgency had increased. Beardsley and Mrs. Draper were of little help, but finally, he had thought to ask the bloody Frenchman with whom his wife got on "quite well." Resentfully, the cook had informed him of her destination.

His eyes fell to the basket, sitting on the floor in one corner of the small cottage. She had prepared a picnic for his brother, hauled the basket here to share with Colin. Alone. The knowledge was a burning coil inside him, winding and seizing his rational thoughts inside a vise. He knew he must contain it. She was gone. And he must find her. That was all that mattered.

"Which way did she head when she left here?"

Colin heaved a sigh and ran a hand through his hair. "The main path through the woods."

"And you did not accompany her?"

"You asked me not to leave the cottage. I did not request that she visit me, Harrison. She simply ... arrived."

The knowledge did nothing to ease his mind. If anything, it made the pain in his gut worse. His eyes fell to the table, where Colin's fists bracketed a peculiar pile of pink ribbons and feathers. "What is that?"

Colin straightened, his chin lifting. "I did not want it. I told her as much."

Harrison snatched it up. It was a pouch of some sort, a reticule. Inside, he found the answer to why she had come here in the first place. His voice grew colder, more deliberate. "This is nearly six hundred pounds."

"Yes. I am aware. She wants repayment at fifty percent. You will be doing me a favor to return it to her. As I said, I will not take her money, nor will I accept her outrageous terms. Fifty percent. Preposterous!"

Blood turning thick and chilled, heart pounding, Harrison shook his head and dropped the reticule. "The pistol I gave you. Bring it to me."

"Do you think I am stupid?"

"Colin," he gritted, giving his brother a deadly glare. "We must find her. Now."

Colin swallowed, his face growing ashen. "You believe she is in danger."

"She would not be gone this long. If someone discovered you were here, and he was watching for visitors ..."

It took his brother only a moment to retrieve the pistol, which he handed to Harrison. "Have a care. It is loaded," he warned, carrying a hunting rifle of his own.

Harrison nodded, feeling slightly sick as he took the gun in hand. He had not fired a pistol since the day he had shot Gregory Wyatt through the heart. The memory was less than pleasant. But if someone had taken Jane, had hurt her in any way, he would gladly put a bullet in him.

First, they searched the perimeter of the cottage, looking for signs of men who might have been lurking nearby. They found nothing—no bootprints, no disturbed foliage. Next, they moved down the path into the woods, retracing Jane's steps. He could clearly see the small indentations of her feet in the moist soil. Trailing behind, Colin whispered, "She came this far."

Harrison nodded and waved him forward, scanning the surrounding woods for motion. Moving slowly and deliberately, he stepped over a prominent root, his eyes constantly shifting from the path to the thick foliage on either side. His pounding heart demanded he quicken his pace; it wanted him to run, to fight, to do violence. His mind knew that would be the worst sort of recklessness. His mind won the battle by the barest margin, but with every second that went by, that margin grew thinner.

He motioned Colin to a halt. There, less than twenty feet before the path emerged at the edge of the wood, her footprints ended. His stomach rolled threateningly, his skin freezing until gooseflesh rose. Another set of prints—deeper, larger—intruded on the path, and then disappeared into the leaf-strewn undergrowth.

Someone had taken her. His wife. His Jane.

He was not a violent man by nature. Killing Gregory Wyatt had been accidental and one of the most horrifying moments of his life. But the part of him that Jane touched without even trying, the part he hid from everyone except her—that part wanted blood. The blood of the villainous whoreson whose bootprints consigned him to death.

THE SETTING SUN SLANTED THROUGH THE WINDOWS OF THE farmhouse, causing the dusty interior to glow a vivid gold. Everywhere Jane looked, there were brightly colored fabrics—yellow gingham framing the windows, apple-green florals on the aged sofa, strawberry-red dotted twill and white lace on the table coverings. She cast a surreptitious glance at the grimy weasel who had pressed a gun to her neck and forced her here. He was wiry and ugly, his face curiously flat, his eyes furtive and pale. He stood at the window, nudging aside the gingham with the end of his pistol. The golden light glinted off his eyes, turning them an eerie, pale green.

"Does your wife know what you have been doing?"

Without turning, he answered, "Haven't got a wife. Now, I told ye, shut your mouth."

"Oh, I was just admiring the many fine colors in this room."

He glanced over his shoulder to where she sat, her hands folded neatly in her lap. She had not moved from the chair since he had shoved her into it upon entering the house. "House belonged to my mother," he said.

"Where is she, your mother?"

Turning back to the window, he muttered, "Dead."

"Ah. So, this is your home. You were raised here."

He grunted. She took it as a yes.

"Then, you are familiar with the Duke of Blackmore."

"Bloody nob. I know 'im."

"You may be interested to learn he is my husband."

He cast her a dubious look. "Right."

"Truly. I am the Duchess of Blackmore."

Snorting dismissively, he shifted his gun from one hand to the other, using his right to wipe his mouth. Jane had noticed he had a tendency to spit when he spoke. "Ye don't look like no duchess to me."

It was strange to hear her own thoughts echoed back to her from the mouth of this foul creature. Strange and irritating. "Regardless, I am a duchess. And, as such, perhaps I can make you a better offer than the one you previously accepted."

"Offer?"

"Yes. Whatever you have been paid for your ... services, I shall double it."

"Ain't been paid for this bit, yet. Only the five quid to watch for the nob's brother. Londoner already knows. Men'll be here in three days. When they see what else I got, I'll get paid more."

Swallowing at the knowledge that Colin's hunters would arrive in only a few days, she continued with her attempts to distract her captor. "And what is it you suppose you have?"

"Lacey's ladybird. Saw ye when ye left the cottage. If the Londoner wants Lacey to go easy, he'll need someone like ye. Pay plenty fer it, too."

She frowned at the nasty ruffian. "I am no man's ladybird."

"Know what I saw. Lacey likes 'em plump, I reckon. Me, I'm not much for the fleshy ones."

"Hmmph. You are a rude man. What would your poor mother say about your appalling behavior?"

The man took several steps in her direction, his posture threatening. She shrank back into her chair. "Ye got a mouth what needs closing. Best shut it before I do it fer ye." He paced back to the window, his boots loud in the silence. "My mother's dead. Before that, she couldn't so much as leave her bed without me, moanin' and shoutin' all bloody day and night. Enough to drive a man mad. I told 'er. Said it a thousand times." His fist hit the windowsill with startling force, causing Jane to jerk in her seat. "Had to die," he muttered. "Had to."

Hearing him speak those words to himself, Jane felt as though she'd been standing on the surface of frozen water, slick yet solid beneath her feet, only to have the ice break from beneath her, plunging her body into the dark, frigid deep. Her fingers went numb; her heart slowed and floundered in an awkward rhythm; the light around her turned from gold to gray.

But she could not allow her horror to show. Could not allow it to stop her from thinking, from finding a way out. Harrison would come for her. She had little doubt of it. She might not be the duchess he wanted, but she was his wife. He would not take her disappearance lightly. But would he find her? And would he do so before …?

She shuddered. Best to devise a plan of escape in the event he did not.

Drawing a trembling breath, she glanced around the room. It was a small farmhouse, set far away from the village, from any other houses. From anyone who might hear her cries, or even the shot of a gun. It had taken them over an hour to get here, with the Weasel yanking her along by her arm, occasionally digging the gun into her ribcage.

Outside, it was a plain, timber-framed house, but inside, it was surprisingly cozy, cheerful. His mother must have had a love of fabrics, as they were everywhere. Perhaps she had been a seamstress. In the corner, Jane spotted a small bookshelf. It sparked an idea.

"M-might I retrieve a book from that case?"

He cast a mean look over his shoulder. "Will it keep ye quiet?"

She nodded. He waved his gun. "Make it quick."

Rising on unsteady legs, she paused to let the blood return to her feet before walking carefully to the back corner of the room. There, she selected the heaviest of the small assortment, a thick, leather-bound Bible. It must have been precious to his mother, as it was well used, but also well cared for and fairly expensive.

"Sit back down," he said flatly.

She turned to see him pointing the gun at her. Swallowing, she complied, sinking back into the chair and opening the book in a show of reading. Slowly, the light began to fade as night fell. The Weasel lit a lantern, so she was able to continue pretending to read, but the darkness outside appeared to make him more nervous. He now paced between the two front windows.

Back and forth. Back and forth.

As the moon rose higher, the echoes of his boots on the floorboards clashed with the songs of frogs and crickets, the light wind sighing through leafy branches. Over the pounding of her heart, she tried to take comfort in the familiar sounds. Tried to devise a plan that would help her escape this hideous man who had quite clearly hastened his mother's death, if not outright murdered her. He was only of middling height, and wiry rather than large, but she knew she could not possibly match his strength. She must, therefore, take him by surprise. Perhaps eventually, he would grow weary and relax his guard. His anxious pacing, however, had not slowed since sunset.

Suddenly, he stiffened, turning sideways along the wall flanking the window. His body now tensed like a filthy, nasty barn cat poised to pounce on a hapless rodent, he glanced back at Jane, his eyes narrowed and glittering. "It's the bloody duke," he hissed.

Oh, God. Harrison is here.

Simultaneously, a warming wash of relief flooded her body while a stone hardened in her chest. She watched in dawning horror as the Weasel sidled to the door, inched it open a crack, and aimed his pistol. The sounds of the night muted and slowed, the stone in her chest growing until her lungs strained at the intrusion, her limbs weighted by lead.

The click of the gun being cocked was cannon fire in her ears. It signaled her body to move.

To leap up.

To grasp the Bible in both her hands, the weight of it lifted by her fury.

To surge toward him.

Raise it over her head.

And bring it crashing down upon his with a mighty thud.

He did not go down. Instead, he covered his head, cursing her loudly. But she could scarcely hear over the screaming. Who was screaming?

"You bloody whoreson! You *dare* point a pistol at my husband, you wretched pile of dung! I shall kill you!"

She swung the book at him over and over, bludgeoning his head and his arms and his shoulders. On her last swing, she caught his wrist, sending the gun toppling to the floor. A loud crack rang through the air. Then came his wrenching yelp as he crouched over his injured leg. With a growl, he swiped out at her, his fist meeting her belly unexpectedly.

Her breath fled in a whoosh, the pain rocking her backwards into the edge of the table. Just then, the door flew open with a resounding crash.

And standing there with silver light behind him, filling the doorframe like a vengeful god, was Harrison. Her Harrison. Tonight, he was not Apollo. He was Hades. Dark and sinister and possessive of what he considered his.

He came to stand over the Weasel, calmly pressed the barrel of his pistol to the man's forehead, and fully cocked the gun with a click. That was when she knew. He meant to do it. He would kill him. His eyes—those beautiful eyes—were pure, blue fire.

"Harrison," she said softly, still catching her breath. She stumbled, reaching toward him. "Harrison, do not. Please."

She couldn't bear for him to live with killing someone in cold blood. Even though the Weasel richly deserved it. Even though she would like to pull the trigger herself. She approached her husband slowly, her hand gently stroking his upper arm. The fine tremors of the muscles there spoke of his control.

"He must die, Jane."

The quiet statement, spoken so calmly, sent chills running over her skin. "No."

"He must die for touching you. For taking you."

She shook her head, though he did not look at her. Instead, he stared unblinking into the eyes of the panting, sweating Weasel kneeling on the floor before him.

"Not by your hand, my love. Not by your hand." She laid a kiss on his arm, wedging herself against him, sharing her heat. "He is not worth the price."

Distantly, she heard hooves thundering the ground outside, men shouting to one another. Harrison's gun did not move, pressing against the Weasel's skin with bruising pressure, forcing the other man's head back on his neck. Wisely, the Weasel kept silent.

Colin appeared in the gaping doorway. Instantly, he took in the scene. "We are here now, brother," he said soothingly. "All is well."

Still, Harrison did not withdraw. Not an inch.

Colin looked to her. "Jane? Are you quite all right?"

Jane nodded and wrapped her arms tighter around Harrison's arm, rubbing her cheek on the fine weave of his coat.

Dunston entered, a long hunting rifle in his hands. "We've brought the magistrate, Harrison. Why don't you let us restrain this scaly wretch while you comfort your lovely wife?"

At last, reason seemed to penetrate. Harrison took a deep, shuddering breath, his hand easing the pressure of the barrel against the Weasel's skull. Slowly, reluctantly, he released the hammer and let his arm fall to his side. Colin and Dunston moved in to haul the Weasel up by his arms and slammed him into the chair Jane had vacated. Several strapping footmen entered, along with a heavily whiskered gentleman who was only slightly taller than Jane and twice as wide.

He bowed to Jane as he entered the now-crowded room. "Your grace. I am Francis White, the magistrate."

She gave him a nod. "Mr. White."

"A travesty, what's happened. I shall do whatever I can to set things right."

Mr. White had kindly eyes and a gentle mien. And though her head was spinning, she managed, "M-my thanks to you, Mr. White. I am certain you will."

He turned to eye the Weasel with a shrewd gaze. "What have we here, gentlemen? Oh, ho! Oswald Hodges." He tsked, waddled over to the ruffian, and bent forward with his hands braced on his knees. "I have been anticipating your return. Thought we would never suspect what happened to your poor mother, did you not? Well, best think again. Your friend Barker told us where you buried her. And you shall hang for it."

Clinging tighter to Harrison's arm, Jane closed her eyes and swallowed against a wave of dizziness. Handing his gun to a footman, her husband turned to stand between her and the others, his arms coming up and cinching tightly around her. Melting at his nearness, she sighed, laying her cheek against his chest. He wore no cravat. No waistcoat. Only a shirt beneath his riding coat. There was not a speck of starch to be found. Nothing to prevent her hearing his heartbeat, steady and strong. She burrowed her nose against him, feeling his hands exploring her back and her neck and the sides of her face.

"You were gone," he whispered, his warm breath stirring the fine wisps of hair at her temple.

"I knew you would come."

His mouth found hers in a sliding, feather-light kiss. "Do not ever be gone again." The command was airless, as if he had not meant to say it aloud.

She stroked his beloved face with her hand, feeling the bristles on his jaw. Her answer was to kiss his descending mouth.

A throat being cleared proved a distracting interruption. "Apologies, Harrison," said Dunston. "The magistrate would like your permission to employ a few of your footmen to haul Hodges to the gaol."

Harrison nodded. "Take whomever you require, Mr. White."

Two of the larger footmen gathered up the bleeding, pale Hodges, who was now tied hand and foot, and hauled him out into the front garden. The magistrate tipped his hat, assuring them he would report all progress directly to the duke, and then followed his prisoner outside.

Jane, noticing Colin leaning heavily on the table she had crashed into earlier, felt a spark of urgency rise again. "Colin," she said. His head came up. "They are coming for you."

He blinked, taking two drifting steps toward her. "When?"

"Three days. He said they will be here in three days."

"Then we shall be waiting." The cold, silky words came not from Colin, but from the man standing solidly at her back. Harrison.

"No," said Colin, shaking his head.

"We must send a message," Harrison insisted. "If he threatens my family, he shall pay a very dear price."

"These men are nothing to him," Colin replied. "Expendable. No. I must lure them away. As long as they are pursuing me, they will be no danger to you."

Jane felt Harrison's rejection of Colin's words as his muscles hardened to steel. "Like bloody hell," he snarled.

"Listen to me. He will never stop. I know that now. I cannot risk anyone else being harmed. You. Or Jane."

"You will not offer yourself as bait in this way."

Colin gave his brother a heartbreaking grin. "It is what you would do."

"Oh, Colin," she whispered.

"I shall give you the funds," said Harrison. "Twice the debt, so he cannot balk."

The sweet-faced boy who had become a weary, hunted man began to protest, but Harrison would have none of it. "That is the end, Colin. We will deal with the men who come here. And you will take repayment to the man who sent them."

After exchanging hard gazes for what felt like eternity to Jane, her husband's brother—now *her* brother, as well as her friend—conceded to Harrison's demand. "Very well," he said, holding out his hand.

Harrison glanced down at the offering. Then he did something she did not expect. Stepping out from behind her, he drew Colin into an embrace. "Be safe," he said, his voice cracking, his hand thumping Colin's back. "And come back to us."

Colin closed his eyes and held his brother in return. "I will."

Chapter Twenty-Four

*"Every man has his moments of foolishness.
Only a foolish woman believes otherwise."*

—THE DOWAGER MARCHIONESS OF WALLINGHAM to her son,
Charles, upon hearing a certain widow's rejection of his apology for
believing scandalous—and inaccurate—rumors.

TWO WEEKS AFTER COLIN LEFT BLACKMORE HALL FOR London, Jane's family arrived with no small amount of commotion. Lord and Lady Berne, Maureen, Genie, and Kate, all invaded her home with their jests and their squabbling and their many hugs. And, of course, Lady Wallingham, as well.

Truthfully, Jane had never needed them more.

"Jane, what is the matter? This is the fourth time you have pricked your finger with the needle. At this rate, your embroidery shall be solid red."

Jane glanced up at Maureen, popping her finger free of her mouth. "It's nothing, really."

"Oh, come now," said Mama. "We have all seen it, dearest."

"You have?"

Every one of the women gathered in the rose parlor gave her sympathetic looks. Even Genie nodded. "I would be out of sorts as well, were I playing hostess to those women."

"Lady Dunston is unpleasant, and I do not like how Lady Mary speaks to you, but I think Cornelius is charming. He is really quite clever, once you spend a bit of time with him," said Kate, her small, rounded chin rising.

Genie rolled her eyes. "He is a dog, you ninny."

"He is a menace," interjected Lady Wallingham. "A flea-ridden, clumsy creature with little useful purpose outside of defecating on perfectly good floors."

Kate took on a mutinous expression. "I think he is adorable."

"Kate," Mama said. "Come sit here and tell me which color to use next, won't you?"

Jane let their comforting chatter drift and flow around her, easing the melancholy that held her in its iron-gray grip. This aching sense of loss was not caused by playing hostess to Lady Mary or her unpleasant mother. It was not even due to Colin's departure on an admittedly dangerous mission.

It was him. Harrison. He was different. The Ice King had reemerged, replacing the man she loved as though he'd never been.

The night of her abduction, they had returned to Blackmore Hall, and he had slowly, deliberately stripped her of every piece of clothing. He had examined every inch of her skin, kissing and stroking and licking every bruise, every part of her, as if he wished to commit her to memory. Then, he had made love to her until she felt her very soul merge and soar with his.

By the next morning, everything had changed. She had

awakened alone. After bathing and dressing, she had entered the dining room for breakfast, seeing him sitting at the end of the table, so handsome he made her ache. He'd been conversing with Lady Mary, who sat to his right. Though his greeting to Jane was polite enough, his eyes had been shuttered, his manner formal. She had assumed it was because of their guests. Surely later, when they were alone, it would be different. He would come to her bedchamber, come inside her again, let her love him again. Be the man he had been only the night before.

But no. She had fallen asleep waiting for him. The next night, determined to reestablish their closeness, wanting to feel his arms around her again, she had entered his chamber—a masculine mirror image of hers—through the adjoining door. He had turned in surprise, his valet pausing in the midst of helping him remove his coat.

"Give us a moment, Fillmore," he had said.

A moment? she'd thought. *Not nearly enough time.*

But the valet had left, and she had approached her husband, who stiffened as though she held a sword to his belly. She'd stopped an arm's length away. "Harrison, I ... I thought you might like to join me. I have missed—"

He turned toward the mirror, fussing with his cravat. "I shall sleep here, as I am rather tired."

"We could sleep together, as we did before."

"No," he'd said flatly. "Not tonight."

Recoiling from the stark rejection, as well as the chill in his voice, she had swallowed. "What is the matter? Are you angry with me?"

Brows arching, he had turned to her briefly before carefully unraveling his cravat with crisp motions. "Not in the slightest."

"Then, I—I don't understand."

"We are married, Jane, not tied together with ropes. There is little need to cling to one another."

Stung, she had flinched. "I did not realize you perceived me as clinging—"

"We have guests now. You should turn your energies to making their stay pleasurable. As their hostess, you shall need your rest."

Not knowing what else to do, she had retreated to her chamber. Alone.

He still had not returned to her bed. He had neither kissed her nor spoken anything more than casual pleasantries to her in a fortnight. In fact, he treated her much like a guest, their interactions cordial but also clogged with starch—and that was when he bothered to interact with her at all. During the days, he spent long hours riding with Dunston or meeting with the magistrate to receive news of Hodges and the other men, who had been captured and returned to London.

For her part, she spent her days arranging entertainments for the hostile and ungrateful Lady Mary and her equally unpleasant mother. Cards and games and music, picnics and rides and walks over the lovely countryside—none of these seemed to satisfy the ladies, who instead often found their own amusements, separate from her. Thankful for the reprieve, she nevertheless felt her failure as a hostess keenly. A better duchess would know how to smooth the wrinkles in this particular bolt of social fabric.

It made her wonder if this was not the reason for Harrison's withdrawal. She had already gone over other possible causes in her mind: his concern over Colin, preoccupation with estate matters or hosting duties or magistrate meetings. None of it made sense. But if he was just beginning to fully realize her deficiencies, and how they could affect his standing with his friends and the rest of the *beau monde*, it might explain the sudden onset of winter in their marriage.

"Dearest, perhaps you should wait to do needlework until you are better able to concentrate on your task."

Jane glanced up at her mother's worried grimace, then back down at the droplets of blood that dotted her emerging rosebuds. Sighing, she tucked the needle into the linen kerchief and folded it neatly. "Yes. Later, perhaps," she said listlessly.

Footfalls in the corridor brought their heads around to the open doors. Lord Dunston and Papa entered, looking flushed and excited after their ride. "Lovely to see you, ladies," said Dunston, with his charming smile aimed at Maureen, who fluttered and blushed.

"My word, if this is not the finest summer we have seen in ages," said Papa, moving to sit beside Mama and leaning over to kiss her cheek, which she readily presented for him. "A far sight better than last year's. The crops still haven't recovered."

"Precisely why one should plan for such contingencies in advance."

The sound of her husband's voice jerked her head around, drove the air from her lungs. He was magnificent today, his riding jacket blue as night, his hair a golden crown, his jaw a line as clean and crisp as a blade's. How she longed for him, for the strength of his arms around her, for the break in his voice as he spoke her name. She missed him as she would miss her own heart, should it be taken from her body.

Presently, his eyes, blank and cold, met hers briefly before deliberately moving on. He advanced into the room, his hands clasped at the small of his back. "A disaster is best mitigated by preparation and discipline," he continued, sounding like the duke she remembered from before their wedding.

The voices around her grew fainter as the gentlemen postulated theories on proper agricultural management. She dropped her gaze to her lap, where red seeped from her finger, wicking into white linen.

"Blackmore lands are surely proof of your masterful governance, your grace," came the unwelcome voice of the newly arrived Lady Mary, followed by the tapping presence of clumsy, brown Cornelius. The pup loped into the room, ears flopping, tongue lolling, droopy eyes shining with excitement.

He headed directly for Lady Wallingham, much to the dowager's dismay. Jane watched the byplay, as it was preferable to watching Mary, Queen of Sweets, flatter and flirt with her husband.

The dragon's initial strategy was to ignore the pup, sniffing disdainfully at his antics as he rolled over onto his back, presenting his round belly for her inspection and possible affection. Cornelius was not easily dissuaded, however, and began snuffling the floor around Lady Wallingham's amethyst skirt, one of his ears comically draped inside-out over his head.

"You are a ridiculous creature," she declared. The pup sat and looked up at her longingly. Her sharp green eyes met the dog's, her white brows drawn low in disapproval. "Your ears are too large. Your legs are too short. You are nothing but loose wrinkles and fleas."

The insults did not seem to faze the dog, who raised his snout and howled mournfully. "Oh, do be quiet, you wretched creature," the dowager ordered. He gave another howl, and Lady Wallingham, quite at her limit of patience, released a hiss of irritation, pushed herself from her chair, and left the room in a huff. Initially confused, Cornelius soon followed, his nose hard at work tracking the dragon's trail.

"Leave off, you brown, wrinkled pest. My skirts are neither a bone nor a privy. If you treat them as such, I shall not be responsible for ..." The old woman's cantankerous voice faded as she made her way down the corridor with Cornelius in pursuit.

Almost against her will, Jane was drawn back to Harrison. He was smiling faintly at something Mary was saying. Suddenly, his gaze collided with hers, stopping her breath. Her heart twisted painfully, an ache settling low in her belly. His lips flattened, nostrils flaring slightly. Then, with the precision of a rapier cut, he turned away from Jane and back to the woman at his side.

The woman he should have married.

All at once, Jane felt the weight of her grief as a gaping wound in her chest. She could not be the wife he needed. The wife he deserved. And, now, he had obviously realized it.

Blinking rapidly, she tried to stop the sobs that clawed to emerge.

But they were coming. And she must go.

"... AND I TOLD MISS SPENCER THAT HER GOWN WAS LOVELY, but she did not believe me! Perhaps next time she asks me to visit the shops with her, I shall simply cry off."

Lady Mary's voice resembled the bothersome whine of a midge in his ear. He did not care a whit what she said. Jane was gone. His wife had turned white, her lips losing all color, then had covered her mouth and left the room with some haste. He wanted to howl and follow after her like that daft pup.

"Harrison."

He did not know how much longer he could bear being away from her.

"Are you listening to me?"

He felt sick with longing. His stomach knotted, his chest torn by a relentless, grinding pain. Truly, it was like some exotic illness. One he must recover from, else be afflicted forever.

"Harrison—"

"Pardon me, Lady Mary. I must speak with Dunston."

Ignoring her offended gape, he stood and joined Dunston and Lord Berne where they chatted near the entrance. He nodded at their greeting, but his eyes were pulled to the corridor, his neck craning to glimpse where she had gone.

"I say, son, that is one fine piece of horseflesh in your stable. Little wonder Wallingham was tempted into parting with one of Remington's get." Lord Berne clapped Harrison's shoulder, snapping his attention back to the older man. When he met those hazel eyes, he saw something he did not like. Knowledge. And compassion.

"Ulysses is as fast as any Ascot champion, I'll wager," added Dunston. "Incomprehensible why you never set him to the turf."

Lord Berne continued to hold his gaze, his hand planted firmly on his shoulder. "Some horses, you prefer to keep close at hand, eh, son? All yours. No one else's."

Harrison struggled to control his breathing. Berne could not possibly understand. No one could. He wanted to shake off that fatherly hand and shove him away. He wanted to find Jane, to take her, to make her his again.

"That is irrational," he said, glad that his voice was steady. "Sentimentality should have no part in such decisions."

Lord Berne smiled, his eyes taking on a familiar twinkle. Jane often wore the same expression when she was teasing him about having too much starch. "Nonsense. Sentiment is merely a reflection of our truest devotion. We may attempt to control it, to civilize it. Perhaps to disguise it, even to ourselves. But it is not so tame a creature."

"Er—are we still discussing Ulysses?" Dunston queried. "I fear I have lost a thread somewhere."

Lord Berne gave Harrison a wink and slid his hand from his shoulder. "Now, then. I must lie down for a while. All this riding has exhausted me. Perhaps I will see if Lady Berne needs a rest, as well."

As his father-in-law ambled over to where Lady Berne sat working her needle and chatting with her daughters, Dunston looked at Harrison askance. "What was that all about?"

"Nothing."

"It seemed like something."

His teeth ground together until his jaw ached. "It is not important."

"Hmm. The duchess has been looking a bit pale of late."

He did not reply. She had been, he knew. Her face was also thinner. He did not like it.

"Perhaps you should find her and ask if she needs a lie-down, as well."

"Dunston," he growled.

"Merely a suggestion."

Lord and Lady Berne paused as they made their way to the door. Lady Berne reached for Harrison's hands, grasping them tightly in hers. "Such a dear boy," she said fondly.

Harrison did not know how to respond. She had been doing these things since her arrival yesterday, hugging him, kissing his cheek, telling him how proud his mother would have been. Was he supposed to thank her? The gestures were both odd and disconcerting to him. Even his own mother had rarely behaved so ... maternally.

He finally settled on, "It is good you are here, Lady Berne."

She grinned up at him, her eyes much like Jane's, dark and rich and alive. "I agree." With that cryptic answer, she squeezed one last time, and accompanied her husband into the corridor.

He did not see Jane again until hours later, at dinner. She entered the dining room—late, of course—wearing an exquisite gown of emerald-green silk. The bodice hugged her breasts lovingly, scooping low to reveal her milky skin. The sleeves came to her elbows, and she wore a loosely woven shawl over her arms.

Her gown was perfect. But Jane was quite obviously miserable. Her eyes, red-rimmed and dull, refused to meet his. She was seated at the head of the table, passing near him so that he could detect a faint whiff of apples.

As the dinner proceeded, he carried on polite conversation with Lady Wallingham, who opined that apricots were "the poor man's peach." But he listened with only half an ear. His eyes were riveted on his wife.

Jane was not eating. She pushed the food around her plate,

occasionally nodding at something Dunston said, but mainly, she kept her eyes down and pretended to eat. He had thought by inviting her family to visit, that she would improve. But, if anything, she appeared worse than before.

"Dogs are useless animals," said Lady Wallingham, continuing her litany of unsolicited opinions. "Anyone with the slightest degree of sense should realize they consume far more than they offer in recompense. And yet, somehow, these wily creatures have convinced us—well, not *all* of us, but those with lesser minds and too much sentimentality—that they are of benefit. Utter rubbish."

Lady Mary, who sat several seats away, but who had overheard Lady Wallingham's canine soliloquy, took offense. "Forgive me, Lady Wallingham, but I beg to disagree."

The dowager raised her chin and slowly rotated her head until her imperious glare landed on its chosen target. "Do you?"

Harrison frowned. The two words did not bode well for Lady Mary.

"Y-yes. Cornelius is descended from a line of superior scent hounds. When he is grown, he will be capable of tracking a stag over as much as one hundred miles."

"And how many stags must he track before he is worth the damage you have incurred to your *skirts* and your *slippers* and your *furniture* and your *floors?*"

Lady Mary shrank back in her chair. "Well," she said. "There is a bit more to it than that. He is also a splendid companion."

Lady Wallingham harrumphed. "Any *real* companion who similarly defiled my slippers as your vile animal did this afternoon would find himself promptly hauled off to Newgate."

In that precise moment, the "vile animal" appeared, his paws tapping and sliding on the wood floors, then thumping on the carpet.

"Oh, dear," said Lady Mary, noticing her dog making a beeline for Lady Wallingham. "Cornelius, come here, darling. Come, Cornelius!"

Dunston, noting the commotion, chided, "Mary, I told you if I gave you the pup, you must keep him confined."

Rising from her chair to rush toward the scampering dog, Mary said, "I did confine him. He was in my chamber. One of the servants must have opened the door. Cornelius, no!"

The dog gleefully snuffled his way to Lady Wallingham's feet, sitting and leaning worshipfully against the dowager's leg. Then, he let out a howl of triumph, having apparently achieved a worthwhile goal.

"You see?" Lady Wallingham sniffed. "Useless. He does not even know his own name."

Lady Mary scooped him up. "That's because he is still a pup. Yes, you are just a babe, aren't you, Cornelius?"

The dowager waved her hand dismissively. "Take him away. I have no desire for fleas in my soup."

The girl looked like she wished to say more, but thought better of it, and carried her dog out of the room.

"Now then," said Lady Wallingham. "Where was I? Oh, yes. Lady Berne simply adores cats. But Lord Berne sneezes every time they come near. Thank God for small mercies. If any creature could be of less value than a dog, it is a cat."

Harrison let the woman's relentless pontificating drift past him, preferring to watch Jane across the length of the table. Dunston leaned toward her and made a grinning comment. She returned his smile with a shy one of her own, her face gaining some much-needed color.

He should be happy. He should want her to smile and chuckle at something his friend said, some witticism or droll remark.

But he was not. It ate at his stomach, burned like coals, slow and deep. *He* wanted to be the one who made those dimples appear, the one who made her blush. The one who heard that dusky laugh and felt the answering tug in his groin.

God help Dunston if he so much as glanced below her chin.

"If you wish to murder your friend, there are more effective methods," came the arch comment from Lady Wallingham. "I have heard you are skilled with a dueling pistol, for example." The dowager calmly slid a forkful of veal into her mouth.

Harrison lowered his brows. "I am not a violent man."

She swallowed then took a sip of wine. "Hmmph. That is precisely what your father used to say. And it was no more true for him than it is for you."

"I beg your pardon?"

"You should. I do not countenance lies."

"What do you know of my father?"

"I know he nearly beat a man to death over your mother. What do *you* know of your father?"

Harrison carefully set his wineglass back on the table. It had been halfway to his mouth when she had begun talking about the seventh Duke of Blackmore. His father. The coldest man he had ever known. "I do not believe you."

"And yet, it is true. Richard Lacey, Lord Branstoke at the time, of course, was mad for Lady Judith. Everyone knew. She was a third daughter of some upstart Whig with more wealth than sense. Personally, I never understood the attraction. But that is neither here nor there. He thought the sun rose in her eyes or some such nonsense."

He had never heard this. Any of it. To the best of his knowledge, his father had chosen his mother the same way he did everything else: with cold calculation. Judith Clyde had been passably pretty, graceful, and above all, proper. She had been the most appropriate match for his father, chosen because of her family's wealth and her carefully composed demeanor. The idea that his father had chosen her based on infatuation, much less the kind of madness Lady Wallingham spoke of, was simply ludicrous.

"Perhaps you have him confused with someone else. Details can become difficult to recall after so many years."

"I am not daft, nor am I senile, boy. The year you entered this misbegotten world, I was already sending my son to Eton. I have seen more than you can imagine."

Harrison nodded his acknowledgement of her sharp rebuke. "My apologies."

She sniffed her disdain then continued. "He was controlled, even then—much like you. But there were stories. I had my sources. Not as superb then as today, but sound nonetheless. They said her father wanted the match, but she resisted. She was in love with some baron's penniless second son. Appallingly short-sighted of her, but youth is often blind to these things.

"Her father forced her to agree to the marriage. Richard believed her willing—until the day he spied her and the second son together, meeting in secret on the road between her father's house and the baron's. They had a terrible row, or so I heard. He threatened to call off the engagement, and she begged him to do so, as it would free her to wed her feckless swain."

Harrison shook his head in disbelief, glancing down at his plate. It could not be. These people she described, they were strangers. Not his parents. His eyes returned to Jane, who was still talking with an attentive Dunston. Something twisted in his belly.

"When he discovered that she desired her freedom more than his wealth and title, your father did what any lovesick fool would do: He agreed. But, he made his offer conditional, for a man crying off a betrothal does great damage to his honor. He demanded that she allow a proper interval for him to win her affection. The swain protested, but it did not matter. She believed in his sincerity.

"Of course, he had no intention of allowing the object of his obsession to escape. But she did not suspect a thing, the poor, dim chit. And so, with time, his attentions, and lavish gifts, she was persuaded to allow the marriage to proceed.

Unfortunately, her swain was not so easily moved. He approached her at her engagement ball, begged her to run away to Gretna with him." Lady Wallingham snorted. "Preposterous. She had a future duke paying homage to her like some pagan goddess. Even the dimmest flame on the candelabra could see where her future lay."

He could scarcely credit it. His father, so deeply infatuated that he had manipulated an unwilling bride into letting him court her. His mother, in love with another man, then seduced by his father into maintaining their engagement. "What happened?"

Lady Wallingham arched a single white brow. "Can you not guess? Your father came upon them just as the swain attempted to kiss her. He lost his head, thinking she intended to leave him. He beat that poor boy with his fists until little remained but porridge. It took three men to pull him off."

Harrison pushed his plate away, feeling sickness wash over him in a wave.

"They married, naturally. And the beating was buried by your grandfather. But I remember everything. Your mother grew increasingly placid over the years, likely for fear of sparking a new conflagration. And your father grew increasingly cold. But you knew that part well, did you not?"

The old woman sipped her wine casually, apparently unaware of the cannon she had fired into the center of his chest.

For as long has he had known his father, the man had been as unfeeling as a block of stone. The seventh duke had behaved with icy politeness toward everyone, including his wife. With his children, he had been rigid and forbidding, insisting on a standard of discipline that did not leave room for laughter or playfulness or affection.

All his life, Harrison had comforted himself with one thing—that deep inside, he was nothing like his father. His father, he'd thought, had ice running clear to the bone.

Harrison, on the other hand, felt too much. He always had.

The sound of his baby sister sobbing for her mother had torn his heart out, while his father had stood over her bed with flat, steely eyes and refused to allow her to be comforted until she had stopped crying.

The sight of Colin, paralyzed and trembling before their grim-faced father, tears streaming down his babyish cheeks, apologizing over and over for bringing a fish into the house. His first fish, which he had caught while trailing after Harrison, as he was wont to do. Harrison had longed to hurt his father that day, had curled his young hands into fists, ready to teach the duke what it meant to be humiliated and scorned.

But he hadn't. Instead, he had done what his father had taught him so well: He had controlled himself and his unruly emotions. He had delayed taking action until later, when he secretly crept into Victoria's nursery long after everyone else had gone to sleep and cradled her in his arms, murmuring his love for her in her tiny ear. When he was not away at school, each day he had awakened before dawn, roused a sleepy Colin, and taken him to the river, out of sight of the house, where he had patiently shown the boy everything he knew of angling.

All along, he had told himself that he could never be like his father. Because, even as he had worked to control his emotions, to carry himself in a way that would bring honor to his family's legacy, his true nature had lived inside him, the riotous tempest of love and hate and need and ferocity battering his will to keep it contained.

That was what had reached out for Jane that day in the old library. That was what had pressed the barrel of a gun into the skull of another human being. That was what had come within a hair's breadth of blowing a hole in the man who had taken what belonged to him.

That was what had so terrified him that he had known he must distance himself from her before his true nature caused him to do something he could never take back.

That was what he had inherited, as it turned out, from a father who was far more like him than he had ever suspected.

Chapter Twenty-Five

*"He refuses to give me what I want—what I deserve.
Well, we shall see about that."*

—THE DOWAGER MARCHIONESS OF WALLINGHAM to her new
companion, Humphrey, on the topic of her son, Charles, and his
failure to provide her with even one grandchild.

ENORMOUS, DARKLY LASHED, BLUE-GREEN EYES BLINKED UP AT Jane in wonder. A tiny arm stretched out toward her spectacles, poorly controlled spinning motions threatening to knock them askew as she laid a kiss on Gregory Wyatt's precious forehead. His scent was angelic—mild and sweet—unlike anything she had smelled since Kate was a babe.

Jane sighed, cuddling the soft, wriggling infant closer. "He is ever so handsome, Victoria."

Stroking a hand over her son's abundant black hair,

Victoria beamed a smile and nodded. "I did not think it was possible for anyone to be more beautiful than Lucien, but Gregory has persuaded me otherwise."

"Ah, but his mama surpasses us both," said the tall, impossibly handsome man entering the rose parlor. With raven-black hair, dark, flashing eyes, and the face of a fallen angel, Lucien Wyatt, Viscount Atherbourne, was quite the most breathtaking male Jane had ever seen. Even Lady Wallingham had once declared herself fortunate to be a generation removed from the dashing lord, or she almost certainly would have ended in scandal, just as Victoria had done.

Moving with athletic grace, Lucien first shot his wife a devastating half-smile, then bent to give her a kiss that lingered long enough to cause Jane's blush. A bit embarrassed by their intimacy, Jane focused on the babe she held in her arms, brushing his tiny, perfect fingers until they clasped and clung around her thumb.

"Please forgive us, Jane," said Lucien, his arm encircling his wife's shoulders as he sat next to her. "It has been nearly an hour since I saw her last."

Jane grinned, as she always did at seeing her two friends wallowing in their own bliss. Even as a part of her grieved her own emptiness, she would not permit her melancholy to spoil her friends' visit. "Entirely understandable," she murmured.

"Where is everyone?" asked Victoria.

"The gentlemen and most of the ladies have gone riding. Lady Wallingham and Lady Dunston had a disagreement over composers, and now they are both lying down. Apparently, debating the merits of Bach and Mozart is rather fatiguing."

Lucien raised a brow. "Incidentally, who won the argument?"

"Lady Wallingham, I believe. Doesn't she always?"

Victoria laughed at her wry response. "Oh, Jane. How I have missed you."

Suddenly, Jane felt her lower lip tremble threateningly. She could not look at her friend. Her tears were choking her. "And

I you," she rasped, focusing with all her might on Gregory's listing eyelids.

Quiet settled in, the silence growing long in Jane's ears. Finally, Victoria said, "It looks as if your son is ready for a nap of his own, Lucien. Would you mind taking him up to the nursery? Roseanna is there now, preparing his cradle. I believe Jane and I shall take a walk."

"Of course, love." He stood and gathered up his son from Jane's arms. The boy fussed a bit at first, but settled almost immediately upon recognizing his father. Lucien bent forward and kissed the babe with reverent tenderness. Just before he left the room, he said over his shoulder, "Don't wander too far, ladies. It looks like a storm is headed our way."

Victoria turned to Jane as the door closed. "Come, dearest. Let us ramble about a bit before the rain comes."

After gathering their bonnets, Jane and Victoria made their way through the south garden, down the long slope to the fish pond, which was more like a goodly sized lake. The breeze rippling the water's surface was laden with the moist scent of cut grass and warm earth, the air heavy and slow to stir in the midsummer heat. But Jane could see the deep, iron clouds from across the valley, just beyond the distant wood. They rose like a great fist into the sky above the trees.

"When Harrison wrote with his invitation, my heart was gladdened," Victoria began, looping her arm through Jane's. "Since your wedding, I fear I have driven Lucien mad with my fretting. Now, I can see for myself how you are faring, rather than bending Lucien's ear about it. He shall be most relieved."

Jane's smile was half-hearted, her gaze turning forward to the path before them. "I am fine."

She could feel Victoria's eyes on her cheek. "No, dearest. You are not."

Slowing to a stop, Jane suddenly gasped once, twice, trying to stem the swell of tears she could feel coming. The humiliating, blasted tears. Her third gasp came out as a sob.

And she crumbled to pieces. Standing right there beside the fish pond, her best friend's arms coming around her shoulders, her body curled into itself, wrenching with grief.

Victoria rocked her gently back and forth, whispering incoherently, stroking her back. "Please," she said gently. "Tell me what's happened. Let me help."

It took Jane several minutes to compose herself enough to speak. Slowly, she lifted her head from Victoria's shoulder and walked a few feet away, toward the edge of the water. She removed her spectacles, wiping them with her skirt, and pulled a handkerchief from her sleeve to mop her eyes before plopping the metal rims back onto her nose.

"I was right," Jane said, her voice hoarse and ragged, her face hot.

"About?"

"He needed a different sort of duchess. Someone more like you. Or Lady Mary."

When she finally spoke, Victoria's voice was hesitant. "Did he say that to you?"

"He says it every time he looks at me. Or, rather, doesn't look at me."

"I don't understand."

Jane turned back to face Victoria, crossing her arms over her waist, suddenly feeling hollow and cold. "He is too well mannered to say it aloud. But it is the only thing that explains how he behaves toward me."

"How is that?"

"Like a stranger. A very polite stranger."

Victoria's soft mouth tightened, her eyes narrowing. "Where is he?"

"Do not be angry with him, Victoria."

"I simply wish to speak with my brother. And perhaps throw something heavy at his head."

Jane swallowed. "He is not wrong. I am hopelessly inept."

Victoria scoffed. "Rubbish. You are more intelligent than

ten of Lady Mary."

"She would make a far superior hostess."

"What makes you say so?"

"I attempted to plan the meals for Lord Dunston's visit. Harrison had already done so without consulting me. You do not do that unless you have little faith in someone's capabilities."

Victoria's blue-green eyes flashed, but she turned her head to the side before Jane could read her expression.

"Secondly," Jane continued, "I have planned many amusements for Lady Mary and Lady Dunston, and they have refused most of them. I have failed miserably."

"What sorts of amusements?"

"Oh, picnics by the pond, rides to the village to browse the shops, that sort of thing. I even hired a woman who sings quite beautifully in the church to come and perform for a night of music, but they will have none of it."

Jane had never seen Victoria's jaw clench in quite that fashion. It reminded her of Harrison.

"And what has my brother been doing all this time?"

Jane blinked. "He is away from the house most of each day. Riding with Lord Dunston and Papa. Hunting a bit. Showing them his new breed of sheep. I believe he acquired it from—"

"Jane."

"Yes?"

"My brother is a dashed fool."

Jane had nothing to say to that. Harrison was not a fool. But it would do no good to contradict Victoria in her present state.

"And you are not a poor hostess. However, Lady Mary and her mother are *exceedingly* poor guests. How many of your planned amusements have your family taken part in so far?"

"Four."

"And did they appear to enjoy themselves?"

That made Jane smile. "Oh, yes. Maureen loved the shop with all the little timepieces. And Genie went mad for a bonnet she found with rosettes of bright-red ribbon. Kate performed beautifully on the pianoforte during the musicale. And, naturally, Mama and Papa adored the picnic luncheon. You should have seen them, feeding bits of Monsieur Renaud's apricot tart to one another. Normally, those sorts of gestures between my parents make me slightly ill, but it was rather sweet."

Victoria crossed her arms and gave Jane a look of triumph. "You see?"

Jane shook her head. "See what?"

"You are a splendid hostess. Splendid! You have anticipated the needs and desires of your guests, and offered ample choices to amuse and delight them without undue pressure to partake."

Frowning, Jane replied, "Well, I did have three seasons as a guest, myself. I simply did what I thought anyone would appreciate."

"Precisely."

"But I am dreadful when it comes to conversing."

Victoria sighed in exasperation. "Jane, has Lady Wallingham declared you a disaster?"

It took her half a minute to answer, as she had to filter through the dragon's many lofty opinions and unsubtle criticisms from the past few days. Her eyes flew wide. "No."

"And would she have, if you were?"

"Unquestionably."

"There you have it."

It was a revelation. One Jane had not even considered. "But, if I am not a miserable failure, then why has he become so distant?" It was bewildering. They had been so close. So close.

"I do not know, dearest. Harrison is ... he is complicated. Do you remember our father?"

She nodded then corrected herself. "Well, not really. I just remember being quite intimidated by him."

Victoria's smile was wry and sad. "Yes. He was intimidating. And very, very cold. Harrison took the brunt of it. He protected us, Colin and me. Loved us in a way our father never did. In truth, Harrison was more a father to us than a brother. He takes his responsibilities quite seriously. You might even say gravely."

Jane recalled Harrison's face when he had described being forced to burn all his favorite books, simply because they allowed his imagination to roam free, which was unacceptable in the future Duke of Blackmore. But he had kept one, buried it like a treasure.

And dug it up only after his father had been buried instead.

She drew in a shuddering breath as a heavy drop of rain splattered on her arm. Her nose flared as she smelled the rain coming.

Victoria's arm came around Jane's shoulders. "I wish I could tell you why he is treating you this way. From your letters, I had thought perhaps you were developing some affection for one another."

Jane smiled and covered her friend's hand where it lay on her shoulder. "Affection? No. Nothing so easy as that." She chuckled, hearing thunder boom in the distance. The storm was closer now, the raindrops more regular. "I am in love with him, Victoria. I love him so much, I could die for the longing." She squeezed her eyes closed and felt Victoria's head lean against hers.

"Oh, Jane," she whispered.

The clouds began to open and pour forth their deluge. Within seconds, the warm, fat drops dripped from the edge of her bonnet and began soaking her sleeves and bodice. But they continued to stand together, Jane and Victoria, staring out at the water.

"He does not love me," she murmured. It was the first time she had spoken it aloud, an agony so deep, she could not alleviate it with tears. "I must live with that."

"You cannot possibly know that for certain. Has he said as much?"

"No. But ever since Lord Dunston and his family arrived, Harrison has treated me differently. First came his doubts about my competence. Then, for the past few weeks, he has been so cold."

Victoria slid around to face Jane, gripping her hands and shaking them. "Then we shall take on each of those problems, one at a time. First, you will demonstrate beyond all doubt that you are more than capable of being his hostess. Then, we shall rid ourselves of Dunston and Mary and their mother—and anyone else who clutters this house and gives him an excuse for his avoidance. Then, you shall work to discover his true feelings for you."

Victoria's grand vision was beginning to make her nervous. "And if it turns out that he has no feelings for me? Or that what he feels most is regret for our marriage, but he is too honorable to cast me aside?"

Her best friend's chin went up, a drop of rain plunking from her brim onto her small, refined nose. "If that is true—and I do not believe it to be so—but if it is, you will come and stay with me at Thornbridge for a while. Until your heart has healed enough to return."

That, Jane knew, might take an eternity. But she did not say so. It was a most generous offer. She nodded her acceptance.

Victoria looked to the sky as another peal of thunder rang out, this time louder. "Perhaps we should return before we are washed away." She looped her arm through Jane's, and they shared small grins as they started back up the path. "We have plans to settle—plans to make Blackmore yours again."

The cry of an infant ringing down the corridor of the upper floor caught Harrison's ear as he headed to his bedchamber to change out of his wet clothes. *What the devil?*

His question was answered by the man exiting one of the guest chambers five doors away. "Atherbourne," he said. "When did you arrive?"

Lucien Wyatt strode toward him, cradling a squirming, squalling bundle. He wore a harried expression. "About two hours ago. Victoria went for a stroll with Jane, and I'm afraid Gregory is a bit put out with missing his luncheon."

Harrison's eyes dropped to the babe's red, angry face. Even furious, his nephew was more handsome than he had been two months ago, his cheeks fuller, his hair thicker.

Atherbourne held his son out slightly toward Harrison. "Like to give it a go?" he said sardonically.

He snorted. "No. I shall leave that to you."

"Well, I suppose you'll have one of your own soon enough."

He felt his stomach drop, his jaw going slack. His heart stopped, then twisted painfully, then started up again with a hard, grinding thump. "Is Jane ...?"

The viscount with the bloody warped sense of humor burst out laughing upon seeing Harrison's expression. "No. At least, not that I know of. But if I were you, Blackmore, I would practice my response in the mirror a bit before that time comes. Women in a delicate condition do not like to be disappointed."

The man's dark eyes darted over Harrison's shoulder, lighting up with a feverish glint. He turned around to see his sister coming toward them. She was sodden from head to toe.

Victoria paused only long enough to greet Harrison and kiss his cheek, then rushed forward to take Gregory from her husband's arms. "What is it, little one? Are you hungry? Mama is here. Not to worry."

He noticed Atherbourne's eyes clung to Victoria the same

way her gown was clinging to her form, his hand dropping possessively to her waist. Without another word to Harrison, the couple disappeared into their chamber.

Turning back to his original destination, Harrison was once again stopped in his tracks. Jane was there, coming toward him.

She was a lush, rounded Venus. And she was all but naked.

Her gown, a lilac-hued, layered muslin dress with a bit of white embroidery at the bodice, was soaked clear through, hugging every curve and mound and hollow. Her nipples were hard, prominent points thrusting out against the fabric of her bodice. Like they wanted his mouth to warm them.

Her head was down, her attention on a small notebook in which she was intently writing with a pencil. If she was not careful, she would collide with him. Her full, generous breasts would press against him. Those hard, ripe nipples would brush his chest. He would have to wrap his arms around her, perhaps grasp her hips to steady her. Then, when she finally looked up and saw who held her, her mouth would open, her lips softening, trembling for his.

But none of that happened. Instead, her eyes seemed to catch a glimpse of him, and she stumbled to a halt, still several feet away. "Har—Harrison."

Oh, God, he had missed her voice, with that little hitch when she said his name.

"You were caught in the rain as well, I see." She gestured to her chamber door, just past his shoulder. "I was going to change my dress." Her lips quirked, and she glanced down at her gown. His eyes followed helplessly. "This one did not fare well at all when the storm loosed upon us."

Her breasts began to move up and down at an increased rate. A tiny droplet of water rolled teasingly across her skin, from the little indentation at the base of her throat, down to the valley between her beautiful, succulent breasts. He pictured his fingers following the same path. Then, his tongue.

Dear God, he was on fire for her, his ballocks aching, his cock full to bursting after only seconds.

This was wrong. An obsession. He must stop. It was too dangerous.

His muscles clenching to tear his gaze away, he stepped back, giving her ample room to ease past him and enter her chamber. But instead of using the distance he had given her, she inched closer to him, her hand coming up and stretching out toward him like a leaf seeking the sun. He could not allow her to touch him. If she did, he would break.

He backed away, his movements stiff, his jaw hardening. Not knowing what else to do, he bowed formally, saying, "I shall see you at dinner."

Her head gave a small jerk; her eyes, so soft and dark, sheened with tears; her lips turned down at the corners and trembled. His response had wounded her. He could see it happening, but could not reverse the damage. Unable to bear it, he reached for her, but she didn't see. She turned her back and fled into her chamber, closing the door with a soft click.

The force that tethered him to her carried him forward, his hand settling on the white paneled wood. He stopped himself from following, but he could not move away from her door. His forehead met the cool surface, the torment of longing and sorrow and regret devouring him until he wanted to tear his entire house to pieces.

"Jane," he whispered, the word almost a prayer.

My Jane. My love.

Chapter Twenty-Six

"All this gazing across ballrooms with longing in their eyes. Bah! I tell you, Humphrey, the only thing less enjoyable than witnessing fools mooning over one another is partaking of the intolerable refreshments."

—THE DOWAGER MARCHIONESS OF WALLINGHAM to her new companion, Humphrey, upon receiving an invitation to Lady Reedham's ball.

"MMM. MORE ORANGE, I BELIEVE."

Monsieur Renaud arched a brow at Jane's conclusion and shouted to a mousy maid, "More oranges!" The girl scurried off to the orangery to gather additional fruit.

Jane took another sip of the punch and nodded. "Yes. The spices are right. A bit more citrus, and it should be perfect."

The cook grunted and returned to kneading his dough.

She set aside her cup as an upstairs maid approached with the cloths for the tables, curtsying and holding them up for her inspection. They were gold-dyed linen with white spangles and embroidered wheat sheaves, which would cause them to shimmer and glow in the light from the torches. "Lovely, Martha. Please inform Beardsley and Mrs. Draper that the tables must be moved onto the south terrace within the hour."

"Yes, your grace."

Opening her notebook, Jane scratched off table linens and punch recipe, eyeing the remaining items on her list. When she glanced up, she saw her mother bustling into the kitchen.

"You should be upstairs changing your gown, dearest. Why do you not let me take over?"

Jane smiled and shook her head. "I have it all perfectly in hand, Mama. Not to worry."

Her mother clicked her tongue dismissively. "Jane, the details involved in hosting a summer ball of this size can be overwhelming even to an experienced—"

"Mama," Jane said with unusual firmness. She looked directly into her mother's startled eyes. "Thank you for your offer. But I have everything well in hand. This evening, you are a guest." She placed a good deal of emphasis on the last word before softening her tone. "I want you to simply relax and enjoy."

Mama's eyebrows arched, her eyes wide and round. Then, much to Jane's dismay, they glazed with moisture, and her mother's chin began to tremble.

"Oh, Mama, I did not mean ..."

Her mother's arms flew out wide, and the next thing Jane knew, she was being crushed into a maternal embrace, knocking her spectacles off kilter. "I have waited for this day," Mama cried against Jane's shoulder. "For so long, dearest."

"This day?"

She pulled back and sniffed, brushing the tears from

beneath her eyes. "The day you become the woman I have always known you could be."

Jane righted her spectacles and half-smiled, still a bit befuddled.

Her mother gave her a watery, fond smile in return, and another quick hug. "Lady Wallingham doubted me, but I told her that, in time, you would learn to take command of your rightful role—and your kitchen, of course. It has happened sooner than even I had anticipated."

"I am happy you are happy, Mama."

"I am more than happy, dearest. I am proud." She beamed at Jane, patting her shoulders before spinning on her heel and bouncing toward the entrance. After only two steps, however, she turned back to say thoughtfully, "Still, you should not delay too much longer before going upstairs. You don't want to be late to your own ball."

Jane just sighed. "Yes, Mama."

On the way to following her mother's advice, she stopped in the music room to consult with the musicians, then in the south drawing room—more of a ballroom, really, which opened onto the expansive south terrace—to ensure Mrs. Draper did not require help assembling the flowers.

"They are exquisite, Mrs. Draper," she said, examining the profusion of crimson peonies, blushing cream roses, yellow sunflowers, blue delphinium, and more. The vivid, lush flowers were all arranged so pleasingly, she was near speechless.

"Oh, thank you kindly, your grace, though I cannot take much credit. Lady Atherbourne composed the first batch, and I have simply followed her pattern. She does have an eye for these things."

Jane smiled. "That she does."

Satisfied that all was coming together splendidly, she made her way up to her bedchamber. The bath had already been prepared, steaming and scented with her favorite perfume.

"You are a treasure, Estelle," she sighed. The maid chuckled and helped her undress. She sank into the deep water, letting it tickle her chin and heat-soak her bones. Her eyes drifted around the chamber, with its rich green silks and lavish furnishings.

Only three days ago, it had been here, in this room, that she had made her decision. But not before she had stood in the corridor, foolishly reaching out for him, near helpless to stop. And he had pushed her away. Again. So complete was his rejection, he might as well have given her the cut direct. After weeping and staring sightlessly out her window for far too long, she'd grown heartily sick of her own mourning.

It was maudlin, really.

So, instead of more weeping, she had composed a letter to Annabelle to express her heartache. And her frustration with herself over being such a wretched watering pot. *Dearest Annabelle*, she had written. *When did I become such a wretched watering pot? In truth, it was my heart breaking which began this pitiful habit, and for that I may blame the duke. However, one may only grieve so long before becoming repulsed by one's own self. And I, dear sister, have reached that unfortunate juncture. I refuse to be miserable one second longer. I shall not weep one more tear for what I have lost. Instead, I shall rid myself of that which causes my misery, whatever—or whomever—that may be.*

Soon after completing the letter, she had made a list of those items and individuals comprising her tapestry of sorrows. To resolve the problem of her ill-behaved guests, she had decided to bring their visit to a natural conclusion by hosting a summer ball. And to ensure they understood it was to be regarded as an end point after which they would be expected to depart, she had gathered up Victoria (for courage) and gone in search of items one and two on her misery list: Lady Mary and Lady Dunston.

She had found them in the gold drawing room, having tea and a discussion that was quickly aborted upon Jane's intrusion. Their haughty stares and dismissive sniffs had shaken her, necessitating a few deep breaths. Victoria had squeezed her arm encouragingly.

"Ladies," Jane had said, heartened by the steadiness of her voice. "I wish to inform you that I will be hosting a summer ball."

"Well now," sneered Lady Dunston. "This should prove interesting. Tell me, is a hostess permitted to be a wallflower at her own fete?"

Lady Mary had snickered at her mother's jest, adding, "One supposes the library is only steps away, should she require reading material."

"That is quite enough," Victoria had snapped, sounding distinctly like her brother. "Need I remind you that you are addressing the Duchess of Blackmore, and that you are currently in *her* home, enjoying *her* hospitality?"

Jane had stared at her friend, wondering how she managed to be so sweet and yet so imperious in her wrath. The two women had flushed unbecomingly, gladdening Jane's heart.

Clearing her throat, Jane had continued the task she had set for herself. "The ball will take place in three days. There shall be music and dancing." Here, she had stumbled a bit, but forged on, knowing it must be done. "I believe this to be the ideal conclusion for your visit here at Blackmore Hall before your departure the following day. A lovely, *final* celebration of summer's bounty."

Lady Dunston's thin mouth had flattened, her ruddy color increasing. Lady Mary had swung disbelieving eyes between her mother, Victoria, and Jane. Finally, she had let out a plaintive, "Victoria!"

Victoria had raised her chin and cloaked herself in aristocratic ice as blistering as anything Harrison had ever managed. "I am Lady Atherbourne. And she is her grace, the Duchess of Blackmore. Perhaps now, you will find your memory—and your manners—less prone to shameful lapses."

Even now, as Estelle cinched her corset tighter, Jane

couldn't help grinning as she recalled Victoria's conversation-ending set-down. It had been a triumph, and she was grateful to have witnessed it.

"What's that smile all about, if you don't mind me asking, your grace?" said Estelle, gathering up hair pins and a brush as Jane sat before her dressing table mirror.

"Oh, nothing in particular." She fell silent as the maid brushed out her long, damp hair. "Estelle?"

"Yes, your grace?"

"I do not like my hair."

The brush stopped. "Beg pardon?"

She frowned into the mirror. "It is always the same. Parted in the center, drawn back into a coil and pinned."

"We could try curling it again."

Jane propped her chin on her hand. "No, my hair simply will not curl. Whenever we try, I always end up looking as if I had been drowned and then dried on the line. But I would like a change."

Estelle bent forward at the waist to meet Jane's eyes in the mirror. "Hmm. There is something. I've been chatting about such things to Collette. You recall Lady Wallingham's most recent lady's maid?"

Jane shook her head. "Is she the fourth one this year?"

"Fifth. She's from France. Very high in the instep. But she knows a thing or two about dressing hair, I must say."

"And she gave you some ideas?"

Estelle nodded, taking pieces of Jane's hair along her forehead and folding them to demonstrate. "See? We trim just a bit of a fringe there around your face. Most ladies who do this have curls, but I suspect it will look quite fetching on you."

Jane blinked, seeing the difference. She had not thought of cutting her hair shorter, in front or otherwise. She had long been, she realized, rather timid with changes of all kinds, particularly with her appearance. But this was not a night for timidity. This was a night to be bold.

She met Estelle's eyes again. "Fetch the scissors."

"FOR THE LOVE OF GOD, HARRISON, PUT THAT AWAY," Dunston hissed in disgust.

Snapping his watch closed, Harrison frowned at his friend. "She is late."

Dunston sighed. "It is her ball. She will be here."

He rubbed absently at his chest, which had hurt for days. Weeks, even. Glancing around the south drawing room, he could not help being impressed. In only three days, she had done this—transformed the room, with its ivory paneled, barrel ceiling and twin chandeliers, into a scene from one of Shakespeare's more fanciful fairy stories. Ivy had been gathered and draped artfully to frame the three sets of glass doors opening onto the broad terrace. Potted myrtles and topiaries had been placed at the edges of the room, giving the impression of a leafy bower. Inside painted lanterns, candles flickered on the soft green walls, casting shadows that danced and flitted like playful sprites.

Outside, long tables were draped in gold, heaped with fruit and flowers and seemingly endless dishes from his kitchen. They were lit by torches placed at regular intervals along the perimeter of the terrace, and the musicians already filled the air with a lively country tune. She had created a midsummer's feast of delights.

And, now, she was late.

"There she is."

Harrison's head whipped around to follow Dunston's gaze. He soon realized his friend was not referring to Jane, but to her sister, Maureen.

"She is beauteous in that gown, don't you think?"

He scowled at Dunston, who was not looking at him.

"Do you suppose she will consent to dance with me?"

"Dunston," he growled.

"Hmm?"

"She is my wife's sister."

"Yes. These Huxley girls do weave an oddly alluring spell."

Feeling a tap on his shoulder, Harrison turned. And lost his breath, along with all sensation in his feet.

She wore red. Deep, fever-inducing crimson silk that shaped and molded to her breasts like a lover's caress. Like *his* hands on her skin. Her dress had no adornment; it was simple and gloriously fitted, dipping in a low scoop to reveal a generous portion of her bosom. Gloves of embroidered, pale gold covered her hands, rising past her elbows. A gold-filigreed necklace draped her throat, dotted with tiny ruby droplets. He wanted to strip off his coat and swallow her up inside it. He wanted to carry her off to the old library, to hide her from everyone's eyes except his.

"Duchess, you are a vision," he heard Dunston say. "Please say you will consent to grant me a dance later this evening." The irritating man took her hand in his and bowed over it, his eyes flashing with appreciation. Harrison wanted to break something. Preferably Dunston.

Jane nodded regally. Something was different about her, but he couldn't quite put his finger on it. "You are most gracious, my lord. I would be delighted."

Grinning, Dunston pivoted to greet Maureen. The bloody fool. If he thought Harrison would allow him to touch Jane, even for a dance, he was either sotted or suicidal. Harrison inspected his wife again.

"It is your hair."

Her eyes flared, glittering dark in the candlelight.

"You have changed it."

Her fingers reached up to brush the short strands which

now framed her forehead and the sides of her face. "Yes. Estelle suggested—"

"I liked it as it was."

Her chin came up a fraction, red rising to color her skin. "Well, I prefer it this way."

"No matter. It will grow back."

"I do not want it to grow back. I am keeping it like this."

"We shall discuss it later."

"There is nothing to discuss," she gritted. Closing her eyes briefly to release an exasperated breath, she next looped her arm through his and tugged him toward her parents, who were just arriving. Late, as usual. He could only conclude it was a family trait. "Let us just get through this evening," she said in a low voice.

He would have asked her what she meant, but they were too near Lord and Lady Berne. After they greeted Jane with hugs and exclamations over her dress and hair, they turned to him.

He bowed to the beaming older couple. Lady Berne waved her hand as though shooing away a bee and rose up on her toes to kiss his cheek. "How dashing you are, Harrison. Such a fine figure. You two make me quite the proudest mother in Yorkshire."

Again, the woman confounded him with her maternal effusions. By now, however, he had learned to simply move on to the next logical response, ignoring his own discomfort. "You are looking lovely this evening, Lady Berne."

"One day, you shall call me Mama. The sooner you do so, the less embarrassment over your reticence you will experience later, I assure you."

"Leave the boy alone, Meredith. Let him come to it in his own time," said Lord Berne.

Soon, he and Jane moved on to greet more guests. She had invited most of the aristocrats and landed gentry from the surrounding area, which amounted to a great many people. He had anticipated having to do much of the talking, but he was surprised by her ease with the strangers. She greeted each one, thanking them for coming, inviting them to partake of the abundant food, games of whist and piquet in the gold drawing room, and dancing out on the terrace.

After a while, he noted a pattern to her conversations. They were all the same, with perhaps a variation on a theme here and there, as though she had memorized a script. By the time they had finished welcoming the vicar and his wife, he was certain. No one said the word "libation" twenty separate times.

As the rooms filled with more and more guests, he noticed Jane's smooth, white neck beginning to tighten, her smile wearing under the strain. "Perhaps we should dance," he said.

She looked up at him with endless, deep brown eyes. For a moment, everything stilled: The sounds of voices, the strains of music, the shuffling of feet and clinking of china. All disappeared. There was only her. Jane. His apple-scented temptress wearing a crimson dress. His book-obsessed, bespectacled, anything-but-plain Jane. The one who made the entire world disappear, who made him forget why he could not have her precisely as he wanted—with nothing between them. Completely, utterly his.

Those lovely lips pursed to form her answer. He hung suspended on her next breath. "No," she rasped. "I cannot dance with you, your grace. My answer is no."

Chapter Twenty-Seven

"The allure of country dancing escapes me. You neither speak to your partner nor discover anything more interesting than his ability to avoid colliding with fellow dancers."

—THE DOWAGER MARCHIONESS OF WALLINGHAM to her new companion, Humphrey, who shook his head in agreement.

SHE DANCED WITH DUNSTON. AND THEN WITH THE VICAR. And then with two more men. Yes, they were country dances with scarcely any touching. But she had refused to dance with him. Her own husband.

With his back leaning against the limestone wall of Blackmore, Harrison took a sip of punch and watched her over the rim of his cup. She was flushed from her exertions, her spectacles slipping down her small, rounded nose with increasing frequency, the wreath of flowers and leaves sliding a bit to one side on her head. At midnight, she had announced in a breathless, wobbling voice that every lady would be given one to wear. With torches casting the terrace in a golden aura, flower-crowned ladies twirling and laughing with their dark-clad gentlemen, and festive music lifting them all on lively waves, the scene fairly glowed with fay enchantment.

Part of him witnessed her triumph, his brave Jane, and cheered with pride. But the darker part sent blood burning through his veins, his need of her and hatred for any man who looked upon her making his head spin as much as the deceptively innocent punch. This was what he must resist. After everything he had learned of his father, after all he knew of who he was and the dear price he would pay should it escape his control, he must find a way to temper his feelings for her. He had thought withdrawing from her company would help. It had not.

"Harrison?" Victoria touched his arm, startling him. "Aren't you enjoying the party?"

She, too, was glowing and happy, having just finished a dance with her husband, who stood like a tall, dark guard behind her. Atherbourne briefly glanced between him and Jane. She was still conversing with Mr. Hargrove, a sandy-haired, wealthy merchant from Leeds. The corner of his brother-in-law's mouth lifted in a knowing smirk.

Harrison glowered at them both. "Do you not have something better to occupy yourselves than monitoring my enjoyment?"

"No need to be cross," Victoria replied. "I was simply going to ask if you have danced yet."

"I do not wish to dance."

His sister's chin went up in a familiar warning sign. "Well, I am glad to hear it, for who would want to dance with someone so sour?"

Harrison did not reply, taking another leisurely sip of his punch and trying very hard to ignore them. Was that bloody merchant inching closer to Jane?

"Your wife, on the other hand," said Atherbourne dryly, "seems rather fond of dancing."

He would have shot his brother-in-law a fierce glare, but he was preoccupied with more important matters. The bloody merchant from Leeds was brushing against her arm, turning so that he could show something to her. Their backs were to him, so he could not see what it was. But it did not matter. Mr. Bloody Hargrove should mind his proximity or he would soon discover how the stones of the south terrace tasted.

"I am simply over the moon for Jane," gushed Victoria. "It is most difficult to plan a ball of this scale in so short a time. But I have always suspected she would make a splendid hostess, if given the chance. She is quite skilled and—"

"He is not listening, love," Atherbourne interrupted.

"He's not?"

"No."

"Then, what is he doing?"

"Obsessing."

She tsked. "Harrison does not obsess. He is highly logical. It is much more likely he is in his cups. That punch is almost entirely wine."

Atherbourne cleared his throat and coughed. "Perhaps you are right, angel. I must be mistaken."

Victoria murmured a bit more before her voice receded. Harrison took little notice. Jane was smiling at Hargrove. Smiling. Her dimples were practically winking at the man.

"It won't help, you know," came Atherbourne's sardonic voice again.

"What?" Harrison growled.

"Keeping your distance. Worsens the effect."

Finally, he tore his gaze away from Jane to meet Atherbourne's dark eyes, which were surprisingly serious. "Whatever you think you know," Harrison said softly, his voice a warning. "You do not."

A slow smile curled the man's mouth upward. "It begins with the small things. The way she smells. A little crinkle at the corner of her eyes when she laughs. Then, you find yourself wondering if you have some kind of illness. A fever, perhaps. Surely that is the only way to explain feeling like a feral beast every time she says your name."

Harrison stared at the other man. It was all he could manage. No one knew this. How could he know? Harrison had not even told Jane.

"The worst is not the wanting, although that is rather frightening in its intensity. No, the worst is when you are parted from her. The only greater agony is in knowing you are the cause of it. And that she suffers for your foolishness."

He did not want to hear more. "You cannot possibly understand," he said hoarsely, his eyes pulled helplessly back to her. Jane.

"Perhaps not. But in the unlikely event that I do, a bit of advice." Atherbourne clapped his upper arm with some force. "Try to avoid doing *permanent* damage."

Victoria waved her husband over for another dance, leaving Harrison alone with his thoughts. Across the terrace, Jane chatted with Maureen, having blessedly lost Mr. Hargrove. Atherbourne's final piece of advice rang in his head. It was the very thing Harrison had been attempting to do—avoid disaster. But his feelings for her had only grown stronger. Now, he could not be certain of anything except this: He must protect her, no matter the cost.

EXHAUSTION HAD COME FOR JANE'S SOUL LONG BEFORE THE last guest's carriage left Blackmore's drive. But she had persevered. She was rather proud of that. Now, standing at the rim of the south terrace, looking out into the velvety-soft night, she gently lifted the listing wreath from her head and set it on the table next to her gloves. The daisies had wilted a bit, much like she had.

"Your grace, the tables have been cleared of food. Would you care for something before you retire?" Mrs. Draper inquired from behind her.

Without turning, Jane shook her head. "Thank you, but no, Mrs. Draper. Why don't you and the others find your beds? The rest of this will keep until the morning."

"You are too kind, your grace. And may I say, it was a magnificent ball."

Jane nodded her thanks, hearing the housekeeper move away, the clink and swish of footmen and maids clearing the debris slowly fading as they finished their tasks and gratefully departed.

Hugging her waist and sighing, she noted the torches had been extinguished, leaving only the stars and a low, setting moon to light the tables and urns of flowers, turning the scene silver instead of gold.

She had done well, she decided. With Victoria's help in formulating the guest list, the vicar's advice on finding worthy musicians, her sisters' willingness to pick wildflowers, and the tireless efforts of Blackmore Hall's superb staff, Jane had managed to play hostess to a grand summer ball without humiliating herself. In fact, she liked to think even an Oddflower might have enjoyed attending as a guest. The most difficult part of the evening had been greeting and conversing with everyone, but the idea for writing a script had come after Lady Wallingham's complaint that most matrons lacked originality in their speech, and that they often seemed to be "reciting lines committed to memory in the schoolroom."

And, of course, Harrison had been there. With every new face, each time she had stumbled over her words, he had stood at her side, sensing precisely when to intervene and when to let her be. He had only left after she'd rejected his suggestion of a dance. She could not explain why she had done it. Too much magic in the air, perhaps. She had needed to keep her wits about her.

Taking one last breath of the warm August night, she turned toward the drawing room. And there he was. She stopped, her heart thudding against her breast as it had earlier, when she had seen him in his black coat and trousers, his gold waistcoat and white cravat. Those simple garments framed him like a portrait of a god. To her, even now, as he examined his watch with exhaustion clear in his profile, he was the handsomest of men.

Drawn toward him almost compulsively, she halted again when she saw who approached from the corridor. Lady Mary, dressed becomingly in green and white, laid her hand on Harrison's arm and smiled up at him adoringly. Acid roiled in Jane's stomach, watching them laugh together, the way he tilted his head to speak with her. The girl's dog followed her into the room, sniffing his mistress's slippers. Jane hoped Cornelius did something vile with those slippers, and that Mary, Queen of Sweets, did not discover it until it was too late.

Instead of her fantasy coming true, however, Mary bent to gather the pup in her arms, and she carried him toward the north entrance hall, presumably so that he could defecate in a more appropriate venue.

Jane watched Harrison's shoulders slump, his head bowing, his hand running through his hair in a gesture more reminiscent of Colin than of her husband. He looked so weary, so worn. Before she could think better of it, she entered the room and said his name.

His head came up in a snap. "Jane. Where have you been?"

"The terrace. It is late. I am surprised you and Lady Mary have not retired before now." Was that her voice, sounding so waspish?

He frowned. "Lady Mary? She was taking her dog outside. She stopped to bid me goodnight."

"Yes, and she just *happened* to find you here waiting for her. How coincidental."

Shaking his head, he replied, "Your implication is absurd."

"Is it, now?"

"Yes. As you can see, she is no longer in the room. Had we desired an assignation, I assure you, it would have taken place in a more private location and lasted considerably longer."

The thought of him in a private room spending "considerably longer" with Mary, Queen of Sweets, produced a strange red haze over her vision. She now felt she was standing outside herself, observing a different Jane speaking words she had never dreamt of saying. "Is that where you go each day, Harrison? Escape your pathetic wife so you can enjoy an *assignation* with that cinnamon-flavored trollop?"

Dimly, she saw his brows arch in surprise then sink low over glittering eyes.

"Is *she* more to your liking? More graceful when she goes to her knees for you? Or is that only something you do with us improper chits?" Who was the bloody harpy saying these hideous things? She couldn't seem to stop the words. "If you'd *wanted* her, you should have *married* her, husband."

Clearly, her exhaustion had worn away whatever armor had carried her through these past few days. There was nothing left of her bravado, of her determination to move on from grief. This was rage. Pure rage, spewing forth in the most undignified fashion, revealing far too much.

"Are you finished?" he said softly.

Considering she wanted to vomit, yes, she was likely finished.

"You are obviously distraught and weary after a trying evening. I shall forget we spoke. Perhaps you will regain your senses by morning." He turned on his heel, his boots ringing loudly on the wood. She followed him all the way to his study.

He was standing at the window inside the dim room before she caught up with him.

"Go on then," she sneered, slamming the door closed. "Walk away. You're becoming rather good at it, aren't you?"

He pivoted and strode back toward her at twice the pace. "Do not push me, Jane. I have had quite enough."

"And what happens when you pass 'quite enough,' husband? Do I then become an acceptable substitute again?"

"You have never been a substitute for anyone. Now, cease this nonsense. You are overtired and raving like a lunatic."

"Do not. Speak to me. As if I were a child."

"A child would have more sense. I do not understand why you are behaving this way."

She held her arms out wide. "Because of this blasted night! I did this, all of it, for you! So you would see that I am capable of it. And you haven't said a word. Not one word." She thought perhaps tears were spilling down her cheeks, but she could barely feel her skin. "You still speak to me like I haven't left the schoolroom. You see me as an incompetent ninny who cannot manage the simplest functions every wife in England performs."

"That is ridiculous. If I had known you wished to arrange such an event, I would have gladly permitted it sooner."

"I do not want you to *permit* me. I wish for you to have faith in me, to encourage me and be proud when I succeed."

"Your shyness is no secret. Hosting a ball of this size is naturally difficult for you. I never doubted you *could*, Jane, only that you desired to."

Her chin rose. "And what is your answer now? Now that I have done it."

His eyes were full of caution, as though watching a shower of sparks fall on a pile of gunpowder. "My answer?"

She swiped at her cheeks impatiently. "For your coldness. Explain it, then, if it was not because you regretted our marriage."

"I do not regret our marriage." His answer was ghostly, almost a whisper.

She stepped closer. "I do not believe you."

He was breathing faster now, his eyes dilating, his face tight. He did not respond.

So she lashed him again. "If Lady Mary were your wife, you would not have treated her as you have treated me. Admit it."

Still, he refused to answer.

"Admit it!" she shouted.

"It is true," he said hoarsely, breaking her in half. "I would not."

Chapter Twenty-Eight

"Never ask a question you do not wish to have answered."

—THE DOWAGER MARCHIONESS OF WALLINGHAM to her new companion, Humphrey, while debating the sinister intentions of her recently dismissed lady's maid.

SOMEHOW, SHE HAD CONVINCED HERSELF IT COULD NOT BE worse, that the gnawing pain of his rejection had been experienced to its fullest, and that hearing the truth would only confirm her worst suspicions, allowing her to finally untether herself from him.

But it was worse. Much worse.

She stumbled backward, her hand forming a claw at the center of her chest, needing to rip out her own heart. Needing the anguish to stop. Turning blindly for the door, her steps were awkward and unsynchronized, the world around her moving out of rhythm.

Someone was saying her name. Someone was holding her from behind.

"I must go," she whispered.

"No, Jane. No."

"I have to leave. I cannot stay here."

"I will not let you go. I will never let you go." The cry was an echo of hers—the same torment. The same need.

She squeezed her eyes shut, his body curving around hers from behind. His arms held her so fiercely, she nearly lost her breath.

"Jane," he groaned, his voice raw, his face pressing into her neck. "My Jane." His hands found hers where they pressed into her abdomen. He clasped one and brought it up to cup his cheek, holding it captive there. "Touch me. Please, Jane. Don't go."

He was holding her up, his arms strong, his heat surrounding her. But she was numb, not understanding why he would cling to her this way.

"You do not want me, Harrison."

He turned his face and pressed his lips to her palm, cupping her fingers so they curved along his jaw. "I ache for you."

She shook her head. "You ache for *someone*. Not me."

"Only you."

"No," she whispered, her denial one of self-preservation. "I am tired, Harrison. Victoria has invited me to stay at Thornbridge. I shall leave with her tomorrow."

"You cannot leave."

"I cannot stay."

"Why?" His voice was tortured.

For long moments, she debated telling him the truth. Everything inside her cried out not to reveal herself. But, in the end, her heart wanted its say. She turned in his arms, facing a man she had not seen since the night of her abduction. "You cut me too easily."

Pain and confusion darkened his blue eyes to the color of an angry sea. "I would never hurt you."

"I know it would not be your intention. But you also will never love me. Not as I love you."

His head jerked back, his eyes flaring.

"Because I do, Harrison. I love you."

"Do not say that."

"Why not? It is true." And it was surprisingly relieving to say aloud.

He pulled away from her, shaking his head. "You cannot love me."

"So many admonitions," she said, softly chiding. "I cannot love you. I cannot leave. Well, here are yours, my darling husband: You cannot prevent it. You cannot control it. You cannot control *me*."

"That is precisely the problem."

"Only for you." She moved toward him, but he maintained the distance between them, retreating step for step. It made her more determined. Soon, she felt like a cat stalking a wolf. Most strange, indeed. "What do you fear, Harrison?" At last, she cornered him near the sofa. "You pull me closer, then push me away. You do not want me to love you, and yet you will not permit me to leave."

"You are my wife. You belong here."

Her body came within a breath of his, her neck craned to meet his troubled eyes. "Do I? Even you admit Mary Thorpe would have made a better Duchess of Blackmore."

Angry indignation sparked in his eyes, the first flash of lightning across heavy clouds. "The devil I did. I would never say such a thing."

Her mouth worked, struggling for words at his peculiar denial. "You—you just did, only minutes ago."

"No. I said I would not have treated Lady Mary as I have treated you. And that is true."

Jane tried twice to speak, succeeding on the third attempt.

"What is the difference?"

He stiffened, his jaw clenching, his neck straightening. "It does not matter."

"It matters very much to me."

"You are a fine duchess. The only one I desire."

"Why would you have treated her differently?"

He looked hunted, his eyes darting over her shoulder, then down to her bosom, then back up to her face. Looking as if he had decided something important, his chin came up a fraction, his gaze resolute. "She is not you. And you are my weakness."

His weakness? She shook her head, now breathless. "That is ... that is merely ..."

His lips twisted. "Lust? No." He stroked her cheek with heartrending tenderness. "I would kill for you. I very nearly did."

In part, it was his words, spoken like a confession. But mostly, it was the way he looked at her—as though she were infinitely precious, as though he had mapped her heart and mirrored the pattern precisely. Jane's body flooded with heat. Tingling sparks showered across her scalp and down her spine, trailing along her arms to her fingertips and down her legs to her toes. They lingered in her breasts and between her thighs, firing her blood. Cupping his hand against her face, she tilted her head and pressed a kiss to his thumb. He took her gesture as encouragement.

"The way I feel is dangerous, Jane. It is a fire. And it must be controlled."

She moved into him, pressing her body against his, laying her head against his chest. Finally, she was beginning to understand. He had not gone cold because he found her wanting. He had retreated because he feared loving her.

"That fire burns inside me, too," she confessed.

His lips rested against her hair. "Not the same," he whispered. "I see you with other men, and I want to take them apart."

"Earlier, I wished for Lady Mary to experience a calamitous indignity involving Cornelius and her slippers. That is unbecoming, perhaps, but not dangerous."

"You don't understand, Jane. Jealousy made my father beat a man so badly, he nearly died. I once believed I was nothing like him, but I now know the truth. He was cold because allowing his true nature free rein was unthinkable."

She pulled away enough to see Harrison's face. He looked quite grave. "Was this something that happened often with your father? Was he a violent man?"

A frown tugged at his brow. "No, at least, not that I ever knew. I only recently discovered the incident. Before they married, he was deeply infatuated with my mother. That came as a surprise to me."

"They were not affectionate with one another?"

"My father was not affectionate with anyone."

Including his son. Harrison didn't say it, but he didn't have to. From everything he and Victoria had told her, she had a clear and unflattering picture of the man who had sired the man she loved. "And you believe the way your father dealt with his 'true nature,' as you call it, was worthy of imitation?"

Stiffening again, he pulled away and paced to his desk. "Can you suggest an alternative? Because I have tried, Jane. God knows I have."

Walking toward him, she began to pull pins from her hair, letting the strands unravel and tumble down her back. Boldness had never come easily to Jane, but if ever a night called for it, this was the night. With Harrison, here, in this moment, she would be bolder than the Jane who had crept through Lord Milton's window. She would be bolder than the plain Oddflower who had dared marry the catch of the season. She would be bolder than the duchess who had demanded two highborn, ill-mannered guests leave her home.

"As a matter of fact, I do have an idea," she said, her voice dusky and low. Drawing up next to her tall, achingly handsome husband, she deliberately brushed his arm with the tips of her breasts.

He sucked in a breath and shifted until his thighs edged the desk.

She did not retreat, but moved around to his back, running her hands slowly up over his broad, muscled shoulders and arching until her breasts flattened against him. "What if, instead of dousing the fire ..." She hooked her fingers inside his collar and tugged until his tailcoat began to peel off. "We let it rage." Dropping the black coat to the floor, she next slid her hands around his waist. Her fingers reached beneath his waistcoat to grasp the linen hem of his shirt and pulled it clear of his trousers. "And you love me fully. With your entire soul. As I do you." She unbuttoned the first few buttons of his fall, just enough to slip inside, where his cock greeted her with heat and hardness. "And we burn together."

He gasped, groaned harshly, fell forward and caught himself with his hands on the dark wood. "Jane," he panted as she squeezed and stroked. "I—I cannot love you."

Her thumb swirled around the very tip, teasing and pleasuring, before she ringed the head with her fingers and tightened just the way he liked. Another groan rumbled through his chest and into her ear where it pressed against his back. "There's the rub, my love," she said, her own voice breathless with arousal. "You already do."

In the next instant, he grasped her wrist, withdrew her hand, and pulled her around until the edge of the desk dug into her backside. His face was flushed and fierce, his need stark. "No," he growled. "I will not love you."

"You will. And quite thoroughly, I'll venture."

His breath sawing in and out, his cock furiously engorged and arched high against his belly, she could see he was close. But perhaps he needed another nudge.

"Furthermore," she said, tugging her bodice and the cups of her corset down until the edge of the cloth scraped her nipples. "You will say it to me." Her fingers delicately teased the hard tips forth from their covering, let the folds of fabric elevate her breasts impossibly high until they spilled over like ripened fruit, lush and swollen with summer's heat. "Before this night is ended, you will say it."

His control was near to breaking. She could see it in his eyes, transfixed on her flushed, hard, naked nipples. "This is madness," he rasped. "You do not know what you are asking."

"Hmm," she purred. "Why don't you show me?"

She expected him to kiss her. Harrison always kissed her. But he did not. His face near unrecognizable with lust, he moved so swiftly, she could not even take a breath, his hands clamping on her waist, spinning her around until her back was to him. The room tilted as he bent her forward over the desk, pressing his hand against her neck, pressing her aching nipples against the hard wood. Cool air whisked across her legs as he raised her skirts, tossing them up onto her back. Then came the warm slide of his fingers, moving through the slick folds between her legs. Two sank deep into her core, as his heated breath stroked her ear. "You wanted fire," he growled. "This is what my fire feels like, wife."

She moaned her pleasure, squeezing his fingers and wriggling her hips. He removed his fingers and replaced them with his cock. The thrust was ferocious—deep and hard enough to bring her up on her toes. His hips hammered into hers mercilessly, and she was helpless in his embrace, her core stretched and pleasured and on fire with the friction. He felt enormous from this angle, a force of nature demanding her obedience. But this was not everything. He must give her everything.

"Harrison," she panted, grunting as his thrusts quickened. "Touch me, my love."

Immediately, one of the hands gripping her hips loosened and glided up her back, the silk of her dress rustling as he passed, a counterpoint to the quiet slap of flesh, the heavy sawing of his breath. His hand tickled over her nape, curved over her jaw. His forefinger teased her lips, demanding entry. She opened for him, letting him slide inside, tasting herself on him. He withdrew his finger then gave her a second one. She circled it with her tongue, suckled briefly. His hand left her mouth and traveled back to her hip, where it curled around her thigh, sifted past her skirts, and used his wet fingers to lay a stunning kiss against her fiercely swollen bud.

The sensations were simply too much—too sharp, too intense. She cried his name, her core gripping furiously, her fists clenching on the desk, body demanding more. And he gave her more. But still, not enough.

Arching her back, she reached behind her to grasp his hand where it dug into her hip. "Come closer," she rasped, her voice all but gone, so near climax, she felt it gathering in her toes.

He slowed his pace and, on the next thrust, held himself deep inside. It was almost too much. "Is this not close enough for you?"

She refused to release his hand, tugging until he bent forward over her, his face dropping next to hers. She pushed herself up until her back was warmed by his front, then brought his hand around to the center of her chest. "Say you love me," she whispered. "For, this"—she tapped the back of his hand where it rested over her heart—"is yours. And I wish to have one for myself."

"Ah, God, Jane." His lips found her neck, his hips now thrusting in small, helpless movements. "I cannot."

"Say it, Harrison. Say it, my love."

"Nooo," he groaned, his voice guttural and raw.

"It is all right. Just say it. I love you."

His thrusts increased in power and pace once again, the sounds from his throat wordless pleas.

But she would show no mercy. He would say it. He would bloody well say it.

And then, as if something had shattered inside him, he

pulled her in tight, his arms hard and relentless across her waist and her breasts. His lips dragged from her shoulder to her cheek.

The first time he said the words, she didn't so much hear as feel them, a hot caress against her skin. "I love you." Then once more, whispered louder. "I love you." Soon, he was grunting the words, growling them in rhythm with his thrusts. "I love you. I love you. I love you." Over and over. The climax that had been standing at the gates rushed in upon her with tidal force. She screamed her pleasure and clawed at his arms. Her hips writhed and ground back against his, and within seconds, he followed her into the abyss, filling her with his seed, taking her heart and giving her his own.

Chapter Twenty-Nine

"If I concerned myself with convention, I would never attain anything worthwhile. That, my dear Humphrey, I shall leave to lesser women."

—The Dowager Marchioness of Wallingham to her new companion, Humphrey, whose response was a single dismissive snort.

The sunlight was near blinding the morning after the summer ball. Birds sang loudly in the oak trees near the drive, while the horses attached to Lord Dunston's fine traveling coach whinnied and shook their heads restlessly.

"I will not leave without him," declared Lady Mary, wiping a tear from her cheek. "He is mine, not hers."

Lord Dunston sighed. "Very well, I shall try to find him. Wait here." He climbed down from the carriage and loped past Jane, giving her an eye-rolling grin before he disappeared into the house.

Lady Berne leaned over to murmur in Jane's ear, "He is rather dashing, that one. I do hope Maureen is not becoming too attached."

Jane gave her mother a questioning look.

"He is dangerous," she whispered. "I won't have my daughter fancying one of Sidmouth's men."

Wondering if her mother had overindulged a bit too much the previous evening, Jane patted her arm. "Mama, Lord Dunston does not work for the Home Office. He is a charming gentleman, not a spy. And the war is long over."

Mama's chin lifted. "Believe whatever you like. My information is sound."

The man in question emerged from the entrance hall minutes later carrying a wriggling, whimpering Cornelius. He handed the pup to his sister, who held her arms out through the carriage door. "Where did you find him?" she asked plaintively, sniffing away her tears.

"He was perched beneath Lady Wallingham's skirts, lying atop her slippers."

"I *knew* she had stolen him from me!" Mary turned to her mother, who sat in the shadows next to her. "Did I not tell you, Mama?"

"Cease your hysterics, girl." The command came from Lady Wallingham, who strode like a purple-clad empress onto the front terrace. "I would not steal that contemptible creature. He is fortunate to be alive after all I have endured."

Mary's red-rimmed eyes narrowed suspiciously. "Then, how did he come to be sleeping upon your slippers without your notice?"

The dragon's nose elevated and wrinkled dismissively. "He is sly. In addition, he possesses an unnatural fondness for my footwear. Since you have failed in your obligation to restrain him, I have become accustomed to his odious weight. For the preservation of my sanity, I no longer take any note of him whatever."

"You are lying. She is lying, Mama!"

Dunston cleared his throat pointedly, quickly sketching a bow to Jane and the others before pushing Mary back onto the coach's seat and climbing in. The door closed with a sharp clack. Moments later, Lord Dunston and his sister and mother departed from Blackmore Hall. Jane sighed her relief.

"Imagine! Accusing me of stealing that loathsome pest. Next, she will posit I have spirited away with her chamber pot. Preposterous."

Feeling almost dizzy from lack of sleep, Jane squeezed her mother's arm and smiled before returning inside. Through the open door, she could hear Lady Wallingham's ongoing outraged grumblings and Mama's noncommittal replies.

The further she walked, the more the voices faded, replaced with the quiet clamor of the footmen carrying her family's trunks down the staircase to stack them in the entrance hall. Genie came tripping down the steps, tying the ribbon of her red-rose bonnet beneath her chin. "Jane, have you seen Mama? Papa says if we do not depart soon, we shall have to stay at one of those dreadful coaching inns." She gave a shudder as she reached the last step.

"I do not know why you find them so objectionable. And yes, Mama is on the north terrace."

"The beds are small and filthy. And I am always forced to sleep between Maureen and Kate. Maureen snores, and Kate kicks in her sleep. I think she dreams of running, but she says she doesn't recall. Perhaps she is really awake and only pretending so that she may damage me with impunity."

Jane shook her head. "Kate has done the same since she was a babe."

Genie sniffed. "Still, purposeful or not, I am not fond of bruises. So, I must hurry and fetch Mama." She headed for the entrance hall, her white dress a lovely contrast with her red bonnet.

Covering a yawn, Jane continued along the corridor, where Mrs. Draper stopped her. "Your grace, the third trunk has been packed, along with the basket of books you requested. Estelle has prepared everything just as you asked, and she should be ready shortly."

Jane swallowed and gave the housekeeper a weak smile. "Thank you, Mrs. Draper. Please inform Lady Atherbourne I will join her outside within the hour."

The woman curtsied and left. Jane wandered through the halls until she came into the old library. There in the stillness, she closed her eyes and wrapped her arms around herself, leaning one shoulder against the dark frame of the window. Absently, she glanced around at her favorite room. It was filled with memories of him. It was where he had first loved her. Him. Not the duke.

And now, after last night, when he had at last revealed himself fully, she knew those memories were not enough. They would never be enough for her. She wanted all of him. Anything less would only hurt more.

"You don't have to leave." His voice came from behind her. He was standing at the door, the length of the room between them.

Without turning, she lowered her head, her mouth curving into a sad smile. "That might be true if I did not love you so."

His long silence was weighted by everything that had been said last night. When he had pulled out of her body after confessing his love. When he had looked at her with heartbreaking fear and told her it could never happen again. When he had disappeared inside the duke's proper skin and declared he would leave, for her sake, and go to live in London.

She had known then that the wounds his father had left inside him would not be mended by her will. If she wished for all of him, she must let him decide whether their love was worth the risk he clearly attached to it.

"I never wished to hurt you, Jane."

It took her a moment to face him. He looked like the duke,

his charcoal coat impeccable, his cravat starched and looped to perfection, his hands clasped behind him. But his eyes—ah, his eyes were agony. Perhaps there was hope, after all.

She took a couple of steps toward him, but he stiffened like a hunted animal, so she stopped. "I know," she said gently. "And I have no wish to hurt you."

"This is your home."

"Yes. It is."

"You belong here."

"Yes. I do."

He went quiet, his jaw tightening. "When will you return?" Though spoken softly, the question seemed wrenched from him.

Her smile trembled. She closed the distance between them, moving slowly and pausing at the door as he stepped aside, out of touching range. Gazing up at him with her heart in her eyes, she let him see how much she loved him. Enough to leave, even while it tore her in two. "When you come for me."

A small crease of confusion appeared between his brows.

Tears filled her eyes, and her smile grew. "You are, above all, a sensible man. I will wait for you to realize it." Then, unable to stop herself, she laid her hand over his heart. "Be brave, my love," she whispered before turning and leaving the old library.

An hour later, after seeing her family off, she climbed into Lucien and Victoria's carriage and gazed out the window as it jerked into motion. The verdant fields surrounding Blackmore Hall had become so dear to her. They rumbled past as the carriage rolled by the fish pond, then beyond the towering oaks and the low stone wall with its ivy and moss. Soon, she closed her eyes, not wanting to see her home disappear from view. Instead, she began a letter in her mind, one she was uncertain she would ever send. *My dearest love,* she would write. *Today, I left you. And it was the hardest thing I have ever done.*

LETTING HER LEAVE WAS THE HARDEST THING HE HAD EVER done. Harder than firing upon a man who had not deserved to die. Harder than allowing Colin to reap the consequences of his actions. Harder than telling her he loved her.

He sat in his study, staring down at the desk where he had taken every piece of his magnificent Jane and given her every piece of himself in return. For the first time in his life, he had felt whole.

Now, he only felt his soul being scraped out of his body, leaving a bleeding pit. He was nothingness, surrounded by the worst sort of anguish.

"Ah, here you are. Brooding, I see." Lady Wallingham's trumpeting voice intruded into the room. "Perhaps you were unaware, but you still have a *guest* remaining."

He could not focus on her words, barely able to breathe for the pain. Rather than continue to face her, he stood and turned toward the window, his hands automatically settling at the small of his back.

"Hmmph. Fine manners, indeed. What would your mother say?"

"My mother is dead."

"Her standards of conduct are not."

Needing her to leave, he inquired, "Was there something you wanted, Lady Wallingham?"

She sniffed. "I have hired a carriage to take me north to Grimsgate Castle. I would like the use of one of your horses and a coachman for the journey. Your village livery stable has only three white horses. I must have four. How would it be perceived, three white and one brown? Appallingly gauche."

"Take whatever you require."

A long silence settled between them. He was not certain

why she lingered. Behind him, he heard the rustle of the dowager's gown, the creak of wood floors as she took several steps into the room.

"You have done the right thing, you know," she said.

He did not wish to hear more, so he did not ask what she meant. But when had a lack of response ever stopped Lady Wallingham from offering her opinion?

"For years, I have told Jane those tales of true love are, at best, lies that will lead to naïve delusions. The girl is plain and painfully awkward. She is fortunate you have an overdeveloped sense of honor, or she would no doubt be a spinster."

He turned, his anger rising. The old woman wore her usual haughty expression. He wanted to shout, but instead said softly, "She is not plain."

She scoffed. "Of course she is. Are you blind? She may trim her hair. She may wear the finest gowns your funds can purchase, but she will always be plain."

"She. Is not. Plain."

The warning note in his voice must have penetrated Lady Wallingham's fog of hauteur, because she did not press further. "Regardless, my *point* is valid. By sending her away, you have done her a favor. No woman wishes to remain where she is unwanted and ill-suited."

His stomach churning, he could feel his patience with the dowager wearing thin. "I did not send her away," he snapped. "Further, she is neither unwanted nor ill-suited. Quite the opposite. She belongs here. It is I who should have left."

"If you find her acceptable, why should either of you leave? Proximity is required for the production of heirs, if memory serves."

At the mention of heirs, his mind flashed to last night. She could be carrying his child. A babe. Part him and part her. His heart, which had died when she left, began beating again, painfully hard inside his chest.

"Your father and mother were not particularly joyful in their marriage, but they did what was necessary for the furtherance of their family line, as all those of noble blood must do."

His mouth twisted. "If you know anything of their marriage, then you should also know theirs is a poor pattern to follow."

One of the old woman's brows went up. "Did I say otherwise? Your mother was entirely lacking a spine, and your father was a horse's ass."

He blinked at the blunt assessment. "Weren't you the one who suggested my father's demeanor was a necessary bulwark against his violent nature?"

She snorted. "I said no such thing. Honestly, after so many years of having been proven right—over and over, mind you—one would think my words would be received with greater care. It is my fault, I suppose. I expect too much of those less capable." She sighed with dramatic flair. "What I said was that he denied his true nature, becoming a horse's ass rather than admitting the lovely-yet-spineless Judith could pull his strings with the twist of her dainty wrist." Her direct green gaze grew piercing. "Cowardice, not nobility, impelled your father toward coldness, dear boy. His pride could not bear being controlled in such a way."

Be brave, my love. It was the last thing Jane had said to him, sensing his fear of what lived inside him, of what reached for her each time she came near.

"Your mother was little better. Do not tell Lady Berne I said so, as she is hopelessly sentimental about the duchess, but had Judith Clyde Lacey reacted with more strength of character, the duke would have been forced to recover his manhood. Believe me when I say the loss of one's manhood is a most unattractive quality."

He winced at the double meaning.

"Fortunately, Jane is not your mother. My influence has surely seen to that. And you are not your father."

Leaning forward against the desk, Harrison dropped his head forward briefly before lifting it again. "You believe ... that my father and I are not the same?"

Her bark of laughter was answer enough, but she elaborated. "Perhaps in superficial ways you resemble one another. Your eyes, for example. Something of his outward manner has transferred to you, but then sons tend to mimic their fathers' postures and habits. My Charles has certainly done so, to my dismay. Beneath the surface, however, you and Richard Lacey are as different as snow and cabbage. The sort of careless cruelty he exhibited would be abhorrent to someone of your character."

He frowned and nodded, acknowledging the truth of her statement.

"Can you imagine your father rescuing a plump, plain, awkward wallflower from her own foolishness?"

No, he could not. But, more to the point, "She is not plain. She is extraordinary."

The dowager dismissed his statement with the wave of her wrinkled hand. "You are clearly suffering a visual disorder of some kind. Perhaps you and Jane should wear matching spectacles."

He did not respond, his head spinning with what she had told him. Lady Wallingham was many things, but obtuse was not one of them. If she believed he and his father were different beneath the skin, then Harrison could rely on her assessment. She had known his parents well, and she appeared to know him better than he would like.

That being the case, he must now revert to the conclusion he had drawn before learning the story of his father's courtship of his mother—namely, that he did not possess the discipline necessary to manage the intense emotions he felt for Jane, despite his father's efforts to instill it. Consequently, he could neither control nor predict his own future behavior with regards to her.

Or, perhaps he could predict it too well: If she were harmed, he would stop at nothing to destroy the source. If she fell prey to the attentions of another man, he would take that man apart. If she—God forbid—died of some disease or the ravages of childbirth or any of the thousand other dangers he had imagined, he would lose himself, never recover his sanity.

That was the risk of loving Jane. And it terrified him.

"You are thinking too much, boy," grumbled Lady Wallingham. "What is going through that foolish head that has you looking like a Frenchman staring down a guillotine?"

"Perhaps I am a coward, too," he muttered, more to himself than the dowager.

"Rubbish," she said. "Do you wish your children to know their father?"

Focusing on her once again, he replied, "Yes, I do."

"Then you shall retrieve your wife and return her to her rightful place."

"It is not that simple."

"Of course it is. Jane is a good girl. Strong. She will ensure you do not fail her."

His pulse quickened as her point struck home. He swallowed, trying to absorb it. In all of his worry over whether he could contain his own wild heart, he had neglected to consider the one element that might make the biggest difference: Jane herself. Over the past weeks, his wife's true substance had been revealed before his eyes. She was a shy woman, and yet had worked to organize a ball for over two hundred strangers. Before he had told her the depth of his love, she had declared her own, knowing he might reject her. She was brave. She was strong. She was determined. And Lady Wallingham was right—she was more than capable of holding his hands steady, of bringing him back to himself. With Jane by his side, he could not possibly fail. It was only when she was gone that he fell to pieces.

"Well, I shall inform your butler to arrange for my horse

and coachman," said the dowager, her expression now curiously serene, even a bit smug. "Would you like your horse saddled as well?" She smiled and lifted a brow. "One must act promptly to recover what one's own stupidity has lost. Wouldn't you agree?"

Chapter Thirty

"Isn't it remarkable how much better everything is when others simply heed my advice?"

—THE DOWAGER MARCHIONESS OF WALLINGHAM to her new companion, Humphrey, on a brisk morning walk through the countryside.

"DO YOU SUPPOSE TEN THOUSAND A YEAR IS SUFFICIENT, Gregory? One may always ask just a bit more, given Mr. Darcy's surly nature." Sitting beneath a great ash tree in the midst of a green field dotted with white sheep, Jane cuddled her nephew and read him tales of silly women obsessed with the annual income of eligible men.

They had just passed the village of Wakefield, making good time on favorable roads. Victoria and Lucien had gone inside the small inn to acquire food and drink while their horses were changed. Meanwhile, Jane and Estelle and Gregory's nursemaid, Roseanna, had spread a blanket beneath a rustling canopy of leaves, opting for a cooler respite from the confines of the jostling carriage.

"'The gentlemen pronounced him to be a fine figure of a man, the ladies declared he was much handsomer than Mr. Bingley, and he was looked at with great admiration for about half the evening, till his manners gave a disgust which turned the tide of his popularity.' Dear me, Gregory," Jane interjected, letting her eyes meet his, blue-green, dark-lashed, and wonder-filled. "I fear generous funds do not compensate for every failing. Let us read on and see what further disturbances we may find: 'For he was discovered to be proud; to be above his company, and above being pleased.'"

"Your grace," said Estelle quietly.

"And not all his large estate in Derbyshire could then save him from having a most forbidding, disagreeable countenance, and being unworthy to be compared with his friend."

"Your grace," said the maid, this time more insistently.

Jane glanced up from her book. "Yes, Estelle?"

But the maid was not looking at her. She was staring across the field, past the sheep, to the courtyard of the inn. Where Jane's tall, handsome, fine figure of a husband tossed his reins to a groom and strode toward her with long, ground-eating strides.

She lost her breath and her composure, filled with a sudden flush that was not due to the August heat. "Oh," she uttered, dropping her book onto the blanket. "Oh, my."

"Your grace, perhaps I should take Master Gregory." Hearing Roseanna's words distantly, she allowed her to lift the contented babe from her arms. Then the girl murmured something to Estelle, and they both departed, moving off toward the inn. She braced her hand against the tree behind her and stood.

Harrison halted while he was still several feet away. "Jane," he breathed. That was all. Just her name, as if it was the only word he knew.

"You—you must have left Blackmore shortly after I ..."

He stared at her with eyes that burned, feeding her starving soul with their fire. "Two hours. Too bloody long, Jane. I pushed Ulysses quite hard, I fear. But I knew I must catch you. To tell you that I ..."

Heart now pounding and melting at once, she prompted, "Tell me what?"

"I want you to come back."

"To Blackmore?"

Looking strangely adrift, he stepped closer, his hands loose at his sides. He swallowed visibly. "To me."

She could not speak, wondering if perhaps she had fallen asleep and was dreaming of him again. Her head began to swivel slowly back and forth in wonderment. No. He was here. He was really here.

"Before you deny me, just listen. I beg of you." He took another step closer, one beseeching hand reaching out then curling into a fist and dropping again to his side. "When you left, I ... I spoke with Lady Wallingham."

That was perhaps the last thing she had expected him to say. *Lady Wallingham?*

"She helped me see, to understand. About my father. That he was a horse's ass."

Jane could not stifle her grin, so she pressed her lips together and her fingers over her mouth. He had spoken those words with utter seriousness: horse's ass.

"I believed I was like him. No, at first I believed we were different, but ... then she told me he was infatuated with my mother. Obsessed with her. And I knew in at least one respect, we were the same."

She tilted her head, her smile becoming less about amusement and more about loving him so much, she could scarcely contain it.

"Because you are that for me, Jane. My obsession. The very heart of me." He took another step closer. Now, he was at the edge of the blanket. "At first, I feared I was not enough like him, that I could not control myself with you. That I would do something rash. When I held a gun to your captor's head—it was a very close thing. Very close."

The heavy, sluggish air, weighted by too much heat and moisture, swayed through the leaves above them, causing sunlight to ripple along his face.

"Then, after Lady Wallingham told me what unrestrained jealousy had caused my father to do, I feared I was too much like him, and that violence or cruelty would be the consequence if I did as I longed to do."

"And what did you long to do?" she asked softly.

"Make you mine. Completely. To let myself love you." He stepped onto the blanket. "So, I pushed you away. Not because I did not want you. God, Jane, never that. Because I want you too much. Need you too much." He dropped his head, staring at his feet, looking startlingly young to her in that moment. When his head came up again, he clenched his fists at his sides, seemingly working up the courage to speak. "I fear what is inside me. But I fear losing you more."

She started toward him, unable to bear it another moment.

"Please say—"

His remaining words were halted by her kiss, her hands seizing his neck and pulling him down to meet her lips in a fiery exchange. His mouth exploded over hers, his arms squeezing the breath out of her. She met his tongue and stroked his face with desperate hands. Oh, how she loved this man. She wanted to climb to the top of him and stake her claim. She wanted to take him inside her body until she disappeared and he disappeared and a new being was born of their ashes.

Together, they rocked and stumbled to their knees. She was grateful, for here she could reach him more easily. Her mouth left his to explore his face, laying adoring kisses along his cheeks and across his eyes. She tasted salt and dampness.

Tears. Whether hers or his, she did not know. They were part of each other now.

He pressed desperate, tender kisses to her jaw and then her throat. She threaded her hands through his hair and cradled him against her. "Harrison," she whispered, her throat tight with emotion. "All I have ever wanted is your love. Without restraint. Without apology. As long as you love me, my darling husband, you shall never lose me."

He groaned and clutched her harder, his head coming up slowly so she could see his eyes. There in the blue, love shone with neither shadow nor veil. For the first time, she could see clear through into his heart. "Then we will be together always, my Jane." He brushed the backs of his fingers against her cheek, sending *springles* down her spine. "For, that is how long I will love you."

IT TOOK AN HOUR TO EXPLAIN EVERYTHING TO VICTORIA AND Lucien before they could send them on their way. Victoria, in particular, wished to know details. "Oh, Harrison," she said damply, dabbing beneath her eyes. "You must have flown upon Ulysses. It is so very romantic."

"Not for the horse, I daresay," Lucien said wryly.

"And Jane!" she wailed, drawing Jane into a third hug. "I am simply overjoyed, dearest. Over the moon for you. Though I shall miss having you at Thornbridge."

Jane smiled and gave her best friend an affectionate squeeze. "I am happier than I ever thought possible, Victoria. Thank you for ... well, for everything." Her throat began to tighten and ache with blasted tears again. "Look at me," she said, pulling back to accept the handkerchief Harrison silently handed to her. She dabbed beneath her eyes, her fingers nudging her spectacles. "I am turning into as much of a watering pot as you."

Victoria sniffed. "I am well ahead of you in that regard. Just wait until your first child arrives. You won't recognize yourself."

Before long, they were saying tearful goodbyes and seeing Victoria and Lucien off with assurances of a Christmas visit. Because Ulysses required rest before being ridden again, and because neither of them could wait several hours to travel to Blackmore, Harrison secured a room at the inn. It was not so grand as her green-silk bedchamber, but as Jane entered the small space, she was reminded of her wedding night at the Pig and Plough—and the following morning, when she had awakened to find Harrison tangled with her in a way that had since become intoxicatingly familiar.

She turned and slipped into his arms as he closed the door. They wrapped her up, tight, strong, and sure. She let her ear rest over his heart, smelled the faint starch and sunshine of his cravat, heard the thud and throb of his blood pumping through his veins. "I love you so," she whispered into the quiet of the room.

"And I love you, my Jane. More than I dreamed possible."

Her fingers flared out as she ran her palms up over the muscles of his chest. Slowly, lazily, she searched for and found the ends of his cravat. She tugged and tossed, unwound the strip of cloth from around her husband, at last sliding it free. Draping it around her own neck, she next went to work on the buttons of his waistcoat and the fall of his riding breeches. As her fingers brushed against his hardness, she could sense his impatience growing.

He pushed her hands away, quickly shrugging out of his riding jacket, shedding his waistcoat and shirt, then his boots and breeches. He stood naked in the daylight from the window, his body a feast for her eyes. She adored his chest, the muscles and light dusting of hair. She loved his belly, with its rippling strength. She lusted for his cock, so high and proud and ready for her.

Turning her this way and that, he made swift work of her gown and corset and petticoat and shift. Then, she stood naked, too. His body brushed hers as he drew in close to remove the pins from her hair. The long strands fell around her face and shoulders, brushing like silk.

"You are so beautiful, my love," he rasped. From any other man, said in any other way, she might not have believed him. Her white, overabundant curves and plain features were exceedingly unlikely to launch a thousand ships. But in Harrison's eyes, she *was* beautiful. She knew it as clearly as she knew those eyes would darken as they did now. That they would spark and flash with desire. For her. Only her.

She reached for him.

He came to her.

Fell to his knees before her.

Pressed his lips reverently to her belly, then upward to her breasts. He nudged one with his cheek then took her nipple into the heat of his mouth. She moaned and stroked his face, arching into him insistently. He breathed against her skin, suckled and laved her nipple until her hips writhed helplessly.

Her knees turned to butter as he left one nipple to pay tribute to the other, letting first the coolness of the air then his worshipful thumb pleasure the first one in tandem.

"Harrison," she begged. "I need you."

His hands stroked over her flesh, curling and teasing along her thighs and buttocks. With his strong hands bracing her waist, he helped her sit on the bed, laid her down gently, then pushed her entire frame up until he could stretch over her, aligning his body with hers.

Oh, the feel of his skin, his weight, his heat against her. Gazing up into his eyes, she breathed his treasured breath. "I love you," she whispered, her hands stroking his jaw, his skin rasping her palms. She brushed her thumb over his lips.

He slid between her thighs, pressed himself inside her. The blue of his eyes glowed and consumed as his flesh joined with hers. "My Jane." Setting a slow, leisurely pace, his chest dragged against her nipples, driving her higher, making her hotter.

His elbows held him braced above her, but his hands played with her hair, sending twirling little thrills along her scalp. His fingers brushed her lips and her cheeks, teasing her dimples when she grinned her happiness.

Between her thighs, his cock slowly stretched and retreated, filled and receded, burned and completed until every inch of her core rippled and wept its joy. He was deliberately angled so his veined, heavy cock caught and slid against the swollen lips of her sex, abrading the center of her pleasure with every slow, ecstatic pulse.

And all the while, her eyes never left his. They held each other suspended, the beauty of their joining nearly blinding, their only reality that precious thread. The one that bound their souls together.

His forehead, now damp with sweat, lowered to hers, but he did not break their link, staring into her eyes, breathing into her mouth. She could see the shift coming, the urgency rising, the fire turning from a smolder to a blaze. His hips quickened their pace. Her legs came up to wrap around his hips. The sparks that consumed her entire body forced her higher, tightened her lungs and curled her toes and spilled all around her. They burst forth in a shower, seized her in an explosion so white-hot, she fell to pieces, sobbing his name. He answered the call with the hard thrusts she needed, the deep pressure once. Twice. Thrice. Then he followed her along the climb, letting her pull him over the precipice into bright white light, tugged by the single thread that refused to break. Blue-gray and dark brown. Harrison and Jane. Bound forever.

He trembled in her arms long afterward, their replete bodies settling beside each other, still tangled in an embrace. "Say that you are mine," he murmured against her ear.

"I am yours."

"Never leave again."

"Never."

While she stroked his arms and his chest, laying little kisses along his jaw, he was silent, letting her explore and soothe him. Finally, he pressed his lips to hers. "It will not be easy for me, Jane," he whispered. "You terrify me."

She smiled. "Me?"

"The way you make me feel."

"And how is that?"

He sighed. "It is too much to describe. I am determined to give you everything. All I have inside. That is my promise to you, and I shall not break it. But please don't ask me to explain, for I haven't the words."

She buried her nose in his neck and breathed deeply, letting the quiet sigh of the breeze outside fill the room for a while. Then, with a touch of mischief in her voice, she said, "I have a proposition."

He stilled. "Yes?"

"Each year, on this day, we will write each other a letter. Not an ordinary letter with notes about the children or the household accounts. But a letter describing one—just one—aspect of our feelings for each other."

"Ah, Jane," he said, his voice filled with affection. "You are far better at such things. I predict you would be woefully disappointed by my efforts."

She propped herself on an elbow, then rearranged his arms so she could roll on top of him, straddling his hips and hovering her face above his. Her dark hair fell like a curtain around them, playfully shadowing the obvious spark of joy in his eyes. Grinning down at her beautiful husband, she laid a tiny kiss on his nose and winked. "Would you care to wager on that, my love?"

Epilogue

"I must say, the foolishness of this younger generation is quite a challenge. Where would they be without my superior judgment and wisdom to guide them?"

—The Dowager Marchioness of Wallingham to her new companion, Humphrey.

December 5, 1817
Grimsgate Castle, Northumberland

THE TEACUP RATTLED IN ITS SAUCER AS LADY WALLINGHAM'S new lady's maid placed it on the small table next to her chair in the yellow parlor. Lady Wallingham glared at the girl sharply. Christina was her name. A local girl. Collette had been too haughty by half, as were many of the French ones. Lady Wallingham had dismissed her last month after an abominable incident with the hair iron. She still had not decided whether the scorching had been intentional.

"For the love of God, girl, leave before you spill the tea and burn us both," she barked. Christina cringed and curtsied, scurrying out of the room. "Hmmph. That one won't last long, I daresay."

Picking up her lorgnette and the first page from the stack of letters in her lap, she proceeded to read the latest reports from her contacts across ten of England's counties. Several pages later, she found herself tsking as she shared the more significant bits of news with her companion, who occupied the chair adjacent to hers. "It appears the Marquess of Rutherford has died, Humphrey. Which means his derelict son, Lord Chatham, shall inherit the title. Most unfortunate. How dreadfully far that dynasty has fallen to have the most disreputable scoundrel in England as its standard bearer. Shameful, would you not agree?"

Humphrey, who had been snoring rather loudly, did not wake to comment.

She took a sip of tea and continued reading. "The Duke and Duchess of Blackmore are rather nauseatingly blissful, or so Lady Atherbourne reports. I expect numerous offspring from that union. Her mother was prolific, and the apple does not fall far from the birthing tree. Additionally, the duke has never known a pursuit which he could not master in short order. Mark my words, Humphrey. Lady Berne will be gloating. I must brace myself for the onslaught."

Humphrey merely shifted and grunted in response.

She shook the next letter to straighten it and held the lorgnette closer to her eyes. "Lady Mary Thorpe has become engaged, it seems. To ... Lord Stickley? Ha! A perfect pairing. They can croon to each other their mutual love of hounds and leave the rest of us in peace."

Grumbling a bit, Humphrey sent her a stare of somber condemnation.

"Yes, well. *They* are tiresome and ridiculous about their affection, Humphrey. Others choose dignity over such an obvious display of sentiment."

His response was to sniff, blink slowly twice, then close his eyes in an attempt to resume his nap.

"Now, here is an amusing report. That red-haired, half-American heiress, Miss Charlotte Lancaster, was mortified when she fell on the ice of the Serpentine and lost control of her skirts. They flew up, apparently, leaving nothing at all to the imagination." She chuckled and shook her head.

Hearing her laugh, Humphrey awakened, yawning widely and sighing.

She raised a brow at him. "I suppose you wish to go for a walk, now."

Eyes brightening, he wriggled to stand on the cushion of the chair, his wrinkled brown body quivering in anticipatory delight.

She set her lorgnette and letters aside, picked up her new pup from his chair, and held him close to kiss one of his long, floppy ears. They were not as large as those of Cornelius, but he was a fine-looking specimen, nevertheless. "Very well. A short one today. It is too cold for one of our lengthy rambles. We wouldn't wish to slip on a patch of ice like the pitiful Miss Lancaster." She set him down and let him chase her slippers across the parlor floor. "I must say, the foolishness of this younger generation is quite a challenge. Where would they be without my superior judgment and wisdom to guide them?"

Rather than answer, Humphrey sniffed the floor behind her until they reached the entrance hall, where she donned her fur-trimmed pelisse, her boots, and her muff before opening the door. The dog bounded out into the snow with joyful abandon, then halted to look back at her expectantly.

"You are most discerning, Humphrey," she said, following him out into the crisp December air, the snow crunching beneath her feet. "They would be lost without me. I could not agree more."

Curious about what happens to the Blackmore black sheep, Lord Colin Lacey? Will he ever be worthy of a love of his own? Find out in Book Three of the Rescued from Ruin series, **available now.** Read on for a sneak peek!

Desperately Seeking a Scoundrel

BY ELISA BRADEN

Desperately Seeking a Scoundrel

August 25, 1817
Whitechapel

DEATH WAITED, PATIENT AND FOUL. BLOOD MARKED COLIN Lacey's wrists where they were bound above him, wetting his arms down to his shoulders, but the flow had long since slowed to a stop, replaced by numbness. The butcher's hook held the ropes fast, held him at the butcher's mercy.

None would be granted.

"Pity you did not exhibit equal reticence at the tables, my lord," the butcher murmured. "A modicum of restraint might have saved us both much aggravation." A sigh, then the snick of a knife leaving its sheath served as reviled punctuation.

Bright, cold agony sliced. Silver light flashed behind swollen eyelids as air hissed through teeth and into lungs. The flesh over his ribs gaped and wept in a warm flow.

"One word, my lord. A name. And this shall end."

His shirt had been torn from his back hours earlier. It now hung in three rags from the waist of his trousers. He fancied if he ever managed to break loose from his bindings, the cloth would prove convenient for soaking up his blood.

Rusty laughter shook inside his chest. He was never leaving this putrid place, thick with late-day heat and the odor of animals that came here to die. No, his bones would join those of cattle and swine. He was not so foolish as to believe a name would save him, either his or anyone else's.

"Come now. You are the brother of a duke. His heir at present, yes?" The butcher paused as though Colin might answer, then answered himself in his oddly soft, cultured voice. "Yes. The heir to the Duke of Blackmore has little need for credit at my humble gaming houses. After the Home Office took an untoward interest in my businesses, the coincidence was rather more than credulity could bear. To whom did you provide information?"

Long silence earned him another stripe, just below the last. This time, although pain flashed, it was but a white peak amidst a range of equally jagged mountains.

A door creaked. Boots shuffled. "Beggin' your pardon, Mr. Syder."

"Benning. I trust this interruption is of a vital nature."

"Y-yes, sir." Boots scraped and shambled again, then the low London voice came from only feet away. "Johnstone sent word the Gallows Club was raided. Roughly an hour past."

If Syder ever grew angry, Colin suspected it would sound like the dark silence that followed Benning's news. But Syder had not built an empire of thievery, brutality, and vice by being a slave to intemperance.

"Who was it?"

"Two of Kirkwood's men, along wif seven more we never seen. Took Johnstone, they did."

More silence, then a sigh from Syder. "My lord, I fear I must leave you in Mr. Benning's tender care. Might I suggest you loosen your tongue? He is less subtle than I in his ministrations."

Reflexively, Colin swallowed against his rising gorge. Footsteps, calm and evenly paced, receded until a door squeaked open and closed. Knuckles popped.

"You lasted longer than most, m'lord. Grant ye that." Benning, whom Colin remembered as a massive, pockmarked brute with hands the size of millstones, shifted near enough that his bulk deadened the noise of livestock outside the door. His breath wafted over Colin's swollen face. It smelled of ale and onions.

"Kill me," he whispered, his aching jaw scarcely able to form the words. "For I have nothing to say to you."

"You're like to die, sure enough." Colin sensed the grin in the brute's voice. "But not just yet." Heavy bootfalls thudded against the hardened dirt, heading in the direction of the table on the far side of the space. It was where Syder had assembled his tools—knives and other blades mainly, but also hammers and saws. After Benning's initial beating, Colin's eyes had swollen shut. In some ways, that had been a mercy. But now, he wished to know what Benning was retrieving, which instrument would be the source of his next dose of agony.

Metal scraped wood as Benning lifted the tool, whatever it was, from the table. Colin's heart lurched into a frantic rhythm. Why he now panicked, he could not say. It could be no worse than what he had already endured. Could it?

Benning drew close. A damp breeze of ale and onions bathed Colin's forehead. A millstone fist gripped his forearm, just below the rope.

Dear God. Was he about to lose his hand?

He heard himself wheezing, struggling, hectic and piteous. His mind flew backward from the horrifying reality, crouching at the rear of his skull.

His hand. He would never play again. Never feel a woman's flesh.

Dear. Holy. God.

His arms jerked. The blade bit. He could not feel it, could only sense the motion and pressure as Benning worked it back and forth. Suddenly, his hands released, his arms falling agonizingly down. His legs left him, and he collapsed. Stunned. Useless. A heap at Benning's feet.

"Eh," the brute grunted, nudging Colin's knee with his boot. "No time fer that, m'lord. I's paid to cut you loose. Not get nipped by Syder."

Colin's blood pounded inside his head, at war with his panting breaths, forming a deafening cacophony. "P-paid?" he managed.

The rope binding his ankles was yanked and severed. "Aye."

Attempting to move his arms, Colin groaned as needles flared across the numb flesh. The fire slowly spread until he had to grit his teeth to keep from screaming.

The scraps of his shirt were yanked from his waistband, torn into strips, and wrapped tightly around his ribs. A massive thumb stretched his eyelid. A blurry, pockmarked face peered back at him, thick lips downturned. "You'll 'ave to force 'em open. They'll come right in a day or two, but by then you'll be dead iffen you don't run fast and far. Understand?"

"Yes." He felt the wormy trembling begin beneath his skin. Sensation returned to his shoulders, making him want to vomit up the pain. He could scarcely move his arms, but at least he still had his hands. For that, he was most thankful. "Who paid you? Was it my brother?"

Benning stood from his crouch and moved to the corner where Colin's coat had been tossed. He stooped to retrieve it. "Nah. Doubtful he knows anything." The man's dialect was thick and round, sounding more like, "Dow'foh 'ee knows anyfing." Before this year, having rarely associated with men of Benning's ilk, Colin might have had trouble following his mutterings. Much had changed.

"Then, who? I took you for Syder's man exclusively."

Benning circled behind him, gripped him beneath his arms and pulled him to his feet in a rough motion. Colin could not stop his pitiful groan as excruciating pain tore through his shoulders. His legs at first refused to hold him. Shamefully, he slumped against Benning, who steadied him with a heavy forearm around his chest and began forcing his arms into the sleeves of his coat.

"Things change. The nob pays better."

Panting roughly, head swimming, Colin paused to catch his breath as Benning came around to face him and quickly fastened his buttons like a nursemaid dressing an infant. "Who is the nob, Benning?"

The blurry brute finished his task and moved to the door, crack it to peer out. "I can get you to your 'orse. No more'n that."

"Whoever it is, he must have offered a princely sum. Syder will not pursue only me for this."

Benning returned to Colin's side, grasped his arm and hauled him forward, dragging his stumbling, bleeding, weakened body toward the door. "It's touched I am by your concern, m'lord. Fact is I don't plan to stay put. Best you do likewise." Benning stuffed a hat onto Colin's aching head, tugged it low over his swollen brow.

The darkness at the end of dusk disguised their movements as they crept through the stockyard. A few cows shifted and lowed at their passing, but no shouts of alarm sounded. Soon they entered a stable, where Benning apparently had already saddled Matilda. The pretty bay mare snuffled Colin's outstretched hand.

"Good to see you, love," Colin whispered, stroking her warm nose. His arms, still weak, quickly fell back to his sides as Benning led her to a mounting block.

"Think you can manage it?" he asked.

Forcing his eyes to open further and swallowing down his lingering nausea, Colin gave his best imitation of his old self.

"The day I cannot mount a female is the day I am cold in the grave, Benning."

The man snorted and waved to the block. "Them's prophetic words, m'lord. Prophetic words, indeed."

WANT MORE OF COLIN'S STORY?
DESPERATELY SEEKING A SCOUNDREL IS AVAILABLE NOW!
FIND IT AT WWW.ELISABRADEN.COM

More from Elisa Braden

It's far from over! There are more scandalous predicaments, emotional redemptions, and gripping love stories (with a dash of Lady Wallingham) to come in the Rescued from Ruin series. For **new release alerts and updates**, follow Elisa on Facebook and Twitter, and sign up for her free email newsletter at **www.elisabraden.com**, so you don't miss a thing!

Plus, be sure to check out all the other exciting books in the Rescued from Ruin series, available now!

The Madness of Viscount Atherbourne (Book One)
Victoria Lacey's life is perfect—perfectly boring. Agree to marry a lord who has yet to inspire a single, solitary tingle? It's all in a day's work for the oh-so-proper sister of the Duke of Blackmore. Surely no one suspects her secret longing for head-spinning passion. Except a dark stranger, on a terrace, at a ball where she should not be kissing a man she has just met. Especially one bent on revenge.

The Truth About Cads and Dukes (Book Two)
Painfully shy Jane Huxley is in a most precarious position, thanks to dissolute charmer Colin Lacey's deceitful wager. Now, his brother, the icy Duke of Blackmore, must make it right, even if it means marrying her himself. Will their union end in frostbite? Perhaps. But after lingering glances and devastating kisses, Jane begins to suspect the truth: Her duke may not be as cold as he appears.

Desperately Seeking a Scoundrel (Book Three)
Where Lord Colin Lacey goes, trouble follows. Tortured and hunted by a brutal criminal, he is rescued from death's door by

the stubborn, fetching Sarah Battersby. In return, she asks one small favor: Pretend to be her fiancé. Temporarily, of course. With danger nipping his heels, he knows it is wrong to want her, wrong to agree to her terms. But when has Colin Lacey ever done the sensible thing?

The Devil Is a Marquess (Book Four)

A walking scandal surviving on wits, whisky, and wicked skills in the bedchamber, Benedict Chatham must marry a fortune or risk ruin. Tall, redheaded disaster Charlotte Lancaster possesses such a fortune. The price? One year of fidelity and sobriety. Forced to end his libertine ways, Chatham proves he is more than the scandalous charmer she married, but will it be enough to keep his unwanted wife?

When a Girl Loves an Earl (Book Five)

Miss Viola Darling always gets what she wants, and what she wants most is to marry Lord Tannenbrook. James knows how determined the tiny beauty can be—she mangled his cravat at a perfectly respectable dinner before he escaped. But he has no desire to marry, less desire to be pursued, and will certainly not kiss her kissable lips until they are both breathless, no matter how tempted he may be.

About the Author

Reading romance novels came easily to Elisa Braden. She's been doing it since she was twelve. Writing them? That took a little longer. After graduating with degrees in creative writing and history, Elisa spent entirely too many years in "real" jobs writing T-shirt copy ... and other people's resumes ... and articles about giftware displays. But that was before she woke up and started dreaming about the very *unreal* job of being a romance novelist. Frankly, she figures better late than never.

Elisa lives in the gorgeous Pacific Northwest, where you're constitutionally required to like the colors green and gray. Good thing she does. Other items on the "like" list include cute dogs, strong coffee, and epic movies. Of course, her favorite thing of all is hearing from readers who love her characters as much as she does. If you're one of those, get in touch on Facebook and Twitter or visit **www.elisabraden.com**.

Printed in Great Britain
by Amazon